P9-DGF-466

ACCLAIM FOR ROGUE WARRIOR II:
RED CELL

ACCLAIM FOR ROGUE WARRIOR

"For sheer readability, *Rogue Warrior* leave[s] Tom Clancy waxed and booby-trapped."

—*Los Angeles Times Book Review*

"Blistering honesty. . . . Marcinko is one tough Navy Commando."

—*San Francisco Chronicle*

"Riveting, suspenseful and tragic, *Rogue Warrior* explodes like a hand grenade . . . a must read. Dick Marcinko is the last of a breed of salty, bigger-than-life characters, and his story is filled with special people who have special courage and spirit. *Rogue Warrior* is a fascinating book—holds the reader like a vise."

—Colonel David H. Hackworth, USA (Ret.), author of *About Face: The Odyssey of an American Warrior*

"Marcinko makes the Terminator look like Tiny Tim. . . ."

—*Virginian Pilot and Ledger Star*

"*Rogue Warrior* [moves at] breakneck speed with the punch of a thriller. . . . you'll learn more about SEAL TEAM SIX than you'll get from any top-secret Pentagon briefing. . . ."

—Richard Perle, former Assistant Secretary of Defense

"Richard Marcinko's bestselling autobiography reads like the plots for about six Arnold Schwarzenegger or Sylvester Stallone movies."

—*Sacramento Bee*

"Marcinko's ornery and joyous agression . . . brought him to grief and to brilliance in war. . . . Here, his accounts of riverine warfare . . . are galvanic, detailed, and told with a rare craftsman's love. . . . profane and asking no quarter: the real nitty-gritty, bloody and authentic."

—*Kirkus Reviews*

"Marcinko recounts his life story with a two-fisted in-your-face style, liberally sprinkled with profanity, rough humor, braggadocio, and violence both on and off the battlefield. . . . Despite, or perhaps because of, a personality that could abrade the paint off a battleship, he's a fascinating man with a compelling tale to tell."

—*Booklist*

"One of the first real peeks inside SEAL TEAM SIX."

—*San Diego Union*

"Special-warfare devotees will find *Rogue Warrior* to their liking. . . . Marcinko's anti-authoritarian behavior, as he improvises his own doctrine of unconventional warfare, makes for entertaining reading."

—*Publishers Weekly*

"Marcinko was too loose a cannon for the U.S. Navy. . . . *Rogue Warrior* is not a book for the faint of heart."

—*People*

Kelly Campbell

ROGUE WARRIOR II
RED CELL

RICHARD MARCINKO
and
JOHN WEISMAN

POCKET BOOKS
New York   London   Toronto   Sydney   Tokyo   Singapore

Books by Richard Marcinko and John Weisman

Rogue Warrior
Rogue Warrior II: Red Cell

Published by POCKET BOOKS

POCKET BOOKS, a division of Simon & Schuster Inc.
1230 Avenue of the Americas, New York, NY 10020

ISBN: 0-671-79957-6

First Pocket Books paperback printing December 1994

10 9 8 7 6 5 4 3 2 1

Cover photo by Kelly Campbell

Printed in the U.S.A.

Once again, to the shooters

And to Everett E. Barrett and Roy H. Boehm,
two old Frogs who have always showed by example what
leading from the front and creating unit integrity are all
about

—Richard Marcinko
—John Weisman

What is the Way of the Warrior?
The Way of the Warrior is Death.

—seventeenth-century
Japanese proverb

THE TEN COMMANDMENTS OF SPECWAR

According to Richard Marcinko

- I am the War Lord and the wrathful God of Combat and I will always lead you from the front, not the rear.

- I will treat you all alike—just like shit.

- Thou shalt do nothing I will not do first, and thus will you be created Warriors in My deadly image.

- I shall punish thy bodies because the more thou sweatest in training, the less thou bleedest in combat.

- Indeed, if thou hurteth in thy efforts and thou suffer painful dings, then thou art Doing It Right.

- Thou hast not to like it—thou hast just to do it.

- Thou shalt Keep It Simple, Stupid.

- Thou shalt never assume.

- Verily, thou art not paid for thy methods, but for thy results, by which meaneth thou shalt kill thine enemy before he killeth you by any means available.

- Thou shalt, in thy Warrior's Mind and Soul, always remember My ultimate and final Commandment: There Are No Rules—Thou Shalt Win at All Cost.

Contents

ROGUE WARRIOR II
RED CELL

Part One

SNAFU

Dick Marcinko

Chapter

1

THE BIG SILVER, RED, AND BLACK JET-FUEL TANK TRUCK SLOWED to about five for the speed bump sixty yards from where I crouched, clutched down, and hump-humped painstakingly, axle by axle by axle by axle by axle, over the obstacle. Then it proceeded at a crawl along the five-meter electrified fence to the unmanned gatehouse, where it stopped long enough for the driver to reach out, insert a pass card, and punch an access code into the electronically controlled, meter-high, ten-ton-defeating ram barrier that barred the way to the ramp closest to Runway 33-W.

That was my cue. I rolled from the culvert like a proper ninja and crabbed my way under the left side of the truck, using the shadows to stay invisible to the surveillance cameras. I slipped between the twin rear axles, pulled myself along the sharp, greasy frame past the trailer hitch, and wedged myself just behind the tractor cab.

Bingo. This was child's play. Hunkered, I checked my watch. It was 0140. I was right on schedule. Then I ran a quick check. The cargo pockets of my black ripstop BDU held wire snips for cutting through fences and surgical tape and nylon restraints for muzzling hostages. In my jacket were a dozen picklocks, two boxes of waterproof matches, fifty feet of slow-burning fuse, and five timer/detonators, dry inside knotted prophylactics. In a small knapsack, I carried

3

half a dozen IED—Improvised Explosive Device—bombs that would attract attention without doing any permanent damage, and a change of clothes, so I could look like any other civilian whenever I decided to.

Inside my left black Gore-Tex and leather boot, a small dagger sat in its scabbard. Knives are like American Express cards. I never leave home without one. Inside my right boot was a leather sap, just in case I had to reach out and crush someone. My face was blacked out with nighttime camouflage grease. My shoulder-length hair was tied back. Over it I wore a watch cap that could be rolled down into a balaclava.

I was wet and I was cold and my joints were as stiff as a horny nineteen-year-old's cock. I'd hunkered in the goddamn culvert for three hours, monitoring the traffic, watching as the pair of television cameras atop six-meter poles swept the gate and barrier area, noting the regular rhythm of the blue-and-white security cars as they passed by. I looked down to see that I'd caught my wrist on something sharp between the culvert and the truck and opened a two-inch gash. I wrapped the wound with one of the three dark blue handkerchiefs in my cargo pocket. Goddammit. This was no way to make a living.

But that's what you get when you're old, you're strapped for cash, and the only way you can make a dollar is terrorism.

Or, as my old friend—I'll call him Tom O'Bannion—put it not seventy-two hours ago, "You may have been a hell of a brain surgeon, Marcinko, but you flunked bedside manner."

I promptly told him, "Doom on you, Tom." That meant he should go fuck himself in Vietnamese. Then I proceeded to explain myself in my usual gentle style: "I'll give *you* a fucking dose of bedside fucking manner. I'll make you eat the fucking bed."

Like me, O'Bannion has a natural way with words. He's a retarded mick O-6 Orion driver—that's a retired Navy captain of Irish ancestry who used to pilot P-3 antisubmarine aircraft to you cake-eating civilians—who works these days as an aide-de-camp to an admiral I'll call Black Jack

Morrison in Black Jack's multimillion-dollar security-consulting business. It was Black Jack who, as the chief of naval operations in 1980, ordered me to design, build, equip, train, and lead the most effective and highly secret counterterror force in the world, SEAL Team Six. He's the one who'd told me, "Dick, you will not fail."

Back in the late seventies, O'Bannion was a Sweat Hog— one of the small group of staff pukes working long hours in the Navy Command Center. They're the Navy's answer men—they develop an incredible network of sources from E-5 grunts at DIA, the Defense Intelligence Agency, who know how to get answers fast, to master chiefs who can slip-slide the paperwork and get results *now*.

The vice chief of naval operations needs to know how long that goddamn Russkie trawler from Petropavlovsk's been trailing a PACFLT (PACific FLeeT) exercise. Call the Sweat Hogs. The secretary of the navy wants to find out how long it'll take to scramble a platoon of SEALs to take down an oil rig in the Persian Gulf. Call the Sweat Hogs. CINCLANT wants to know—well, you get the idea.

Anyway, O'Bannion, who was a real pig for punishment, spent three years hogging sweat. Then Black Jack plucked him from obscurity, gave him a fourth stripe, the title of deputy executive assistant to the CNO, and ordered him to protect my hairy Frogman's ass, since he knew so many people and they all liked him, while I, the knuckle dragger with the Neanderthal eyebrows and temperament to match, was persona non grata at most Navy installations.

It didn't take much ordering either. While O'Bannion's not a mustang—a former white hat like me who came up through the ranks—he still drinks and swears like a chief and chases pussy like a priapic adolescent. As I built Six, O'Bannion ran interference for me—a Sweat Hog turned offensive lineman. He protected me from the assholes who tried to scuttle me with paperwork or chain-of-command bullshit; he made sure I got all the equipment and the money I needed. He kept them off my tail.

But in doing so, he earned the everlasting enmity of the Annapolis mafiosi who really control the Navy system.

Then the bottom fell out for Tom. Black Jack Morrison retired in 1983 and O'Bannion lost not only his one rabbi, but his future, too. Admirals, after all, have long memories. And when it came time to give out the stars, O'Bannion somehow didn't rate a promotion to flag grade in the post-Morrison Navy.

He didn't go up, so he got out. Now Tom's retired, living with his third—or is it fourth?—wife in Hawaii, and working as a factotum, troubleshooter, and cutout for Black Jack Morrison. That is, when he's not out on his thirty-six-foot Grand Banks humping six-foot swells, trying to catch something bigger and meaner than he is.

A cutout? Yeah. Four-star admirals do not meet with ex-felons, and I am an ex-felon.

Let me explain. Despite O'Bannion's help, I managed to tread on a shoe store full of toes when I commanded SEAL Team Six. I made more enemies than I could count when I created another unit, Red Cell, at the request of my sea daddy, Admiral James "Ace" Lyons. Ace was then the OP-06, which is Navyspeak for deputy chief of naval operations for plans, policy, and operations. Ace wanted the biggest, baddest wolf he could find to test the Navy's antiterrorist capabilities.

Enter *Canis lupus* Marcinko, huffing and puffing and blowing Navy bases down, stage right.

It didn't take but six weeks for me to prove that the Navy had no antiterrorist capabilities. But I kept demonstrating that happy fact for two years, rubbing their noses in *merde* time after time and enjoying the hell out of it.

Then, in 1985 I lost my rabbi, too. Ace Lyons was promoted from OP-06 to CINCPACFLT—Commander-IN-Chief PACific FLeeT. He and his beautiful, tough-as-nails wife, Renee, were posted to Pearl Harbor. Thereafter, my ass became grass, with the Navy establishment playing the part of lawn mower.

Because once Ace was gone, all the old farts with scrambled eggs on their hats—not to mention their faces—got even. They called in the best headhunters in the Naval Investigative Service—the Admirals' Gestapo—and turned 'em loose on me. They code-named the investigation Iron

Eagle. In all, the Navy spent five years and $60 million trying to prove I stole $118,000. They failed.

But after I'd been forced into retirement, NIS, which holds grudges, took its case to the feds. And after some prompting, the feds went after me.

A couple of years, a couple of hundred thousand dollars in attorney's fees, and two trials later, I was finally convicted on one count of conspiracy to defraud the government—despite the fact that there was no concrete evidence against me. And three months after the judge's gavel slammed down, I was serving a year at the Petersburg, Virginia, Federal Correctional Institution.

Petersburg wasn't so bad. I've been quartered in worse places. There was CNN and HBO on the cable TV, I worked out three times a day on the weight pile, and I even had time to author a best-seller, *Rogue Warrior,* that spent eight months on the *New York Times* best-seller list—a month at the No. 1 slot, much to the Navy's horror. But it was jail. My phone calls were all tapped. There was no beer, no Bombay gin (and worst of all, no pussy), and the money I got for the book all went to pay my lawyer's fees.

Now I was out, and, like I said, I was strapped. So Black Jack, God bless him, found some work for me.

That was like Black Jack. When he was CNO, we'd been on a first-name basis. He called me Dick and I called him Admiral, and we'd gotten along real well. I admired the former CNO. Unlike most of your Navy four-stars, who majored in diplo-speak or bean-counting and think that war is a dirty word, Black Jack Morrison was a tall, gaunt aviator who'd flown 188 combat missions over Vietnam and been shot down twice.

According to O'Bannion, the admiral had kept track of me from the huge, wood-paneled office in Honolulu with the bird's-eye view of Pearl Harbor that serves as the hub of his international consulting business. And just a few short days after I said bye-bye to my cellmates at Petersburg, he had Tom O'Bannion call and offer me this here job—a thousand bucks a day plus expenses to play terrorist in the Land of the Rising Sun.

Black Jack, it seemed, had been hired by Fujoki, the

Japanese corporation that ran Tokyo's Narita Airport, to upgrade their security apparatus. Fujoki wanted somebody to makee-makee everything state-of-the-art, and they were paying Black Jack Morrison seven figures to do the job.

As part of his "show-and-tell" security-enhancement package, Black Jack told Fujoki he'd contracted with someone to infiltrate the airport—hired a certified Peck's Bad Boy who would roam the place at will, leaving calling cards wherever he went, and even plant "explosives" in the most secure areas, to show the Narita folks where, and how, they'd screwed up in the security department. Then Black Jack would explain how he could fixee-fixee makee all better, and in the process he'd charge them another few million, to "harden" the airport properly.

To play the role of chief Pecker, he needed someone who could think and act like the Japanese Red Army or Abu Nidal; someone who didn't mind getting dirt under his fingernails, or a few bruises if necessary. For some reason, he thought of me.

Which is why Dickie was now wet, cold, dressed in basic black without the benefit of pearls, bleeding, and breaking into Narita to place the IEDs, which I carried in my waterproof ballistic nylon knapsack, where they'd do the most "harm" to the airport, and the most good for me.

The truck turned right, moving southwest onto a well-lit roadway that paralleled the taxiway, heading toward the Number Four Satellite building, which protruded off the south wing of the main terminal. As it slowed past the terminal and rolled through a huge shadow created by a pair of docked, darkened 747s, I let myself slide back through the frame, lowered myself between the wheels, and let the truck run over me.

Then all of a sudden the goddamn knapsack got in the way, I hit my coccyx on the concrete trying to straighten myself out, and my head snapped back and bounced off the apron a couple of times.

Shit—that hurt. I rolled to my left, scrambled to my feet, and hustled into the shadows between the ramps.

Since the planes were empty, there was nobody watching. Narita was no different from the hundreds of other targets

I'd hit. Human nature is the same, whether it's Japanese or American.

Who'd want to screw around with an empty plane, right? Only Dickie and his explosives.

I made my way under the fuselage and climbed into the nosewheel well. A red plastic streamer was attached to one of the struts, a reminder to the mechanics to check for hydraulic leaks. I attached an IED—I chose a yellow smoke bomb with a whistle screamer—to the strut and tied the end of the streamer to the detonator. Whoever pulled on *that* was going to get a nice surprise.

It didn't amaze me that nobody'd discovered me yet. I'd simply slipped between the security cracks. Most airports are sieves—Narita was no different, just bigger. It handled an average of three hundred and fifty flights a day from an assortment of forty different airlines. At any one time somewhere close to five hundred security people were at work in and around the grounds. But that didn't necessarily mean they were on the job.

Why? Segmentation. Each airline at Narita hired its own rent-a-cops, whom they paid minimum wage. Most can barely read and write—they're no threat to anybody. That's one. The perimeter of the airport, as well as the warehouses, cargo buildings, operations center, and admin spaces were patrolled by Narita's private security force—that's two— while the terminals, concourse, gates, ramps, and other public areas were under the jurisdiction of several Japanese Defense Force units—that's three. The roads outside the airport perimeter, including the two-lane blacktop that ran along the fence and the Tokyo expressway, were patrolled by national highway police. That's four.

And, as always, the left hand seldom knew what the right hand was up to. Example: communications. The airline security people had one brand of walkie-talkies, while the Narita rent-a-cops had another. The army and the real cops, meanwhile, talked on two other frequencies. And if an airline rent-a-cop needed to talk to a real cop? Well, there was always the public phone. Sure, there were cameras and electronic fences; there were locked doors and access codes and all the nitnoy dip-dunk security bullshit common from

Tempelhof to Taiwan. But none of it worked together, in concert, as a team. Each element was separate—each reported to a different authority.

In the Navy, we called these sorts of organizational compartments stovepipe commands. Like, the hospital at Subic—when we had a base at Subic—didn't report to the admiral there. It reported to a three-star at the National Naval Medical Center in Bethesda, Maryland. The security officer at Pearl Harbor doesn't report to CINCPACFLT, he reports to the one-star in charge of Naval Investigative Services at the Washington Navy Yard. In peacetime, this stovepiping creates a paper chain that gives the bureaucrats something to do.

In war, it's a goatfuck.

In wartime, by the time you say "May I?" to some asshole halfway around the world, the bad guys are pulling your skivvies down around your knees and humping you like a prison ho.

I started to lower myself. Footfalls. Somebody was coming. Back up into your hole, Marcinko.

I squeezed up into the wheel well and tried to make myself invisible.

I saw the back of a head, and a wooden shaft. It was a broom man. At Narita, they've got guys who sweep the tarmac clean. Talk about your anal retentive society.

He was sweeping—and doing a great job—when he stopped and peered at something on the ground. I caught my breath when I saw what he was looking at. It was blood. My blood.

Obviously, he thought he'd found an oil leak. He took a rag out of his pocket and wiped the droplets off the concrete, then looked to see where the drip was coming from. He looked straight up at me. The broom clattered to the apron.

His mouth opened in astonishment. But before any sound came out, I dropped on top of him.

"Murrf—"

I cupped a hand over his lips, wrapped an arm around his neck, and began to apply a sleeper choke hold to his carotid artery.

The son of a bitch swiveled, dropped, turned, and threw

me over his shoulder. I bounced off the concrete. "Shit."
The little motherfucker knew judo.

He turned to run away and sound the alarm. There was no
time to fool around. I tackled him from behind, knocking
his legs out from under him. I reached into my boot for my
sap as I lay on top of him. Then I let him have it gently but
firmly behind the left ear—*thwoock.*

He collapsed. I rolled him over and dragged him and his
broom under the plane. He was going to have a hell of a
headache. I hoped I was covered by Black Jack's
insurance—I didn't want the SOB suing me.

I bound his hands and feet with nylon restraints, gagged
him with tape, then tied him to the nosewheel of the 747. I
unpeeled a sticker, which I attached to his overalls. It read,
in Japanese and English, "Dead hostage. Security exercise.
Fujoki Corp. Have a nice day."

It was time to say sayonara to the tarmac and do some
serious damage elsewhere. My goal tonight was to get into
the underground baggage area and leave a series of IEDs to
illustrate how terrorists could devastate the entire baggage-
handling capability of Narita with one or two well-placed
explosive charges. I had a second goal, too: showing how
dismal the security of the baggage-transferring system was.

If you can slip a bag into the system and get it on a plane,
you can blow up the plane. I was going to scope out the area
this evening. Tomorrow, I'd come back with a suitcase and
slide it into the system, onto a Hawaii-bound plane, where
O'Bannion would retrieve it.

The Narita most tourists see when they arrive comprises
only about one-third of the airport. Two-thirds of the huge
complex is below ground—three subterranean floors filled
with acres of cargo bays, miles of roadway and baggage
conveyor belts, endless conduits filled with electrical wiring,
air-conditioning ducts, and fuel lines. They prepare all the
airline food at ground level, store it two levels down in huge
drive-through refrigerators, then truck it out to the planes.
All baggage is shuffled, shifted, and transshipped below
ground. Freight, too, is moved by a series of underground
shuttle trains to one of the five huge cargo warehouses that
sit directly to the north of the main terminal area.

I was at the Number Four Satellite, the southernmost tip of the passenger area. I moved under the nose of the plane, walked ten yards, and stared down a long ramp. It was from there the baggage-handling carts, service vehicles, and catering trucks drove up onto the apron. The path was clear. I moved the knapsack, wrapped the kerchief around my hand so I wouldn't leave a bloody trail for the good guys to follow, and started my descent. This was going to be fun.

Two and a half hours and a $175 cab ride later, I was back in my room on the fourteenth floor of the Okura Hotel, nursing a $15 Bombay and soaking my tired old bones in the huge Japanese tub. My first night on the job had been a success: I'd planted six IEDs without any trouble. That would get their attention. The only snag I'd run into was my bomb-on-the-plane plan.

Narita—like most big airport facilities—had recently installed a sophisticated system for checking cargo and baggage. Using a combination of electromagnetic and sensory devices, any container holding explosive or radioactive components was immediately flagged, isolated, X-rayed, and searched. The system worked on all forms of plastique and nitro-based explosives. It was, I'd discovered, virtually foolproof. Well, doom on me.

After half an hour of hot-water therapy, I dried off, wrapped myself in one of the thick terry-cloth robes that come with the rooms, turned out the lamp, and peered out the window. My room faced north. I could make out half a dozen government ministry buildings and, in the distance, the lights on Uchibori-dori Avenue, which ran around the perimeter of the moat surrounding the Imperial Palace and its formal gardens.

Tokyo hadn't changed much in the decade since I'd been here with Red Cell. The city was bigger now, and more expensive. But it was still the bustling, hustling city I remembered. Twelve million people lived and worked here, packed like sardines without benefit of oil into a metropolis that had been built for half that number.

I refilled my Bombay from the minibar. Another $15 in expenses added to the Fujoki Corporation's tab. It would be light soon. Time to grab some shut-eye before writing a few graphs on my night's work and faxing them back to O'Bannion. I killed the gin and headed for the futon. That was just like the Japs—to name their hard-as-nails bedrolls "fuck you" in French. Devious little sons of bitches.

My head had hardly hit the mat when a Klaxon horn interrupted a perfectly good dream about a perfectly good woman. I groaned and reached for the telephone.

"Marcinko-san? *Ohayo gozaimasu* and fuck you, you round-eyed, hairy-knuckled son of a bitch."

I hadn't heard the voice in ten years, but I knew who it was. "Good morning to you, too, Tosho, you little yellow monkey cockbreath. How the fuck are you?"

"I'm pissing away half the morning on the phone with you, *gaijin*. Pick your ass up off the mat, throw your body in gear, and haul yourself down to the Terrace Restaurant. I'll be waiting."

"Aye, aye, Sergeant."

"That's lieutenant inspector to you, dog breath."

"No shit—okay, Tosho, I'm on my way."

Toshiro Okinaga was a sergeant—no, a lieutenant inspector, now—with the Kunika, a so-called Special Action Unit of the Japanese National Police. In English, that means he was, like me, a SpecWar operator.

The Kunika used extensive undercover operational, surveillance, and counterintelligence techniques and were targeted against terrorists, guerrillas, and most recently, organized crime. Tosho and I first played together when I brought the Red Cell to Japan to test readiness at the joint U.S.-Japanese naval base at Yokosuka. Tosho was assigned to be my point of contact with the Japs, and we'd worked together like old swim buddies from the very first day.

In many ways he was more like a SEAL than a Japanese cop. He had a roguish sense of humor. He chased women. He liked his whiskey, his sake, and his Kirin Ichiban beer in copious amounts, and he could even be persuaded to take a drink of the Deadly Bombay once in a while.

He was also an expert pistol shot and a seventh-degree black belt, and he'd rappelled down the sides of buildings with the best of 'em. But that was all to be expected of someone who represented what I thought of as classic Jap warrior personality.

What I really liked so much was the fact that there was nothing Tosho wouldn't do. I'd thrown him out of a plane and tossed him into the ocean, but he just kept coming back for more. He was absolutely fearless.

And he could pull the trigger, too. I respect a real hunter—a man who can kill another man face-to-face. Tosho had gone nose to nose with the Japanese Red Army— twice. The score to date was Tosho three, JRA zero.

He was working on a stack of pancakes and a side of bacon when I got there. No fish, pickled veggies, soup, dried seaweed, rice, and raw egg for Tosho in the A.M. Not when he could be visited by his favorite relative—Aunt Jemima.

He looked up from his syrup-drenched plate and waved me over. "C'mon, c'mon, sit down."

He hadn't changed at all. Maybe a tinge of gray around the temples, but he was the same solid, Japanese fireprug he'd been a decade ago. Tosho was built like a running back— five eight or so, 180 pounds, most of it thighs and biceps, a narrow waist, and a bull neck atop which sat a round face.

His unaccented English came from four years at Notre Dame (BA in poly sci), two at Indiana, where he'd received a master's in criminal justice and married a big-hipped, round-eyed woman named Katie, who was as Midwest as Jell-O–mold salad. Yeah—Tosho's English was perfect and idiomatic, although he liked to fraunt his *l*s and *r*s like a Hollywood Japanese villain, circa 1943, if he thought he could outrage somebody by doing so.

He poured me a cup of ¥1,500 coffee from the ¥6,000 thermos decanter he'd ordered for the table. "So, Marcinko-san, how does it feel to be a convicted felon?"

"You stay current, don't you?"

Tosho nodded. "Intelligence is the name of the game, bub. Like Sun Tzu said, 'Every matter in war requires prior knowledge.' "

"Then you already know that it feels lousy."

He nodded. "I guessed it."

"Especially because I was innocent."

Tosho waved his finger at me. *"Innocent* isn't a word that

could ever be applied to you, you stupid asshole. But I'll bet you weren't guilty of the charges they threw at you."

He had a point. "I wasn't."

"I believe that. Want to know why?"

"Sure."

"Two reasons." He rubbed a forkful of pancake wedges into the sticky puddle of syrup on his plate, stuck them in his mouth, and wiped a dribble of Vermont Maid off his chin. "First, because you're such a devious son of a bitch that if you'd wanted to steal money, you'd be a millionaire by now. You were working with a goddamn black budget, for chrissakes—millions of dollars, much of it in cash."

He was right. If I'd wanted to steal, I'd had ample opportunity: Red Cell carried cash by the suitcaseful. "Thanks for the vote of confidence, Tosho."

"You haven't heard the second reason."

"What's that?"

"You're too stupid, Marcinko-san. You could have never carried it off." He pointed at his forehead. "You have fucking rocks up there." He laughed. "Rocks. Anybody who thinks throwing himself out of a plane at thirty thousand feet is fun has rocks for brains. And anybody who does it with a stress fracture of their right leg is certifiable."

What could I say? He was right. I'd once gone seventeen months with a stress fracture in my right leg. "But I let the dentist use Novocain."

"Where? In the balls? Is that why they call you numb nuts?" Tosho laughed and scooped up another load of pancakes. "So, you're here on a security detail."

"Your intelligence net really is working overtime I see."

Now it was the bacon's turn to be washed in syrup and consumed. He nodded his head while he chewed. "O'Bannion called. I help him out occasionally. Black Jack was always good to us, so I'm not averse to an occasional favor for the admiral."

"Ah, so."

He wrinkled an eyebrow in my direction. "Cut the inscrutable-Oriental shit. Anyway, Tom asked me to keep an eye on you. He wants me to make sure you don't kill anybody."

"That sounds boring—"

"Or if you do, it's legal."

I laughed. "That's better." I sipped the coffee. I hated Japanese hotel coffee. It was so weak I could see the bottom of the cup. "Speaking of killing," I said, "what're the chances you can get me a little piece?"

His eyes mocked amazement. "You want to get *raid?*"

"I always want to get raid. But that's not what I'm talking about."

Tosho looked hurt. "You're asking me, a police officer sworn to uphold the law, to supply a gun to you—a convicted felon?"

"That's the general idea."

He smiled. He nodded. "Sure thing. Say, you want a Blowning or a Grock?" Tosho liked to think of himself as funny.

I prayed arong. "I'd rike a Ruger or a Luger, but I'll settle for a Grock."

"Glate." Tosho chortled. I hated when he chortled. "I rike Grocks, too. Accurate. Easy to crean. Rightweight. Big capacity."

I switched back into English. "And an extra mag or so, if it's not too much trouble."

"No prob, guy." He slurped his coffee. "Now why don't you give me a dump about your trip."

"Sure." I drew him a quick verbal sketch. He liked what he heard.

"It's about time. That place is a mess. What makes it worse is that we're not allowed inside—our jurisdiction stops at the fence line. It makes trying to keep tabs on all the bad guys a big prob."

"Who are they, these days?"

"Same old faces. JRA tangos." Tosho used the radio slang for Japanese Red Army terrorists. "Heroin smugglers from the Golden Triangle. North Koreans. Our own Yakuza mafiosi, and occasionally some right-wing kooks. The usual cast of characters."

"My kind of people. Makes life worth living. I'm going back today to walk the concourses, maybe try to get into the food area. Maybe tomorrow I'll probe the underground cargo areas."

"Want some company?"

"Do brown bears shit in the woods? Sure."

"Good. It's been a while since I got to play those sorts of games with you *Amerikajin* assholes."

"Don't you work with the Cell when it's here?"

"Yeah." Tosho's impassive face screwed up into a frown. "But they don't get here very often anymore."

I knew what he was talking about. I'd heard the rumors from other SEALs while I was in prison. They spoke carefully—all my calls were monitored—but I could read between the lines. Leadership sucked. Nobody fought for the men anymore. A CO's slot was just another ticket to be punched on the way to an admiral's star. So you took no chances. You saved money by cutting back on travel and training. You played it safe—and you screwed your men.

Tosho cracked his knuckles. "You know that these days they do most of their exercises by building a computer model and playing the war games on a screen. And when they do get a chance to deploy, they're required to wear uniforms. Polo shirts that say *Red Cell,* and black hats with some kind of logo on them."

"That's crap." How the hell could they function like that? The whole idea of Red Cell was to infiltrate and exploit the facility's weaknesses, just like real terrorists would do.

"May be crap indeed. But that's the way they're doing business these days. They've been cut back to a single squad."

I knew that.

"Still a couple of your people there, though—Nicky Grundle and Cherry Enders."

Grundle and Enders *were* my people. My shooters. I'd raised them from tadpole trainees into Frogman hunters. I'd selected them for SEAL Team Six. Then I'd brought them to Red Cell. "They're the best of the best."

"May be. But they're not doing very much these days. Fact is, Dickie-san, you embarrassed too many base commanders."

"That was my job."

"Yeah—but you did it too well."

He had a point. "Well, it was fun while it lasted."

"Yeah—but you're out. Retired. Red Cell's still limping along."

"I know. Sometimes, I get to thinking that I'd like to be back in the Navy just long enough to take my shooters on one big, balls-to-the-wall op."

"So?"

"So—then I come to my senses."

"Smart, Marcinko-san." Tosho drained his coffee. "So, how's about you come downtown with me and we'll get you your Grock, and we can make some plans for your stay here. Like dinner tonight, followed by a tour of a bar or two. I assume you've got a huge expense account."

"You assume correctly." I pulled out a two-inch-thick wad of yen notes and dropped ¥17,000 on the table. "That should cover your appetite."

"Better leave another twenty-five hundred," Tosho said. "Aunt Jemima don't come cheap here anymore."

Chapter

2

IT WAS A TWENTY-MINUTE WALK FROM THE HOTEL TO TOSHO'S office. We cut through back streets and alleys, shouldering our way through the crowds on their way to work as we meandered past dozens of municipal and national government agency buildings, high-rises, modernistic office towers, and corporate headquarters. Even the best city maps can't do justice to Tokyo's random pattern of streets and avenues —the place is a maze. For a round-eye like me, who'd only been to Tokyo half a dozen times before and had a hard time making sense of the few street signs, the best thing to do was try to memorize landmarks and work from those.

Just south of Hibiya Park we cut into an alley behind the Nippon Press Center and followed it around a corner to a dead end. A windowless, six-story building blocked our way. "Back entrance," Tosho explained. He slipped a key into a gray steel door, opened it, and bade me enter.

We walked into a dimly lit hallway painted the same dull puke green as the police stations in New Brunswick, New Jersey, when I was a habitual truant and the cops liked to pick me up and give me a hard time. Tosho led the way up three flights of stairs, then past a long line of tiny offices— cubicles really—where dozens of Nip cops in cheap suits plied their trade, tapping endless information into desktop computers, working phones, and shuffling papers. Then it was down another corridor, through a series of security checkpoints, up another flight of stairs, and suddenly there we were, in the Kunika ready room.

The walls were covered with organizational charts and mug shots of the Japanese crime families, as well as national and international terrorist organizations. An HK poster displayed the prowess of SAS troopers using the MP5 submachine gun as they assaulted the Iranian embassy in London back in 1980. A big, framed, black-and white photograph featured Norwegian Jagers on a high-speed water infiltration. Four SEALs, their M16s and MP5s at the ready, graced a U.S. Navy recruiting poster. There were plaques and mementos from Herr Gen. Ricky Wegener's GSG-9 antiterrorist squads in Germany, an oversize replica of the unit insignia from the Incursari, Italy's happy-go-lucky, trigger-crazy, hairy-assed frogmen based at La Spezia on the Ligurian coast, and a pair of mounted bayonets from France's crack GIGN hit teams.

I wrinkled my nose. The familiar, acrid odors of bore cleaner, sweat, and tension were unmistakable. A pair of shooters just in from the range, their countersniper rifles in hard, dull, waterproof black Pelikan cases, still reeked of primer as they climbed out of their black assault coveralls. In the corner, a young pup in spandex cutoffs, Bundeswehr tank top, and net-backed, leather weight-pile gloves was pumping iron, grunting as he worked at what looked to be three hundred or so pounds of plate. He was sweating nicely, too.

A sudden wave of nostalgia swept over me. This place, more than half the way around the world from my home, had the same sights, smells, even the same spiritual gestalt as the locker room at Red Cell's headquarters at Dam Neck, Virginia, just outside Virginia Beach. I stopped in my tracks, took a deep breath.

God, I missed my shooters. That was a sentiment I hadn't let myself express until now. Not in jail, and not in the days afterward. But it was true. I missed my men—terribly. Of all the things the Navy did to me, the most severe was that they took away my men. Because I wouldn't compromise with the system, I was unceremoniously removed from command, first at Six and then three years later, at Red Cell. After my precipitous retirement, both units were turned over to commanders who ordered them to conform to the Navy system, and in doing so they turned my effective, unconventional warriors into conventional sailors who got killed and chewed up in Grenada, Panama, and elsewhere.

Even worse, so far as I was concerned, they'd tried to split the men up, so that the unit integrity I'd inculcated, built, and nurtured would be forever dismantled. During my trial and subsequent imprisonment, I'd been told stories that my senior chiefs were being scattered far and wide, dispersed so they couldn't operate the way I'd taught them to or pass my values to the next generation of SEAL shooters.

"You okay?" Tosho's arm dropped onto my shoulder.

I nodded. "Yeah—I'm fine. It's just nice to see a bunch of working stiffs again."

"They're a good group of kids."

"Seems that way."

"C'm'on." Tosho pushed at a door, led me down a carpeted hallway, and plunked me in a six-by-eight office. "Welcome to your home away from home."

I looked around. No window. The place was barely big enough for a small desk, two chairs, and a tiny bookcase. Tosho pulled open his desk drawer and set a pristine Glock 19 on his oversize blotter. "That's for you."

I reached for it, but he covered the weapon with his hand. "Not so fast, Marcinko-san. There are a couple of conditions."

"Such as?"

"First, that if there's a chance you're going someplace where you'll be using this and I'm not around, you call me so I can come along for the ride."

"No prob, Tosh."

"Good. I don't need nasty surprises at this stage of my career. Then—" He extracted a copy of *Rogue Warrior* from the desk. "You gotta sign this."

The sticker told me he'd bought it at the airport book store and paid ¥8,500—more than $65—for the $22 book.

To a Japanese cop—even a lieutenant inspector, that was a wad of money.

I was touched. I scrawled a properly obscene inscription and slid the book back to him. In return, he pushed the pistol across the desk.

I opened the slide and locked it to make sure there was no round in the chamber, then I dropped the empty magazine and hit the slide release. The pistol snapped closed with a satisfying whack. I dry-fired it, noting the easy trigger pull. Impressive. Quickly, I field-stripped the gun, making sure that the surfaces were dry and not overlubricated. I checked the barrel, firing pin, and extractor. Everything was perfect. I reassembled it, slammed the magazine home, and pulled the trigger again to put the gun into its "safe action" position. The trigger was smooth as silk—a terrific feel. Probably shot that way, too. "Nice action, Tosho, *suki desu*—I like it." I inclined my head in a traditional Japanese gesture of respect. *"Domo arigato*—thank you. What a great trigger."

Tosho nodded back at me. *"Do-itashi-mashite*—you're welcome. Yeah—Glocks like this normally come with five-pound triggers. But they make a three-pounder for their target model, so I bought a bunch and had our armorer install them instead. It makes a difference—except you'll probably fire six shots instead of two because it shoots so easy."

"Not likely." I slid the gun into my waistband. It fit beautifully. "Now—what do I shoot when I want to wax somebody, or do I just wave this in their direction and say, *'Banzai'?"*

"Ah, of course." Tosho picked up the phone, punched three keys, and barked into the receiver. In a moment, a youngster with a punkish haircut, leather jeans, and a Ralph Lauren T under his Elvis Presley motorcycle jacket entered the room. He bowed to Tosho, handed him a box of ammunition and a second magazine, said something in Japanese, and left.

"For you."

It was fifty rounds of Black Talon—Winchester's police-grade, man-stopping hollow-point. Not as good as the handmade hot loads we'd carried at SEAL Team Six, but it would do. "Who's the kid?"

"Yoshioka—Yoki. He works the club scene—places in Akasaka like Tangiru, where they do a fifties and sixties number. It's the latest craze—cocktails and Budweiser beer, and a Wurlitzer jukebox playing lots of Beatles, Beach Boys, Herman's Hermits, and Dion songs, and a heavy cocaine trade in the bathrooms. We keep an eye on 'em."

"Heavy drug problem these days?"

"It's growing. It's indicative of what's happening here. Face it, Dick, we're losing our identity, becoming just another Western nation, with all the associated problems— drugs, welfare, unemployment—the whole bit."

"Shit, Tosho, aren't you overreacting to a couple of fast-food joints, an amusement park, and some Elvis CDs?"

"It's not just McDonald's on Ginza Square, or Disneyland at Narita. Or the rock and roll and the Levis, and the fifties clubs. It's deeper than that. More dangerous."

"Come on, Tosho—you're sounding hysterical."

"Maybe it's time to get a little hysterical. Look, Dick, for years, we were isolated, self-contained, monolithic. Now we're a cosmopolitan superpower, and I'm not sure that's so good. Japanese society is like a sponge, and it's been soaking up too much of the bad stuff."

"It isn't just happening here."

"No, but it's Japan that I'm worried about."

"You're pretty Western."

"True. But I've been steeped in classic Japanese culture, too. I took a second master's degree at Kyoto University, in our philosophy and history. I study kendo—the way of the sword—and other classic martial arts two evenings a week now. These things made me change the way I look at the world. In some ways, we have to be Western—in my job, for example. But in others . . . no. In fact, we've got to turn back the clock in a few areas."

This from a Notre Dame grad who liked his Coors Right? I was amazed. "Tosho—"

"Even here—in my unit—things have changed, too. My

men work twelve-hour shifts, six days a week. Now, the government's telling me I have to give them two days off every week, and I can only work them ten hours a day."

It still sounded like slavery to me. "What's so bad about that?"

"They'll lose their Japanese-ness," Tosho said wistfully.

"Their *what?*"

"Their Japanese-ness. Their moral center. The thing that makes us different from everybody else."

"Tosho—"

"You're *gaijin,*" he said, a sad smile clouding his face. "You can't understand." He touched his heart. "It is in here. It is the key to our souls." His expression had become a mask, and I wasn't about to try to penetrate it.

"Whatever you say," I said.

The cloud disappeared. "Okay," Tosho said. "Tell me what you want to do first out at Narita. We'll grab a car and go have some fun."

Instead of a car, we grabbed some soup and noodles at a mom-and-pop soba joint around the corner from the police station, slurped our way through two economy-size bowls of broth and noodles, flavored with delicate green onion and a dash of soy. I would have ordered seconds, but mama-san behind the counter'd already poured our tea. We made a quick pit stop at my hotel for some goodies, then headed for Ueno Station to board the Keisei Skyliner express to the airport. Japanese trains are efficient, clean, and—given the astronomical cab fares to Narita—cheap. We paid ¥1,650 a ticket—just over $13. I nodded at the express check-in. Tosho shook his head. He understood. Bags were being checked, but not checked.

It reminded me of one of the major vulnerabilities of cruise ships—the lack of inspection of the on-board luggage. You could put a 40-Mike-Mike mortar in your steamer trunk and no one would discover it until too late. Same thing with the Skyliner—the train was completely vulnerable. Only at the airport would the passengers cue up for a bag inspection—and that would be cursory. I made a quick notation in the spiral book in my jacket pocket.

We wandered the six-car train once during the hour-long trip, but mainly I sat, nose pressed to window, looking at the ever-expanding megalopolis called Greater Tokyo as it passed in front of me at sixty miles per hour. We reached Narita Airport Station within thirty seconds of the arrival advertised in the printed timetable.

There, Tosho and I split up. He would observe, while I did the actual sneak-and-peek. That way he'd get to see how the *Nihonjin*—Japanese—reacted to this big, ugly, bearded *gaijin*.

Almost immediately, we realized that the news would not be good: here I was, carrying a pistol and extra magazine, and my suitcase was filled with explosives. But just being a round-eye was apparently sufficient to get me a friendly nod from the airport rent-a-cop, and a quick wave through the security barriers onto the buses that carried commuters and passengers to the other side of the airport and the main terminal. Give that man an F.

The policeman at the gate also flunked—he waved me through, although he searched the Japanese passengers. I saw Tosho grimace in disgust. It was more than evident that despite all the memos about my arrival, not to mention the IEDs I'd left behind the previous evening, the security personnel were still oblivious to their situation.

I abandoned the overnighter next to a trash container and walked to a bank of phones ten yards away. Would someone try to steal the suitcase? Would it flag the rent-a-cops? The answer to both questions was negatory. So, after ten minutes I retrieved it and moved on.

There were, according to the briefing I'd had before I left, roughly five hundred security personnel on duty at Narita, twenty-four hours a day. Were they all asleep? The fact that my actions hadn't tickled anybody's sensors seemed to indicate that they were. Their attitude was bad—complacent and self-satisfied.

This is a condition endemic to security directors, who tend to be former cops—in other words, tight-assed, rigid, numb-nutted bureaucrats. They, in turn, hire minimum-wage idiots and don't bother to train them properly.

What evidence do I have of this? I give you, your honors, a

list of hijacked and bombed flights as long as my thirty-five-inch arm, starting with TWA 847 and Pan Am 103. The terrorists could have been thwarted if decent security had been provided by airlines and airports.

There are two airlines—El Al and Swissair—that train and test their security personnel on a continuing basis. The number of Swissair and El Al flights hijacked in recent years is zero.

Thus endeth the lesson.

So, needless to say, my suitcase bomb was still intact and undiscovered. What to do with it? I could have placed it in the temporary holding area within the main terminal and let the timer run off by itself, or been fancier and used a remote firing device, creating casualties in the men's room or at one of the half dozen bars or restaurants on the mezzanine level.

Moreover, despite the cops, the undercover agents, the JDF soldiers, and the security checkpoints, I was wandering around the terminal packing heat. What Narita needed was metal detectors at all the front doors. That solution, Tosho and I knew, was unlikely.

But that wasn't the question of the moment. That question was where we'd leave our suitcase bomb to make the most impact.

We linked up, stopped at a bar, and I ordered two Kirins. "Time to place this little toy," I said. "Any ideas?"

"What are you thinking?"

I suggested the luggage claim area.

"Too obvious." Tosho also rejected the storage room and the lockers.

"What about hitting them so obviously they'll never realize what's happening?"

"Huh?"

"I'm thinking of rent-a-cop HQ."

"Brilliant. Coals to Newcastle." Tosho laughed out loud.

Yup—it was a terrific idea. I played with the timer while we sipped our Kirin, then took the suitcase—IED smoke bomb inside and timer set for twenty-five minutes—to the rent-a-cops manager's office. I knocked. No answer. I walked inside.

"Hello?"

No one answered. I peered into the office. The place was empty. That figured—after all, the door had been open.

I saw a bulletin board, with my picture mounted and a note scribbled in Japanese below it. Someone had left his wallet on a desk. I put it in my pocket. Then I slipped the suitcase next to the desk. It was all so simple. Just like when I was an enlisted Frogman back in the sixties, and we did what they call Zulu-5-Oscar, or Z/5/O, exercises in Norfolk harbor.

Z/5/Os were evade-and-escape drills in which Frogmen like me would try to attach limpet mines to ship hulls, while the ships' crews tried to catch us in *flagrante delicto,* otherwise known as *bombus interruptus.* No matter how hard they tried, they never caught us. Why? Because the officers in charge, just like the security supervisors at Narita, were idiots. They yelled and screamed, but never gave their men any real incentive (such as a twenty-four-hour pass) to catch us.

Here at Narita, things were much the same as they'd been in Norfolk three decades ago. The officers in charge weren't motivating the enlisted men, and it showed. An example? You want an example? Okay. Your safety depends on the security guards who man the metal detectors and X-ray machines, right? Right. And how much are those people paid? Minimum wage.

So how do you motivate them? I'd give 'em a big fat bonus for every piece of contraband they discover. But that solution is too simple for most airlines. What they do is yell and scream. So, what you get is a security guard who doesn't give a rusty fuck whether I'm carrying an attaché case filled with papers or an attaché case filled with grenades.

I armed the timer and closed the suitcase. Well, maybe this would teach them something. Doom on you, assholes.

In less than two minutes I was back at the bar. I gave Tosho the wallet, drained my beer, and stood up. "Time to prowl and growl. Save my place."

With Tosho watching, I picked a lock and descended two flights into the commissary area. To my right lay the access ramp from the dock where the food trucks drove up and delivered their cargo. A brace of freight-elevator doors sat off to the side—keyless operation, too. That meant anybody could ride them. Down a long passageway to my left, the quarantine area and employee locker room doors were visible.

The main kitchens were straight ahead, through a set of double pneumatic doors. I pushed and stepped inside and was greeted by a blast of frigid air. The temperature must have dropped by twenty-five degrees. No salmonella here. The place was all white tile and bright, green-tinged fluorescent light. It reminded me of the kitchen at Petersburg prison. Well, time to move around. I started toward the big reefers, where I intended to leave one of my MARCINKO THE TERRORIST SAYS HAVE A NICE DAY stickers, but a sumo-sized cook in a white jacket and paper chef's cap intercepted me before I'd gotten ten feet. He was carrying a cleaver in extra large.

"Sumimasen?"

"Excuse me?"

"Wakarimasu ka Nihongo?"

"Eigo—English," I said. "No Japanese."

"No come here," said Sumo sternly. "No come here."

Smoke and mirrors time. I bowed. "My name is Marcinko. I'm an American journalist writing a story about airline food preparation in Japan."

"Oh."

"Hai—yes."

"Oh."

"Can you show me around? I'd like to see the facilities here. I visited Haneda yesterday." Haneda was Tokyo's other airport—smaller, and much closer to the city.

Sumo shook his head and explained in halting English that I would have to make an appointment to view the commissary areas with the airport authorities. Furthermore, he explained, I would need a health certificate. "It is too easy to contaminating the preparation areas otherwise."

He ushered me back up the stairs and opened the door for me. I heard him double-check the lock before he returned to work. That guy would get an A in my memo.

I retired back to the bar in the passenger waiting area.

Tosho had moved us to a pair of stools with a better view of the security office.

I checked my watch. "Should be coming up soon," I said.

Three minutes later, we heard a muffled whomp, and the door flew open to reveal thick yellow smoke. Half a dozen rent-a-cops came stumbling out into the crowded passageway, coughing and gagging. There was screaming and yelling, and within minutes dozens of cops, soldiers, and security people were outshouting each other, while they tried to figure out what the hell had happened to them and who was to blame.

After a few minutes, two blue-uniformed men with oxygen rigs on their backs and fire extinguishers shouldered their way through the crowd and back into the office. Tosho laughed at the mess across the hall. "What a clusterfuck."

We prowled and growled for another hour. Despite the fact that the airport had been put on alert, it was absurdly easy to penetrate supposedly "secure" areas, and heads would roll when I wrote my report.

Tosho and I took the train back to town. He wanted to spend the rest of the day hitting his favorite bars, but I begged off and cabbed to the Okura, took a shower to collect my thoughts, then wrote another long cable to O'Bannion. At about five I ambled downstairs to the Garden Lounge, where I sat watching the sunset and nursing a Bombay until seven-thirty, when I was accosted by something small, buxom, blond, and Australian. For some wonderful reason, Aussie women just love me. Maybe it's the way I say "Sheila." Maybe they think I look like a koala. Maybe I remind them of home. Maybe it's the promises I make. Whatever the case, half an hour later we were upstairs in my big Japanese tub with a triple order of room-service sake and I was assaulting Mount Suribachi yelling, *"Banzai."*

By 0-Dark Hundred—that's the wee, wee hours of the morning to you civilians—the pressure relieved, I was back in my favorite culvert, dressed in my basic black, cold and wet, watching and waiting.

I slid the Glock from my pocket, checked the magazine,

then chambered a round. Better safe than sorry. It hit me that I hadn't fired the gun, but it was in perfect shape, and what the hell—what's life without a surprise or two? Then I thought of Tosho—oh, shit, I hadn't called him. Well, it was better that way. Why keep him up all night when he could be in bed lolling in the hay or whatever Japs do.

I caught a ride on a Coca-Cola delivery truck, jumping for the rear bumper while the driver punched in his access code, and holding on for dear life as he jounced over the speed bumps going down the ramp to the subterranean passageways. He parked near the concourse elevators, so I figured I was right under the main terminal area—the perfect location for ten pounds of C-4 explosive. I rigged an IED so it would go off when the elevator doors were opened, then placed a sticker nearby. Then I wandered along a series of hundred-foot-deep, six-foot-high concrete bays where drivers parked and recharged the electric delivery vehicles that shuttled baggage and packages up and down the three miles of underground highway. Peering and poking at cargo that had been parked between flights, I made my way toward the short-term freight area to do some other damage.

I moved along the walls from bay to bay, using the shadows cast by the crates, containers, and vehicles to my advantage. It took three hours to move the thousand or so yards down the subterranean road, examining each bay for signs of pilferage as I moved through the dimly lit passageway. Nothing. So I affixed my have-a-nice-day stickers to crates and left seven IEDs behind, each rigged with a slightly different booby-trap mechanism. Doom on you, security forces.

It was four A.M. as I eased into the rearmost departure bay. I stopped short. Flashlights shone at the far end and I heard the scraping of wood on concrete. The hair on the back of my neck stood up. My whole body tingled with a delicious mixture of fear, anticipation, and tension. It was like the first patrol in Vietnam, or the first jump from thirty-five thousand feet—a mystical sense of apprehension coupled with the exhilaration of finally being able to get the job done. At last, I'd come upon something unexpected. I moved forward, inch by inch, to see what was going on, easing my way around a pile of six-foot containers, working my way toward the noise.

I squinted in the dim light. By the sound of it, someone was muling around large crates. I didn't understand why they weren't using the forklifts I'd seen in the main passageway—except that perhaps they didn't want to attract attention. I crept closer until I could make them out—four men, jabbering at each other as they worked on a crate with a crowbar.

I watched for a few seconds, wondering whether they were ripping off an incoming shipment or stashing drugs in an outgoing container. I worked my way closer, and all of a sudden the rhythm and cadences of their chattering hit me like a club. Geezus—these guys weren't Japs, they were Koreans.

Shit. Koreans have no sense of humor. Zero. Zippo. None. How could they? They live on kimchi, which is a foul mixture of garlic-laden sour cabbage laced with hot peppers, poured into a clay pot, buried like a rotting corpse, and left in the ground to ferment for months. It is impossible to eat kimchi and have a sense of humor.

I dropped and scuttled across the floor to get closer. But I wasn't alone. Mr. Murphy of Murphy's Law fame had snuck up on me in the dark, and he hooked my foot on a dolly handle as I crawled. *Kerrrrang!* It hit the hard concrete with a ring that sounded like Big Ben. Doom on you, Dickie.

The Koreans turned in my direction and broke out firepower. I did, too. I raised the Glock. I hadn't shot a gun since before I'd gone to jail, but what the fuck—they say that shooting is like riding a bike.

As the first of them charged in my direction, I dropped him with a double tap. From my vantage point and pucker factor it looked like a gut shot at four P.M. and a rise to the neck. Was it the surge of adrenaline that made me squeeze and heel? Who cared—the SOB went *down*.

My heart was doing about a hundred miles per hour. I rolled right to draw fire. It worked—a piece of wood splintered somewhere above my head and I saw a muzzle blast at ten o'clock.

April fool, motherfucker. I rolled again and came up on a

knee, my Glock's night sights three even green dots in the semidarkness.

Bingo. Kimchi Number Two was right in my sight picture six feet away, his round face amazed that this bearded gringo ninja had him and he was about to meet his ancestors.

"Fuck you—" I pulled the trigger three times and rocked him back, a triangle of holes in his chest. Doom on you, asshole.

I rolled again, my shoulder smashing into the concrete as I scrambled for cover, firing wildly down the bay while I shifted. A ricochet came too close and I felt wetness on my cheek. No time to check how bad it was, just move, roll, and fire. Shit—the mag ran dry. I reached for the backup in my pocket.

Goddamn—where the hell was it? I fumbled around, cursing.

The pause to change magazines must have given them a thirst for success or some other damn kamikaze syndrome because I heard a big scrambling of feet, and the next thing I knew, one of them was on top of me. I could see the whites of his eyes as he rounded a crate at full gallop, his hand wrapped around a big knife. My gun was still empty.

I could almost hear the profane growl of my old UDT platoon boss, Chief Gunner's Mate Everett E. Barrett, in my brain as the kimchi rushed me. *Do not be a fucking fumble-fingers, Marcinko. Take the fucking magazine. Now, put it in the motherfucking gun, release the fucking slide, and shoot the son of a bitch. Do not screw up. I said, shoot the son of a bitch, Marcinko, you shit-for-brains no-load cockbreath pus-nuts pencil-dicked asshole geek!*

It felt like it took me a week, but I finally wrapped my sweaty fucking fumble-fingers around the magazine, pulled it out of my pocket, slapped it home, dropped the slide, and shot the son of a bitch—all in the space of about a second and a half.

Not a moment too soon, either. By the time I'd loaded and locked he was on top of me, charging like a bull, his face ratcheted in anger or fear or both, knife coming for my eyes, a scream in his throat. I never even had a chance to raise the weapon. All I could do was fire from a crouched position and hope he'd fucking drop like a stone.

It was so easy to pull the three-pound trigger I put five rounds in him before I could stop. Shit—don't waste bullets, you asshole. What if they had reinforcements outside—what the hell was I going to do, wave my lizard at 'em?

Kimchi Three went down but his momentum carried him into me. I ducked the blade and hit him in the face with the side of the gun to knock him away. He stopped moving. I rolled him over and shot him again in the head at close range to make sure he was dead. After all, when there's a question, leave no doubt. I gave the kimchi a quick once-over. I'd walked the rounds from his right thigh through his groin to his heart and then shoulder. It was reflex firing—and lots of luck.

Now on to Kimchi Number Four. There was movement at my two o'clock. I saw him scramble for the main corridor, about fifteen yards away. I tried to get a sight picture but I was so pumped up I was shaking. I braced my forearm on top of the nearest crate, acquired front-sight picture, and squeezed off a controlled three-round burst as the Korean was silhouetted against the passageway light. Controlled burst—like hell. Only one of them hit, but he still pitched forward. Goo-bye.

Sure I shot him in the back. I have no pride about things like that. A back shot is still a shot, and whether you believe it's fair or not, it does the job—it kills your enemy.

I collapsed, sweaty, bleeding, and still shaking. But as I lay on the cold concrete, I flashed on something great: all the days of stress-firing at SEAL Team Six had paid off. I don't remember how many times I'd chased through rooms full of furniture and boxes, firing at moving targets, dinging my old shins and brittle elbows on sharp edges, trying to impress my baby SEAL shooters with the importance of being able to shoot when you're pumped up and under incredible stress, your heart is going a mile a minute, and you don't know what the hell's gonna happen to you next.

They'd bitch at me. Complain that they knew all this shit and there was no need to do it again and again and again and again. "Fuck you," I'd tell 'em. "The more you bleed in training, the less you'll bleed in combat." I felt I was right, but I had no proof. But I said it anyway because it made perfect sense.

Now, lying out of breath on my back in the subterranean cargo bay, the pulse racing in my ears, I remembered how, over cold beer with the troops after we'd spent the day stress-firing, I'd count my newly gained scar tissue and wonder if it really *was* all worthwhile.

Tonight, I could answer that question unequivocally.

Tonight, I'd been alone. Sans backup. Sans friends, allies, or fellow shooters.

It was the edge I'd honed during SEAL Team Six training that got me through.

Chapter

3

TOSHO AND A CREW OF SIX ARRIVED IN TIME TO PICK UP THE pieces. It took them less than half an hour from Tokyo, which meant he'd probably scrambled a chopper. Actually, he'd scrambled a pair of them, and as it turned out the expense was worth it. The kimchis turned out to be North Koreans—citizens of a country not recognized by the United States, but legal residents in Japan. The papers they carried indicated they all had jobs. One worked at the North Korean embassy as a clerk. Tosho knew about him—he was an intelligence agent. Another did menial labor in Tokyo. And two carried corporate IDs from Matsuko. I knew that name—and I didn't like it very much. Matsuko had made millions by selling top-secret, seven-axis milling machines to the Soviets back in the late seventies. The two-story-high, three-hundred-ton tools had made it possible for the Soviet Navy to build eleven-bladed submarine propellers that ran as quietly as the ones on U.S. attack subs. In its quest for profits, Matsuko had forever changed the dynamics of undersea warfare.

Before he got down to business, Tosho gave me a dressing down that would have done Ev Barrett proud. "You dumb cocksucking shit-for-brains asshole," he began. "What the hell did you think you were doing blowing people away without calling me first?"

He answered his own question. "You were fucking up!" he shouted, his nose about an inch from mine. "You were fucking up and causing me great personal loss of face." Pause. "Goddammit, Dick—"

I tried to get a word in edgewise. Tosho was having none of it. "Not a fucking word until I see what the hell happened here."

He calmed down when he discovered what I'd blundered into. The goods the kimchis had been muling around in the cargo bay when I interrupted them was a container of high-speed detonators—electronic switches virtually identical to krytrons, the small, precise electronic triggers used for nuclear weapons.

These were small detonators, the kind that could be used on tactical missiles such as Tomahawks. I'd seen similar ones during Red Cell infiltrations of naval weapons depots. This crate had been innocuously labeled ACME AIR-CONDITIONING PARTS and shipped to Narita through a roundabout odyssey that included London, Frankfurt, and Rome. The final destination on the polyglot manifest stapled to the side of the box was an electronics firm in Hong Kong.

Obviously, I'd interrupted the Koreans playing a Pyongyang version of three-card monte, in which the detonators were the ace in the hole, and the kimchis' sleight of hand would cause them to end up in the North Korean nuclear program, while the empty crate continued to the Crown Colony.

Two of the tangos were still alive—I guess my marksmanship wasn't what it used to be—and Tosho had them transferred under heavy guard to a hospital where they'd be patched up before interrogation. I received first aid for the ricochet wound on my cheek, then he and I choppered back to Tokyo, where I debriefed at his HQ and called O'Bannion to let him know about my adventures and the capacitors, so he could inform Fujoki about the Koreans.

I was still in overdrive. My mind was moving at warp speed, reliving the shootout, trying to extract whatever I could. But I kept getting the same error message every time: "Something is wrong with this picture." I was just too crazy or tired or hyper to figure out what the bad element was. Doom on me.

By then it was 0900. Tosho's researcher told me the company that made the capacitors was called Jones-Hamilton. I got on the computer and played with Nexis and Dow Jones for a while and discovered that Jones-Hamilton was a California-based contractor that did a bunch of hush-hush work for the Defense Department, mostly because one of its directors was a former secretary of defense named Grant Griffith.

I vaguely knew Griffith's name—he was some big muckety-muck. Probably a crook, too, given the fact that it was illegal to ship nuclear detonators. While I played Sherlock, I had Tosho run a trace on the air-conditioner company on the manifest. It was owned by one Grant Griffith. One time can be an accident. Twice is not. This guy was dirty.

We called Hawaii. When I told O'Bannion what I'd discovered, he instructed me at once to pass the word on through channels. Between the nuclear detonators and the involvement of a former SECDEF, the proper authorities would want to know.

Tosho drove me to the American embassy. I phoned the naval attaché's office from the Marine security booth and asked for an immediate appointment. His royal highness Commander Blivet Sphincter, Jr., or whatever his name was, was too busy to see me right away, so while I waited, I dropped by the commissary to pick Tosho up a case of tax-free Haig & Haig "Dimple" Scotch as a way of saying thanks for the Glock, the ammo, and the moral support.

"Think of this as a bribe," I told him.

He stowed the package in the trunk of his car as lovingly as if he were dealing with an ancestor's ashes. "Absolutely, Buster Brown, you know it," he said. "Don't forget—I was educated in your country. I'm familiar with your customs."

Then we sat in a reception room on the third floor of the huge embassy building watching the passing State Department apparatchiki in their pin-striped suits as they twiddled their thumbs and rocked on their heels and jingled their pocket change. We made small talk and read six-month-old issues of *People*.

After a two-hour wait I was finally admitted to naval Valhalla. The attaché, a ship driver, wore a starched shirt, an Academy ring, and a bored expression. He didn't bother taking notes. I was in and out in ten minutes.

That steamed me. We were talking tactical nuclear weapons parts after all, and all this guy could do was nod. Well, fuck him—I'd call my old friend Tony Mercaldi when I got back to the States. Tony works at DIA doing God's work. He'd move on the info. Meanwhile, I'd kissed all the necessary signets here in Tokyo, and I was free to go.

Well, I was almost free to go. Tosho kept me under wraps for twelve hours.

He explained why during a walk we took in the park just outside the old Imperial Palace, a venue where Tosho said it would be almost impossible to bug the conversation. "This is one of those awkward things, Dick."

"Shoot, Tosho."

He shrugged. "Look—we've got problems here. First of all, when we took the crates apart, we found three passive omnidirectional monitors."

"The shipment was bugged?" That blew me away.

"Yup. And the stuff appears to be American made."

Had I strolled upon a scam run by Christians in Action— the SEAL nickname for the CIA—or some other alphabet-soup agency? What the hell was going on here?

Tosho said he hadn't the foggiest. "But I do know there's a former U.S. secretary of defense involved in what appears to be a weapons smuggling operation to North Korea. I'd like to question him—and I've let my superiors understand it in no uncertain terms. Trouble is, he has a few friends in very high places here in Japan, and they've been able to keep Kunika's hands tied for the present. The orders were real simple: quote, Do not proceed. Full stop, end quote."

"Sounds like the start of a cover-up to me."

"That's the way I look at it, too. Officially, we've been told to lay off. But my boss isn't willing to let go so easy."

"Even though I've never met him, I like him already."

Tosho grinned. "He's an ornery old bird. Irascible curmudgeon. Independent. Very un-Japanese. But he gave me a shrug, a wink, and a nod—and I know how to read his body language. He was telling me to move ahead, but very, very cautiously."

"Are you?" If Tosho was planning to move ahead with an investigation, I'd want to be a part of things.

In fact, I'd already decided to pursue Grant fucking Griffith on my own when I got back to the States.

Why? you ask.

Good question. The answer is simple. Look—the Navy may have fucked me, but it's still the Navy in which I served for more than thirty years. It's the same Navy that took me in, educated me, gave me brave men to lead, and the opportunity to hunt and kill my enemy.

And when some goddamn millionaire lawyer runs a scam that could end up costing Navy lives, I want to plant his ass in the ground.

I looked at Tosho. "So?"

"Dick, I need a favor. You still have your old connections and their fancy computers at DIA and Langley. Dig up whatever info you can find on Grant Griffith and what he's up to, and pass it along to me. In return, I'll share my stuff with you."

I didn't answer. Instinctively, I didn't warm to the idea. I didn't mind a collegial relationship with Tosho. When I ran Red Cell, he and I were each representatives of our governments, and we shared official information on that basis. But now, I had no official status. The bottom line is that he was trying to make an agent out of me. That's what an agent is—a foreign national who gives information to an intelligence officer. And in Japan, I was a foreign national, and Tosho was an intelligence officer. You think I'm splitting hairs? Well, call it what you will, the bottom line was that I'd be Tosho's spy.

Still, the arrangement made a certain amount of sense— if I could shimmy it in certain directions. Certainly, there was no possibility I'd use my connections at DIA or CIA to pass information to a foreign government. There's a word for that—it's called treason.

But Tosho had access to information I didn't. He represented an official agency and had the use of all its facilities —whether or not he was operating covertly. Me? I was a retired ex-felon. And if my information—what there would be of it—stayed nonclassified, there was nothing wrong about sharing it with him.

"Deal." I shook his hand.

Tosho made sure I was on a plane home by the end of the day. He'd managed to keep the Narita story under wraps and didn't want me hanging around just in case the press or anyone else got nosy. So he drove me to the Okura, checked me out, ferried me to Narita, walked me through security, got me upgraded to first class, and bowed like a fucking movie samurai at the gate. I watched him through the window—he stayed right there nose pressed against glass until they pulled the ramp away, backed the 747 onto the apron, and wheeled it toward the taxiway.

Like Ronald Reagan used to say to Gorbie, trust but verify. *Sayonara,* Tosho. I spent the next fifteen hours alternating between working the three-pound laptop computer O'Bannion had given me, snoozing, and sipping Dom Pérignon as we flew nonstop back to Dulles. As I wrote the first draft of my report to Black Jack Morrison, I mused that, all in all, it had been a successful trip. I'd hit some bad guys, gotten laid, eaten lots of raw fish, and even had a few days of fun and games while sneaking and peeking. Who says life ain't great?

The only snake in the woodpile was the former SECDEF whose company was smuggling forbidden fruit to the kimchis. Don't get me wrong—I'm no Boy Scout. But, like I just said, I spent thirty-plus years in the Navy, and even though I think the system sucks, I believe in the men who do the job.

I shut off my computer, switched my attention to the bubbles in my flute of champagne, and thought of ways to check this guy out.

There was a string of messages as long as my cock when I got back to Rogue Manor, my house in the woods about sixty miles from Washington, so I poured a Bombay on the rocks and listened to them both. That is a joke. Mostly, they were nasty calls from creditors, bitchy threats from my ex-wife, pleas for money from the kids, and calls from assorted friends asking where the hell I'd been and when could we get together for some Bombay and gossip.

Most gratifying, there was a short, sweet "Fuck you very much," from Nasty Nick Grundle. Nick's twenty-five-second message told me he was calling from a pay phone somewhere on the road—operational security and all that —but that he and the boys would check in with me, real quietly, the next time they hit D.C. "Life is terrible, the CO's a piece of shit, and we're all bored because nobody lets us shoot and loot anymore. Hoist a Bombay for us, Skipper —we need it bad."

Damn—there were actually tears in my eyes when I replayed the message the third time. Nicky—and the rest of the Navy's clandestine SpecWar community, which is called Naval Special Warfare Development Group, or DEVGRP these days—had been ordered not to communicate with me. DEVGRP's CO, a senior four-striper named Hal Mushnik, known as Captain Mush Mouth to the men, sent a memo to all hands. It said that any sailor who contacted Dick Marcinko would lose his security clearance. For those of you who don't understand the significance of that, suffice it to say that without a security clearance, a SEAL cannot deal with classified material. And almost everything the SEALs in DEVGRP deal with is classified.

I'd heard about Mush Mouth's memo through the SEAL grapevine. There were even whispers that my home phones were tapped and my mail checked. Whether or not the rumors were true, the warning worked. Until now, I'd been successfully excommunicated from the men I'd led.

Nasty's message meant there'd been a change. What was behind it? Who knew. Who cared—so long as it meant I'd be able to see my SEALs again.

Finally, there were eight separate messages from a secretary at something called Allied National Technologies, asking if I'd call back about a personal protection job for the company's CEO. After the third message, the secretary's voice took on a tone of urgency. By the eighth and final call she sounded downright frantic.

I wasn't anxious to call back. I've tried to stay away from VIP protection. I had to do it in order to pay for a lawyer and two criminal trials, but I vowed that I wouldn't do it again. Mostly, the work is boring, and the people you're paid to protect are assholes. You are basically a well-paid nursemaid—I charged $2,500 a day plus expenses and first-class travel—who's treated like a cross between a servant and a chauffeur. I've had CEOs' wives order me to polish the silver and their daughters try to diddle me while Daddy's turned the other way. You can't drink and you don't get to eat very often, and the hours are long.

Every once in a while there are thrills and chills. Just before I went to prison I had a terrific assignment in Pakistan, for example, when I played offensive lineman for an oil company exec who'd been targeted by local gangsters. I kept his ass safe, slapped around a couple of bad guys, and got to eat some of the hottest food this side of Jalapeño. But in 99 percent of the cases, you are a mere bump on a log. A well-paid bump, but a bump nonetheless.

Besides, I'd had my fill of VIP protection in the Navy. During the mideighties, I was assigned to protect the CNO, Adm. James Watkins, on a trip to Central America. There had been significant terrorist threats against his life, but he didn't want a big entourage traveling with him. Besides, he hated the Naval Investigative Service, which was formally responsible for his safety, and I was asked to head a one-man detail to replace the ten no-load, shit-for-brains NIS dip-dunks who normally traveled with the CNO.

I went in uniform, all beribboned and medaled. I carried a leather briefcase that looked just like the CNO's. His was made by some fancy luggage maker like Crouch and Fitzgerald. Mine was made by Heckler & Koch, the Kraut gunmakers. It had an MP5 submachine gun inside, and the briefcase handle contained the trigger. The rig wasn't accurate—if I unloaded, I'd take out friendlies as well as bad guys—but my job was to protect Watkins, not worry about assholes getting in my way.

The MP5 wasn't my only option. I was actually a walking, talking arsenal. In my pockets I carried an assortment of minigrenades, each about the size of a Ping-Pong ball, each about as lethal as a cluster bomblet. I had a leather sap, a knife, and a trusty, palm-sized Detonics .45-caliber Combat Master Mark I automatic concealed on my person. Behind my belt was a garrote. The belt buckle hid a dagger. And I never left the CNO's side. I tucked him in bed at night and I rousted him in the A.M. I slept in the room next to his. We ate, drank, and even peed and shat together. It was the first time I'd ever been overseas that I didn't get a piece of ass or a drink of wine. I liked CNO Watkins—still do. And the first trip was okay. But not the second, third, fourth, fifth, or sixth. It was then that I decided VIP protection sucks. It's no way to live. Not for me.

So I took my time about getting back to Allied. I finished my report for Black Jack Morrison and sent it out Federal Express. I cut, chopped, and split two cords of wood, shredded three cubic yards of chips for the English garden, and finished off about a fifth of Bombay down in the Jacuzzi. I also turned on the computer and ran Grant Griffith's name through Nexis and a few other databases.

He'd been profiled not six months before in the *Washington Post*—one of those fawning Style section blow jobs that made him into a goddamn Boy Scout and his fucking influence peddling sound like public service. There was a more interesting—and valuable—article in *Business Week,* which covered Griffith's extensive web of influence. I photocopied it and used it as the basis for an organizational chart.

I also called Tony Mercaldi at DIA and asked for a meet. We rendezvoused at the Officers' Club at Bolling Air Force Base, on the eastern bank of the Anacostia River just outside Washington, and spent a two-hour lunch catching up while I briefed him on my trip to Japan, and the official ennui with which my findings had been greeted.

Tony shook his head. "Assholes," he said. "They don't understand how close the North Koreans are to building a bomb. Without getting into classified areas, we estimate they're less than twenty-two months from having one."

"What's holding them up?"

"Things like the detonators you ran into. They have capacitors from the Soviets—" Mercaldi rolled his eyes skyward. "Sorry, they're Russians now. Anyway, capacitor-detonated bombs are iffy—inconsistent. So they need state-of-the-art elements to make modern nukes. Electronic. Transistorized. Miniature."

Mercaldi's information was dovetailing nicely into what I'd seen. So I relayed my suspicions about Grant Griffith. Much to my surprise, Merc told me I was way off base. "He's one of the good guys, Dick."

"Yeah? Well, then why the hell is he back-channeling nuclear detonators?"

Mercaldi brushed a crumb from the blouse of his Air Force colonel's uniform. "Don't know. But if Grant Griffith did it, he had his reasons."

He explained that Griffith had helped the Pentagon before in solving cases of high-tech smuggling to the Soviet Union, and it was entirely conceivable that he was doing so again.

I wasn't entirely convinced, but what Merc had to say mollified me somewhat. Still, I made him promise that he'd check out the situation and get back to me soon. There was something about Grant Griffith that made me uneasy, and my instincts about things like these have always been good.

I faxed a bunch of press clips to Tosho along with a note that I'd be in touch soon. Then I climbed back onto the computer and began to research Allied. There wasn't much. ANT was a small firm that did 90 percent of its business with the Navy. End of story. By then it was the evening and the morning of the sixth day and I returned Allied's call.

I was told that the company's CEO had gotten a death threat. I suggested they go to the police. I was told the threat wasn't concrete enough for police action, and my name had been dropped by someone in the Navy.

I was suspicious. Was this what they call in the intelligence field a "dangle," a Navy-inspired sting to try to get me to commit conspiracy to murder?

I told Allied in plain English that my protection work was just that—protection. It was defensive, not offensive, in nature.

That's what we're looking for, the man said.

I suggested an outrageous fee. I was told they'd been

quoted much higher prices, and my bid sounded good. I kicked myself and grudgingly suggested that I meet the VIP in question before they commit. Maybe he'd hate me. Maybe I could insult him. Maybe I'd stiff him. Maybe.

On the one hand, I didn't want the trouble. On the other hand, I was broke, and in my immigrant family, one worked for a living. What's his name? I asked.

Joseph Andrews, I was told. He's an engineer by trade. Great. A WASP named after a Henry Fielding novel who does his diddling with a slide rule.

Against my better judgment we set up a meet-and-greet in Old Town Alexandria, at a restaurant on the Potomac called the Chart House. I like the place. It's like a comfortable living room—the decor's informal, the food's good, the drinks are big, and the waiters don't hover. We'd meet for dinner. He'd pick up the check and, more importantly, the bar tab.

I knew him the moment he walked in the door. Thin, sixtyish, white haired. But it was the Ross Perot pompadour, generic pin-striped gray suit, white polyester shirt, blue tie, and plastic pen-holder in his breast pocket that gave him away. You see one engineer, you've seen 'em all.

Michael, the manager, led him to my table.

He looked down at me as if he'd come upon an alien. My hair lay in a single braid that came below my shoulders. My beard was somewhere between Tartar and Visigoth. "Mr. Marcinko?"

"C'est moi." I stood up. *"Enchanté."*

"Joe Andrews. Puleezed to meetcha."

We shook hands. He had a firm, dry grip. I liked that.

We sat. He ordered diet Coke. This was not a good omen. I drained my Bombay, ordered another triple, and made small talk. I figured I'd give him a couple of hours, hit him for dinner, and split.

He stared at me through thick glasses. He was one of those guys who look naked without a pocket computer in their hands. He blinked a lot, too. I thought he resembled a slightly bemused chipmunk. I gave him the mental radio handle of Alvin.

We sparred for about half an hour, doing the touchie-feelie stuff that you always gotta do. We played Jewish

Geography—the game of who do you know—and tried to figure out where we might have crossed paths.

To my surprise I discovered that we had more in common than I might have imagined. His name hadn't always been Andrews. He'd been born Josef Amajuk, the eldest son of a Croatian immigrant shoemaker, in a two-story row house in a tenement neighborhood in North Philadelphia. That made us both Pennsylvanians from working-class families—I came from a long line of Slovak coal miners and I was born in my grandmother Justine Pavlik's tiny frame house in Lansford, Pennsylvania. So we both knew about sweat, heartbreak, and slivovitz—although I was the only one who still drank it.

Like me, he was a bootstrap guy who'd worked his way up from poverty. He'd put himself through college—Temple University and grad school at MIT. For twenty years, he'd worked as a designer for International Dynamics, helping to build many of the guidance systems that went into the Navy's stealth underwater systems. Then, abruptly, he'd quit because, as he put it, the system was screwing itself, and he wanted to make waves, not pour oil.

He'd built his own defense-oriented business, designing guidance systems for Navy missiles, and made it prosper by doing it the old-fashioned way—sweat and blood. He had a wife he'd married while he was a grad student, and three grown kids—all doctors. I told him I should be so lucky. My kids are in their twenties, but they haven't grown up yet. Maybe someday.

Me, I'd taken the Navy route—a high-school dropout who joined at seventeen to escape reform school. I became a Frogman because I wanted to kick ass and take names. Then, because of incessant prodding by my first sea daddy, that wonderfully profane, delightfully obscene Underwater Demolition Team platoon chief named Ev Barrett, whose voice I always heard in my brain during times of stress, I got my high-school GED, went to Officer Candidate School, and was commissioned. Then I became a SEAL. And then it was more than twenty years of shooting and looting, hopping and popping, raping, pillaging, and burning. I served as an attaché in Cambodia, where I body-surfed on the Mekong River under Khmer Rouge fire. I commanded SEAL Team

Two. I earned a college degree, and even an MA from Auburn.

And then, in 1980, I was ordered to build the Navy's answer to Delta Force, SEAL Team Six. I retired ten years later, the subject of a $60-million investigation. Twenty-three months after that I was indicted by the Department of Justice, suffered through two criminal trials, and ultimately did a year in a federal pen.

They investigated me at about the same time they were investigating Ollie North. They got him for shredding paper. They got me for shredding people.

I had more fun doing my shredding than Ollie did doing his.

But enough about me. What makes you tick, Joe?

Well, he said, he was fifty-eight, his kids were grown, and he wanted to work not for them, but for himself. He was a small businessman in a world of multinational corporations and defense cutbacks, but the challenge suited him, and he wanted to win. That sounded good to me. So why, I asked, did he feel he needed protection?

He explained that he was making his bread and butter designing telemetry systems for a new Navy missile project. But that his soul belonged to a new project: he'd gone ass over teakettle in hock to buy an Italian company that built toroidal-hulled diesel minisubs, appropriately named Focas, or seals. Focas were small, maneuverable craft that could carry eight to twenty-five people and were especially effective for SEAL operations. But so far, the Navy had rejected anything to do with Andrews's sub, refusing even to evaluate it. If it was diesel, he was told, the Navy wasn't interested.

That made perfect sense to me. I'd found it out in 1974, when, as the commanding officer of SEAL Team Two, I'd tried to get the Navy to buy a sub remarkably similar to the Foca—a twelve-man dry sub for CALOW, or Coastal And Limited-Objective Warfare use. I was turned down back then, just like Joe was being goatfucked now, because of an internal dispute between Surface Force, which funds and controls SEALs, and Submarine Force, which funds and controls submarines.

I could write reams on the subject, but the bottom line is

that Surface Force can't buy subs, and Sub Force won't buy diesels.

It meant Joe was getting screwed by a system so inflexible, narrow-minded, and rigid that even if he'd had a perfect vehicle, the Navy would reject it. So far, he said, he'd poured more than 2 million of his own dollars into the Foca. He'd hocked his house and taken bank loans. But the payoff would be worth it. If the Navy bought twenty-five Focas at $4.5 million each, he'd gross over $110 million and net more than half.

That's big bucks, Joe.

"Bet your ass, Dick." About the only hope he had left, he continued, was to hire a lobbyist to take his case directly to the top echelons of the Pentagon—the offices he hadn't been able to crack on his own.

So, I asked, what's stopping you?

The fee. Joe explained that there was only one man in town who could convince Sub Force to buy a diesel sub. That was Grant Griffith—the former SECDEF. But he charged $1,500 an hour, with a two-hundred-hour minimum up front. "That's a third of a million dollars, Dick—I don't have it."

That name made my ears prick up. If this guy wanted to be represented by Griffith, I was interested in sticking to him like glue. Especially since he was building the exact kind of underwater vehicle countries like North Korea could use to smuggle nuclear materials.

I asked about the death threat, and how he'd gotten to me.

"I got to you because I talked to a friend of mine at DIA and asked if he knew anybody I could call."

"What's his name?"

"I'd rather not say."

"What's his job?"

"He handles Spec Ops stuff."

"What branch?"

Joe looked at me and smiled. "Can't say, Dick. If I did, you'd know exactly who I was talking about—and he wants to stay out of it. But he told me that if I wanted the best, then I'd hire you. He says the Navy railroaded you."

Well, I knew fifty guys like that at DIA—from Air Force weenies like my old pal Tony Mercaldi to SEALs I'd schooled at Team Six to Army assholes I'd cross-trained with at various times in my career. And as for the fact that the Navy screwed me—I agreed with that sentiment whole-heartedly. "Okay—let's say I'm not being set up here. Why do you think you need protection in the first place?"

"Cluster bombs," Joe said.

That made no sense at all. I called for another triple Bombay, my third since he'd arrived. Joe sipped his original diet Coke and explained. He was involved in a new design for the cluster bombs used by Navy Air, making them more efficient, by which, of course, he meant more deadly. At one stage, the work involved animals—research on wounds—and it had somehow attracted the attention of a bunch of animal rights activists. It had all begun suddenly, about the same time I'd been in Japan. One day everything was normal. The next, Joe's tires had been slashed, his car spray-painted, and a dozen obscene phone calls left on his answering machine. Two days later, he'd received the first of a dozen threatening notes—he brought them to show me—complete with snapshots of him going to work. It was enough to make him very nervous.

"What about the cops?"

"They say if something happens they'll take action."

Of course. What had I been thinking? I perused the pictures and documents. He wasn't just another paranoid CEO who wanted to look important. He'd actually been threatened. We got down to the nitty-gritty over grilled swordfish. He didn't balk when I ordered a nice, flinty white Graves to go with the fish. He even had a glass. Okay, half a glass.

By the end of the evening, I'd agreed to help. By working for Joe, I could learn more about Griffith's modus operandi and get paid at the same time. When I got back to the manor I faxed Tosho, requesting any info he had on ANT, and nutshelling Joe Andrews's situation. Six hours later, I received a one-line memo from Tokyo: "Clips you sent are total bullshit. Get real. We have nada on ANT. Keep head down. Luv & kisses, Tosh."

You know how when your car develops a tic and you take it to a mechanic, there's no way the tic will surface? Well, as of the minute I went to work for Joe Andrews, there were no further threats against his life. I even tried letting him go out alone, making him an inviting target while I trailed at a discreet distance.

On Wednesday morning Joe climbed into my car and displayed an envelope.

"Good news," he said.

"What is it?"

"An invitation." He was like a kid, pushing the envelope on me. "Read it, read it, read it."

The envelope was expensive—the thick kind of cotton rag paper you can't find at Office Depot. I slid the heavy, hand-lettered card out and fingered it.

"Read, Dick."

"Okay, already. Geez."

Allied National Technologies, Inc.

Is Invited

To Send a Team

To Participate in

The Fifth Annual Combat Simulation

Friday, November 22

The Hustings

Upperville, Virginia

I recognized the address. It was the horse-country retreat belonging to Grant Griffith. I knew about The Hustings because I'd been doing beaucoup homework. Grant McKendrick Griffith had been Lyndon Johnson's thirty-seven-year-old Secretary of Defense back in the late sixties, and a military adviser to all the Republican and Democratic administrations since. He was always being interviewed on "Nightline" and CNN and the Sunday-morning talk shows—a tall, distinguished, somewhat reptilian-looking asshole with thick eyebrows and prematurely white hair who wore gray pinstripes, spoke in measured tones, and used polysyllabic legal-babble instead of English. I thought of him as a FMR. Those are the letters on the TV screen, explaining that he was a FMR secretary of defense or a FMR Reagan adviser or a FMR member of the such-and-such commission for the nonpartisan study of pigeon entrails.

Griffith was part of the permanent Washington establishment—one of those lawyer/lobbyists like Robert Strauss or Clark Clifford or Leonard Garment who make their millions no matter who's in power.

I also knew that once a year, Griffith ran a war game on his estate in horse country. He invited ten teams. The winner got a trophy. It sounded like so much bullshit—like *Soldier of Fortune* wannabe stuff.

"So, what's the big deal?"

"I told you the night we met I'd love to get Griffith to represent us, but his fees are too rich. He wouldn't even talk to us. And now—here's an invitation to his home."

I wondered about that. I wasn't going to say anything to Joe, but there were too many coincidences going on here. On the one hand, I don't believe in coincidences. On the other, a foot in the door is a foot in the door. "Didn't you tell me that if the Foca deal goes through you'd net more than fifty million bucks?"

"Uh-huh."

"Then use the war game."

"Huh?"

"The invite gets you in the door. You take Griffith aside.

You tell him if he represents you, you'll give him fifty percent of the profit—that works out to about twenty-five mil, right?"

"Ask him to work on a contingency basis?"

"Yeah."

"I'd never thought of that." Joe scratched his chin. "You think he'd bite?"

"For that kind of money? Who wouldn't."

"But what about the game?"

Game, shmame. "What about it?"

"Wouldn't we have to do well to impress Griffith?"

That brought me to a full stop. Joe was probably right. Well, nothing was impossible. "You ever do this sort of thing before?"

He shook his head. "Not since I was a Cub Scout."

"And the people you'll be bringing with you?"

"Geez, Dick, I don't know. A couple of 'em were in the Navy."

"How long before we have to play soldier?"

He glanced at the invitation. "We're supposed to show up at The Hustings two weeks from this Friday."

I threw the car into gear and swung into traffic—Brer Rabbit Marcinko was being tossed into the fucking brier patch one more time. "Joe," I said, "welcome to boot camp."

Chapter

4

I'VE ALWAYS BELIEVED THE SINGLE MOST IMPORTANT ELEMENT IN creating a battle-ready special-ops force is unit integrity. Unit integrity means your men think and act in concert, each supporting the others, not as a disparate bunch of no-loads, each out for himself. Unit integrity also means they'll die for each other if the need arises. Unit integrity is the emotional, physical, and psychological epoxy that holds SEAL boat crews, Marine Recon platoons, and Special Forces A-teams together. In John Wayne war movies, the Duke always makes a speech to his grunts or pilots or sailors about what they're fighting for. But in real life, pilgrim, men do not fight to the death because somebody's just mouthed off about abstruse values like freedom or liberty or democracy versus the Red menace, or because they've gotta defend their country against *narcotraficantes* or Abu Nidal–inspired terrorism.

Real men fight for their buddies: for their squad or for their platoon. But hardening that man-to-man epoxy—the bonding process that builds unit integrity—can take weeks and months, months of training, working, hanging out, and, yes, even fighting together until the kinks have been loosened and your guys start thinking like a big collective sphincter, not a bunch of singular assholes.

For SEALs, unit integrity training starts in BUD/S (Basic

Underwater Demolition/SEAL) training, when pairs of tadpole Frogmen are literally tied together as swim buddies on their first day and stay lashed as a team for the next six months. When they become real SEALs, the inculcation continues during combat training.

When I formed SEAL Team Six in 1980, we ate, slept, drank, and fought together for eighteen weeks without stopping, cramming a year's worth of training into less than five months of intensive, high-pressure exercises. My men shot more, jumped more, climbed more, and trained harder than any unit in the history of the U.S. military.

When we were at home, our days began at 0-Dark Hundred with PT. When we were on the road, we'd begin with predawn assault exercises or parachute jumps. At home or on the road, the day usually ended way past midnight at a bar, some friendly saloon where my ninety SEAL Six rogues drank their Coors, downed tequila shots, ogled the lovely ladies, and argued the issues of the day, a combination of activities that often resulted in their beating the shit out of each other—unless outsiders offered differing opinions or objected to the ogles, in which case my beamish boys would turn on the unfortunate commentators and reduce them to sausage. The result of all those self-inflicted bruises, lacerations, contusions, and bloody noses was a unit filled with men who'd drink each other's piss—*that* was how close they became.

My current problem was to give Joe's dweebs a combination of BUD/S course and SEAL Team Six inculcation in less than a week, in order to build them into something that resembled a unit. I knew that when it came to the war game, I'd be the one doing the heavy lifting, so believe me, I wasn't shooting for integrity—I just wanted to keep them from stepping all over themselves.

The list of tasks they had to learn was formidable. They needed basic outfitting, land navigation, patrolling, ambushing and counterambushing, concealment, camouflage, survival, food preparation, weapons tactics, marksmanship, tracking, first aid, night movement, and some consideration of cold-weather training. At least I didn't have to worry about sleeping accommodations—there'd be no time for sleeping.

Okay, so I was faced with what you might consider an impossible task: turning four no-load, pus-nuts, engineering-dweeb dip-shits into a finely tuned fighting machine. Well, fuck you—I don't accept the word *impossible*. But to accomplish my mission, I knew I'd have to break them down into basic animals, then give them a common goal. That wouldn't be hard. I'd faced more difficult challenges and broken down more impregnable personalities.

Besides, I had a plan: Mother (fucker) Marcinko's Basic ERA Technique. My version of ERA is to treat everyone alike: just like shit.

The breakdown would be done at Rogue Manor. I told Joe to pass the word that for seven days everyone would be incommunicado, so leave the cellular phones at home. Isolation and concentration were the keys. The area around the Manor—two hundred acres of opaque woods, complete with cold streams, mucky bogs, and even a couple of small lakes—is enough quiet space to help wreak a quick transformation of civilized creature into killer animal. I have neighbors, of course, a few hundred yards away, but the thick forest between houses acts as a terrific buffer.

As for the common goal, I'd motivate the dweebs to think collectively by force of my shy, retiring, introverted personality. They'd all pull together toward something that could be defined in two words: "Get Marcinko."

I gave Joe a shopping list that must have made his local army-and-navy store think Christmas had come early. The team needed all the basics: camouflage fatigues, boots, sweat band/scarves, gloves, handkerchiefs, lighters (or waterproof matches), notebooks, pencils, watches, compasses, spoons, can openers, penlights, field knives, space blankets, emergency rations, canteens, insect repellents, camouflage make-up sticks, medical kits, spare socks, heat tabs, toilet paper, individual cammo netting, as well as any personal medicine they felt they might need or consume on a regular basis.

Weapons and ammo would be addressed after I saw who was going to survive the basic bushman's course. My goal was 100 percent.

I scheduled arrival for 0800 Monday, and being scientific nerds, they all pulled their Volvos into the driveway within seconds of each other. Joe made the introductions. Dweeb One was David Fisher, a sallow-skinned, four-eyed electronics maven with a Cal Tech Ph.D.—an abbreviation that, as we all know, means "piled higher and deeper"—who parted his hair in the middle and had a big cowlick. He bore an uncanny resemblance to Dagwood Bumstead —which is what I named him.

Engineer Number Two was Norman James, who was actually wearing a three-piece suit and black wing tips. I asked sarcastically why he'd left the tie at home, and he said in a serious tone of voice that he'd left it at home because he was coming to the country. I dubbed him Normal.

Bringing up the rear was Francis Albert Schivione, a short, bearded guinea with curly salt-and-pepper hair and a thick Baltimore accent. He was yclept Crabcakes.

I fed them coffee and doughnuts and told them to get dressed in combat clothes. Half an hour later they reappeared on my front porch looking like something out of "McHale's Navy." Shit—I was living in the middle of a fucking sitcom.

I smiled at them. "Good morning, gentlemen."

They all answered politely.

It was wake-up time. "Fuck you all," I said in my best Ev Barrett growl.

That opened their eyes.

"That's right—fuck you. You know why? Because you're a bunch of worthless motherfucking cocksucking shit-for-brains pencil-dicked no-load dip-shits. I don't give a shit about pee-haich-fucking-dees, or where you went to school. Because this isn't a fucking office—it's the real world, where you get cold and wet. Here, success is judged by how well *I* think you're doing, not how well you write memos or keep your files alphabetized. This is boot camp, assholes. Know what that means? It means, if you don't camp well, I'll give you a boot—right up your ass."

Shock works. Especially on people whose whole life has been spent in civilized activity. I didn't give them a chance to catch their breath. "Here, your lives depend on doing what I tell you to do—when I tell you to do it. And you don't have to like it, cockbreaths, you just have to do it.

"Here, if one of you screws up, then all of you will suffer. That's the way it is from now on—so get used to it."

They started grumbling immediately, of course. Dagwood opened his mouth to say something. Before he could get a syllable out, I was in his face.

"You complaining already, dweeb?"

"I—"

"Get down and give me twenty."

"Huh?"

"Push-ups, asshole. Twenty. On your knees."

He balked. I shoved. He sat down hard on the macadam.

"Okay, roll over and give me twenty."

His eyes flashed. His jaw worked. But he rolled and assumed the position.

"Hold it." I looked at the others. "What are you shit-for-brains no-loads waiting for? Didn't you just hear me say that if one of you fucks up, you all suffer?"

Joe stared at me in disbelief. He hadn't figured on this kind of treatment. The look on his face said, "Hey, I'm paying you." He gave me The Face. It is a look all bosses have mastered. It is guaranteed to work on employees. "Now, Dick—" he began pedantically. Then he closed his jaw and took a good look at me.

Except for the day we'd met, Joe had always seen me in a suit, tie, and polished Gucci loafers. When it rained, I wore a Burberry trench coat. I was every inch the gentleman.

Today, things had changed. It was November. It was about thirty-five degrees in the morning chill. Joe and the dweebs were shivering. Yet, I was standing there dressed in six-pocket fatigue shorts, a T-shirt that had a picture of a malevolent alligator named Phideaux on it, and thong sandals over bare feet.

My hair and beard looked as if they hadn't been combed in about three days. There was a nine-inch, handmade Field Fighter battle knife in a black ballistic nylon sheath on my belt.

I put my big, broad Slovak nose about an inch from Joe's. "You talking to me, asshole?"

He saw I meant business. He dropped. The others did, too.

Good. They didn't have to like it—they just had to do it. I counted off while they performed. Joe did eight push-ups. Dagwood and Crabcakes made it through four each. Normal managed about two. Holy shit. I was working with corpses.

I told them to stand. "Okay—let's get your equipment dirty and break in your boots."

Crabcakes wheezed, "Can we catch our breath first?" Joe asked for a break.

I laughed sinisterly. "What are you, crazy? Give me twenty more."

As they groveled and did more push-ups, I walked up and down like a drill sergeant and explained how we'd be starting with a basic land-navigation course. I'd marked a series of trees stretching across a nearby pasture with yellow paint. They'd follow a compass course from tree to tree, reading the azimuths and degrees, which would allow them to get comfortable with the compasses.

I watched as they worked their way across the field, moving deliberately from point A to point B to point C to point D. They were engineers. They knew which end of the needle to follow. No problem.

After an hour I extended the course beyond their line of sight and made them start pacing the distances, so they'd have an idea where the markers—I was using a bunch of old Kewpie dolls I'd bought in a thrift shop—should be. So far so good.

By midday the four of them had made progress—albeit as individuals. Each was able to follow his own compass and walk in a straight line through a series of fallow fields. The quartet was happy with its progress. Good. Now it was time to start the mind games.

I brought them back to the Manor for a quick bowl of hot chili and a couple of beers. Joe and Normal wanted diet Cokes. I insisted on beer. The alcohol would loosen them up—and help disorient them. I let them use the facilities, then set them off on their first dogleg course through the underbrush. I instructed them to form pairs. That would begin basic teamwork—and instill competition. I also took away two of the compasses.

They hardly noticed. By now, they figured they'd mastered land navigation, so they set out confidently, galumphing through the dry vegetation like a herd of moose.

Joe and Dagwood took off first, followed by Normal and Crabcakes. That made sense to them. Joe was the boss, and the men would expect him to lead—even though he might not be the best point man. Well, I thought, they'd discover things like that later. Meanwhile, I brought up the rear, loafing behind, watching their pace, movement, and level of confidence, and listening to the office gossip. They'd learn not to talk later.

To keep 'em honest, I'd reduced the size of the targets. Instead of whole dolls I used only doll heads now—and, oops, I forgot to inform my guests. And guess what? Oops again—I'd partially concealed the heads, too. Doom on you, dweeb dip-dunks.

Did they notice? No way. They were filled with the kind of dumb self-assurance that gets men killed on patrol. They even started cracking jokes—and missed the first target. In fact, they marched right past it, flapping their lips like Lucy and Ethel, and their arms like a bunch of merry mummers on New Year's Day.

It was Joe who finally realized the error of their ways. About forty yards too late he called for a head-shed and suggested a circle search.

He also wondered aloud whether I'd changed the targets in any way. When asked directly, I admitted they were smaller and might be a wee bit harder to find.

More grumbling. Now I introduced another element: time. I gave them nineteen minutes to find the next marker. They set off again, this time slower and less confident. Real life was beginning to set in: the terrain was no longer flat and the honeysuckle and briers were starting to fuck up their pace count. I watched as Joe and Normal argued over whether they'd gone forty-eight or fifty-eight paces at 230 degrees. Joe won—and he was wrong. I watched as they passed the marker and thrashed through a quarter-acre patch of what had, last summer, been poison ivy, following Joe's lead. The man was a masochist.

What the hell. The fresh air was invigorating, the day was getting warmer, and the woods were as lovely, dark, and deep as any Robert Frost had ever written about. So I let my Boy Scouts march on. And on. And on. After half an hour Joe realized that something was probably amiss. He called a halt and walked back to where I leaned against a tree. "Okay—you got us."

"I didn't get you, Joe. You got you. You were all so fucking sure you knew what you were doing that you screwed up."

I called a powwow. "Look," I said, "this is harder than it looks. But it's not impossible." I explained how to simplify the task. It made sense. They nodded. "Think KISS," I said.

"Huh?" Crabcakes was befuddled.

"Keep it simple, stupid. That's the SEAL way. That's how you stay alive." I let the concept sink in.

Dagwood cleaned his glasses. "What you mean to say is that by discarding all the extraneous elements and concentrating only on the most consequential matters at hand, we'll enjoy a longer MTBFR."

I was stymied. "What's that? A motherfucking titsucking bastard French renegade?"

Crabcakes and Dagwood laughed. Joe giggled.

Normal tsk-tsked and wagged his index finger under my nose. "Everyone knows that MTBFR stands for 'mean time between failure rate.'"

Everyone but this SEAL. "Could you put that in English for me, cockbreath?"

"Sure," interrupted Joe. "More time between fuckups." That broke them all up.

I clapped him on the shoulder. "Spoken like a true Frogman." I pulled a map from my pocket. "Now, let's see if you can act like SEALs and find your own way back to the Manor." I gave them the map—a 1:5,000 geographic survey on which I'd marked the location of the Manor. I took a pen and showed them where they were.

"It should take you half an hour—maybe forty minutes— to make it home. If you come to a river, you've gone one hundred and eighty degrees the wrong way. If you're not back by morning, we'll send out the dogs for you." I waved as I struck out down a narrow footpath. "See you."

They straggled back to the Manor six hours later—just after 1700. They looked as if they'd been on the road for weeks. Their clean BDUs were now filthy and stained. Their new boots were scuffed and caked with mud. They were hungry and thirsty and looked as if they wanted to murder me.

I greeted them from the second-floor porch. I'd showered and changed into a clean set of black BDUs and a pair of high-top Gore-Tex boots.

I'd spent an hour punching the computer databases to see what I could find out about Grant Griffith's war games—and had come up dry. That puzzled me. The man was a publicity hound. But there were some areas of his life—the games were one—over which he seemed to have drawn a curtain. His ability to do so intrigued me.

I also got a fax from Tosho that detailed one of Griffith's Japanese connections. The minister who'd tried to quash the Kunika investigation was one of Japan's leading ultranationalists—he was a real Jap military hero, one of the pilots who'd attacked Pearl Harbor. He and Griffith owned real estate in Tokyo and had met through one of Griffith's clients, Matsuko.

The name was familiar—I'd just started to go through my files when I heard grunts and groans outside. That would be my nerds approaching. I sauntered out on the balcony, holding a glass of Bombay in my fist. I saluted the men with the gin. "Have a nice day at the office, boys?"

No one answered, but if looks could kill, I would have been a dead man.

I let them wash and dry their equipment and shower while I rustled up dinner. We ate grilled T-bones and salad in the basement, where they looked longingly at the sauna and Jacuzzi. Over our steaks we reviewed the day's events and discussed options that might have made things easier for them. I talked about the history of small-unit tactics—handing out copies of the nineteen rules of warfare written by Maj. Robert Roger in 1756.

Roger was the commander of what came to be known as Roger's Rangers, the original unconventional warfare unit in the New World. Roger's Rangers fought in the French and Indian War, pioneering tactics in patrolling and reconnaissance that are still used today.

His rules may sound rudimentary, but they are as valid today as they were more than two centuries ago. I read them off to Joe's dweebs:

- Don't forget nothing.
- Have your musket clean as a whistle, hatchet scoured, sixty rounds, power and ball, and be ready to march at a minute's warning.
- When you're on march, act the way you would if you were sneaking up on a deer. See the enemy first.
- Tell the truth about what you see and what you do. There is an army depending on us for correct information. You can lie all you please when you tell other folks about the Rangers, but never lie to a Ranger or an officer.
- Don't never take a chance if you don't have to.
- When we're on the march, we march in single file, far enough so one shot can't go through two men.
- If we strike swamps or soft ground, spread out so it's hard to track us.
- When we camp, half the party stays awake while the other half sleeps.
- If we take prisoners, we keep 'em separate till we have time to examine 'em so they can't cook up a story between 'em.
- Don't sleep beyond dawn. Dawn's when the French and Indians attack.
- If someone's trailing you, make a circle, come back on your own tracks, and ambush the folks that aim to ambush you.

I finished Roger's list of dos and don'ts, then went on to explain how a squad works, and what role each man plays. I told them about fields of fire, and how to carry weapons in the field. Their bobbing heads may have indicated that they understood what I was saying, but their body language said, "This is in-one-ear-and-out-the-other material." They probably thought I was just telling war stories.

Wrong. As the grizzled chiefs who taught my classes at Organized Chicken Shit (that's OCS, or Officer Candidate School) used to say, "You will see this material again, assholes."

I watched as the quartet ate and drank, letting the day's hardships slip away from them. They approached life from an office worker's point of view. They'd done their eight hours—and they now considered themselves home for the night: dinner, a little down time in front of the TV, then seven hours of flower dreams tucked in beddy-bye.

Fat fucking chance. Not in Marcinko's Navy.

While they snored in front of the fireplace with an Alan Ladd western on AMC, I hit the trail, stashing goodies.

I rousted them at 2300 using my ship's bell and a police whistle. The resentment was immediate and vocal.

I, however, was brooking no flak. "Listen up, you worthless, stinking trainees, you've got six minutes to dress and turn out in front of the manor house, ready to prowl and growl." They were about to experience an abbreviated version of hell week.

The fifth week of BUD/S training is called motivation week in the training manuals. In real life it is known as hell week. Usually, about 50 percent of the BUD/S class drops out during hell week, five days of unmitigated torture. For the trainees, hell week tests their ability to keep going despite pain, discomfort, lack of sleep, and intense psychological pressure. For the instructors, it is the time to discover who has the guts and the heart to make it through an intensive, brutal series of nonstop exercises, and who gives up. Often the gazelles—the sailors who have done the best in swimming or running the obstacle course during normal training mode—are the ones who give up when the going gets tough. The grunts, guys who ran in the back of the pack and so always had to tough it out, just keep going and going. It is grunts, not gazelles, who make it through hell week.

Grunt story. There was once a big, strong, barrel-chested young sailor from Colorado named Harold Aschenbrenner who wanted to become a Frogman. Finally, the Navy sent him to Underwater Demolition Team Replacement Training, as it was called in those days.

The first day at Little Creek, Ash took the basic Frogman test—which, in those days, meant that he was given two buckets of stones and ordered to jump into the deep end of a fifty-yard swimming pool. The idea was that you jumped in holding the buckets, released them on the bottom, surfaced, then dove for the buckets, grabbed 'em and swam them as far as you could, then surfaced, breathed, dove for the buckets, swam as far as you could, and so on and so forth until you got to the shallow end of the pool. It was supposed to test your endurance and basic swimming skills.

Ash grabbed the buckets and jumped. But instead of surfacing, the instructors watched him as he held the buckets tightly and schlepped them the entire length of the pool, underwater, without surfacing once.

A crusty mustang Frogman lieutenant named Roy Boehm (who later went on to become the first commanding officer of SEAL Team Two) was waiting for him at the shallow end. "What the fuck do you think you're doing?" Boehm asked the sputtering Aschenbrenner, who was depositing his buckets of stones on the rim of the pool.

"I can't swim," said Ash by way of explanation.

"Aw, shit, we can teach you to fuckin' *swim,*" said Boehm, a World War II veteran who'd been a chief boatswain's mate and had a destroyer shot out from under him long before he became an officer. Mustangs like Roy Boehm knew enough to appreciate Mark-I Mod-0, nonquitter grunts when they saw them. "Welcome to the fuckin' program."

"Gentlemen, what we have here is called a night exercise. That is because it is night and you need exercise. If you perform well, you'll be in the woods less than three hours. If you fuck up, you will still be there tomorrow at this time.

"We will rotate jobs. Joe will begin as point man, Dagwood as squad leader, Normal as deputy, and Crabcakes as machine gunner. Then after a half-hour interval, we'll switch. They'll probably be taking captives in this goddamn war game you-all want to play so bad, and each of you has to know everyone else's job."

I gave three of them four-foot lengths of four-by-four lumber to carry. I gave Crabcakes a five-and-a-half-foot length of compressed pine six-by-six. They groaned as they hefted the timber.

"These are your weapons. Three HK-93 assault rifles and an M60 machine gun. You'll carry 'em as if they were loaded. Remember what I said about fields of fire?" I was greeted by blank stares. I repeated myself, adding some Everett E. Barrett spice to the language.

"There are three targets tonight. The first is a bright red Cyalume stick. The second is a bright green Cyalume stick. The third is a bright yellow Cyalume stick. They can be seen from ten yards away. But the red stick has a life of only three hours, and I lit it an hour and a half ago, so you'd better find it fast."

They stood, feet shuffling and arms uncomfortable with their wooden "guns" as I went on to explain that we'd be going over familiar terrain, and that the real purpose of the night's events was not so much the navigation, but learning how to cope with darkness. I added that we'd act like a "real" five-man patrol—the same way we'd be functioning in the war game.

"I'm going to play rear security and keep my mouth shut. All the decisions will be made by the squad leader—so if he fucks up, you all fuck up.

"One more thing. I want you to consider this night patrol a mission through hostile territory. Act accordingly."

They laughed at that. Except I wasn't making a joke. We were in the middle of hunting season, which meant the local good ol' boys were running packs of dogs on foxes, the wild turkeys were out, and we were deep enough in the woods to have local poachers, who sure as shit wouldn't appreciate a band of unidentified merry men in cammo stumbling around their backyards. I knew that many of my neighbors would respond to their dogs' barking by firing a few rounds off the back porch. That would keep this squad alert—and probably cause a few wet trouser legs as well.

We struck out moving west from the house, creeping down a long gully and fording a small stream. We hadn't gone ten minutes before the bellyaching began. They complained about wet feet, sore backs, branches whiplashing faces, and the considerable evening chill. Joe, who was the first to lose his patience, pushed the point man aside and began forging through the underbrush like a baby bull.

His tantrum lasted about six minutes. At which point, a loud *craaaack* that could only be a high-powered rifle about fifty yards away sent my squad of greenhorns scrambling for the deck.

There was a chorus of "What the fuck!"'s and "Goddamn"'s.

Normal crawled back to where I hunkered and stage-whispered, "What the hell was that?"

"That was one of my neighbors. You assholes are making so much noise that you probably woke him out of a deep sleep. He's letting you know he doesn't appreciate it."

"You mean there are armed people out here?"

"Of course. This is the backwoods, asshole."

"Holy shit. You're going to get us killed."

"Not if you do things the way I've told you to do 'em." I made the universal sign for circling wagons and drew the men close.

"Listen up. You guys are dressed in camouflage clothing, so no one can see you. And you're moving like a herd of goddamn animals. So, my neighbors are going to think you're deer." I paused. "Guess what, assholes—out here, they shoot deer without benefit of hunting licenses." I let that sink in. *"Think,* goddammit. We are a patrol. We are supposed to move quietly. The probs and stats of success— that's MTBFR in your language—are in inverse proportion to the noise we make. Got it?"

There was a chorus of nods and uh-huhs.

"Okay—change point man and move out, quietly."

Dagwood led the way. I watched as he slithered through the underbrush. The boy showed promise. He moved carefully, his toes testing the ground, his body working around the undergrowth, his eyes constantly moving, sweeping the area ahead of him—even though he wasn't quite sure what he was looking for. He wasn't Patches Watson, my old point man from Bravo Squad, Second Platoon, Vietnam, 1967. But Dagwood was doing okay for a cake-eating civilian. He had the right instincts—I just had to develop them.

Of course, he led them straight into a bog. Now they were wet and cold. The wood firearms were getting heavier by the second, increasing their misery index in geometric progression. I didn't permit any talking, but from my position in the rear I could hear a lot of cursing through clenched teeth. We'd passed the red Cyalume stick by four hundred yards before Dagwood realized the error of his ways. To atone for his sin he marched straight back into the bog, where Joe lost a boot.

It served him right. At dinner, Joe'd asked why I tied my shoelaces in big, fat, tight knots, instead of floppy bows. I explained that they stayed on my feet that way.

"But it's a waste of money," he said, whining like your typical bottom-liner. "That means you have to cut your boots off every time you wear them."

"That's the idea." I told him about combat training in Panama, where you had to worry about three feet of slimy mud, or quicksand. I explained how slackly laced boots have the tendency to come off when you're sucked out of a plane at 150 miles per hour.

As I spoke, I took a good look at him. Joe was nodding. His head was bobbing up and down. But he wasn't listening. I could almost hear my words bouncing off the wall as they came out his other ear.

Shit—I wasn't doing this for my benefit. In fact, Joe's attitude was similar to the shit-for-brains demeanor of a SEAL captain I had to deal with when I commanded SEAL Team Six more than a decade ago—a guy whose attitude was so bad that he still pisses me off even though I haven't seen him in almost ten years.

The asshole in question's name was—well, I'll call him Pinkney Prescott III. That's close enough without being libelous. I always referred to him as Pinky the Turd. Pinky was destined for great things. His daddy, Pinky II, had been a four-star. So had his granddaddy, Pinky da foist, who had been foisted on the Navy because he was a younger son sans trust fund from a pseudo-aristocratic Main Line Philadelphia family.

Like his ancestors, Pinky went to Annapolis, where he was a mediocre student. He graduated in 1972, too late to go to Vietnam. Uncertain of what to do, he somehow ended up in Navy SpecWar. How he made it through BUD/S no one knows. But evidently he graduated, because in 1973 he was sent to UDT-11 in Coronado, California. He lasted about a year at the team, then was shipped back east, where he was assigned to UDT-22.

While other officers clamored to deploy with their troops, Pinky always favored desk jobs. He jumped quarterly, dove semiannually, and shot only once a year, the bare minimum according to the regs. Indeed, for more than twenty years Pinky held a series of staff positions at Little Creek, where the East Coast Underwater Demolition Teams and SEALs were headquartered, and—as he rose through the ranks—at PHIBLANT (that's AmPHIBious Forces, AtLANTic), at LANTFLT (AtLANTic FLeeT) HQ in Norfolk, and finally in the bowels of the Pentagon.

There, planted safely behind a desk, he mastered the art of writing memos full of bureaucratic doublespeak. Somewhere along the line he also perfected the delicate art of kissing admirals' asses without swallowing too much shit.

By the time I became CO of Six, his years of obfuscating and puckering had paid off handsomely. He'd made it to the Olympus of staffery: he was commodore of all East Coast Navy SpecWar and had just been frocked to rear admiral. He was also famous for his nitpicky memos. They were known as rockets.

Well, Pinky rocketed me early in 1981 to tell me I'd spent too much money on shoelaces. I am serious. This is no joke. Polysyllabically he ordered me, forthwith, to instruct my men to tie their boots with bows, not knots.

I paid a call on the good commodore and told him in my own polyfuckingsyllabic style where he could put his cocksucking motherfucking shit-eating rocket, and what I'd do to his scrawny little pencil-dicked pus-nuts sphincter-faced body if he wrote any more like them.

For some reason, my approach did not sit well with soon-to-be-admiral Pinky, who tried (but failed) to get me court-martialed for attempted murder. He hated me. So what? Fuck him—let him get in line.

I was more patient with Joe than I had been with Pinky. I went over the ground again, explaining that knots are fail-safe. With knots, tied as tight as you can do 'em, there are no bows to come undone when you've been mud-sucked by knee-deep ooze. My lips flapped in the wind. The lights may have been on, but no one was home.

Because obviously, he hadn't listened. Half an hour later we retrieved his shoe—bow and all. It was filled with muck. Boy, was his foot going to hurt. He turned his back on me as he put it on, but from the angle of his shoulders, I could tell that he was tying knots in his bootlaces. Better late than never.

By the time we got back to the house at 0440 with all the Cyalume sticks stashed in my knapsack, I was pleased at the progress they'd made, although I was careful to hide it. Joe had relinquished the position of squad leader to Crabcakes, who turned out to be a grunt of the strong, silent persuasion. Joe became second-in-command—the detail man. Like Crabcakes, Dagwood toughed things out in silence. He'd grit his teeth, hunker down, and do whatever he was told. I'd have liked to see a bit more initiative, but I was perfectly happy to take yes for an answer. Normal still spent too much of his time fussing over extraneous matters, like whether we'd survive the evening. But when I snared a wood snake, he actually touched it—albeit with one finger—and along about 0100 he stopped complaining and complaining and complaining about his wet feet.

His silence made me happy. I know it doesn't sound like much, but in my line of work you take your pleasure where you can. And Normal's acceptance of his condition told me he was making progress, too.

I let them sleep until 0615, then over coffee we rehashed the night's events. I handed out some copied pages from a

SEAL training manual that showed pictographs for silent field signals. "Instead of talking, we'll be using these," I said. "Memorize them. The quiz begins at zero nine hundred."

By the end of the day we'd made real progress. Before lunch, we were forming skirmish lines and practicing fields of fire. The afternoon was spent working on camouflage. And in the evening, we repaired to the tree line bordering the manor house to set up our first ambush position. I broke out my supply of air rifles, provided eye protection, and watched as they blasted away at a series of paper plates I'd stapled to trees and stumps, while they crawled along the edge of the lawn.

Even Normal was getting into the spirit of things. He'd blackened his face, wore a knit stocking cap low across his eyebrows, and used the F-word at least once a sentence. That night, we patrolled twenty-five yards from my neighbor's house without alerting his dog. As we took a five-minute breather about ten yards farther on, we heard the door squeak. We watched my neighbor amble outside, take a steaming leak off the porch, shake himself off, and wander back to his TV.

Normal gave me a big double thumbs-up. The shit-eating grin on his face told me he was having the time of his life. Was he ever. After only seventy-two hours, he didn't even flinch when a wood snake writhed through the dead leaves, skimmed over his leg, and slid into the underbrush. "Fuuuuck you, cockbreath," he murmured as the reptile disappeared. When I heard that, I knew we'd just passed total breakthrough.

Slowly but deliberately I led them through a SpecWar Genesis, similar to the one I'd experienced almost three decades before. I'd purified myself in battle in Vietnam, where I was forged on an anvil of blood and live fire. Joe's dweebs sanctified themselves on a different altar, fortified by the heat of their newly burning muscles, and the iciness of the mud in which they played.

Ah, they were as clay in my hands, and verily, I formed them and shaped them and made them into, well, weekend warriors.

- The First Day I taught them how to play with the toys of SpecWar.
- On the Second Day they learned about camouflage and how to crawl on their bellies because a man must crawl before he can walk.
- On the Third Day they studied the fruits of intelligence and learned how to read the signs of the land and the waters.
- On the Fourth Day they discovered the joys of booby traps.
- On the Fifth Day they learned about surprise attacks and were taught the precepts of ambush. And verily, they memorized the watchwords of their new faith and recited them upon demand: "An ambush is a surprise attack by a force lying in wait within a concealed position upon a moving or temporarily halted target, sir."

When they failed—and fail they did—they were punished and forced to do hard labor and give me twenty, thirty, forty push-ups.

And then it was the evening and the morning of the Sixth Day, the time to create a training operation in my own image, to see whether they could put together everything they'd learned and function as a unit—even, verily, a unit with some integrity.

And so I rented five complete paint-ball outfits—semiauto paint-ball submachine guns and pistols, thick goggles and face masks, and a thousand rounds of Splatmaster ammo in visibility orange, fluorescent pink, bright red, chrome yellow, lime green, and turquoise, and I sent my guerrillas into the woods as a colorful four-man infiltration team of rainbow warriors.

Their mission was to find, and neutralize, a VC command facility—that was me—by a specific time, working their way point to point along a series of markers that required them to use all the navigational and patrolling skills we'd learned. I explained that there might be surprises along the way, so they'd have to keep their eyes open for booby traps, minefields, and other assorted battlefield obstacles.

I gave them the coordinates of the first checkpoint (telling them at the last minute that they'd find directions for each subsequent marker at each checkpoint), a set of maps, four waterproof radios with lip-mikes and earpieces, and turned them loose.

Ten minutes after they left the house, I slipped into the woods and began tracking them. It didn't take long for me to catch up. On the one hand, they were leaving a fat wake behind them: lots of broken branches and muddy footprints made their trail easy to pick up. On the other hand, they were moving well for amateurs—counting their paces and keeping their eyes open.

They made the first marker way ahead of schedule, shifted coordinates, and moved confidently on, counting paces. I'd set a small booby trap fifty yards beyond the marker—a snare-and-pit arrangement. Dagwood almost stepped into it. But he didn't. He stopped, he looked, and he listened, just as I'd taught him to do.

His fist clenched, he held his arm level with his shoulder —the sign for an emergency halt. Then he gave the sign to take up temporary defensive positions.

Joe, Crabcakes, and Normal dropped and fanned out on each side of the trail, their paint guns sweeping the under-brush in complementary arcs. I clenched my fist in triumph. Yes!

Dagwood crept forward and looked. Then he crawled to Crabcakes and whispered in his ear. Crabcakes nodded. The squad detoured around the trap, counting paces, then found the trail again and resumed their patrol. This was terrific— much better than expected.

The next two markers were harder to find. So, all the time they'd gained they now lost. That was good: during the upcoming war game, they'd have to contend with my old adversary Mr. Murphy, of Murphy's Law fame. It was time to learn how to work despite the omnipresent Murphy.

I watched as they made their way through an area in which I'd left some obvious tracks. Crabcakes and Dagwood conferenced, then Dagwood led the men in a wide circle through the underbrush. They were following Roger's Rule and circling back to ambush whoever was tracking them.

Goddamn—they'd listened, and they'd remembered. They were running an A+ so far as I was concerned.

When I left to make my way to the VC bunker, they were working their way around a second series of booby traps—a simulated minefield filled with IEDs that was bordered on one side by a long trench filled with spikes, and on the other by a bog about six feet deep, with a foot of soft mud—and some pressure-plated IEDs—at the bottom. They'd use the bog if they were smart. That would add the elements of cold and wet to the mix. They'd survive if they were careful. I hoped Joe'd remembered to knot his boots.

Meanwhile, I repaired to the ambush site. I'd set my VC position carefully. It was a hootch built a yard off the ground at the end of a thirty-yard-wide spit of land that extended about three hundred feet into the biggest of my lakes, about a mile and a half from the Manor as the crow flies. As the patrol maneuvers, however, it's about a five-mile hike. The minipeninsula was sparsely vegetated and slightly elevated, which afforded me a two-hundred-degree view of the ground from the raised, four-by-eight-foot plywood porch.

The only way they'd get within firing range was to use the water. The dweebs would have to swim across the lake or around the spit and attack from the blind side at the rear of the hootch.

I'd run a similar action in Vietnam in 1967, on a nutmeg-shaped island called Ilo-Ilo, which sat at the mouth of the My Tho River where it ran through the Mekong Delta into the South China Sea. It was there I'd developed by chance a common-sense, KISS strategy that allowed me to kill beaucoup VC without taking any casualties: hit through the back door whenever possible.

Instead of coming up the river on Ilo-Ilo from the west, where a big, wide canal ran eastward in a series of inviting S-curves, some primal SpecWar instinct made me hit the island from the east, infiltrating through a thousand yards of impenetrable, backbreaking marshland and thornbushes. I lucked out. The VC had set all their ambushes and booby traps on the canal, facing west. I was able to hit 'em from the rear and decimate 'em.

Doom on you, Mr. Charlie.

Now, I wanted to see if Joe's dweebs would make the same kind of decision I'd made. If they came at me from the land side, I'd make hamburger out of them. But if they attacked from the water, they'd be able to hit my position and win the exercise.

I extracted a Stroh's from the cooler I'd stashed in the hootch and took a pull, while I attached the detonator wires to the dozen Claymore IEDs I'd rigged across the peninsula. I checked the empty beer cans strung on wires along the water's edge. Any attempt to crawl over them would set them jangling—and give me advance warning of a waterside attack. I pulled my black T-shirt over my head. They'd be at least another half hour getting here and I wanted to grab some rays while I could. I finished my beer, popped the top on a second, closed my eyes, and relaxed.

The sound of snapping twigs brought me out of a half doze. I pulled my shirt on, slipped the goggles over my eyes, brought my paint-ball submachine gun up, turned on the CO_2 supply, and cranked a round into the chamber. There was movement to my ten o'clock.

They'd fucked up and taken the land approach. Joe's dweebs were assholes and I was about to hunt 'em all down. How many times had I told 'em—unconventional warfare means just what it says. Unconventional. Dirty. Spooky. Nasty. Unfair. The Marquis of Queensberry, I explained, was a queen, and he was buried.

It was time to teach them a lesson. I grabbed the detonator, swung over the porch rail, and dropped onto the ground, just in time to see the glint of a paint-ball gun barrel veer in my direction from a clump of rattail ferns. I hit three Claymores and watched as geysers of sand exploded fifty yards away. I hoped no one was lying on top of the mines—even though I wasn't using real ordnance, the sorry bastard who got too close would be sore for a couple of weeks.

I rolled left and fired a quick burst, rolled again and scrambled for cover under the hootch, taking the detonator with me. I fired another charge.

The first of my prospective victims stuck his head up. It

was Crabcakes. I could see his beard as he tried to find a sight picture for his paint-ball gun. His eyes went wildly from right to left—he was disoriented and couldn't pick me up.

Doom on you, Crabcakes. I fired another burst, this time catching him splat in the face with my red paint. I fired the rest of my IEDs, then slammed a fresh mag into my gun, whooped and charged out from the hootch. A good offense being the best defense, I'd scare them off with an in-your-face frontal attack.

Shiiiit. I was machine-gunned in a rainbow of colors as I came out from under the hootch. The paint snapped as it hit, too—I'd have welts tomorrow.

Now they were shouting and charging, their "war faces" primordial and fierce, water dripping from their mud-soaked BDUs.

Goddamn—they were coming from both sides, too. Terrific—the fuckers had used Crabcakes as a diversion. He was cannon fodder—expendable. Meanwhile, while I diddled with their dangle, they'd snuckered and puckered around the back, flanked me from the water, and hosed my ass.

I rolled onto my back and lay there like a movie corpse. Somebody shot me behind the ear, administering a coup de grâce in visibility orange.

"Die, scumbag." It was Normal's voice. The little dweeb had turned into a stone killer.

Another *smaaaack* in the back of the head bounced me on the ground. "Fuuuck you, cockbreath." From the triple-knotted boots standing by my face, I realized I'd just received a bouquet from Joe.

"Doom on you, Dickhead." Dagwood shot me in the testes with turquoise paint, giving the phrase "blue balls" new and painful meaning. I tucked my knees, curled my toes, and vowed silently to return the favor someday.

"Okay, okay—I give up," I wheezed. "Now which one of you assholes is going to carry my corpse back to the Manor so we can have a proper wake?"

"Shit," said Crabcakes, who stood watching from afar, "we're not schlepping you anywhere. We're gonna skin you and frame you. You've got so much paint on you, you look like a fucking Jackson Pollock."

"You mean Jackson *Polack?* Fuck you, cockbreath—I'm a Slovak, and proud of it."

They all laughed. Joe looked down at my Technicolor BDUs. "Say whatever you will about being Slovak, Dick, but you look more like a fucking canceled Czech than anything else right now."

Chapter

5

THE FIRST RULE OF SPECWAR IS: NEVER ASSUME. NEVER ASSUME your enemy isn't waiting to blow your ass away. If the CO of SEAL Team Four—the team that had assaulted Hato Airport during Operation Just Cause—had followed Rule One, his men probably wouldn't have been chopped into hamburger by the Panamanians. SEAL Team Two's commanding officer, Norm Carley, followed Rule One during Just Cause, and his ops went more or less as planned. He didn't assume *anything*—he anticipated every possible fucking contingency, and his planning paid off—he fulfilled his mission without losing a man.

It didn't matter whether I was in command of a six-man squad or a hundred-and-fifty-man unit. I never assumed anything. I always planned my tactics as if everything would go wrong. Why? Because things always go wrong. Mr. Murphy is always going to come along for the ride.

Rule One: Never assume. You will see this material again.

The second rule of SpecWar is: Never give a sucker an even break. That translates to keeping your opponents off guard, never allowing them to get ahead of you, either physically, mentally, or tactically. As the CO of SEAL Team Two, and later as CO of SEAL Team Six, I used whatever it took to get my way: threats, intimidation, booze, blackmail —whatever. I took Rule Two to heart. I used it against my

77

enemies in the field, and against the Navy system, when it got in my way.

I have often been accused of not playing fair. I plead guilty. What's your point? I always thought the saying went, "All's fair in love and war."

Which leads me to the most important rule of SpecWar: Win. Do whatever it takes, but win. When Roy Boehm, the true godfather of all SEALs, conceived, designed, and selected the original unit back in the sixties, the crusty, froggish ex-boatswain's mate begged, borrowed, and stole whatever he had to, to make sure his men were properly equipped and ready for war. The system worked against Roy—so he went around it. On occasion, he went directly through it—leaving shattered bodies when he thought it necessary.

Black Jack Morrison told me, "Dick, you will not fail," when he ordered me to create SEAL Team Six.

The only possible correct response was the one I gave him: "Aye, aye, sir." And I did not fail. Like Roy—who was one of my sea daddies—I found ways to go around the system or through it.

There is, incidentally, one final rule of unconventional warfare. It is that there *are* no rules.

Now, applying all these maxims to the situation at hand, i.e., Grant Griffith's war game five days down the pike, I realized that I was in trouble.

Rule One applied. Did it ever. After all, I was working with Joe's greenhorn dweebs, guys who meant well but lacked the finesse and field experience of real-world SpecWarriors. I liked Joe, Dagwood, Normal, and Crabcakes, but I couldn't assume that they'd perform under pressure. As previously noted, I couldn't assume anything.

That meant Rule Three was out the window. Certainly, a win was virtually impossible given the current personnel.

That left Rules Two and Four. To apply them, I got on the horn to a thirtysomething machinist's mate first class I'll call Stevie Wonder.

I call him Stevie Wonder because he always wears wraparound shooting glasses in amber, rose, or smoke, depending on his mood. He also has a permanently stiff neck, out of which he works the kinks by rotating his head right/left/right, left/right/left, doing a passable imitation of . . . you got it . . . Stevie Wonder.

Stevie's an ex-Marine staff sergeant who joined the Navy because he was bored with civilian life and tired of teaching assholes karate. His neck is permanently stiff because he got blown off a mountain in North Vietnam or Laos or Cambodia during one of those ninety-day behind-the-lines classified missions you volunteer for when you're a seventeen-year-old Force Recon lance corporal and don't know any better than to offer to become cannon fodder. Anyway, Wonder had so much fun killing Japs that he never took time to let the bone chips and fragments heal properly.

Three weeks ago, one of the smaller frags detached itself from the muscle surrounding his neck and worked its way due west, coming out through the bottom of his left eye socket. Boy Wonder thought it was a bad hangover at first. That should tell you something about his lifestyle.

Wonder first worked for me at Red Cell. When I discovered him he was an MM2—machinist's mate second class—detailed to security at the Pentagon. I wore four stripes thin those days, but he treated me as if I were a chief, with all the appropriate F-words and compound-complex profanity. My kind of guy. So I shanghaied him out of his detail and found a slot for him at the Cell, where he fit right in amongst the other dirtbags.

SEALs are normally suspicious of anybody who hasn't earned a Budweiser—the trident all Frogmen wear on the left breast of their uniforms. It took my shooters about a week to get used to Boy Wonder. His acid wit—some say it's only half-acid—helped. So did his capacity for Coors Light. So did the fact that he'd killed more people both in and out of combat than anybody at the Cell except moi.

He turned out to be a valuable asset, too. After his career as a Marine, Wonder'd served on nuclear subs, so he spoke the right language when we infiltrated the sub base at Groton, Connecticut. He'd had other extracurricular experience as well, playing back-room dirty tricks for the invisible men at the NSA Annex, and spending some time with the black-bag communications boys out at Vint Hill Station, west of Manassas, Virginia.

He's a shooter and a looter and a red-hot root-toot-tooter, and whether it's a bar brawl outside Subic or some Hezbollah nasty boys shooting at you in Beirut, you wouldn't want your back up against anyone else's except Boy Wonder's well-broken-in forty-two long.

Yeah, Wonder is rock steady, and as competent as they come. It's not his fault he looks like a cross between Ted Koppel and Howdy Doody.

He's still pulling active duty down at the Navy Yard, so it took him about two hours to shitcan his work detail, get ten days of approved leave, and hustle his butt out to the Manor. We sat on the deck, working on a six-pack of canned pork chops—that's Marine slang for beer—while Wonder plinked away at the empties with his trusty Browning High Power.

I explained my problem.

Wonder scratched his chin, drained his beer, and emptied another magazine downrange. "Shit, man, the solution to that one's simple. Cheat."

See why I like him so much? I toasted him with Stroh's. "My sentiments exactly."

He leaned back, lifting the front two legs of his chair six inches off the ground, and pondered my dilemma for half a minute or so. Then he let the chair fall back onto the deck with a *thwock.* "What you need to do is stash a bunch of goodies so's you can deal with any contingency."

"I was planning on that."

"I keep forgetting you're not as dumb as you look." He smiled behind the rose lenses that told me he'd gotten laid last night. "Then, you'll need a Mr. Outside, with the right comms, and a bunch of proper black-bag toys. That way, when you get into trouble—and knowing you, you will get into trouble—there's somebody to bail your sorry Dickhead ass out."

"Can you think of anybody who fits the bill?"

Wonder's head swiveled in its trademark slow half-circle. He didn't say anything. He just giggled.

* * *

We went shopping that afternoon at Vint Hill Station. Vint Hill's just over the ridge across the river and up the road from Rogue Manor, which kind of backs up to Quantico. So far as any casual observer is concerned, it's just another Army post. But if you look carefully past the third set of razor-wire barricades that lie behind the commissary, to the left of the medical unit, and diagonal to the cafeteria and the other miscellaneous creature features, you'll discover more spooks than you'd ever find on Halloween.

Because, behind Barrier No. 3, Vint Hill is actually a clandestine intelligence-gathering facility run by NRO—the National Reconnaissance Office. NRO is the unit that flies all our Keyhole, Lacrosse, and VELA spy satellites. Does that sound like intelbabble? Let me translate. Keyholes— the KH series, combine LASP (Low-Altitude Surveillance Platform) technology with computer imaging and infrared capabilities. Lacrosses can penetrate thick cloud cover and use thermal imaging. VELA satellites are targeted at nuclear facilities. The unit's commanding officer—actually he's a supergrade named Ulysses Robinson who's on a three-year TAD (Temporary Additional Duty) from No Such Agency at Ft. Meade—sits behind a triple set of locked doors on the Pentagon's fourth-floor C-ring. But Useless, as he's known to everyone, also runs three operational commands in the National Capital region: one at Bolling Air Force Base, another at Dahlgren, Virginia, and a third at Vint Hill Station.

NRO somehow manages to spend just over $5 billion a year—and that figure, in case you weren't aware, is the largest single intelligence expenditure in the federal budget. Larger than CIA's cut of the $29 billion we spend on intelligence gathering every year. More than the Defense Intelligence Agency—DIA—gets. More, even than—well, you get the idea, and the place I was about to mention is still classified.

Useless Robinson runs what's known in the trade as a hardware outfit. That means NRO oversees the design, building, and launching of satellites. It also tracks 'em, through the Satellite Control Facility, or SCF, in Sunnyvale,

California, and eight other tracking stations worldwide. Using such networks as SDS, or the Satellite Data System, NRO retrieves the information, which it then channels to NSA, the National Security Agency, DIA, CIA, or a half dozen other alphabet-soup organizations that can't be found in any telephone books.

The information NRO gathers can be in the form of COMINT and SIGINT, or COMmunications and SIGnals INTelligence, which is a fancy way of saying electronic eavesdropping, ELINT, the acronym for ELectronic INTelligence, or the scooping up of *non*communication electromagnetic radiations, or it can be visual—infrared, pictures, analog telescopic photographs, computer-enhanced laser readouts, or radar images.

Its satellites can pierce cloud cover and ground fog; they can differentiate between cloth-dummy trucks and real ones; they can provide clear pictures of a license plate from more than 22,000 miles. When I led SEAL Team Six on a covert raid to Libya early in 1982, for example, NRO's Lacrosse-IIa/3fl satellite, serial number 153296/Zulu, provided CIA director William Casey with a real-time picture of me and my eleven shooters on the ground as we waxed six people sleeping in three tents, and thirty Libyan soldiers guarding them. The primary targets—two Irish nationals, a West German woman, an Israeli, and two Italians—had been rehearsing an assassination scenario to be carried out against Pres. Ronald Reagan.

The people we killed were all professional hitters, recruited by Libyan leader Muammar Qaddafi and paid more than a million dollars each for their services. Casey was able to see us administer the coups de grâce, watch as we fingerprinted the corpses and took Polaroid portraits for the intel files, and observe our extraction by STOL—Short TakeOff and Landing—aircraft flown by our support group from Task Force 160, the Special Ops squadron out of Ft. Campbell, Kentucky.

What's my point? Point is, if you want state-of-the-art communications goodies, NRO is a great place to start looking for them. Unfortunately, I am persona non grata at

Vint Hill. Sure, I drive over there once a month to buy groceries or show up to visit the occasional sawbones or tooth-yanker, but I never get beyond the Army-base portion of the place.

Luckily for me, Wonder, whose job at the Navy Yard is classified (he won't tell me what he does, either. "I could," he once said, "but then I'd have to kill you"), is friendly with a bunch of the Vint Hill spooks beyond Barrier No. 3. He got on the horn, half an hour later the walls of Jericho came tumbling down, and we went shopping.

By the end of the day, we'd trucked about three hundred pounds of equipment back to the Manor. We borrowed a half-meter satellite communications system with burst transmitter and digitized scrambling capabilities, with two pocket-size transceivers that could pass as cellular phones. We also took a multifrequency scanner and several other pieces of electronic wizardry, an assortment of night-vision devices, and—thanks to a Special Forces master sergeant I'd known during the planning stages for the Tehran hostage rescue back in 1979—six cartons of assorted explosive devices, ranging from cherry-bomb squibs to C-4, from M80 smoke grenades to MI pull-fire devices, artillery simulators, and Claymores. I took pressure pads, trip wire, fuses, timers, and detonators.

The war game commenced on Friday at 1800 hours. This was 1735 Monday afternoon. That gave us just over ninety-six hours to work our magic. Within the next forty-eight hours, Wonder and I would set up a base of operations for him a few miles from Grant Griffith's estate. After we'd gotten him settled, we'd infiltrate the property and cache a selection of war toys.

I'd have liked to run a penetration or two of Griffith's house—there was probably valuable intelligence to be gained there. But there wouldn't be time. A proper B&E, which is breaking and entering without the subject's knowing that you've come and gone, takes time—it's not a spur-of-the-moment thing. So a visit to Griffith's house was out of the question.

I had no idea what the rules of the war game would be. Basically, there are two ways to go. The first is Red Force/Blue Force. That's the way Eighth Platoon played in Panama before my second Vietnam tour. In RF/BF, teams are run against aggressor forces. The second format is Capture the Flag, in which teams run a set course and compete against the clock. A lot was at stake here—both for Joe and for me. So, I wanted to take no chances—whatever form the games took, I'd be ready.

The topographic survey maps I pulled from my files told me that The Hustings, Griffith's 2,500-acre estate, lay three miles north of Route 50, which runs approximately due west all the way from Washington, D.C., to Winchester, Virginia, through the middle of some of the most beautiful (and expensive) real estate on the East Coast. Griffith's place was about two-thirds of the way between the small town of Upperville and the smaller town of Paris, dead in the middle of Virginia's exclusive hunt country. Two miles down the highway was Pamela Harriman's huge estate where the president was rumored to spend occasional private weekends when his wife was back in Little Rock visiting her mother. A fifteen-minute drive down Route 50 and up a side road brought you to the pseudo-plantation house and six hundred acres once owned by CIA renegade Edwin Wilson. Closer to Middleburg sat a twenty-five-acre estate the CIA still used as a safe house. One recent DCI felt safe enough to use it whenever he needed to "relieve the pressure" with his secretary.

Next, I pulled a 1:25,000 Loudon County survey map from my files and scoped out the area. From Route 50, you turned north toward the Blue Ridge Mountains on a numbered blacktop county road and meandered through foothills interspersed with pasture and an occasional stream. Three miles later, you bore right onto a narrower, brown-top road, swung left at a fork, pulled hard right onto two-track paved asphalt, and drove another six-tenths of a mile. Then it was hard left onto a macadam country road and across a hundred-year-old wooden bridge—the map showed a historical marker at each end—that spanned what looked like an old millstream. At that point, you intersected a quarter-mile driveway that led, we gathered, to the main house.

Steve and I packed his Ram Tough truck, tarped it, and headed north toward Middleburg. As his command post, I'd selected the 1763 Inn, which sat on Route 50, just about due south of Griffith's estate. The Inn, which was once owned by George Washington, sits on fifty gorgeous acres. More to the point, it has a restaurant that features some of the best German cooking in the state.

The 1763's owners, a gregarious couple named Kirchner, are also fans of the U.S. military. On the wall, as you head from the main entrance down a narrow hall to the dining room, are a series of framed oil portraits of America's great World War II generals—Ike, Patton, Marshall, MacArthur, and Bradley—and a brand-new picture of "Bear" Schwarzkopf, the hero of Desert Storm.

It took us about sixty-five minutes to get from the Manor to the Inn. We were greeted by an old black Lab named Leroy, who immediately fell in with Wonder. I paid $1,500 in advance for seven nights in the Inn's honeymoon cottage. The cottage—actually it's a two-room suite built in an old barn—sits about three hundred yards behind the Inn, way up on a hill, hidden in a grove of hundred-year-old oak trees. It is secluded, quiet, and completely invisible from the road. No one would see our satellite dish or other electronic goodies.

I made small talk with Uta and Don, the 1763's owners, as I counted Franklins.

Wonder, ever the smart-ass, squeaked, "Are you gonna carry me over the threshold, sweetie pie?" when he heard me ask for the honeymoon cottage.

"No, poopsie-whoopsie," I answered sweetly. "I'm going to pull your fucking nostrils back over your fucking ears, roll your head up your ass, and bowl you through the fucking door from fifty yards away."

That brought a guffaw from Uta. "You ever in the Navy?" she inquired.

"Retarded O-5. How'd you guess?"

"Our head groundsman's a retired chief. You sound just like him."

That brought a smile to my face.

"What brings you to our neck of the woods?" Don asked.

"We're here to do some quiet research," I said noncommittally, explaining that Stevie would be staying for the week, while I'd come and go.

The conversation played on while I examined the bar. I was delighted to see they served draft Dortmunder Union beer. I'd developed a taste for Dortmunder thanks to General Ricky Wegener, the commander of Germany's *Grenzchutzgruppe*-9, or GSG-9 counterterror commando team. In the early eighties, SEAL Team Six and GSG-9 staged combined training exercises in Europe. Herr General Ricky had introduced me to two new experiences: Mercedes armored tactical jeeps and Dortmunder Union beer.

"Could we have a couple of Dortmunders, please, Uta?" I pointed at the tap.

The beer was cool and fresh—real German draft. Wonder and I drained our glasses quickly and ordered refills.

"Boy, that's good," he said, smacking his lips.

I wiped foam from my mustache and nodded. "You might want to order an extra keg, Uta"—I hooked my thumb toward the Dortmunder—"because we'll drink this stuff by the gallon."

A smile a yard wide crossed Uta's face. *"Jawohl, Herr Fregatten-kapitän,"* she said. "I'll get right on it."

By midnight Wednesday we'd done half a dozen sneak-and-peeks, leaving goodies stashed behind. The Hustings covered just under four square miles of paddocks, meadows, and woods. It ran from the foothills of the Blue Ridge Mountains, where hikers roamed the Appalachian Trail, down through a series of thickly forested woods to the meadows and grazing land for Griffith's purebred French Charolais cattle and his Arabian racing horses and polo ponies.

The property was bordered on the east and west by two-lane blacktop roads that ran on a north-south path from Route 50 into the Blue Ridge. From northwest to southeast, it was bisected by a small river, and from southwest to northeast by a paved county road, which divided the land into four roughly equal quadrants. I named them Alpha, Bravo, Charlie, and Delta, starting at six o'clock, which is the quadrant where the main house was located.

Then we subdivided the quadrants, using map coordinates that ran south/north and west/east, so that I could call Wonder and tell him I was at Charlie 16/10 or Delta 20/21, and he'd be able to locate me within one hundred yards. Since we had no idea where or how the game would be played, we cached quadruple sets of supplies. No matter where the ANT squad ended up, we'd be able to lay our hands on extra goodies within minutes.

I called Joe early Thursday morning and suggested that we all link up prior to the formal assembly at Griffith's place. I didn't tell him about Wonder, or our forays onto Griffith's property. He had no need to know that we had any aces in the hole. We agreed to rendezvous at the Hidden Horse Cafe, a friendly tavern in Middleburg, at about 1500 hours on Friday, then move as a group to Griffith's place. I reminded him to bring extra laces for his boots. He reminded me to wear a suit.

The five of us drove to The Hustings in a civilian version of an Army Hummer that Joe had rented specially for the occasion. I was all for making the trip in Steve's pickup—so we'd look like a truckload of Tehran terrorists driving up—but Joe insisted we had to arrive dressed fashionably, and with appropriate quasimilitary style. During the fifteen-minute drive, I had the dweebs recite Roger's standing orders to his eighteenth-century Rangers like a SpecWar mantra.

I'd worn my best suit—a gray flannel, double-breasted number—and a white shirt. My hair was tied back with a black band. I was glad Joe'd insisted I dress formally, because as we crossed the wood bridge over the old millstream, turned hard right, and crunched onto the crushed-stone driveway, I saw we were being followed by two black stretch limos with diplomatic plates. So it looked to be a high-style, high-power weekend, and I knew from my days as a naval attaché in Phnom Penh that diplo-dinks prefer to mix and mingle with people wearing suits, not Skivvies and sandals.

It was already growing dark as we pulled up in front of the house, so you couldn't see the expanse of manicured grounds that stretched a hundred yards in each direction. But the house, which was lit by dozens of hidden lamps, was impressive enough.

I snuck a look as we pulled our bags out of the Hummer. The centerpiece of the estate was a stone field house that bore the words *The Hustings* and the date 1788 above the doorway. A wood addition that looked nineteenth century by its architecture sat to the right; a fieldstone addition was joined to the left side of the original house by a passageway.

A trio of butlers appeared as if by magic, shooed us away from our baggage, slipped hotel claim tags on them, gave Joe the stubs, and whisked the bags away.

"You will find your luggage in your rooms, gentlemen," Butler No. 1 said in the Queen's English. "Please follow Cedric into the drawing room, where Mr. Griffith is awaiting you."

Joe nodded, and we moved off just as a new crew of handlers appeared to welcome the stretch limos behind us.

We walked through the foyer, down a pegged-pine corridor covered with what I assumed were antique Oriental rugs, and through a narrow hallway lined with framed eighteenth-century French military prints. We hadn't gone thirty feet when we came to a huge archway.

Beyond it was a massive atrium that had been built onto the old colonial house. It must have been fifty yards wide and twenty yards deep, with glass walls twenty-five feet high. The huge space was divided into separate entertaining and dining areas by a series of marble pedestals on which stood full medieval sets of armor.

The outside brick wall of the original house looked as if it had been sandblasted. Suspended from it was a breathtaking collection of Revolutionary-period firearms. A pair of Civil War cannon formed the base of a huge dinner table. Couches were flanked by old mortars. Through the atrium window I could see a display of World War II American and

German tanks, dramatically illuminated by hidden spotlights.

Grant Griffith was waiting for us just inside. I'd seen pictures of him on the TV news shows and in the papers for years. Whenever the news media did a story about "Whither the Military," they quoted Grant Griffith. There was good reason. Griffith had served as secretary of defense for Lyndon Johnson and done such a good job that when Richard Nixon was elected, he'd asked Griffith, who had just opened his own law firm, to advise him on defense matters as well.

Every administration since, whether Republican or Democrat, had solicited Griffith's advice on defense policy. Gerald Ford appointed him to a commission on Vietnam policy. For Jimmy Carter he had worked to assuage veterans groups when the Georgian wanted to declare an amnesty for Vietnam-era draft evaders. Ronald Reagan made him chairman of the task force that developed SDI; for George Bush he made quiet trips abroad, forging critical military and political support for Desert Shield and Desert Storm. Between his quasi-official commissions, Griffith worked as a lawyer and lobbyist for what Pres. Dwight D. Eisenhower called the military-industrial complex.

Only the current president, who had made preelection vows to ban influence peddlers and the government/industry revolving-door circuit from his administration, had banished Griffith from the Oval Office.

Now, here he was in the flesh, a wide, inviting smile on his tanned, reptilian face. I had to admit, his pictures didn't do him justice. He was tall—gaunt, even—and regally white-haired, with that sort of wrinkled complexion that told me he either had his own ultraviolet tanning bed somewhere in the house or he spent three days a week in Puerto Vallarta.

Griffith's eyebrows were as thick as Brezhnev's, except they were absolutely snow-white, making them all the more prominent against his pecan-colored forehead and setting off his bright blue eyes. He waved us over with long, aristocratic hands, ending in perfectly manicured fingernails that I could see from five yards away had been buffed and polished. On his right pinky was an antique Roman ring. I knew it was antique and Roman because I'd read about it during my research. The ring had once belonged to Julius Caesar, and it had cost more than the national debt of most Third World (and a few Second World) nations.

He was dressed in the way only the rich can afford to dress—a bespoke suit (I knew it was custom-made because the bottom two buttons on his coat sleeve were unbuttoned) in somber, ministerial gray that, while reeking Savile Row propriety, was genteelly shabby at the elbows and lapels. His shirt and tie were also English. The shirt had broad stripes of purple, blue, green, and black, a wide, long-point collar, and starched French cuffs held together by small, gold monkey's-paw knots. The tie, unfashionably narrow, was black pin-dot. His black cap-toes had the soft patina of gentle buffing on the best kidskin. Spit shines were just not this guy's style.

I've done my share of entertaining. I gave regular diplomatic receptions when I was a naval attaché in Phnom Penh; I threw parties in my home when I commanded SEAL Team Two. I have attended hundreds of dinners, downed probably tens of thousands of cocktails, and munched on several tons of hors d'oeuvres while attending countless receptions thrown by a spectrum that includes weapons-makers, business executives, Navy leagues, Kiwanis and Rotary clubs, company picnics, and manager's training sessions.

But nothing prepared me for the opulence of Griffith's home, or the grandeur of his style. It was simply not a factor of my life experience.

Griffith extended his hand to Joe. "I'm delighted you could attend," he said. His voice was as perfectly manicured as his fingernails.

"We're happy to be here, Mr. Griffith," Joe said.

"Grant. Call me Grant, please. Now, whom did you bring with you?"

Joe introduced his team, saving me for last. I watched Griffith's eyes. They flickered. "You wrote *Rogue Warrior,*" he said. "You were on '60 Minutes.'"

"That's me."

"Great book. Wonderful stories. But you screwed up in the end, didn't you? The Navy got you."

"Some people think so."

He grunted. "You served time."

"A year—in Petersburg."

"Know why?"

"Tell me."

"You had the wrong lawyer," Griffith said, a wry smile on his face. "You should have come to me."

"Probably. But I couldn't afford you, from what I hear."

"Sometimes, I take cases that interest me on a pro bono basis."

"If I'd known that, I'd have called—and saved myself two hundred grand."

"Not to mention the year in jail, eh, Commander?" He reached over and squeezed my upper arm, checking my biceps. "Still stay in shape, I see. Good."

He paused, patriarchically surveying his domain. You could tell from the look in his eyes that he saw that It Was Good. His hand remained on my biceps. It was making me uneasy. I do not like to be touched by men I don't know.

Griffith was oblivious. "Give me a call sometime. Come and visit. I've got a lot of friends on Four-E," he said, using the Pentagon shorthand for the row of fourth-floor office suites with river views on E Ring, where the secretary of the navy, the chief of naval operations, and most of his deputies reside. "Maybe I can help you straighten things out with the Navy."

Then Griffith removed his patrician paw and turned to Joe. "Please make yourselves at home," he said warmly. "We'll be eating at seven-thirty. The exercise starts at midnight, with a briefing at eleven."

"Will you be doing the briefing?" I asked.

"Heavens, no." Griffith's cotton-puffball eyebrows fluttered briefly. "It will be conducted by Major Brannigan." The ex-secretary's head moved vaguely to his right. "Last I saw of him, he was somewhere over there, talking to the gentlemen from General Dynamics."

Griffith smiled benignly and shook Joe's hand in a way that hinted we should move on. Indeed, he was already looking toward the next group of arrivals.

I knew a Major Brannigan. Thomas Boyd Brannigan, aka

Buckshot. A lean, mean fighting machine from Nashville, Tennessee. He'd had a long history in special ops. As a lieutenant he'd been a raider for Bull Simon's assault on the Son Tay prison in North Vietnam back in 1970. In April of 1975, he'd stayed behind in Saigon after the North Vietnamese took the city, setting up an underground railway to get his ARVN people out of the country under the Communists' noses.

When Charlie Beckwith formed Delta Force he'd picked Captain Buckshot Brannigan as his ops boss. Buckshot had been on the ground with Charlie in the Iranian desert during the disaster that was Operation Eagle Claw. In the mid-eighties, as a major, Buckshot was part of what became the Army's Intelligence Support Activity, or ISA.

A "black" operations group jointly tasked with obtaining intelligence and acting on it, ISA's missions ran the gamut from trying to locate and extract U.S. POWs still held in Southeast Asia, to maintaining covert support for the anti-Sandinista army the CIA maintained in Central America, to locating and rescuing the American hostages in Lebanon.

I was running SEAL Team Six in those days, and it was as if we were all part of a big, covert fraternity that had special handshakes, high-signs, and decoder rings. We felt we were invincible. Unstoppable. Immortal.

Obviously, we suffered from hubris—and our nemesis, punishment by the gods, was inevitable. Indeed, like me, Buckshot had retired under a cloud.

First, a retired Special Forces lieutenant colonel named "Bo" Gritz inadvertently blew ISA's cover. Gritz had been working in concert with—but not for—ISA in Asia. One of the nation's true Vietnam-era heroes, he was convinced that Americans were still being held in Laos and Cambodia, and he went there to investigate. A *New York Times* story about Gritz appeared, which also mentioned ISA's activities. Congress, which had been told nothing about what was going on, immediately started its own investigation.

By the end of 1986, two dozen of the Army's best SpecWarriors had either resigned or taken early retirement. Among them was Buckshot Brannigan. He'd kicked around

Fayetteville for a while, hobnobbing with his old friends at Delta Force. Then he moved north, to Washington, where he had scores of contacts from his SpecOps days.

In the late eighties he worked as a Class A contract agent for the CIA, helping to coordinate anti-Soviet resistance activities in Afghanistan and Pakistan. In 1989, he'd been hired by a Saudi prince as a security consultant. That was the last I'd heard of him.

I excused myself and threaded my way across the room, checking faces. I'd seen many of them in the newsmagazines and on television. Buckshot's back was toward me and he was in animated conversation with a blue-suited asshole wearing a monocle and a rosette in his lapel.

I bumped him gently with my shoulder. "Yo, bro."

He turned. It took him six seconds or so to identify and confirm. I could see the Rolodex cards whap-whap-whapping behind his eyes. "Dick—great to see you. God, it must be what—five, six years."

He turned back to Monocle Man. "Sir Aubrey, this hulking, hirsute creature is Dick Marcinko. Dick, this is Sir Aubrey Hanscome Davis, who's visiting from London. Sir Aubrey is deputy minister for defense. He carries the CT portfolio."

Translation: Monocle Man was a spook who ran counterterror operations for the British Foreign Ministry. I shook the Brit's hand, which was as cold and limp as their bacon. "Pleased to meet you."

Buckshot rested a hand on my shoulder. "Don't let the hippie disguise fool you, Sir Aubrey. Dick was the first commander of SEAL Team Six. He built the unit from scratch."

"Of course he did." A look that might have passed for a smile crossed Monocle's face. "Trained with our Royal Marines in the North Sea, as I recall."

SIX and the SBS—Special Boat Squadron—had indeed spent many freezing fucking hours in thirty-degree water, practicing joint assaults on North Sea oil platforms. "That's right, sir," I said. "They're first class, too."

"Yes, they are, Commander. You should come over and see how they're doing these days. There's a new boy in charge—young Geoff Lyondale. A real go-getter." He looked me up and down again, then dropped the monocle from his eye and backed away. "Well, I'm running off at the mouth when you chaps probably have some catching up to do."

He was right, and neither Buckshot nor I protested too loudly as he veered off to starboard, heading toward a waiter bearing a tray of champagne.

Buckshot looked prosperous. He'd put on some weight, and his butterscotch hair had gone gray at the temples. The eyes were the same, though—blue-gray killer's eyes, hooded as a cobra's.

"Whatcha up to, asshole?"

"Gone into business for myself."

"Making money?"

"Hand over fist." He wagged an index finger at the champagne waiter, retrieved two glasses, handed me one, and touched the rim of my glass with his. The glasses chimed. They were goddamn crystal. From the sound of it, goddamn good crystal, too.

"Security company. We call it Centurions International." He laughed.

"What's so funny?"

"We call it 'international,' but I still haven't gotten overseas."

"Who's the 'we'?"

Buckshot's head tilted toward the house. "Secretary Griffith and me." He sipped his champagne. "I did just over three million last year."

"Impressive." I finished my drink.

So did Buckshot. "Thanks. What's up besides the book?"

"Not much. Scratching to fill the wheelbarrow." I nodded toward Joe Andrews, who was deep in conversation with a small Japanese man. "Working for Allied National for a while."

"Making money?"

"A little."

"We could always use another body at Centurions, Dick —keep it in mind."

"I will." Fuck him, I thought. I'm not just another body.

I looked out toward the woods. "What's the deal here?"

"A weekend of fun and games. Nothing more than we used to do at Bragg."

"How rough can it get?"

"That depends," said Buckshot.

"On what?"

"On who's playing." He looked at me through his cobra's eyes. "I get the feeling that this year's game is going to set a new record for nasty."

Chapter

6

WE KNEW WE'D GET OUR FIRST REAL LOOK AT THE COMPETITION just before 2300, when Buckshot Brannigan was scheduled to conduct the briefing. So right after dinner, we met in my room for a quick head-shed and discussed how to act around the other teams. Then we got dressed, met up, and headed back downstairs at 2250.

The atrium had been cleared out, the round dining tables replaced by a rostrum and lectern, map display, and a phalanx of neatly arranged chairs. Except for the museum-quality armor display and the weapons on the walls, it looked like a think-tank presentation, right down to the Centurions International pennant hung on the lectern.

I waved at Buckshot and received a friendly smile, then parked Joe, Dagwood, Crabcakes, and Normal, just as planned, in the back row. That way, we'd be in a dominant position. We could eyeball everybody as they came in without shifting and squirming in our seats like some nervous-Nellie assholes. Anybody wanting to take a look at us, however, would have to turn around.

Buckshot, still in his suit, lounged near the lectern, scanning a thick, loose-leaf briefing book. His hooded eyes took quiet but professional notice of each corporate team as it wandered in, making silent evals, checking probs and stats.

I perused, too, making mental notes as they wandered by. They were dressed in an assortment of camouflage BDUs, fatigues, hunting gear, yuppie-scum, down-filled, high-fashion weekend gear, and blue jeans, and wearing accoutrements that ranged from Eddie Bauer backpacks to assault vests. Most of them looked monumentally underprepared.

We, however, were ready. It being November, and Virginia, *and* because I'd been crawling all over Griffith's property, I'd called Joe on Tuesday and told him to special-order five sets of Super Slam Dry-Plus BDUs from Cabela's hunting supplies in Nebraska, then run them through the washer twice to get the sizing out. I wanted our team to wear an exclusive camouflage pattern called Brush, which matched about 70 percent of the denuded forest and scrubby underbrush on The Hustings, and even worked well in Griffith's open pastures. Instead of long johns, I'd bought four sets of active-sports underwear for the dweebs to wear under their cammies. The polypropylene would wick dampness from their bodies, so if they got wet, they'd dry out quicker.

I had other equipment for them, too—but there was no way I was going to let them carry it where the other teams could see. All in all, I was vaguely optimistic. I'd watched my own men with a critical eye as they fell to. I hated to admit it, but the dweebs looked good in their cammo gear. They wore it with authority—not like the others, who tended to look self-conscious in their BDUs. It turned out that this quartet of engineers had done more than play at snakes and lakes out at Rogue Manor. They'd learned something. Moreover, they'd even adopted some of the virile gestalt of the warrior—the physical and mental bearing that differentiates the warrior from the rest of humanity.

Okay, okay, I can see you shaking your head. What's this bullshit psychobabble? you're asking.

It is like this. Warriors are different. Whether you are a master of the ancient Chinese martial art of tai chi chuan, a sniping instructor at the Marine sniping school at Quantico, or a master chief at BUD/S out at Coronado Island, you have the same goal: to teach your students to neutralize the enemy by any and all means at their disposal, as quickly as they can. To instill this principle so that each man can carry it out takes time and effort.

First, they must be willing to work hard. To learn the craft of killing. Then they must learn to work as a group—remember all that preaching about unit integrity? I told you you'd see it again. Then they must learn to be flexible, both in body and mind. In Eastern martial arts, for example, you learn how to turn your enemy's energy against him. The same doctrine can be applied in running a Marine platoon, a SEAL squad, or an Army Ranger battalion.

Finally, you must inculcate in your men a warrior's soul. The soul of a true warrior is always prepared for death. What that means in plain English is, give your mission everything you've got—because in the end, you're gonna die anyway. So the warrior gives everything he does 110 percent. This, then, is the core of the warrior. The resolve that allows him to kill, face-to-face. The determination that keeps him going despite any adversity.

The warrior sees things through to the end, because in the end, there can only be death. I could lead my SEAL Team Six shooters, for example, out of planes at thirty-five thousand feet because of this principle. They followed me because they had true warrior's souls. They were ready to die. Not anxious to do so. But prepared nonetheless.

Now, sitting in Grant Griffith's atrium, watching the teams as they sauntered in, chatting amongst themselves, making jokes and wisecracks, or laughing nervously, I realized that Joe and his three engineers had it all over the others. They'd caught on—just a little bit. They realized that this game was more than a game. It was a microcosm of life. It had to be played all-out—110 percent. The determined looks on their faces told me they were ready to do so. That made me very happy.

We'd be competing against nine other teams—fifty men total. And despite the fact that I don't know a lot of executives from Fortune 500 companies, I still saw my share of familiar faces. It appeared that Joe wasn't the only businessman to hire a ringer or two for the weekend. I recognized a couple of Special Forces veterans, a guy who was in my class at the Air Force Staff and Command College in Montgomery, Alabama, even a SEAL I'd turned down for Six, a petty petty officer named Nacklin (his handle was No-Load), who'd finally been up-or-outed from Team Three on the West Coast. I nodded at him in the vague way you nod at somebody you don't know very well and whose sorry ass you are about to kick.

The sixth group to arrive was made up of five Japanese look-alikes who wore nylon jackets that read MATSUKO TOOL & DIE on the back. They were also wearing white shirts, ties, the same blue pinstripe suits that they had been wearing at dinner, and wing-tip shoes.

Buckshot looked up, concerned, as the quintet of Nipponese nitnoys slid into a row looking like the five Marx Blothers. He shook his head and ambled over to where they sat. There was a quick conference, with a fair amount of gesticulating on Buckshot's part, and then the Japs departed.

A fucking lightbulb went off in my shit-for-brains Slovak head. Two of the kimchis I'd shot at Narita had been carrying Matsuko ID. Now there was another Matsuko-Griffith connection. And guess whose dummy company had shipped the detonators in the first place. And guess whose friends in high places got Tosho's investigation quashed. My mind was moving at warp speed. What the hell was going on?

I ambled over to Buckshot. "What's up?"

"Fucking Japs didn't bring any equipment."

"You gonna disqualify 'em?"

Buckshot shook his head. "No can do. They're worth about five million bucks of billable time to Secretary Griffith. They'll be allowed to play. I sent 'em down to the office to get outfitted. And they'll get some TAC help from one of my people. I got a guy who can speak some Japanese."

"Who's that?"

"Manny Tanto. You know him, don't you?"

The hair on the back of my neck stood up. It always did when I heard that name. "Manny Tanto? He works for you?"

"I ran into him in Saudi. He was under personal contract

to one of the princes—the one who runs the intelligence service. I made him a better offer."

Manny Tanto. He was the meanest thing I'd ever come across. I'd first met him in Vietnam, back in 1968. Six feet seven inches of uncontrollable mayhem. Back then, he was a Special Forces master sergeant who'd already spent almost six years in the boonies, most of it on his own, waging a one-man war against the VC, the North Vietnamese, the Khmer Rouge, Pathet Lao, and anyone else who got in his way. Manny was part Japanese, part American Indian—a malevolent, treacherous, demonic half-breed who combined the worst qualities of both his ancestries.

His mother, a full-blooded Apache, had met his father when papa-san, a nisei from Los Angeles, was interned at Manzanar during World War II. They'd made the beast with two backs on a cot in the California desert. Their offspring turned into Rosemary's Baby.

I knew about Manny Tanto because on Valentine's Day, 1968, I and a Black Irishman SEAL I'll call Mike Regan went out on a five-day, two-man patrol in the Seven Mountains region of Vietnam, up near the Cambodian border.

I always felt comfortable with Mike Regan. Like me, he was a New Jersey boy. Except he'd grown up with money to burn, in a big, stone house near Princeton, while I was the product of the New Brunswick public housing projects, and empty pockets. Still, he was my kind of guy—a big, hair-trigger lad who liked to use his fists in bars and didn't mind if someone tried to rearrange his face.

In Vietnam, he turned out to be the kind of man you want up against your back when the going gets rough. We'd done five two-man hunts in the past three months, killing a total of thirty-six VC between us. Of those three dozen, Mike had bagged twenty-two.

We began our excursion at a Special Forces A-Team camp near Chompa Mountain, ferried in by a chopper we'd caught in Chau Doc. The next morning, we volunteered to carry some mail to a Special Forces major named DeVine, who was the regional military adviser based in Tri Ton, about thirty miles to the southwest.

When the captain, a gung ho kid named Jackson, asked me how I planned to get to Tri Ton, I told him Mike and I would walk.

"You're shitting me."

I shifted the Swedish K submachine gun to my left shoulder. "Would I shit you, Jackson? Look at it this way—we're dressed in black pajamas. We look like a pair of fucking Russkie advisers." I extracted the letters from Jackson's hand and gave them to Mike.

"You're a fucking crazy SEAL asshole, Marcinko. You're supposed to be operating in a maritime environment—this is the mountains. We're up two thousand feet and nowhere near water."

"Water?" I slapped the canteens on my belt. "Cap," I growled in my best Ev Barrett imitation, "I have fucking water in my fucking canteen—and that's fucking close enough for me."

We ambled into Tri Ton twenty-two hours later, to find a crotch-scratching, straight-legged, home-boy sergeant—regular Army, not Special Forces—waiting for us in the middle of the dusty single street that ran past a series of ramshackle, tin-roofed hootches.

His shirt was half-buttoned, his fly at half-mast, and his 'fro was flecked with lint. I guess we'd busted up his siesta—or his nooner.

He gave us a noncommittal once-over. "They said round-eyes was coming."

"That's us, Sarge."

Mike set the butt plate of his AK down in the dust and leaned the weapon against his leg. He extracted half a dozen envelopes wrapped with a red rubber band from his shabby pajama blouse and waved them in the sergeant's direction. "We brought your major some mail."

"Major?"

"Ain't there a Major DeVine here? Special Forces Regional guy?"

"Used to be. But he moved on last week. Set up new RHQ at Kien Giang near Rach Gia—they got a airstrip there." Home Boy's right hand dropped into the deep pocket of his fatigues and worked his groin area. "Ahhh." Then he retrieved the envelopes from Mike's hand. "I'll make sure they get passed on." He scratched again. "Where you guys come from?"

"Special Forces A camp above That Son," I said.

He shook his head. "Evil neighborhood, bro." He looked around. "Where's the chopper? I didn't hear nothin'."

"We didn't come by chopper."

"No chopper." He began to look perplexed.

He worked his balls again. The son of a bitch must have had a hell of a case of the crabs. "Then how you get here, bro?"

"We came by foot."

"You come by what? Through all those damn VC? What kinda crazy muthafuckers you be, bro?"

"We be SEALs, bro—Navy SEALs."

"SEALs? Navy SEALs?" He just stood there, pickin' and grinnin'. "Okay, bro—so you say you be SEALs. So you say you walk from That Son." He scratched and scratched and scratched while he mastered the possibilities. "Well, if you be Navy SEALs and all, how come you didn't fuckin' *swim?*"

Home Boy roared with laughter. "Come on up to the compound." He turned to trudge point, shoulders hunched against the sun. "You crazy muthafuckers want some cold beer?"

"Fuck you like a *mule,* bro," Mike said. "I been waiting all day to hear somebody ask that question."

We marched into the village behind Home Boy, thirsty as hell. But we forgot about beer when we got to the compound.

We forgot because Manny Tanto was there. Right outside the wood-and-razor-wire gate. Big as life. Stripped to the waist, sweating in the heat, but nonetheless working his ass off in the way men of great dedication pursue their craft.

He was impressive. Big. Big, hell—he was huge. And he was muscular in the way great football wide receivers are muscular—probably less than 1 percent body fat on him. His thick, black hair was shoulder length and worn in Comanche-style braids. His hatchet face was set off by Cro-Magnon-sunken, almond-shaped eyes the color of coal.

Strung around his neck on a double-thick piece of rawhide was a turquoise and silver medallion about the size of a scallop shell. He wore rip-stop, olive BDU pants tucked into knee-high, beaded moccasins that he'd soled with tire rubber. A huge bowie knife hung off one side of his garrison belt; a Smith & Wesson "hush puppy"—one of the silenced, 9mm automatic pistols carried by Special Forces—rode the other side.

He'd built a ten-foot-high tripod out of thick bamboo. Hanging upside down from it, just like you'd suspend a field-dressed deer, was a naked North Vietnamese soldier.

Manny was skinning him. He'd finished about a third— he was somewhere between the genitalia and the lungs at the moment, working downward, toward the head.

The NVA was still alive, too. He was beyond screaming, but I could see him breathing.

Manny looked up from his endeavors as we trudged up. "Hey, bros, welcome to Tri Ton."

His arms were bloody to the elbows. He was using a short-bladed deer-skinning knife with an ivory handle. He wiped the blade on his fatigues, slid it into its sheath, walked up to us and extended his wet hand. "Manny Tanto. Fifth Special Forces. Where you palefaces from?"

"What the hell is this?" I was outraged. Upset. Angry. This was no way to win hearts and minds. Don't get me wrong—I have no qualms about roughing up prisoners. Occasionally, I'd been known to use electrodes on VC testicles to encourage them to answer my questions. But my strong-arm tactics always had an objective—saving the lives of my men. Everything you do has to have a purpose.

This was torture just for the fun of it.

"Cut that son of a bitch down."

Manny went back to the tripod, deliberately retrieved the skinning knife from his pocket, unsheathed it, and took six inches of skin from his victim. Then he turned and looked me up and down with distaste. "Who the fuck are you?"

"Marcinko. Lieutenant, U.S. Navy."

He turned back to his work. "I don't take orders from fucking pussy sailors."

Before he could make another slice, I slung the Swedish K across my shoulder and pumped two bullets into the NVA's head, putting him out of his misery.

Manny Tanto swung around, skinning knife pointed in my direction. I put a bullet in the ground six inches in front of his right foot. "Don't even think about it, cockbreath."

His eyes told me he wasn't going to follow orders. I put another round in the ground. "Believe me, asshole—"

He charged. God, he was fast—he was more than ten yards away, but he covered the distance in less than a second.

I didn't have time to think—all I could do was react. I sidestepped, brought the Swedish K up, and backslapped him across the face with the muzzle of the gun as he careened past me. That slowed him, momentarily. As he staggered, I reached in my pajama pocket for a spare magazine, took it like a club, and whapped him upside the head, drawing blood.

The straight magazine bent into a banana clip, but it did its job—Manny went down like the sack of shit he was. Just to make sure he wasn't going anywhere, I hit him a couple of times more for good measure.

Mike and I cut the NVA corpse down and threw a tarp over it. Then we dragged Manny Tanto over to the tripod and strung him up by his feet. We weren't gentle.

Finally, we finished. "Hey, Home," I shouted.

Home Boy sergeant ambled up.

"Leave this sack of turd hanging where it is for a day or so."

"No way, bro."

I shook my head. "What you say?"

"If you be gone and I leave him hang, then I be dead two minutes after I cut him down. He is one mean motherfucker. He keeps fucking VC scalps in his hootch. Nobody gets in his way."

"The major let him do this kind of thing?"

"The major, he figure Manny's a kind of one-man psy ops. Manny do his thing. Word spreads. VC stay beaucoup far away up north where you come from. Leave this fucking region alone. The major, he thought it was effective fucking tactics."

Fucking tactics was right. Well, each to his own. "We're gonna stay the night. You let him hang there. Tomorrow, when we're gone, do what you have to."

"Manny's fucking crazy, you know that?"

"Sure I know." Buckshot grinned. "But sometimes, you need crazy. Look—he's manageable. He follows orders."

I wasn't convinced. There were too many stories. After Vietnam, Manny'd gone freelance. It was said he'd been promised a million bucks to teach interrogation techniques to the Iranian secret police, SAVAK, then lost it all when the shah and his family fled Tehran. He'd been sighted in Chile, Argentina, and Mexico. He'd reportedly advised Pres. Ferdinand Marcos on counterterror and worked with the Indonesian government against Tamil rebels.

In the eighties, the SpecWar rumor mill put him in the Falklands, laying booby traps that killed British soldiers, then Guatemala, then Salvador. Then he'd disappeared. Now he was part of Buckshot's staff. It gave one pause. "Who else is on your crew?"

"Biker Jordan, Sally Stallion, and Weasel Walker."

The man had taste. It was in his ass, but he had taste. He'd recruited four of the biggest dirtbags in the history of Special Warfare. Four stone killers, all combat tested, all combat proven.

Biker Jordan was one of those fad-crazy, California-cool dudes who always seemed to ride bright red rice rockets, wear French sunglasses with ice blue lenses, and attract big-titted women. He'd lost his cherry in Laos working on covert assassination ops. Later, he worked for Charlie Beckwith and Buckshot at Delta Force, where his specialty was room-clearing with a silenced HK MP5 submachine gun. Charlie and Buckshot liked him, although I always thought he'd eaten too much tofu as a child and turned his brain to soy.

Salvatore Stallone—aka Sally Stallion—was from Brooklyn. *Suo padre* was a made guy—a button man for the

Gambinos. Sally'd thought about the family business, which was hijacking, but instead he'd decided to become the best that he could be. He joined the Army and went to Ranger school. The son of a bitch won a Silver Star in Vietnam when he surprised a company of NVA regulars and killed twenty of them single-handed. His specialty was booby traps, and he knew how to use a straight razor better than any Harlem pimp. I'd played against him during war-game exercises in Panama and at Eglin Air Force Base. He was good—for a guinea who always reeked of garlic. Sally loved garlic. He ate it raw—by the clove—to improve his circulation. You could smell him ten yards before you'd see him.

Weasel Walker was a red-haired, freckled, skinny merink, as my Slovak mother Emilie Pavlik Marcinko would say, from somewhere up north like Minnesota or Wisconsin. He weighed about 140 pounds soaking wet and had a face like a buck-toothed rat, set off by big, jug-handle ears. In Vietnam he'd been a sniper, killing VC cadres at ranges up to a thousand yards with a specially modified Remington 700 bolt-action rifle in .308 caliber.

In the late seventies he'd spent a year with the British Special Air Service, drinking best bitter in Herefordshire with SAS's Twenty-second Regiment and shooting IRA tangos in Ireland, where his coloring allowed him to blend in with the locals. His hobby was running—he ran marathons as warm-ups. His serious events were one-hundred-to-two-hundred-mile endurance runs in such hospitable places as Death Valley or Fairbanks, Alaska. It didn't matter to Weasel how hot or how cold it was. He was like that rabbit in the battery commercial—just kept going and going and going.

Buckshot looked past me. "Gotta go, Dick. Duty calls." I turned. The Japs, only four of them now, dressed in woodland camouflage, were on their way back into the room. They were followed by Manny Tanto. He was older and wider, and there was gray around his temples. But he was still the big, ugly, dangerous behemoth I remembered from Vietnam.

His black eyes played range finder as we drew closer. His

face expressionless, he guided his charges into their seats, muttering to them in Japanese. Our eyes locked as we drew abreast.

In a split second, his arm shot out, his elbow catching me in the back of the neck. I staggered, catching myself on the back of a chair.

"I slipped." Manny smiled malevolently, revealing white, even teeth.

I glanced at the ceiling. His eyes followed mine. Without looking, I kneed him in the groin as hard as I could. He sank to the floor. "I guess I fuckin' slipped, too." I continued to my chair, sat down, folded my arms, and waited for Buckshot to begin.

Chapter

7

THE GAME WAS BOTH SIMPLE AND DIABOLICAL. IT COMBINED THE best features of Red Force/Blue Force and Capture the Flag. It worked like this: pairs of teams set out from different points on the estate at the same time. Both teams were assigned an identical series of five objectives, which had to be achieved within thirty-six hours—by noon on Sunday. Some objectives served as targets for more than one pair of teams; others were exclusive to a single pair.

At each objective, the team would retrieve a card, as evidence that it had reached its target. It would also discover the location of the next target. As an afterthought, Buckshot mentioned that some of the sites contained prepositioned booby traps.

The competition had been well thought out. You worked against the clock, but also against the other teams. The winning team would have the best time, most cards, and least casualties.

Buckshot explained that we could "kill" our opponents by shooting them with Simunition, a Canadian-made training ammo made of wax bullets filled with fluorescent pink indelible paint. Simunition, with which I was familiar, has a range of fifty feet, is reasonably accurate, and administers a nice welt wherever it hits. It feeds through submachine guns and most 9mm pistols. Squibs made of the same paint material were available for booby traps and IEDs. And, Buckshot said, it was also permissible to take an opposition soldier out with your bare hands—you had to attach an unremovable nylon and Kevlar bracelet to their wrists or ankles without having the same done to you.

Certain types of foul play, he emphasized, were forbidden. Destroying another team's cards, for example, would cause immediate disqualification. So would removing the directions to the next site. Buckshot assured the assembled players that cheating would cause severe repercussions.

But, he added, there was nothing wrong with laying additional booby traps at the sites if you got there first. Or lying in ambush and waiting for your competition to show up. I caught a glimpse of Grant Griffith's expression when Buckshot said that. The former SECDEF looked like he was getting a Manila whorehouse blow job. Then Griffith saw me peering at him and the look on his face changed. He smiled, showing his teeth. There was incredible cruelty in that atavistic, reptilian grin.

I shifted my attention back to the lectern. Buckshot was explaining that the bottom line of this game was simple: there were no friendlies. All forces were to be considered hostile. He pointed in my direction. "Dick understands that, don't you, Dick?"

The few people in the room who knew me laughed.

I did, too. Well, why not? Let him have some entertainment at my expense. I'd have my fun later—in the field.

Overall, I was impressed. It was an ingenious exercise because you weren't just being pitted against one team but everyone. And, since all fifty players were going to be out in the woods at the same time, there was bound to be a lot of bumping and humping along with the prowling and growling, which suggested adequate quantities of bruising and contusing during the thirty-six hours of cruising. I liked that part. I am all in favor of full-contact sports.

Of course, we were paired with Manny Tanto and his Japs. Buckshot saw to that. He always did have a nasty sense of humor.

We were timed out at 0025 from the log-cabin slave quarters that sat five hundred feet west of the main house's west wing. Manny's crew left from the old mill half a mile to the east. The first objective was in his favor—it was in quadrant Delta, at coordinates 11 and 27. That meant we'd be doing a diagonal traverse of the property, covering just over a mile and a half as the crow flies—and about three times that on the ground. Once we were well away from the cabin, I handed each man a map of Griffith's estate marked with the coordinates Wonder and I had agreed on, and a radio with earpiece and lip mike.

"Put these on."

The dweebs set their equipment. While they did, I called Wonder on the digitized transmitter I carried in my pocket to give him the location of our first objective. He reminded me there was a cache at 13/28 Delta, and I'd want what it held. Then I checked the team's weapons. We'd been given Glocks with specially modified barrels, and three fifteen-round magazines of Simunition per man. That was sufficient. I didn't think we'd be needing more.

I took point. It wasn't that I didn't trust Crabcakes, but with Manny out and about, I didn't want to take any chances.

The moon provided ample light. We moved north across a plowed field that had once held corn. It had rained recently and the furrows contained enough water and mud to make me thankful for our Gore-Tex equipment. Using the cover provided by the natural contour of the land, we crossed a hilly field on which rye had grown, then slid into the wooded area bordering the pasture, turned east, forded a stream, and humped along a low ridge, down a slope thick with honeysuckle and thistle bush, to the bank of the small river that I knew ran northwest to southeast, cutting The Hustings more or less in half diagonally. So far, we'd seen or heard no one else.

The river was about thirty feet wide and too deep to wade. There was a bridge about a half mile to the east, but that was too obvious a route. We'd ford here. To get across we'd need a fording bridge.

I had seventy-five feet of nylon coiled around my waist. I looped one end around a sapling, then went into the chilly water. I hate cold. But you can't be a Frogman and not be cold. So in I went. Thank God for the quick-drying underwear. The current was worse than expected, and I had to fight my way across. I hauled myself up the bank, then tied the nylon off.

I waved the team on. Man by man, they pulled themselves across. We rechecked our equipment. The sound of gunshots came from the south. At least one of the teams had engaged.

"How far away was that?" Dagwood asked.

"Maybe half a mile—maybe more. Sound carries out here."

Joe took a pull of water from his canteen. "I wonder which team it was."

"Do you really care?"

He grinned. "Nah. Just so long as it wasn't us."

"Right." I took point again, heading on a northeasterly tack. I tried to guess how Manny would think. Knowing him, he'd probably cheat—he'd use the road on the eastern border of the property, even though it was marked out of play. Then he'd set up an ambush on the western approach to the target. That's what I'd have done if I'd started from the mill.

So we stayed away from the road, moving parallel to it but six-tenths of a click in, then fishhooking at the last minute, to the split-rail fence line where my cache of goodies was hidden in the hollow, deformed trunk of a hundred-year-old white ash that sat twenty-five feet from the roadside.

There were three old, reliable M-1 pull-firing devices, two spools of trip wire, a pressure-switch device, two Wham-O slingshots, a handful of cherry bombs, a dozen M-80 smoke grenades, and three IEDs of various potencies.

"What's up?" Joe watched as I dropped the toys into my rucksack.

"Insurance."

"How—"

"Joe, were you a Boy Scout?"

"Sure—Eagle Scout."

"What's the Scout motto?"

"Be prepar—" His round face broke into a smile. "Why, you cunning son of a bitch."

Now it was my turn to smile.

By 0340 we'd snaked and slithered our way south, coming up on the target from behind, paralleling about eighty yards west of the obvious course. We'd moved pretty well. The boys stayed quiet, even though we'd heard a dozen bursts of gunfire during our three-hour crawl. Still, I hoped that by giving Manny a wide berth—although I saw a few signs that suggested he, or someone who knew his business, had been prowling—we'd avoid contact and hit the target clean. That, not shooting up the other team, was the real goal of the exercise.

After about thirty minutes of slow but steady movement we'd pulled within two hundred yards of our goal. I called a halt. It gave the men a chance to relax their muscles and pay attention to the night sounds.

While the dweebs looked and listened, I backtracked about fifty yards and rigged an M-1 pull-fire device with an M-80 smoke grenade just in case Manny had circled his own trail and was sneaking up from behind, just like Robert Roger's Ranger rule number seventeen says you're supposed to do.

The eight-inch-long M-1 cylinder is simple to use. You attach your explosives and a detonation cord to the bottom end and a trip wire to the pull ring at the top. Then you rig your trip wire. Finally, you remove all the safety pins, and the M-1 is armed and dangerous. When someone hits the trip wire, it allows a spring-loaded striker to hit an old-fashioned percussion primer, which in turn fires a flash that ignites the det cord, and the bomb goes boom.

I rejoined the men and indicated for Crabcakes to take the point. Just as I gave the silent signal to move out, Crabcakes tensed. He pointed east and silent-signaled that he'd heard something. I listened. I nodded.

Something was moving out there—maybe thirty to forty yards away. It could be deer—the place was crawling with fox and deer, and with all the teams in the woods the herds would be disturbed, churning up from the thickets where they normally stayed.

But it could also be Manny, or another team. I decided to play safe. We rerouted to the west again, circled 360 degrees, then back-angled on an azimuth that brought us up on the target from the northern back door—shades of Ilo-Ilo Island allo-allo over again.

After about half an hour of slow patrol, Crabcakes called a halt and conferred with Normal, who was the team's pace man—he was the guy who counted the steps between compass points to give us our location. Normal scratched his head. He was just about to say something when Crabcakes' arm went out and his thumb pointed straight down at the ground.

It was the silent signal for "enemy seen." He followed it with the signal for "get down."

The men deployed, scattering into the underbrush on each side of the narrow track we'd been following in a textbook example of rapid offensive deployment. Who says engineers can't learn? Twenty seconds later, the point man of another team came around a horseshoe bend in the trail. From my position I could see him wander blindly as he took the outside track of the curve. Asshole. The outside track gets you killed.

He stood out like a dickhead. He'd rubbed camouflage all over his face—but he'd left his neck, ears, and hands bare. The moonlight, filtering through the bare trees, made him glow like neon.

Dagwood lay three feet away. I gave him a silent signal to let the point man pass, but keep him in sight, then kill him. A big smile crossed Dagwood's well-camouflaged face.

The rest of the team followed hard on their point man's tail—not more than three or four yards behind, and not even a yard apart. Assholes. Thus, in war, are casualties caused. The rear guard could be heard thrashing and splashing five or six yards behind them.

At my signal, whispered into the lip mike of my radio, we sprang.

I grabbed the patrol leader—he was an overweight asshole wearing hunting coveralls in wetlands camouflage—from behind, cupped my hand over his mouth, slapped him with my sap, and watched him collapse on the ground. I turned to see Joe and Normal struggling with another big man in an L.L. Bean ski jacket. I reached out and touched him with the sap, too. Two down. Crabcakes was already sitting astride a third man, running surgical tape around his mouth from the rolls we all carried. Hot damn—the boy'd learned fast.

That left Point Man and Rear Guard.

Two shots rang out from the front of the skirmish line. Shit—I'd forgotten to tell Dagwood that I wanted everyone to kill their targets silently. Now the rear guard knew something was amiss. I got my ass in gear, cutting back, parallel to the trail, moving as quickly as I could without making noise.

I saw him before he saw me. It was No-Load Nacklin, the asshole SEAL from Team Three.

He'd dropped into the approved defensive position and was scanning the trail with his eagle eyes. I let him scan. He may have been looking, but he wasn't seeing anything. Shit—he was like so many of the young ones today. They loved maneuvers and war games. They spent all their time jumping out of planes and diving. But they'd never killed anyone, never knew what it was like to get their asses shot at.

So they did everything by the book because that's how their worthless no-load shit-for-brains pencil-dicked pus-nutted sphincter-sucking tight-assed officers, who'd never been to war either, told them to do it.

Remember Rule Four? There are no rules.

I tossed a twig behind him. He rotated 180 degrees. Just like all those Jap sentries in John Wayne movies or Arab assholes in *Delta Force Part XXI*. Before he could swing back, I was on top of him. I applied a helping of leather sap and trussed him like a heifer. I used the tape liberally, binding his arms and legs and gagging him. Then I grabbed him by the collar of his Official U.S. Navy Issue BDUs and dragged him back to the ambush site.

We sat them all in a row like captured VC, propped up

against trees, linked one to another by the nylon and Kevlar bracelets.

"What do we do with Team General Dectonics?" Joe asked.

"Kill 'em," I said, removing my fifteen-inch-long, razor-sharp Field Fighter knife from its scabbard. I loved the look of panic in the prisoners' eyes when I did that. They went wide as saucers.

"Be serious."

"I am."

"Dick—"

"Okay, okay. We tie 'em up to trees and we leave 'em. Buckshot's people'll find 'em sooner or later. But we booby-trap 'em. Let's make it quick because we're behind schedule."

It was close to daybreak when we finally reached the first objective—a half-demolished shed about one hundred yards from the county road. I signaled for everyone to take up defensive firing positions while I belly-crawled to the target. That way, if I got caught in an ambush, the dweebs could kill the bad guys. It took me about fifteen minutes to make the approach because I took no chances, coming from the blind side through a patch of dead poison ivy and live huckleberry bush.

When I finally got there, I was happy for two things. First, that I had come in alone, and second, that Ev Barrett had taught me to do things the hard way.

From my position at the side of the building I could see the instruction envelope. It was wedged in a crack of an old board about fifteen inches above ground level next to the doorframe. That was just too inviting to be true. I double-checked the ground, and about a full body length out, right in front, I found a monofilament trip wire about ankle high running parallel to the doorway. I tracked it and discovered one end of the wire attached to a sapling; the other end was rigged to a paint-filled IED. The device wasn't camouflaged, which told me that either the damn thing had been placed there hastily or whoever'd rigged it thought we'd storm the target area in the dark.

It took a couple of minutes to defuse the squib. Then I back-crawled to the doorframe and ran my hand around the upright as tenderly as if I were getting ready to finger-fuck a virgin. Rule One, as Ev Barrett had knocked into my thick Slovak skull so many times, was never assume.

I could hear his throaty New England–accented growl rumbling between my ears even now. *"You know what happens when you* ass-sume, *Petty Officer Second Class Marcinko, you worthless blankety-blanking blank-blank blanker-bleeper bleeper-blanking no-load geek? Every bleeper-blanking time you* ass-sume, *you make a blanking ass of you and me."*

Once again, I had to give credit to Ev. The envelope was attached to something. I investigated further. It had been secured by wax to a hair-thin wire . . . it was a goddamn pull device. That fucking ingenious bastard Manny.

Holding my breath, I eased the envelope back into the crack so I wouldn't accidentally pull it. Then, sliding a razor-sharp Emerson CQC6 Close Quarters combat folding knife out of my BDUs, I carefully slit the envelope about one-third of the way along its upper edge. Gingerly, I slipped the directions and our team card out without disturbing the wax-and-wire arrangement. By the time I'd copied the new location into my notebook, I was sweating copiously.

I double-checked to make sure I'd copied everything correctly, then I slid the directions back up into the envelope, sealed it with tape, and withdrew.

Our first goal was to get the hell away from the target. So we crawled directly north for about ten minutes, moving quickly but carefully. I led the way, probing for booby traps and antipersonnel mines and IEDs with the Field Fighter. I was anxious to put as much distance as possible between us and the shed. We finally stopped, winded, just below the crest of a small rise. While Joe and the boys read the new directions, I rolled over the top and called Wonder on the secure transmitter.

"Yo, bro."

"Yo, asshole."

"Anything?" Stevie was tasked with monitoring all communications from The Hustings.

"Nah. Lots of normal message traffic. A lot of it is cellular—in Japanese."

That was interesting. I wondered if it was significant. "Sounds—" Our conversation was interrupted by an audible explosion back at the target site. I smiled at Joe. Somebody hadn't been paying attention.

"What the hell was that?" Wonder asked.

"It used to be the competition."

He giggled. I could just see his head swiveling.

I explained about Manny. He whistled. "Anything I can do?"

"Not for the moment. Keep your ears open. If you hear something, call."

"Roger-roger."

Joe watched as I put the phone away. "Who're you talking to?"

"That's compartmented, Joe."

I planned on reaching the second objective just before 1330. It would be a long morning—marching through seven miles of foothills, meadows, and high pastureland, taking a circuitous path right up to the edge of the Appalachian Trail, where Target Two was located. We stopped on the way at 14/12 Charlie to pick up another package of goodies Wonder and I had stowed during our sneak-and-peeks. This cache sat in a waterproof pack tied to the southeast concrete foot of the county-road bridge that crossed the river about two miles due north of Griffith's house.

It was at the bridge we received a gift from God. Before I retrieved my package I checked the bridge for booby traps. Attached by a wood frame to the underside of the concrete span, which sat about five feet above the shallow water, was a big envelope. I went into the water and checked for wires and other trigger devices and, finding none, tied a rope to the wood frame and pulled myself up. There were three separate booby traps attached to the envelope. I disarmed them, retrieved the envelope, brought it back to shore, and opened it carefully to see which team's objective we'd blundered onto.

Eureka! There was a Team ANT card inside, along with a

Team Matsuko card, as well as directions to Target Number Four. Joe and I high-fived. It wasn't even 0930 hours yet. This put us way ahead of the game.

The smart thing now would be to play it safe—proceed alone to the second target, retrieve the ANT card, and then cruise on to the fourth and fifth targets, hours ahead of the others.

But something was gnawing at me. Something was not right. Suddenly it struck me: Buckshot had pitted Manny and me against each other because he—or more likely Grant Griffith—wanted us to go at it. A couple of knuckle-dragging gladiators engaged in blood sport for the gentry's amusement. They'd all be expecting us to face off at the last target—if we both got that far. Probably have video cameras going. That pissed me off. If the goddamn former SECDEF wanted to see me kill somebody, let him pay me for the pleasure. He could afford it.

So, fuck him. Doom on you, Grant—I'd take Manny here, in private, for my own enjoyment.

First, I showed the dweebs how to rig a pair of pressure mats (they look like shower mats but they have a built-in switch that detonates when weight's put on them) to Claymore mines, each rigged with Simunition red paint and an artillery simulator. I anchored the pads on the muddy river bottom underneath the bridge and wrapped vines around the det cords. We stuck the Claymores on the vertical bridge supports, then Normal camouflaged them with mud.

Then, we built a series of booby traps laid in concentric circles out from the bridge. We ran M-1 pull detonators attached to trip wires. I planted multiple pressure mines attached to paint squibs. I set a series of Claymores. Dagwood looked at my wiring and shook his head.

"Negatory, Dick."

"What's the prob?" I'd never had a problem setting this kind of trap before.

"You have set the charges serially. If you set them this way"—he changed the wiring—"they can be fired from either direction, or from the middle out."

Son of a bitch. He was right. It was so simple it was

elegant. "Fuck you, Dagwood. I'm gonna get you a job teaching booby traps at Little Creek."

He smiled back at me like a toothpaste billboard. "Anytime, Dick. Anytime at all."

As we finished preparing our tenth old-fashioned smoke-grenade trap, Joe wondered aloud whether I was perhaps overcompensating.

The maniacal look on my face told him *that* was a question that shouldn't be asked.

The idea, I explained as we worked, was to run Manny's Matsuko team through a gauntlet of explosives and funnel them into a killing zone, where we could decimate 'em. We worked at a frenzied pace. Even so, it took us just under two hours to rig the explosives.

As soon as we finished—just after 1115—I got on the horn to Wonder. Eight minutes after I called, Stevie's maroon Dodge Ram approached the bridge.

I opened the right-hand door and motioned Joe and Dagwood over. "Get in."

Joe was confused. I stuck my thumb in Stevie's direction. "This is your tour guide. He'll take you to Target Two."

"But—"

"Hey, Joe, this is no time for discussion." I handed Wonder the directions. "Bring 'em both back alive, okay?"

He grinned from behind the wraparound shades. "No prob."

I went around to the back and pulled a cammo tarp off the truck bed. "Later, bro."

Under my direction, the squad dug two long, deep pits in the soft loam of the heavily wooded areas directly to the north and west of the bridge. I lined them with pieces of Wonder's tarp, and we camouflaged the tops with brush and leaves. Then I found two good-sized downed trees and secured each of them to a sapling.

With Normal and Crabcakes' help I bent the saplings back and tied them off, setting the triggers with monofilament trip line.

The concept was KISS-simple. I'd leave a hint of a trail for Manny and his team to follow. Not too much, or he'd get suspicious. But enough so he'd take the bait. The Japs would move along the path, trip the wire, and the trees would swat them into the pit. I'd used the same device successfully on VC. If the traps didn't get them, the IEDs at the bridge would do the job—or we'd shoot 'em all from ambush.

The traps took two hours to finish. I was nervous—we were pushing the edge of the envelope so far as the opposition was concerned. Manny was good. And he'd be coming soon.

The traps finished, I supervised Crabcakes and Normal as they dug in. What I wanted were SAS-styled ambush positions from which we could maintain fields of fire that crisscrossed the entire bridge area, while remaining invisible, even to Manny's practiced eyes. I had the men hunker in their shallow holes and camouflage themselves with loose vegetation. Then I double- and triple-checked their positions to make sure they were invisible even to me. I used the 5-S system that we'd learned in SERE, or Survival, Evasion, Resistance, and Escape school. I watched for Shape, Shine, Silhouette, Smell, and Sound.

By the time I'd finished adding a wisp of brush here and a branch there, or painting an exposed ear with cammo cream, I didn't care how good Manny was—there was no fucking way he was going to see my squad before they blew his ass away.

I dropped into my own foxhole and figuratively pulled the covers up under my chin. Now came the hard part. The wait.

The ambush has come a long way since Odysseus dropped out of the Trojan horse, the Robin Hood gang swung down from their trees in Sherwood, or the minutemen popped up from behind that stone wall outside Concord, Massachusetts. Today, there are a panoply of wonderful mechanical and electronic devices to help us kill our enemy. We've got UGS—Unmanned Ground Sensors—that trigger Claymores and other explosive devices when an enemy force moves into the area. There are infrared trigger systems, microwave activators, radio-controlled devices, and laser detonators.

All of these gadgets are marvelous. They are also expensive. And they only work when your enemy is kind enough to walk along a path where you've painstakingly set them up and trip them.

It's possible, of course, to convince your enemy to follow a specific route—you can make him believe you're unaware he's around. Or that you've got something he wants. You could drop money on the trail and let him follow you, picking up the coins as he goes.

But nothing in warfare is guaranteed. Remember Rule One. Never assume. So, maybe Mr. Bad Guy is independently wealthy and he doesn't need your coins. Or he's smart, so he takes the back door. Or maybe he's lucky, and the batteries in your million-dollar laser system run dry. Or perhaps the company that made your UGS cut a corner or two and it's not as waterproof as it's supposed to be. You catch my drift.

Bottom line: when it comes to an ambush, the old-fashioned way is the best. You use intelligence to tell you where your enemy's going to be. Then you set up, and you wait for him to show. Then you kill him before he knows what's happening.

I had the right intelligence—I knew where Manny had to be. I'd set my traps and put out my bait. Now, it was time to wait.

He showed up at 1445. By then we'd been in the holes more than a hour, and everyone was fidgety. Despite liberal applications of insect repellent, the creepy-crawlies were doing their creepy-crawling up and down arms and legs, in and out of shirts and pants. The November sun was hot, and we were all sweaty and uncomfortable. I knew Crabcakes and Normal wanted to take a piss because that's the way I felt, too. But you couldn't even piss in your pants because Manny would smell it a hundred feet away, and the big mean bogeyman would come and scalp you dead.

He was still good. Was he ever. You didn't hear anything —*anything*. No rustle of brush. No change in the way the insects buzzed or the birds chirped. It was just that, all of a sudden, he was *here*. Manny. The Predator.

It was like a chapter out of *Zen and the Art of the Ambush*. The hair on the back of my neck stood up. It took all my self-discipline not to move, not to crane my neck to see if he was coming up in back of me.

I waited. The silence was excruciating.

It took another six or seven minutes before I actually saw him. He was coming from downstream, working his way through the woods on the southern bank of the river. The approach was proof of his professionalism—he was coming through the back door, just as I would have done.

And, like me, Manny was alone. He'd left his Japs behind, probably somewhere safe in the woods nearby, while he did the recon solo. Just the way I'd hit Target One earlier in the day.

We had our radios on. I whispered, "Quiet, steady," and, "Four o'clock," into the lip mike, hoping the men would understand.

He was bare chested. His muscular body was covered in camouflage war paint that blended almost perfectly with his tiger-striped BDUs and the cammo rucksack he carried over one shoulder. He'd tied a cammo kerchief over his long Indian hair, and he wore another around his neck. In one hand Manny carried a CAR-15. In his other was a wicked bowie knife with which he probed the ground, testing for mines. Manny moved at a slow, consistent pace, his eyes making a methodic sweep of the area, his moccasins leaving no tracks in the soft earth. He knew enough to look in a 360, watching above and below as well as side to side.

He came upon the first of my IEDs—an M-1 pull device attached to a series of squibs by a trip wire secured a foot above the ground. That is high for a trip wire. But I'd wanted Manny to see it.

Bingo. His eyes followed the path of the wire as it led across the leaf-strewn path, to where the detonator was concealed behind a tree. Slowly he moved his hand into his shirt pocket. He withdrew an M-1 firing pin and inserted it into the pull device's safety. Then he snipped the trip wire. The booby trap was disarmed.

He paused, looking around, as if asking himself who it was who'd done that. You could see his nostrils flare, as if he were trying to sniff out the opposition.

He stopped. He slipped the rucksack off his shoulder and

hung it on a convenient tree. Then he backtracked, peering around to see what the alternatives were, should he need them. He knew about Rule One.

He tacked away from the path, moving in my direction. I held my breath as he edged closer, inch by inch, toward my SAS position. I could hear my heart pounding in my ears. I prayed that Manny couldn't.

He stopped, two yards away, and looked right at me. When someone does that, the only thing to do is nothing. If you believe you are invisible, you will become invisible. I willed myself to be invisible, and Manny looked right through me. It seemed like he stared for an eternity, even though it was only a few moments. Then, having seen nothing, he moved on.

I didn't breathe again until he was ten yards beyond me. Then I watched as he crept in a thirty-yard circle, backtracking to his original position. Smart.

Now, he began a systematic search of the area for other booby traps. One by one he found them, each time getting closer to the bridge. My concentric lethal circles were being peeled like an onion.

It took him an hour to sweep the southern approach to the bridge alone. Then, having deemed it safe, he vaulted over the rail and began a systematic search of the bridge itself. He went over every nook and cranny. He'd do the bridge itself now, then search the northern approach. I had to admit it: Manny was good. Nothing escaped him. That worried me. We'd concealed ourselves on the north side of the bridge— and I knew he'd discover us. It was just a matter of time.

I watched as he lowered himself into the water. I held my breath. We had two pressure plates down there. If he touched bottom—and it was less than six feet deep under the bridge—then he'd go boom.

No way. Manny floated downstream on his back, looking up at the envelope secured to the concrete five feet above his head. Then, as I watched, he breast-stroked against the current, then dead-man-floated downstream. He was looking for booby traps. This was one careful half-breed.

Okay, I know you're wondering why I just didn't stand up and shoot the son of a bitch. I mean, here I am, all camouflaged, locked, loaded, and lying in ambush. So why not ambush Manny right then and there?

The answer is that I didn't know where the others in his team were. I was certain he'd stashed them in the woods. But, if he was a pro like me, he'd have left them in a defensive posture, weapons ready. Even if they were complete assholes, they'd be able to fire their guns or toss a grenade or two, and I'd be dog meat. Good-bye, game; good-bye, Joe Andrews; and most important, good-bye, Grant Griffith. No—this was an all-or-nothing deal, and I wanted it all.

Finally, Manny began sniffing around the envelope like it was a bitch in heat. He swung himself under the bridge and worked his way up and down the structure. He disarmed the booby traps attached to the envelope. Then he took the cards and the directions and slipped them into his BDUs.

Not kosher. Allegedly, another team—ours—would be using the site as well. And Buckshot had been specific about taking the directions. That was verboten.

Except, in SpecWar, of course, there are no rules. Doom on us.

Manny unlatched the flap on his rucksack and withdrew something. He hustled over to the bridge, sat on the abutment, and began to rig an IED. Obviously, he was going to booby-trap the envelope. Then I saw what was in his hand: a mini fragmentation grenade, about the size of a tangerine. This was no IED—it was the real thing.

It was clear to me what was going on. Manny also knew that the game was between the two of us—and he was trying to make it very dangerous for me. He was playing for keeps.

I was going to have to act. But not until Manny had finished playing with the grenade. My inventory of deadly weapons was decidedly less complete than his—so I wasn't about to mess with him yet.

He slid under the bridge. Wedging himself in position, he slid the envelope halfway back into its wooden retainer. Then he pulled the pin on the grenade and placed it between the envelope and the concrete, with the spoon against the envelope.

Whenever some anxious asshole named Marcinko moved the envelope, the spoon would drop, the grenade would detonate, and it was *sayonara, ciao, au revoir,* Mr. Shit-for-Brains.

It was a Keep It Simple, Stupid booby trap, as in gimme a little KISS, will ya, huh. Cheap, effective, and deadly. Precisely the sort of thing I'd do myself.

Satisfied with his handiwork, Manny extracted himself from under the bridge. He slid the rucksack over his shoulder, picked up the CAR-15, and began to work his way out, moving toward the east, directly away from the northernmost man-trap we'd built.

It hit me right then with the sort of absolute clarity that clobbers you like an epiphany—*Manny was alone.* He'd stowed the Japs. That was the foreign-language cellular stuff Wonder had heard. While Manny waged war, they were doing business as usual. Of course—just like Vietnam, Manny Tanto was doing what he did best: playing a solo act.

Two could play that game. I came out of my hole, murder in my eyes. Manny's shoulders shifted in my direction. A wicked smile came over his face. His hand dropped toward the huge bowie knife on his belt.

"Die, you goddamn son of a bitch!" It was Normal. The asshole dweeb actually came out of his hole like a fucking pocket rocket and ran toward Manny, firing his Glock wildly, screaming obscenities at the top of his lungs.

The half-breed turned, swiveled the CAR around, and fired from the hip. He stitched Normal with six shots of Simunition. Normal looked at the splotches of paint on his BDUs and kept coming. He tried to club Manny with his pistol. Manny hit Normal only once—a gut-wrenching sucker punch that lifted him about six inches off the ground and dropped the poor asshole like a brick, unconscious.

"Hey—fuckface, let's keep this between pros." I charged, knocking Manny off Normal. We rolled around, each of us trying to get some kind of advantage.

"Uhh—" He rolled away, sucking air.

I came at him. He caught me upside the head, chopping at my ears. I went down. Now it was his turn to jump my bones. He caught me with a knee in the groin, and as I reacted, he got my ear in his mouth. I gouged his eyes and he opened his jaw before he'd chewed completely through.

Time to go. I threw him off me, rolled away, caught his hair, and yanked his head around, smashing at his face with my forehead, drawing blood.

That got his attention. He came at me with his knife. I threw dirt in his face and got out of range, then regrouped and went in low before he'd recovered. I knocked him down and kicked him in the head.

That only made him mad. But, as he tried to stand up, I hit him with my elbow twice, then shouldered him backward against a stump. I bounced his head off the wood, tagged him twice with my sap, then got out of the way as he charged me.

It was like fighting a goddamn raging bull. I stepped aside and tripped him—*Ole!*—and he went flying forward into a tree. He turned, dazed but deadly, and came for me.

It was exactly what I wanted. "Hey, Manny—you foul-smelling cockbreath—over here, you worthless slant-eyed pussy."

I knew where I was—just a yard from the man trap's trip wire. I took six measured steps backward. Now the wire was between us. Manny followed, the knife in his hand and murder in his eyes. And like the asshole he was, he was too busy watching me to pay attention to the ground.

Whooomp. He hit the fucking trip wire. The log came around and caught him in the rib cage just under his armpit, knocking him into the pit.

"Timber!" I jumped on top of him and beat him senseless with my sap. Then I rolled him over, tied his arms behind his back with surgical tape, bound his legs together in three places, and gagged him. He looked like a goddamn bloody mummy by the time I finished.

I climbed out of the pit and ran over to Normal, who was still out of it. Crabcakes was at his side.

I beeped Wonder on the burst transmitter. Three minutes later he returned the call on his cellular.

"Yeah?"

"What's up?"

"Fucking piece of cake. Got the card you need. Your guys are both okay."

"Then get your ass back here and stop loafing. I need you. I need the truck."

"Yo, Holmes, don't sweat. I'm on my way."

It didn't take him ten minutes to show. While I waited, I took the team cards and directions out of Manny's pockets. When Stevie arrived, we loaded Manny on the back of the truck. Then we picked up Normal and stowed him, too. Joe and Dagwood carried him to the cab. Then I told Wonder to head back to the 1763.

"Whaddya want to do with the oversized pile of shit?"

"Roll him in a tarp and leave him on the truck. We'll figure something spectacular out later."

Joe and I regrouped the team at 0430 and showed up at the main house at 0525. Wonder and I took the final two sites by ourselves, meeting no opposition. I had no qualms about cheating. Remember Rule Four? Well, my goal was to win. Joe needed Grant Griffith for business reasons. I had other objectives. I wanted to get inside—to see what this multimillionaire asshole did, and how he did it. From what I'd seen so far, the best way to do that was to impress the shit out of him. And if badass Manny Tanto, trussed like the turkey he was, didn't do that, nothing would.

The five of us rousted Buckshot from his slave quarters office and insisted that he wake up Grant Griffith.

When the former secretary finally appeared a quarter of an hour later, he was wrapped in a long, muted red, blue, and green ancient madder silk dressing gown worn over tan slacks and an open-necked brown silk shirt. His suede Gucci loafers were worn without socks. Joe made him a formal presentation of our five site cards.

"This means you've won," he said. "Congratulations." He slid the cards into the left-hand pocket of his robe. "We'll make the formal award at noon tomorrow, in front of the assembled teams."

Griffith appeared about ready to go back upstairs when I asked him to come out front and receive another trophy we'd taken during our session in the field.

We made him a presentation of Manny Tanto, who lay trussed and writhing in the driveway.

Joe Andrews pointed at Manny. "I want to lodge a formal complaint. It has to do with him."

"Yes?" Griffith's eyebrows rose. There was respect in his eyes when he stared at me.

Joe continued, "We were given to understand that teams are required to operate at full strength unless members have been killed in action."

"That's correct," said Griffith.

"Please ask him where his team is," said Joe.

I ripped the surgical tape off Manny's face so he could talk. It took some skin and eyelashes with it, but I didn't give a damn.

Griffith looked at his bloodied behemoth. "Manny, where is the team from Matsuko I requested that you advise?"

The half-breed turned his face away. Griffith walked around his head and nudged his cheek with a Gucci-clad toe. "Manny, I'm asking you a question." He tapped his toe in front of Manny's recumbent nose.

"They're resting, sir," Manny finally said. He pronounced it s-i-r but he was spelling it c-u-r. I knew because it was the way I'd addressed so many of my own superiors.

Griffith paid no notice to the ex–Green Beret's insubordination. "Resting? Where?"

Manny shrugged. "At the inn in Paris—just down the road. I told 'em it was okay—they were unprepared anyway, and I didn't see any reason for 'em to have to spend two days in the woods. They would have lost face."

"Lost face?" Griffith snorted. "You have caused them to lose more than face."

He turned to Buckshot. "Team Matsuko is disqualified," he said evenly. "Please make sure they are picked up from the inn and shown every courtesy. And convey to them my deepest regrets. But they are disqualified. Those are the rules."

The lines around Griffith's mouth hardened. "I am not happy about the manner in which your man has performed," he said, addressing himself to Buckshot's general area. "He has brought dishonor on me. We'll discuss this more later."

The former SECDEF turned his back on Buckshot. He put his arm around Joe's shoulder. "Congratulations, Mr. Andrews," he said warmly. "Your team has performed admirably—you set a new course record."

Then he smiled his carnivorous grin at me. "Mr. Marcinko, you are as advertised."

I wondered what the hell he meant by that, so I asked.

"I have heard a lot about you from all sorts of people."

That didn't tell me anything either. "The problem with that is most people are assholes."

"By which you mean?"

"I mean we should talk things over, Grant." I shot a dirty look in Buckshot's direction. "But in a more private venue. After all, I'm in the security business, too. Let's meet next week and see what good I could do for you."

"I was thinking along the same lines." Griffith ran his tongue along his lower lip. "Please come and see me on Tuesday at my office. At noon. We'll do lunch. I believe you like your steak rare and your Bombay gin on ice."

Chapter

8

GRIFFITH MUST HAVE WANTED TO SHOW ME OFF, BECAUSE THE minute I arrived, we went back downstairs and limoed the five blocks from his offices on Farragut Square to the Palm, the steak house mecca for Washington's top lawyers and lobbyists. It's over on Nineteenth, just above M.

I'd eaten there only once before—three days after I was released from jail, when Charlie Thompson, the ex-Navy brown-water sailor who produced Mike Wallace's "60 Minutes" segment based on *Rogue Warrior,* took me out for an expense-account B² lunch—it was built around Bombay and blackened tuna steak.

That time, Charlie and I were seated at an anonymous table in the rear after fifteen minutes of pacing in the foyer. When I walked two paces behind Grant Griffith, the Palm's owner/manager, a mustachioed, Italian New York transplant named Tommy Jacomo, greeted him like the *capo del tutti capi* and me like the capo's favorite button man. We were immediately whisked to the center table in the front room, where half a dozen waiters and busboys bowed and scraped as they brought bread, butter, Perrier water, and a huge bowl of half-sour dills, pickled tomatoes, and radishes and placed them all reverently on the checkered tablecloth.

Griffith obviously enjoyed every minute of it. To be honest, I didn't think it was so bad, either.

130

I looked around the room as a double Bombay on the rocks was put in front of me. I recognized at least half a dozen of the self-appointed "experts" who appear regularly on the nightly network news shows. Other familiar faces stared down at me from the walls, where scores of caricatures provided a visual *Who's Who in Washington*. Griffith's face was prominently displayed—his picture was larger, and more favorable, than the president's.

The former secretary watched me reconnoiter as he sipped on a huge goblet of iced tea in which a sprig of crushed mint had been dropped. Finally, he toasted me with his Lipton. "Your health."

I returned the favor. "And yours." I don't think either of us meant it.

"Quite a win last weekend. I hadn't expected it to come out the way it did."

I'll bet he hadn't. I underplayed it. "Joe's a good man."

Griffith nodded graciously. "Yes, he is. You helped him a lot."

"You mean the war game?"

"Yes, but I mean the protection angle, too. Your being around seems to have chased the threat away."

I was surprised he knew about the threat against Joe. Belay that. I wasn't surprised by anything about this guy. "Yeah."

"Does he still need protection?"

"Well, I gave him the name of a good friend if he does." I have a friend I'll call Old Blue Eyes—a retired SEAL with whom I went through training back in 1961. These days he sometimes hires out as a mercenary—most recently he did some sniping for the Croatians against the Serbian Army. He waxed three Serb generals in less than a week—and received $50,000 for his efforts. He's well versed in personal protection, and I figured that if Joe needed a repeat performance, I'd throw a little cash in Blue Eyes' direction.

"That was generous of you."

I stared at Griffith. "I have bigger fish to fry."

He stared back. "I'll bet."

There was about a thirty-second lapse in the conversation. My mind was racing. It was like a chess game, trying to stay three or four moves ahead of this guy. I'd spent the past forty-eight hours cramming like a student for a fucking final. I rattled my network of chiefs, spooks, intel squirrels, and shooters, poking into whatever dark corners of Griffith's life I could. What I found worried me. This guy had reach. And the kind of juice that made him a power unto himself. He could do more than most cabinet secretaries, generals, or admirals.

I talked to Tosho, to see if he had any new angles for me, but he came up dry. Things in Japan were status quo—which means he was still getting pressure to do nothing. I passed along word of Team Matsuko at the War Game and mentioned Manny Tanto's presence. The Matsuko angle pricked Tosho's ears. After all, two of the kimchis I'd shot at Narita were Matsuko employees. Tosh said he'd follow up.

I also called Hawaii and shot the shit with Tom O'Bannion. That call was worth the money—I discovered that Griffith had received a full readout on my activities at Narita from Black Jack Morrison. According to O'Bannion, Black Jack had even sent the former SECDEF a copy of my report. That was significant.

Why had Black Jack sent my report to Griffith? I'd asked.

"Because Griffith ordered him to," O'Bannion said. "Something about your fucking up a classified op."

Classified op? This was a fucking maze.

Griffith coughed discreetly, bringing my mind back to the conversation at hand. I asked, "What about Joe? Are you going to represent him?"

Griffith's eyes brightened. "On the minisub? Yes—I think the Foca has great possibilities for the Navy's mission in the nineties. CALOW requirements, the ability to bottom, and its two-hundred-mile range all make it very attractive and potentially extremely profitable. I've agreed to take him on in return for a small percentage."

So, Joe had been able to convince him to take the business on a 50-50 contingency basis. Small percentage indeed. I sipped my Bombay. "I agree. SEALs need a sub like the Foca. But you're going to have a hard time getting it past the barons at Sub Force."

"I don't think so."

"How come? They're pretty entrenched."

"True," said Griffith, dipping a radish in a small pile of salt and nibbling it. "But CNO's a ship driver, not a submariner, and he generally sees things my way. So does the secretary. We've traded favors since he was a freshman congressman back in the early seventies. Besides, the Navy's looking for a little good publicity these days—and Special Warfare is the best place to get it. Nobody doesn't like SEALs. I had my people research the subject yesterday. All the media stories about SEAL missions over the last five years have been one hundred percent positive. So, between the Tailhook mess, the *Iowa* investigation screwup, and the way frigate captains keep launching live missiles at our allies during exercises, a cheap, effective new submarine that'll help SEALs achieve their missions is just what the doctor ordered to help the Navy upgrade its image."

"You're awfully sure of yourself—doc."

He laughed out loud. "Coming from you, that's a real compliment. The pot calling the kettle black."

I drained my Bombay. It was immediately replaced by a fresh one.

We shot shit balls at each other for about half an hour, playing verbal Ping-Pong. He lobbed various subjects in my direction and watched to see what kind of English I put on them. I played the role I thought he wanted me to play: the profane, outrageous, deadly, and amusing ex-SEAL. ("You know what SEAL stands for, Mr. Secretary—Sleep, Eat, And Live it up. I learned that way before I retarded—excuse me, Mr. Secretary, that's *retired.*")

Because my sleeve length is thirty-five and my inseam is thirty-two, people tend to underestimate me. All they see is another knuckle-dragger who loves to use the F-word in various ingenious combinations. They forget that I have a master's in international relations from Auburn, and that I speak three languages conversationally and half a dozen more well enough to get me by.

They know that I am proficient at killing. They forget that I am also a reasonably capable corporate politician. You can't *not* be a corporate politician and rise to the positions I held in the Navy, which included command of SEAL Teams

Two and Six, naval attaché in Phnom Penh, Navy liaison to Operation Eagle Claw—the rescue of the Tehran hostages—and SpecWar briefer to Secretary of the Navy John Lehman. It's impossible.

But that's okay with me. I'd rather be underestimated. It gives me an edge. It allows me the advantage of surprise.

Anyway, after about half an hour of foreplay, Griffith got down to fuck-you business. "I hear you've had some interesting adventures recently."

I was all innocence. "Really?"

"I called Black Jack Morrison. We had a fascinating little chat."

"How is old cockbreath?"

Griffith's thin lips turned upward in that crooked, yellow-toothed smile of his. "Just fine. He asked the same about you."

"Yeah—Black Jack was one of the few admirals I could ever say *fuck* to—and vice versa."

The former SECDEF nodded. "He told me about your assignment at Narita—and the incident with the, ah, intruders."

"Interesting he should bring it up."

"We're old friends. We've done a lot of business together—I know he's consulting for Fujoki because I opened the door there for him. He and I talk frankly." Griffith took a sip of his iced tea. "Besides, he was concerned. Your report worried him—especially the references to me. Fortunately, I was able to explain that events in Japan weren't exactly as they might have seemed to you at first glance."

"I don't quite understand what you're saying." Actually, everything was pretty cut-and-dry to me.

- Item: Griffith was a director of the Jones-Hamilton Corporation. It paid him $48,000 a year plus expenses to attend four meetings in Los Angeles. Nothing wrong with that. But he was also—on paper at least—a part owner of the nonexistent Acme Air Conditioner company of Redondo Beach, California. *That* made him dirty.

- Item: I knew that included in the inventory of defense-related items currently manufactured by Jones-Hamilton were electronic detonators for such tactical nuclear weapons as Tomahawk missiles. Griffith had access to that information—and had used it. That made him dirty.
- Item: I had discovered that despite federal—even international—prohibitions to the contrary, the firm had sold several dozen of these state-of-the-art detonators to front companies in Britain and Germany. That made him dirty.
- Item: Somehow, the detonators, mislabeled as air-conditioning parts and shipped by a nonexistent company Griffith "owned," ended up at Narita, pawed over by the nasty quartet of kimchi-sucking Koreans I'd had the misfortune to run into—including two who worked for a corporation that paid Griffith $5 mil a year. Dirty, hell—*that* made him a fucking traitor.

My reverie was interrupted by the former defense secretary. "I know you don't understand," Griffith was saying, "because if you had understood, you would have kept your nose out of things instead of making a total mess."

"Huh?" Now I actually *was* confused.

"You blundered into a sting operation, you idiot," Griffith growled at me. "We'd set it all up—Jones-Hamilton shipped dummy goods. We were hoping to scoop up the whole goddamn network that's been smuggling prohibited materials for the past five years."

"We? Who the hell's 'we'?"

"DOD—the Navy—the Japanese authorities, Interpol. All with my encouragement, help, and cooperation. And then you came along—huffing and puffing and blowing our house down."

I was not impressed. In fact, I was dubious—despite the tidbit from O'Bannion about my screwing up a classified operation in Japan. The Navy does not let civilians run ops. Not even former SECDEFs. I said so to Griffith.

His eyes frosted over. "I am not your everyday former

secretary of defense," he snapped. "I have served administrations since Johnson's. There are few people I do not know, and few places I cannot go."

He was right—I'd found that out already. But I wasn't about to appear impressed. "No shit."

Griffith's tongue flicked across his lip. " 'No shit' indeed. And then to make matters worse you tried to investigate on your own—had that Jap cop of yours trace the shipment back to Acme Air Conditioner in Redondo Beach. And of course you discovered that there is no Acme Air Conditioner company in Redondo, or anywhere else."

I let him talk.

"And so you set out to check my bona fides, didn't you, Captain?"

"I guess you could say that."

"I guess I will say that. And what have you discovered?"

"That you are one powerful fucking juju man, Mr. Griffith."

"Call me Grant."

"You are one powerful fucking juju man, Grant."

"I know I am. And what else did you find, Dick?"

I thought about things for a few minutes while I finished my second Bombay and a third gin was put in front of me. If my newfound friend Grant was trying to loosen my tongue with alcohol, he had a long way to go. Back in 1973, I spent six months in spy school before I was assigned to Phnom Penh as the naval attaché. We actually had courses in cocktail parties where they taught us how to drink competitively—not that I needed any schooling in that discipline. I decided to take him back over some old ground. "So, Black Jack didn't know anything about your sting."

"Of course not—not then. If he had, do you think he'd have given you the Narita assignment?"

I thought about it. That, at least, made some sort of sense. But there were still too many loose ends; too many convenient coincidences. Thirty years of active duty in unconventional warfare had taught me that there are very few convenient coincidences in life, but lots of inconvenient conspiracies. "So, whose operation was this alleged sting?"

"Pinky Prescott. He's the OP-06 these days—deputy

chief of naval operations for plans, policy, and operations. Good man."

Pinky da Turd. My nemesis from SEAL Team Six. I bit my tongue.

He watched my face closely. "Oh, I know all about your long and bitter relationship with Pinky. You don't like him, and he doesn't like you, either. He insists you tried to kill him."

"He's a liar. If I'd tried to kill him, he'd be a fucking corpse today. I'll tell you all I know about Pinky. He's an asshole and a coward and he has the brainpower of a fresh cowpie."

Griffith licked his upper lip again. It reminded me of a lizard. A particle of spittle remained, tucked in the upper left corner of his mouth. "Don't be wishy-washy, Dick." The tongue darted and dabbed. The spittle disappeared.

It was time for reveille. "Fuck you, Grant. Cute doesn't work well for you. Bitchy, maybe. But on you, cute sucks."

I slammed down my Bombay in a single gulp and returned the glass to the table with a thwack. "Look, you silver-haired, lip-licking schmuck, *you* may like to do business with fucking companies that build things that kill American servicemen—I'm talking Matsuko here in case I'm being too fucking subtle for you—I don't. You may *have* to do business with no-load dip-shit sphincter-sucking pus-nutted assholes like Pinky Prescott on a regular basis. I don't. I did my fucking time. I did it in the fucking Navy and I did it at Petersburg. I don't owe anybody a goddamn thing. I gave the fucking country fifty fucking years, and I've got the fucking scars to fucking prove it. The next fifty are mine—and I plan to take advantage of 'em. So, if you have something to offer me, then do it. Otherwise, thanks for the Bombay, fuck you very much, and *sayonara,* asshole."

You remember those commercials where E.F. Hutton talks and everybody else listens? Well, that's what happened to us. Griffith and I suddenly realized that the entire restaurant had come to a complete fucking stop.

Tables of men in fifteen-hundred-dollar suits peered disapprovingly over their half-glasses in our direction. The eighty-three-year-old thrice-married grande dame of the

Democratic Party looked so pop-eyed outraged I thought she was going to bust her latest face-lift. A quartet of Chanel-clad suburban matrons began to fan themselves with their menus. Waiters, mouths open, stood bearing their trays of food. Vietnamese busboys holding gleaming pots of steaming coffee or armfuls of soiled napery stood transfixed like jacklighted deer. Tommy Jacomo, who had been ringing something up on the register, peered over the top of the cashier's partition like Kilroy.

Our own waiter—a well-fed Brooklyn boy who called himself Joe but was born Giuseppe—was standing, order pad in hand, pencil poised, just behind Grant Griffith's shoulder as I did my monologue. He looked down at me and asked, "And just how would you like those fifty fucking years done, sir?"

I wagged my eyebrows at the four ladies with their makeshift fans and made a noise like a horse whinnying in heat. "Extra pussy on the side, please, Joe."

I let Griffith do most of the talking until we got back to his office. My outburst must have affected him like a laxative because he ran off at the mouth for the next hour. I hardly got a word in edgewise. That was all right with me. I'm leery about chatting in restaurants anyway. I used to teach my guys at Red Cell to listen hard when they went to restaurants and bars. A lot of good intel is picked up when people drink and eat. Somehow, when there's a good steak on the plate, a bottle of wine at hand, and a couple of good-looking women in the area, the classification stamps just seem to slip away.

I asked Griffith if he had his office swept for bugs. He told me it was done by Buckshot's people every week.

That didn't tell me anything one way or the other, but I decided to let it pass. "Okay, Grant, a couple of things," I said. "First, you're trying to bullshit me, and I don't like it."

He gave me this real concerned-type look. "How, Dick?"

"First, those were no dummy detonators. Come on—I've been in and out of nuclear weapons facilities hundreds of times. What I saw at Narita was the real thing."

Griffith played with his Roman ring in silence.

"Second—what's this crap about a sting? I ran into four

Koreans playing 'Hijack the Nuclear Material.' Nobody else was doing diddly. There were no undercovers lurking in the shadows—because I was lurking there all night myself. And the bad guys I shot weren't any fucking double agents. I knew that by the time I left Tokyo, thanks to Tosho. They were the opposition."

"Everything you say is literally true," Griffith said. "Look, Dick, we're not dealing with amateurs here. We had to use real detonators. But we always knew where they were. We had passive monitors in the crate."

"That's a load of crap."

"Why do you say that?"

"Because they're fucking passive—there was no active surveillance in play, Grant, I was there."

"We knew where the goods were at all times."

"And what if they'd been taken to Pyongyang?"

"What's your point?"

"You had no way to stop things once you'd set the ball rolling."

He nodded grudgingly. "You have a point."

"Who built the monitors?"

"NIS had them built."

"Naval Investigative Service? Are you out of your fucking mind, Grant?"

"That's who Pinky assigned to the job."

Pinky again. "When I ran into the bad guys, they were switching crates."

Griffith nodded. "That concerned me deeply. I would have hated to lose the trail."

"You would have lost more than the trail, goddammit—you would have lost the fucking detonators." He sounded so bloodless. He sounded like every other goddamn bureaucrat; the kind of no-load, pencil-pushing, bean-counting supergrade who makes strategic decisions that can cost the lives of thousands of men on the basis of a penny or two saved.

He was talking as if lives didn't depend on his following the fucking trail. It got me steamed. "That's why passive monitors and most of that other electronic garbage is such a goatfuck when it's used by itself," I explained pedantically.

"If you assholes had been thinking, you'd have used operators in addition to the electronic stuff. Guys trained to work in the shadows. Shooters who would have stuck to the trail like glue—no matter where it led."

"You're talking about SEALs?"

"That's what I know best."

"You're probably thinking your old unit Red Cell should have been given the assignment."

"Why do you say that?"

He rubbed his chin. "Well, they do fit the mission profile for the job."

"Oh?"

"Dick, Dick, Dick—I know all about Red Cell's two-tier capability. OP Zero Six Delta slash Tango Romeo Alpha Papa was the original designation, I believe, using the code-word designation of Waterfall Weatherman."

Shit—the guy *was* plugged in. Very few people knew about that. When I'd created the Cell, Black Jack Morrison had me design it as a unit within a unit. Tier one—OP-06 Delta—was the security-exercise designation. We acted the part of bad guys to test naval installations and teach them how to counter terrorism. The other tier—Tango Romeo Alpha Papa and code-word secret—was to operate as an elite unit under Red Cell cover, performing covert ops worldwide, as dictated by CNO and the National Command Authority. That sounds very broad. It was. We were charged with everything from proactive elimination of terrorist elements (that translates into assassinations), to the destruction of nuclear facilities in unfriendly countries, to the scuttling of unfriendly vessels.

"You may have designed things that way originally," Griffith said, "but that was ten years ago. Today, both you and Black Jack are retired. And the Cell's mission requirements have been modified substantially."

"For the worse, I've been told."

"Some say for the better. These days, Red Cell is a valuable training tool—and that is all. It's been recast as an integral element of the Navy's command structure."

"You're feeding me a load of horse puckey, Grant. 'Valuable training tool'? That's so much crapola. I've heard what goes on. The men are ordered to wear goddamn Red Cell uniforms—T-shirts or windbreakers and hats—so they can't infiltrate the targets in mufti. If they deep-six the outfits, they're cited for being out of uniform. The exercises are designed to let the good guys win every time. That's not real life. Worse, it doesn't teach the base commanders anything."

"But their morale is better."

"Fuck morale. We're talking life and death here. And what about Red Cell's morale? They're the shooters who end up going over the rail whenever the shit hits the fan."

Griffith sighed and shook his head. "You still don't understand."

"Understand what?"

"That every unit—especially Red Cell—has to be a part of the chain of command."

"I disagree. To succeed, the Cell has got to exist outside the system."

"Why?"

"Because if it's part of the problem, it can't be part of the solution."

"You can't have a rogue unit, Dick."

"I agree—most of the time. But when Black Jack let me design Red Cell, he realized that in some circumstances, a unit has to be able to operate outside the chain of command. That's why Red Cell reported directly through CNO to the secretary of defense and the president, not through some asshole Navy SpecWar commodore, or a thumb-sucking admiral on E Ring."

"You're talking about Pinky again, aren't you?"

"What if I am?" I knew damn well what Red Cell's problem was. It was Pinky da Turd.

Griffith chose to disregard my protest. "Politically, Red Cell is in the doghouse these days. Frankly, Dick, it's still recovering from you. Several of the men are being investigated by NIS. It's considered a déclassé operation. No self-respecting officer wants to lead it anymore."

"What you mean is that it's not a ticket-punching slot, so Pinky's assigning any asshole he can find as CO."

"Describe it any way you want—the bottom line is the

same. Red Cell is in trouble. So, there was no way I was going to use it to perform a delicate mission. There was never any question about that."

"You were going to use it—give me a fucking break. Civilians don't pick the units to carry out missions."

Griffith's reptilian eyes burned in on me. "In case you forgot, Dick," he said, a pedantic tone in his voice, "the military is still under civilian control in this country."

"But not under your control."

"Not officially. But there are those who still seek my advice, my counsel, my opinion. And when it was suggested by one of the few officers brought in to work on this smuggling problem that the Navy use Red Cell to keep an eye on the monitors, I vetoed the recommendation."

Sure he did—the guy was dirty. I knew it. I felt it in every bone. "Why—because they might have succeeded?"

"No, because Red Cell isn't suited for that kind of work these days. It is a training tool, pure and simple."

"Maybe that's because there's no leadership anymore. Maybe the shooters need a real CO for a change—a guy with balls. Somebody who's not looking to earn his stars by fucking his enlisted men."

Griffith looked at me intently in silence for some seconds. "Maybe you're right, Dick," he said quietly. "Maybe it does."

Part Two
TARFU

Cherry Enders Photograph

Chapter

9

DEPARTMENT OF THE NAVY
OFFICE OF THE CHIEF OF NAVAL OPERATIONS
WASHINGTON, DC 20350·2000

IN REPLY REFER TO

SER 07BL/3Q3056191
22 December

FROM: CHIEF OF NAVAL OPERATIONS (OP00)

TO: COMMANDER RICHARD [NMN] MARCINKO, USN (RET) 156-93-083/1130

SUBJ: INVOLUNTARY RECALL OF RETIRED OFFICERS TO ACTIVE DUTY

REF: (a) SECNAVINST 1811.4D
       NMPC-213 (8/1/91)
     (b) 10 USC 688
     (c) 10 USC 672 (d)
     (d) SECNAVINST 1920.7

1. Delivered by hand.

2. In accordance with Ref (a) you are hereby recalled to active duty. You are ordered to report immediately to RADM Pinckney Prescott, III, no later than 1100 hours on December 22. The period of your active duty is at the discretion of this office.

3. Failure to respond immediately will force this office to implement other means available.

4. (Signed): Arleigh L. Secrest
             Admiral, U.S. Navy
             Chief of Naval Operations

Chapter

10

THEY CAME TO GET ME BY CHOPPER. I WAS OUT BACK, WORKING ON the weight pile when I heard them closing—they were in a UH-1H from the whump-whump-whumping sound they made. They must have landed way out on the south forty—that's what I call the ten-acre cornfield beyond the mailbox—because it took 'em about fifteen minutes to hump up the road, down the driveway, meander through the house, and discover me bench-pressing 350 pounds of iron down in the little hollow behind the deck.

Outdoor PT was a routine I'd begun in jail. The weight pile at Petersburg Federal Peck's Bad Boys' Camp and Medium Security Prison was about two hundred yards downhill from the dorms, on a hundred and fifty square feet of concrete slab sitting next to the White Men Can't Jump–style basketball hoops. Every morning at six, seven days a week, rain or shine, I'd walk past the tower, wave to the guard, then set about doing my PT. I dressed only in a pair of nylon running shorts, a pair of Nikes, and a headband. I dressed that way whether it was ninety-five degrees out or fifteen degrees. I did it for a couple of reasons. First, it was mental exercise for me—to see how much self-discipline I could muster day after day after day. Second, it was a mind game I could play on the other prisoners. I wanted them to know—without my having to say anything overtly—that I was not to be fucked with.

Guess what? No one messed with Demo Dick, or, as I came to be known at Petersburg, Lobo the Wolfman. The crooked politicians, drug dealers, snitches, white-collar criminals, and mafiosi all took one look at me working the weight pile bare chested in January, my fingers freezing to the steel bar, and knew that I was absofuckinglutely crazy. They saw me come back from an hour's workout with steam rising from my body, ice in my matted beard, and a madman's gleam in my roguish eye, and they understood that I wanted to be left alone.

Funny thing was, I discovered—this is typical for a Frogman, incidentally—that I actually *liked* the no-pain/ no-gain feeling I got when I did my PT outdoors. So, when I bought the Manor—which came complete with a sauna and Jacuzzi for heating up my old, tired, and soon-to-be C-O-L-D bones, I poured ten by ten feet of concrete slab, set an industrial-strength weight bench and a ton of iron on top of it, and got back to my daily prison routine.

This particular morning it was about eighteen degrees at the Manor. I'd been lifting for half an hour and there was already ice in my beard and steam on my chest when the pair of staff four-stripers in heavy bridge coats, plus two burly security types in dress blues and Dixie cups, showed up, all huffing and puffing from their half-mile walk. They looked funny from my point of view, but I wasn't about to interrupt my routine, so I lay there pumping iron and staring up their nostrils.

Finally, the tall one with dark nose-hair spoke. "Commander Marcinko?"

I did five more reps. "Who wants to know?"

"I'm Captain Tobias, this is Captain Burger. We're from CNO's office."

"I'm impressed. Does that make you archangels or something?" Another five. "So, why the visit?"

Tobias walked over to the head of the bench and stared down at me. He put his hands on the weight bar, which rested just above my chest. "You're being recalled to active duty. Please get dressed and come with us."

I let him spot for me, did ten more reps, replaced the bar, and swiveled off the bench. I shook the ice out of my beard. "Fuck you very much, gentlemen, but that's a BTDT so far as I'm concerned."

Burger, a tall dip-shit who had both freckles and dimples, growled, "Huh?"

"Been there—done that. No need to repeat myself."

"You're not volunteering," said Tobias, a pretty boy wearing an Academy ring. He presented me with an unsealed envelope.

I opened it and read the bad news. There is a naval technical term for what they were doing to me. The term is *goatfuck.* "You can't do this."

"Beg to differ, Commander," said Burger, brushing the dandruff off his shoulders. "It's both legitimate and binding. I'm CNO's legal adviser, and you can take my word for it."

"But—" For once in my life I was speechless.

"So, if you please," said Tobias, "you can either get dressed and come with us on your own, or we'll have these first-class boatswain's mates here bring you along in manacles. Choice is yours, bub."

Pinky had changed for the worse in the five years since I'd laid eyes on him. He was the same dour-faced, nervous, skinny beanpole as always. His uniform was swimming on him—the Budweiser on his uniform breast seemed oversize and out of place. Indeed, how he'd become a SEAL I never knew. He didn't have a muscle in his body. As he rose from his armchair when I came through his door, he seemed to do it in stages, unfolding himself the way tall clowns extricate themselves from those tiny cars in the circus ring, joint by joint by joint. It struck me that he was completely pliable, like whalebone, or, more aptly, chicken cartilage.

He'd aged—badly, too. His hair, once dirty blond, had now gone slate gray, something that gave new emphasis to the sepulchral qualities of his face. And he'd become more stoop-shouldered than ever, as if he'd been worn down by carrying the great burdens of his office. He had the overall look of a harried accountant.

When he saw me, his eyes went wide as saucers. I don't

know whether it was the nonregulation hair and beard that bothered him most or just the fact that I was still alive and kicking.

I extended my hand. "Hey, Pinky, still getting hazardous-duty pay for counting those beans?"

"Hello, Dick," he said sullenly, turning away toward the window so he wouldn't have to shake my hand.

But Pinky wasn't alone in the office. Grant Griffith was there, too. The former secretary of defense sat behind Pinky's desk, looking like the Cheshire fucking cat, twiddling with his Roman ring. In his three-piece, pinstripe suit of ministerial Oxford gray, starched white shirt, and sincere blue pin-dot tie he looked right at home in the high-backed judge's chair—the only thing missing was a gavel. It was he who began speaking.

"Dick—Pinky, please." Griffith pointed toward the two armchairs that faced the desk, indicating that we should take our places.

We sat as directed. Then Tobias and Burger opened a heavy leather dispatch case and presented me with a half-inch-thick pile of papers, all marked with an *x* and highlighted where my signatures were to go.

The agreements were filled with wheretofores and herebys and hereafters and notwithstandings. If they were ever translated into English, they would have said that I'd been involuntarily recalled to active duty because of my unique and irreplaceable expertise in certain areas—notably the area of sending bad guys to their just rewards. I was, furthermore, now frocked as a captain, which meant I had all the rights of a four-striper, except I hadn't been (and would never be) confirmed by the U.S. Senate. I knew about that. I'd been frocked to captain before, until my enemies—Pinky Prescott among the leaders of them—got to Secretary of the Navy James Webb and convinced him to remove my name from the list.

The promotion was the good-news part. The contracts also stipulated that if I ever repeated a word of what I heard, read, saw, or was told during the time of my activation, I'd be thrown in jail for the rest of my life sans benefit of due legal process. Furthermore, I pledged never to write another nonfiction book about my activities unless I got written permission to do so in advance from the Navy. Okay—I'd write fiction from now on. There was nothing in the agreement about writing fiction. Doom on you, Navy.

I signed. I found it ironic that, with the stroke of a pen, I gained a stripe but lost most of my First Amendment rights. Now let me ask you—is that Newton's Law at work, or Murphy's?

The paperwork over, Griffith flicked a glance at my two four-striped escorts, who nodded and withdrew as silently as the Victorian butlers they were.

"I guess the cliché would be to say, 'You're both wondering why I called you here today,'" Griffith began, his long index fingers pressing together in a steeple. "Well, let me explain."

It wasn't Moses and his tablets, or the Sermon on the Mount, but it was close. Grant's monologue, which went on for the better part of half an hour, contained the following major points.

First, he'd managed to convince his pal the CNO to recall me because he believed I could help the nation solve its most critical security problem—to wit, the hemorrhage of nuclear technology to North Korea, as evidenced by the episode I'd witnessed at Narita.

Further, it was apparent to Griffith there was an organized program of clandestine nuclear theft going on, and that Red Cell—led by me—should be used to stop it before the media got wind of the problem. That way, everything could be handled quietly from within the defense establishment.

After all, Griffith rhapsodized, administrations come and administrations go—but the system stays in place forever. The system is eternal.

Griffith grinned at us. Wasn't he proof of that point? He, after all, was the personification of the system's immortality. That little joke aside, he explained, it was the system that had to be protected, not the political goals of any particular president or the objectives of a single administration.

Why? Because by safeguarding the system, the nation's security was also protected. That was the long-range view, as he—along with the CNO and others of his ilk—saw it.

Moreover, it was the safe way of doing business. Any program—from Middle East policy to health-care tax proposals—the current administration tried to undertake would unquestionably leak to the press. The White House was a sieve. The Pentagon was little better. And as for the Hill—well, we all knew that the Hill was filled with petty, small-minded, selfish assholes each out for himself. Griffith laughed cynically. "I've been here for three decades and I've never yet met a congressman or senator who's ever even offered to pick up a lunch or dinner check. The only thing they're interested in is money and getting reelected."

He apologized for the digression. Congress, he confessed, was the one aspect of his work he wished he could dispense with. But they did make the laws—with his help, of course.

Anyway, he summarized, the bottom line was this: the only way to get the job done would be to accomplish our goals covertly. At that sort of thing, Griffith went on, I was a master. There was no one blacker or spookier or dirtier than Demo Dick Marcinko. Therefore, I was the one to volunteer for the mission.

When Pinky snorted, Griffith shut him up by saying that he—Pinky—had blown it thus far. He commended da Turd's administrative abilities, then chastised him for his poor operational sense. Pinky glowered, but kept his mouth shut.

Now, Griffith continued, came the carrot and the stick so far as I was concerned.

I was, he explained, an enlisted man's officer—one of those four-stripers who preferred drinking with his chiefs in the goat locker to sipping port in the wardroom. Well, he continued, if I was actually concerned about the fate of my men, I'd better do the job right. Because if I failed, Red Cell would be decommissioned, and its shooters scattered to other SpecWar units. Furthermore, all the men with whom I'd served would be either reassigned or up-and-outed. He'd hate to see that happen, of course—what a waste of talented manpower. But it would happen—don't doubt it for an instant.

So—I was to be given command of Red Cell—with the full approval of the chief of naval operations, of course. I would, as noted, hold the rank of captain. But, Grant added, with my newfound prestige would come responsibilities. In this scheme of things, he explained, I would answer to Pinky. Pinky would be my only point of contact with the Navy.

That brought a smirk to Pinky's ugly face.

This specific chain of command, Griffith emphasized, would be observed at all times. Otherwise, news could leak. Word could spread. The operation could become fatally compromised.

I saw what they were doing, of course, and I didn't like it at all. I was fucked in every orifice. If things went well and I saved everybody's ass, then Pinky would take all the credit and I'd be retired again—quietly—with no threat of a "60 Minutes" piece or another *Rogue Warrior* to upset his apple cart. If I screwed up, then it would all be my fault, and they could court-martial me behind closed doors and send my ass to Leavenworth for ten or twenty years. Or they could, as they used to say on "Mission Impossible," deny knowledge of the enterprise and say I was a one-man rogue operation who'd hijacked an entire military unit and used it for his own purposes.

It's not inconceivable—they've done it before. That's one of the raps they tried to pin on Ollie North, for example. And who better to call me a rogue than the man who'd used reams of Navy paper doing it already, Pinky Prescott. This was a real lose/lose situation for Dickie.

The room fell silent. "So," said Griffith finally, "what's your answer, Dick?"

He'd planned this operation well. He'd done his homework. He already knew damn well what I'd say. It was too big, too impossible a challenge to turn down without looking like a pussy in my own eyes. He'd probably pulled my fitreps. He knew what was in them—which is, that I never, ever accepted the word *impossible;* never accepted that there were limits to what I or my men could accomplish.

"Fucking A. You got a deal," is what I said. Doom on me. Doom on Demo.

"Good. Your TAD begins today." That was Navyspeak for Temporary Additional Duty.

I chose to think of it as Traveling Around Drunk and said as much. Griffith laughed. "Always irrepressible, aren't you, Dick?" Then he looked over at da Turd, who sat balefully white-knuckling the arms of his chair. "Pinky?"

He was met by silence.

"Pinky, I'm *wait*ing." A look appeared on the former SECDEF's face that can't be described except to say that it was frightening, even to me.

Pinky's gray pallor grew even grayer—as if he'd swallowed cordite. "Okay, okay. But I don't like it."

"Oh, you don't have to *like* it, Pinky," said Griffith. "You just have to *do* it." His tongue flicked across his upper lip twice, right/left, right/left, and he looked at me with a wicked smile that told me everything I had to know. "Isn't that what real SEALs say, Dick?"

Griffith left Pinky and me to work out the details. He had a meeting over at the White House, he said. Something or other to do with the Office of the U.S. Trade Representative and one of Griffith's Japanese clients. The Jap assholes from Matsuko in their Blooks Blothers suits came to mind. Manny Tanto or no Manny Tanto, Matsuko was still a priority client, and there was money to be made.

With just the two of us there, Pinky dropped all hint of cordiality. He assumed his rightful place behind his desk (wood, executive grade one), plunked his two-starred ass into his chair (high-back, senior executive grade one), and drummed his long, aristocratic fingers (dumb-shit, grade one) on the desk pad.

"Let's get something straight right away," he said by way of introduction.

"I'm all ears, Pinky."

"I am in charge," he said, his face growing flushed. "Secretary Griffith said so. CNO said so." Now he began to hyperventilate. "There will be a chain of command. You will follow orders. Follow orders. Follow orders. So far as you are concerned, I am fucking God, do you hear me? God!"

I leaned forward, my elbows on Pinky's desk. "What's your point, Pinky?"

I thought he was going to have a heart attack. "Goddammit, Marcinko—"

Crack! I slammed my palm on his desk. He looked as if I'd shot him. He pushed off on his oversize casters, swiveled his chair, and rolled backward a couple of yards to put distance between us. "Look, you simpering, limp-dicked asshole, I don't relish this arrangement either. But the fact is, we're stuck with it—for the present."

Pinky's voice floated petulantly in my direction. "Don't talk to me like that. I am your superior."

I'd grown soft as a fucking civilian—I decided to try tact. I gave the back of his chair an earnest look. "Face it, Pinky, I don't like the fact that you're in charge any more than you like the fact that I'm here at all. But that doesn't change the situation—which is, that we're going to have to work together."

Holding on to the arms of his chair like a walker, Pinky umbrella-stepped closer to his desk. "So?"

"So, I suggest we work out an arrangement."

"I have already worked out an arrangement," Pinky insisted. "The only thing for you to do is work within the boundaries."

Tact, schmact. Nothing had changed. Da Turd was the same closed-minded, intractable, pigheaded dickbrain he'd been his entire career. "Would you mind spelling them out for me?" I asked.

"Not at all." He slid a single sheet of paper out of his top desk drawer, slipped a pair of half-frame glasses on, and read the chicken tracks that he'd laboriously set down word by word.

"'One: Marcinko will be responsible for Red Cell's prearranged schedule of security exercises in addition to his other duties. The first of these will be a comprehensive sweep of the Washington Navy Yard, which has been scheduled by this office for next Friday at zero eight hundred hours.'"

"Next Friday? Geezus, Pinky, get real."

He never even blinked. "'Two: Marcinko will be accompanied at all times by representatives of the Judge Advocate

General's Office and representatives of the Naval Investigative Service to ensure that he does not exceed the bounds of military propriety or behavior.

"'Three: Marcinko will keep this office informed at all times in writing of all his activities—in advance.

"'Four: Marcinko will requisition all supplies through this office.

"'Five: Marcinko will coordinate all intelligence activities through this office.

"'Six: Marcinko will file a report on his and Red Cell's activities by COB—close of business—every day.

"'Seven: Marcinko's outgoing message traffic will be approved by this office before transmission.

"'Eight: Marcinko will conform to Navy grooming standards during his active-duty tour.'"

He looked up at me, his eyes all scrunched up, his nostrils flared, and his lips contorted in a sneer. "'Nine: In other words, Marcinko will not fucking breathe unless I say it is all right to breathe.'" He slid the paper back into his desk. "Now—you got that, *Dick*-head?"

Sure I got it. And there's a Santa Claus. And Elvis is still alive. "Loud and clear, Pinky. Loud and clear."

I worked for countless assholes like Pinky when I was in Vietnam, inflexible, small-minded officers with pea-brains, who refused to see how SEALs could be utilized imaginatively. Instead of using us as the tip of the tactical spear to terrorize and disorient the enemy, they assigned us brief supporting roles for their slow, blundering, ineffective armadas of riverine craft—SpecWar spear carriers whose mission was badly conceived and ill-defined.

The reason behind their incredible lack of vision was that they had all been trained as ship drivers, aviators, or nuclear submariners, not as lean, mean, badass jungle fighters. They thought of war in the conventional way—a static affair in which the lines don't shift very much; in which one side attacks the other with huge numbers of men to take territory.

But as we all know now—and a few of us knew back then—Vietnam was an unconventional war. It wasn't about territory and huge armies facing off the way it had been done since the Assyrians. Vietnam was a brutal jungle war largely waged by small groups of highly motivated insurgents backed up by large numbers of highly motivated troops. To succeed, you had to hit the enemy the way he hit you: get in, beat the shit out of him, and get the hell out before he knew what had happened. Most of the naval officers with whom I worked just didn't get it.

Why? Some of them were stupid. Others were cowards. Others were bean-counters who led from behind their desks. Still others were ticket punchers—staff pukes who needed six months in a combat zone to further their careers. The most dangerous believed they were the twentieth century's answer to von Clausewitz. They designed missions guaranteed to provide 80 to 90 percent casualties to the American forces involved, while doing Mr. Victor Charlie little or no damage whatsoever.

I developed an effective technique for dealing with them all. It was called UNODIR. Whenever I took my men out hunting, I filed my ops plans—as ordered—with the task force HQ. My messages always had the same theme: UNODIR (UNless Otherwise DIRected), they began, "I'm going to go out in the boonies and kill a bunch of Victor Charlies as brutally as I can. To do this, I'm going to commandeer a PBR [Patrol Boat/River], grab as much ammo and ordnance as me and my men can carry, and head off into the boonies. When we've run out of ammo and hostile bodies, we'll be back. Love & kisses, Demo Dick Marcinko, LT, USN."

Then I'd give my UNODIR message to the communications shack and order the radioman to send it half an hour after we'd left.

Of course, the assholes back at HQ would try to reach me and countermand my ops plan. Guess what? For some reason, every time they tried, my radio was turned off. Well, we'd been ordered to maintain radio silence out in the bush, and I was just following normal procedures. After about two months of UNODIR missions, the assholes left me alone and I was able to kill Victor Charlie in peace.

So, Pinky's list did not intimidate me. There were ways to

get around it. What bothered me more was the schedule—
we had to keep up Red Cell's normal schedule, as well as
perform the covert missions that were the real reason I'd
been shanghaied back to duty.

For example, he wanted to turn me loose on the Navy
Yard. Why? Why detail the Cell to do a bunch of stupid
exercises when the national security was being buggered by
a bunch of Kimchis?

Besides, the Navy Yard is where NIS headquarters is
located. It's where the CNO has his office. It seemed to me
that if there was one place Pinky wouldn't want Demo Dick
Marcinko, Shark-Man of the Delta, sticking his big Slovak
nose, it was the Navy Yard.

That was on the one hand. On the other hand, Pinky was
one of the dumbest assholes I'd ever come across. Maybe he
just didn't care where I growled and prowled—maybe he
figured I'd pull my punches if I was going up against NIS.
Maybe he figured they'd catch me and throw me in the
brig—and he'd be rid of me once and for all.

Fat fucking chance.

Chapter

11

LESS THAN A DAY AFTER I'D BEEN SHANGHAIED BY CNO, I MET with my new unit at Shooter McGee's, the bar on Duke Street East in Alexandria that served as the unofficial headquarters for the original Red Cell. It seemed fitting. Shooter's is where we used to stand in the parking lot and watch Snake and Pooster the Rooster race up the outside of a seven-story apartment building to the penthouse Pooster shared with Snake and his gorgeous wife, Miss Kitty.

But that was then. Snake, Pooster, Trailer Court, the Gold Dust Twins Larry and Frank, Ho-Ho-Ho—all of Red Cell's plank owners, which is Navy talk for the men who originally form a unit—they were all gone now. Some had retired. Others had been retired. And still others, fortunately for me, were in senior SpecWar slots and scattered all over the world—my own, personal fifth column of master chiefs.

The current Red Cell, then, was composed of second- and third-generation rogue warriors, kids who'd been through BUD/S in the mid-eighties, child-warriors who were only babies—seamen second- and third-class petty officers—when I created SEAL Team Six back in 1980. I'd selected a couple of the most precocious of these tadpoles for Six during my last months as CO. When I created Red Cell in 1985, I'd shanghaied a few of these gifted Froglets for the unit.

Now, most of these "kids" were first-class chief petty officers and junior chiefs; others had earned their senior-grade petty officer's stripes. They were platoon leaders now, passing on what they'd been taught to a new generation of Frogs. But it wasn't easy.

As the CO of SEAL Team Two I had about one hundred and fifty men under my command. There were less than three hundred active SEALs nationwide back then—Team One in Coronado, and Two at Little Creek—and I knew every SEAL in America by name. Today, there are thousands of SEALs in more than half a dozen SEAL teams. Indeed, SEAL Team Six, supposedly the most elite of all SEAL units, is bigger than SEAL Two was when I commanded it in the mid-seventies. That dramatic growth has meant more money, more opportunities, and a higher profile for SpecWar, especially in these days of Pentagon cutbacks. But it has also meant more bureaucracy. More layers of management. More conventional thinking applied to unconventional warfare.

Worst of all, hordes of unqualified officers—admin pukes like Pinky, intel weenies, and Academy-educated ticket punchers—are elbowing their way into Navy SpecWar because of the rapid advancement potential, the increased visibility, and the larger budgets. The officers they displace are operators—the hunters who don't give a damn about anything but getting the job done.

SpecWar's rapid growth has also led to paralysis—and worse, it has led to endemic butt-covering. Today, for example, there is such a convoluted chain of command that SpecWar units—which were designed as quick-reaction teams—cannot in fact react quickly. There are so many "May I?"'s that have to get asked, so many forms to be signed, so many rules of engagement that have to be explained, that the bad guys escape before the SEALs are wheels up.

Please, your three-starred sanctity, may I receive your blessing to go after Abu Nidal, who just assassinated our ambassador in London, then raped and eviscerated his wife and children?

Of course, my Froggish son. But first you must sign for each and every bullet you requisition. Also, here's another form—this one guarantees you won't kill anybody. Killing deeply offends the ACLU, NOW, and the hundreds of Hollywood liberals who spend time in Washington when they're not making violence-filled movies.

Please initial this. It's an affidavit saying you agree to take a legal adviser on your mission, so he can inform the bad guys of their rights before you do anything. The pink form is your request for a political cadre who'll make sure none of your sailors uses language or gestures that might offend some minority or pressure group while doing the nation's business. After all, we don't want any gay-bashing or other politically incorrect actions in our Navy.

The green form—sign on the dotted line please—ensures that you won't ding up any of our equipment. Policy guidance regulations state that the Navy doesn't care whether your equipment works or not, just so long as it looks good and it remains on your unit inventory sheet as an operational asset.

Another thing: we can't have bad press. So, my roguish killer, you must take a media adviser with you, too—just sign this contract here, and date it. That way you're committed to hold a press conference on CNN explaining each and every move you're going to make, one hour before you attack.

Now, finally, please put your John Hancock on this one last pledge statement.

What is it, your flag-rank panjandrumcy?

It's a sworn attestation that you are doing this on your own. This operation was your idea—no one else's. It says that if you fail, you agree to fall on your sword.

Ah, good. Now, then, just prick your finger and add your initial in blood by this last clause, too.

What's that, your gold-braided worshipness?

It's the ultimate contingency rider, my hairy-assed child. It says that if your mission succeeds—which is exceedingly unlikely because of all the strictures we've hung on you—and you and your men become heroes, which would greatly astonish us because that would glorify warriors (and the one thing our new Navy does not want to do is glorify warriors), then you go straight back to your cage, and I get to take all the credit.

In its heyday, in the late eighties, Red Cell comprised roughly three dozen shooters, each with a specialty such as lock picking, mountain climbing, or long-range sniping. Now, after five years of nickel-and-diming, the unit had been cut back to the bare bones—eight men. Leadership was nonexistent. Money was tight.

Why? Because the Navy was protecting itself from a perceived threat—and I don't mean terrorism. The system didn't see Red Cell as a positive force, to be used to solve its real-world problems. The system saw it as a liability.

Example: Commodore Rat Shit is in charge of Naval Station Echo. If Red Cell infiltrates Echo easily, the commodore will be embarrassed. Not because he might be responsible for the deaths of scores, perhaps even hundreds of his men in the event of a real-life attack, but because his failure to keep the Cell out will become a part of his next fitness report. Bad fitness reports mean no promotions. In this world of downsizing, no promotion means early retirement.

Therefore, Commodore Rat Shit makes sure that Red Cell does not infiltrate his station. He makes them wear hats and shirts that say BAD GUY in big bold letters. He takes an active hand writing the scenarios.

Guess what? *Surprise!*—Rat Shit's security force wins the exercise. The fact that his installation is not prepared for a real-world terrorist threat doesn't concern him. The important thing is that his ass has been covered. His fitrep will be outstanding. His promotion is assured.

So these days, if you believed the fitreps, Red Cell was made up of misfits, iconoclasts, and renegades. The admiral to whom the unit reported was Pinky Prescott. He hated Red Cell because it had been created by yours truly, and he took it out on the men every chance he got. Slowly, their numbers, like the days of December, dwindled down to a precious few.

There was, then, a single SEAL squad—eight men— gathered around the end of the bar sucking down Coors Light when I walked out of the afternoon rain into the smoke-tinged atmosphere of Shooter's.

The unit may have been small, but so far as I'm concerned, the sailors Pinky saw as malcontented, troublemaking scum were representative to me of the best that Navy SpecWar can offer. They're Warriors—dirtbags, grunts, shooters, hunters—who will do the job no matter what it takes, no matter how dirty they have to get to do it.

The platoon chief's name is—well, I'll call him Nasty Nicky Grundle. Nasty is about the size of an NFL linebacker, and twice as mean. The gargantuan California surfer received his handle in Panama, where he'd been a part of SEAL Team Two's attack on the Panamanian gunboat *Presidente Porras,* a twin-diesel job about one hundred and fifty feet long tied up in Balboa Harbor.

Nicky was responsible for designing the C-4 explosive charges that he and another SEAL attached to the boat, after swimming half a mile with them. The "recipe" called for half a pound of C-4. Nick used two pounds in each charge. The resulting explosions blew two three-ton diesel engines one hundred and fifty yards down the harbor. SEAL Two's CO, Comdr. Norm Carley, who led the underwater attack— the first underwater assault on a warship since World War II, incidentally—told Grundle, "That was real nasty, Nick," and the name stuck.

I liked the fact that Nicky could be nasty. But what I liked even more was his dedication. I'd selected Nick for SEAL Team Six even though he was a youngster because of his size and his aggressiveness. I didn't know how much heart he had—but he proved it to me. Three months after he'd come aboard we went out on a HALO—that's High Altitude, Low Opening—night jump exercise out of Marana, Arizona. That night, one of the newest men in the platoon, a shit-for-brains radio operator, screwed up. Nick went after him, free-falling to just under four thousand feet before he caught up with the asshole, took hold of him in midair, and untangled the fouled-up chute so it would deploy.

Then it was Nicky's turn to get down safely. Of course, with his having just saved one man's life, it was time for the ever-popular Mr. Murphy to make a guest appearance. Nicky pushed off and free-fell right to the edge of the low-altitude envelope before he deployed his chute. But in the darkness, he flew straight into a triple line of high-voltage lines. He tucked over the first, but couldn't clear the others. So he cut away at sixty-five feet and dropped face-first into the desert.

The fall—think of it as jumping face-first off a seven-story building onto a pile of rocks, because that's exactly what it was—would have killed most people. Not Nick. When I found him, he was trying to walk back to the assembly point. The whole right side of his face was gone. Every nerve had been severed. His right eye had been popped back right inside the skull and they thought he'd lose it.

But Nicky's a tough puppy. He not only survived his ordeal, he was back on duty within six months. The doc allowed him to make his first jump less than one hundred days after he was back; ten days after he jumped, he requalified as a diver. His vision is perfect; so is the rest of him. Of course, these days he sets off the metal detectors at every airport he goes through, since the whole right side of his face is made of titanium. But that hasn't stopped him. In fact, it's actually improved his looks.

Sitting next to Nasty was Duck Foot Dewey. Allen Dewey was a short, barrel-chested farmboy from Maryland's Eastern Shore. He grew up hunting Canadian goose, deer, rabbit, squirrel, duck, and anything else that could be cooked and eaten, on his father's seventy acres of soybeans and corn. He must have been affected by the low rumble of explosions coming from Aberdeen Proving Ground, directly across the bay, because at seventeen, he up and joined the Navy.

Even as a SEAL the kid was an irrepressible hunter. In fact, since he's based less than four hours from home these days, Duck Foot makes the drive virtually every weekend, grabs his shotgun, and heads for the woods or the ponds. The SEALs he serves with always eat well because their freezers are stocked with an unending stream of mallard and Muscovy ducks, Canadian geese, and venison sausage.

I hadn't worked with Duck Foot, but he came highly recommended. All that sneaking and peeking in the woods made him a stealthy son of a bitch, and he'd won his spurs in Iraq, where he'd been attached to SEAL Team Five. Duck Foot's assignment was to infiltrate Kuwait City and bring communications equipment such as cellular phones and video cameras, intelligence materials, and ordnance for booby traps to the Kuwaiti resistance. He made more than two dozen trips in and out without being seen. In fact, Duck Foot is the only petty officer third class who holds the Exalted Order of the Eastern Star, the highest military decoration the Amir of Kuwait can bestow.

Next to Duck Foot stood Cherry Enders. Cherry was the youngest sailor who'd ever been selected for SEAL Team Six—he was six weeks past nineteen at the time. But he had language skills—he spoke gutter Spanish with almost no accent and could make do in French and Arabic. Don't ask how he had acquired the skills, although the joke was that he'd spent his childhood in whorehouses. A big, rangy kid with ham-sized hands and a round, innocent face, he grew up fast at Six. Now he was a master chief who'd led platoons in Grenada and Panama.

Cherry was the senior enlisted man during SEAL Team Six's covert foray into Haiti in December 1991. Back then, twelve of deposed president Aristide's family and political allies were brought out during an operation code-named Raw Deal.

Acting on orders created by an Executive Intelligence Finding typed at the White House and signed by Pres. George Bush, SEAL Team Six's Green Team traveled clandestinely to the Navy Station at Guantánamo, Cuba. From there, they dropped out of a plane onto Navassa Island, an American protectorate thirty miles off Cap Carcasse, on Haiti's westernmost tip. There, two Mark III Mod-4 Blue Lightning boats had been prepositioned by naval SpecWar units. The BLs—1,500-hp chase boats that had been confiscated from drug dealers and given to the Navy—had been brought on a tramp steamer from Naples, Florida, and secured and camouflaged on the uninhabited island.

Aristide's people were waiting by prearrangement in a small Haitian fishing village called Dame Marie, on the north side of Cap Carcasse. The SEALs landed at night in small rubber boats, found the Haitians, brought them back to the swift boats, and exfiltrated, covering 125 miles of open sea to Guantánamo in just over three hours.

The operation remained secret for almost nine months. It was leaked to *San Diego Union* reporter Greg Vistica—the guy who broke the Tailhook story—during the 1992 budget fight, by a disgruntled West Coast SpecWar captain who hoped that Congress, which had not been notified about Raw Deal, would cut the SEAL Team Six budget.

"Hey, Skipper, fuck you!" That froggy growl came from Half Pint Harris, a Coors Light in his size-six fist, down at the end. Half Pint, a pug-nosed, curly red-haired squidge of a SEAL, real name Mike, stands five foot five. He'd weigh about one hundred and fifty pounds—*if* you soaked him in mud for a couple of days and it all stuck to him. But the surly little squirt can bench-press three hundred pounds, and he's a fast little motherfucker with his fists. He's probably part turtle because he can snap out at you in any number of ways. He loves to drink and brawl (his most recent claim to fame in the teams is that about a year ago he bit off an Airedale lieutenant's ear in a bar fight at the Ready Room, a saloon just outside the back gate of Oceana Naval Air Station). The son of a bitch also swims like a fish—he moves like he's turbine driven—and he is *the* man if you're doing sub ops. There's nothing he doesn't know about getting in and out of underwater situations.

For the last thirteen years, Half Pint's played Mutt to Piccolo Mead's Jeff. The Pick, as he's known in the teams, is the tall, thin drink of water who was assigned as Half Pint's swim buddy at BUD/S by a master chief with no sense of humor. Well, doom on the chief, because they've been inseparable ever since. They graduated from BUD/S tied in ranking. Both made CPO the same day. They went to Six together, where Half Pint was the dive ops boss, and Pick was put in charge of EOD—Explosive Ordnance Disposal. Question: how good an explosives man is he? Answer: after five thousand demolition jobs he can still count to twenty on his fingers and toes. Which is good, because Pick's hobby— flying—demands both hands and feet. He's instrument-qualified on multiengine aircraft, which means he can fly everything from a P-3 Orion sub-hunter to a C-130 Hercules, should the need arise.

I liked that. When I'd commanded Six, I'd encouraged my enlisted men to take flying lessons. I wanted the unit to be self-contained, so that if the need arose, we could handle our own tactical demands without calling on the Air Farce. After I left, flying was put back in the hands of officers. The Navy considers it improper for enlisted men to fly because they are not gentlemen, and flying is a gentlemen's art.

Anyway, Mutt and Jeff had played at Dam Neck almost six years. They got there just after I left and managed to survive the assholes who thought that discipline was the way to tame SEAL Six, not to mention the hell-raising duo. Finally, after Six was taken over last year by an ass-kissing intel weenie four-striper named Don Pitch, to whom all forms of bodaciousness are a sin, things came to a head. The ear-biting incident was too much for him, and Half Pint was asked to leave or spend some time in the brig. When he went, so did the Pick. And, much to my current delight, they had both volunteered for Red Cell purgatory.

The other three I didn't know—so they were immediately yclept Wynken, Blynken, and Nod. Wynken was Dale, a chunky twenty-six-year-old with a round baby face, hair the color of butterscotch toffee, and size fifteen shoes, who wasted no time telling me he loved shooting and looting. Okay, I said, I'd give him an opportunity to prove it. Blynken was Carl—an olive-skinned, mustachioed Black Irishman whose dark, liquid eyes probably made him successful with women. I didn't mind my men being slaves to their dicks and told him so, which brought a big, wide smile to his face. And then there was Nod—Eddie DiCarlo was one of those strong silent types who are more common to Special Forces than SEALs. A brooder, from the look of him, he's the kind that usually makes a good point man. I asked why he'd joined the Cell. He said he'd kicked the crap out of the master chief at Team Five when the guy told him he couldn't go to Iraq because he looked Jewish.

"Hell, Skipper, I *am* Jewish—half-Jew anyway. So I kicked his ass." He drained his beer and tilted his jaw toward me like a sinister bulldog. "Any problem with that, *sir?*"

"You look kosher enough to me, asshole. You'll do."

In fact, they all appeared okay, except they were sort of clean-cut for my taste. But that was a problem with all young SEALs these days. Besides, they managed to suck down the

Coors like real men, and they didn't mind when I used the F-word. They were, I guessed, suitable cannon fodder.

A word about that. You're probably groaning now and saying why the hell is he talking about cannon fodder again. God, what an insensitive, politically incorrect schmuck this Marcinko chap is.

Well, gentle reader, cannon fodder is a reality of warfare. There are times when, as a commander, you make a decision that will probably send some of your men to their deaths. Period. Full stop.

When I created SEAL Team Six, I chose several of the younger shooters knowing that if I had to make that call, they'd be the first ones to go into the jaws of death. I did it without remorse or guilt.

I did not feel remiss about this because, as a SEAL, I am the Navy's cannon fodder. SEALs are expendable. In fact, all SpecWar units are expendable. That's the way it's always been. Indeed, the UDT teams at Omaha Beach in June 1944 lost more than 50 percent of their men. The planners on Ike's staff had known how bad it would be, and still they assigned those naked warriors their mission. The Frogs at Omaha Beach were cannon fodder. So were the brave Canadian commandos who lost 80 percent of their men at Dieppe.

But the generals who created those missions weren't villains. Nor were they callous. Sometimes, war calls for men to sacrifice themselves for a greater good. And when the order comes through, you don't have to like it—you just have to do it. No matter what the consequences may be.

So, the fact that I can and will send men to their deaths does not mean I do not love them, or that their deaths will not affect me. During my thirty-three-year Navy career I lost only one man in combat—Clarence Risher, who was killed at Chau Doc during the Tet Offensive of 1968. His death still tears me apart. I believe that all the men who work for me also know that I will never ask them to do anything I will not do—that I am as much cannon fodder as they are. That we are all in this together.

So please, no more touchie-feelie bullshit or pantywaist complaints about "using" my men as cannon fodder. It is part of the job. You volunteer to become a SEAL or a Green Beret or a Ranger or a Force Recon Marine, knowing that you are expendable. I did. I still do.

Thus endeth the lesson.

It didn't take long for me to give them all the customary no-shitter about our situation. I explained the relationship between Grant Griffith, CNO, Pinky, and me. The way I saw it, Grant had some kind of hold over Pinky. Maybe it was a J. Edgar Hoover—that's my way of saying blackmail of one kind or another—maybe it was something else, like the promise of a quarter mil a year when Pinky put his papers in. But whatever the case, the bottom line was the same—I was the designated fall guy.

I was interested to see that the men were also quick to pick up that something about Griffith didn't quite fit. It takes a dirtbag to know a dirtbag, I guess. But the boys had lots of questions about my week in Japan, and where Griffith and his security company fit into the scheme of things. To an operator, very little is coincidence. The fact that Griffith was working with the Navy on the North Korean nuclear problem made all their antennae as erect as dicks.

I told them about the war game, and how Griffith was a SpecWar wannabe, complete with a museum of war toys and a mouthful of Asian martial-philosophy buzzwords. And I gave them a readout on Buckshot's operation, and especially on Manny Tanto.

I added that the way I saw it, everything was tied together—I just didn't know how or where.

For example, it was conceivable, I said, that Buckshot had been sneak-and-peeking in Tokyo when I was there. Had I been under surveillance? Who knew. Was I part of a bigger scheme? It was altogether possible. Had Griffith engineered the bodyguarding job with Joe Andrews to make sure I ended up at The Hustings in Upperville for the war game—and Manny Tanto's live-grenade booby trap? It wasn't inconceivable.

Who the hell knew. It was all a clusterfuck, and the only thing to do was call for another round.

The waitress, a buxom Scottish lass whose name was

Tammi, leaned up against my back. She had a firm, firm chest. "What's the order, Dick?"

I loved it when she talked dirty to me. "Hay for my horses, wine for my men, and mud for my turtle, sweetcakes."

When I told the Cell we'd be operating under UNODIR, my words brought a smile to everybody's face. And there were actually grins when I dropped the news about the security exercise at the Navy Yard. Duck Foot said it was a chance to screw with the system. I liked the fact that the nasty boy in each of my shooters was never far from the surface.

A Navy Yard hit had advantages, too: NIS headquarters was ripe for the plucking—and they probably had something in the files on Grant Griffith. CNO's files could be burgled—he and Griffith were tight. Bottom line: I'd come away knowing more than I did now.

Half Pint was ready to go—now! "The only thing to do is clusterfuck 'em back, Skipper. And we do it before they realize what's happening. That way, while everybody's pissing and moaning, we can get some real work done."

I liked that sort of thinking. When SEAL Team Six had been tasked for the second hostage-rescue mission in Iran, one of the planners, an Air Force two-star with all the imagination of a pet rock asked what I'd do if we got caught behind the lines. I explained gently that he might want to call NRO.

"Why?" he asked.

"So you can read the satellite photos and watch the trail of fires I leave behind on our way to the Turkish border, sir," I said, spelling it with a *c* and a *u*.

The way I look at it, Pinky had given me the perfect excuse to run through the system like *merde* through an *oie*. The only question was how and when we'd begin. So, I was delighted to discover that my men were thinking the same way I was.

Duck Foot drained his beer. "When's the exercise scheduled—next Friday, right?"

I nodded.

"So let's hit 'em on Tuesday. Quick and dirty."

Pick snapped his fingers. "Yeah—when security is normal. Which is to say fucked-up."

Nasty grinned. "Take apart CNO's office." The chief of naval operations had a huge office suite at the Navy Yard.

Duck Foot nodded. "Visit NIS headquarters. And maybe borrow some equipment from Building Twenty-two."

That was a good idea. Building 22 was a huge warehouse in which NIS's Technical Security Division built and stored its eavesdropping and surveillance equipment—the monitors for Grant Griffith's sting operation at Narita, for example, were the products of Building 22.

Cherry chimed in, "Not to mention kick officer ass and take officer names." Cherry Enders hated officers. He'd made the embarrassing of officers his full-time avocation. The Navy Yard gave him scores—nay, hundreds—of possibilities.

It all made perfect sense to me. Like Red Cell's two-tier mission, I had a number of reasons for wanting to stage an assault on the Navy Yard, and I wasn't about to explain all of them. On the overt level, I wanted to get some sense of how my men performed under stress. On the covert level, I wanted to target areas in which I was likely to come up with information about Grant Griffith and Pinky Prescott.

I sketched out an agenda to the men. The schedule was tight—but doable. We had the weekend to sneak and peek—do the recon necessary to see what objectives were the most vulnerable and start figuring out how to get inside them. We'd formulate our mission plan on Monday, do the dirty deed Tuesday, and have the results on the CNO's desk before close of business Wednesday.

That way, Pinky would learn what we'd done from the CNO—and there'd be nothing he could do about it. Marcinko's first rule of nature is that it is easier to drop turds from above than have them bubble up from below. Pinky could screw with me—but he was powerless when it came to the CNO.

Something else as well had to be done over the weekend. I needed a secure location for us to discuss the covert side of Red Cell's assignment. Shooter's was not the place for it. I finished the Bombay, slapped the glass back on the bar, and wriggled my mustache playfully. "Okay, cockbreaths, here's the plan."

The Washington Navy Yard is a sixty-six-acre site that has been in operation since the early nineteenth century. Most of the buildings on the "old" side of the Yard—that is, the westernmost portion—are humongous, six-story, red-brick warehouses that were built around the time of the Civil War. The Yard is home to NIS, as well as the Navy Museum. Behind its fifteen-foot walls, the senior admirals have their quarters, up on Admirals' Row. CNO lives there. So does Pinky Prescott and twenty-five other of the Navy's top brass. On spring evenings, you can see the wives walking their dogs around Admiral Leutze Park, or wandering down Dahlgren Avenue to the Anacostia River, where an old destroyer escort, the USS *Barry,* is moored.

Of course, the Yard sits between Sixth and Tenth streets, on the southern side of M Street, Southeast, plunk in the middle of what's become one of Washington's worst and toughest neighborhoods, so all the dog-walking and jogging takes place on the grounds. One admiral's wife strayed off the Yard a few years back. She was found a couple of days later cut up into serving-size pieces and stowed in a Dumpster.

So, to keep the flags from getting nervous (or mugged), the base is patrolled by its own police force, as well as government rent-a-cops, on a twenty-four-hour basis. It is, however, wide open. As I'd discovered, it didn't take much to get onto the Yard clandestinely, and it would take even less to get off. Indeed, if any of the brothers from Southeast actually put their minds to it, they could pick Admirals' Row clean before anyone ever noticed. Because of that, it occurred to me that maybe we should boost a couple of the flag homes just to show what could be done by enterprising minds and willing bodies.

But the admirals' quarters would have been too easy. Instead, we targeted the headquarters of the Naval Investigative Service, which was in the four-story Forge Building, the CNO's office, the security-detail HQ, and the Yard's power plant. Those were all legitimate "terrorist" targets so far as I was concerned. And they'd also cause the most embarrassment.

I did my first recon on Saturday at noon. I tucked my hair up into a green corduroy baseball cap, climbed into a pair of black trousers, a Polo shirt, and a brown leather jacket, and huff-puffed right through the gate onto the Yard. I waved at the guard, who had my picture up on the gatehouse wall—a publicity picture for *Rogue Warrior* that featured me with shoulder-length hair and a Charles Manson beard. Doom on you, asshole. I had a camera in my pocket and malice in my heart. "Have a nice day, sailor."

I snapped pictures of NIS headquarters, accenting the routes we'd take to break inside. I asked a nice admiral's wife who was walking her dog to take my picture outside NIS, and she obliged. That would make a nice addition to my scrapbook. I peered through the doors at Building 22 and made notes about the security situation. It was nonexistent. I went over to the power plant and checked the locks on the doors. They could easily be picked.

I ate a leisurely lunch in the cafeteria, then went to the base gym, where I worked out for an hour, pumping iron, taking advantage of the sauna and steam room, and stealing three ID cards from a trio of officers who were taking showers and had conveniently left their lockers open.

Feeling both fulfilled and well-conditioned, I sauntered past Building 200, where the CNO had his office. I walked inside and took the stairs to the second floor, wandered down the hall, and checked the doors to his suite.

A Marine was posted outside. He was carrying a holstered sidearm—a .45-caliber pistol—which I noticed lacked a magazine. That made sense. If he'd carried a *loaded* gun, he might be capable of shooting intruders. Like me, for example. But not in the new kinder, gentler armed forces. No—he'd die holding his dick in his hand.

He challenged me. "Sir?"

I flashed a quick smile and one of the stolen ID cards— my thumb conveniently across the picture—which identified me as a captain named Cook. I patted my pocket, laughed nervously, and shrugged helplessly. "I left my keys at home, Lance Corporal. But I've got a report to write—

and if I don't finish it, CNO's gonna have my butt for lunch on Monday."

"No problem, sir." He opened the door to the suite. I went inside, slipped on a pair of surgical gloves, and rifled the desks and file cabinets until I found a set of keys. I pocketed them. Then I checked to make sure everything was replaced the way I found it, borrowed an empty file folder, which I stuffed with Xerox paper, and made my exit, stage right, smiling.

"Thanks, Marine."

He saluted. "Pleasure, sir. Have a good weekend."

"I'm planning on it." Outside, I deposited the folder in a convenient trash can. Then I jogged back through the main gate, waving at the guard and calling out, "Have a nice day," as I left.

On Sunday, I took the guys to the Yard for our preliminary sortie. The Pick and Half Pint went through the General Services Administration forty-five-acre supply facility on the Navy Yard's westernmost border. The GSA main gate is always unmanned. They wandered over to the chain-link fence that separates the GSA and Navy Yards, cut the chain on the personnel gate, and replaced it with the lock and chain they carried with them. Cherry, whose new ID card identified him as a lieutenant commander, sauntered into the officers' club and ransacked the coat-check area. He came away with three wallets, two briefcases containing classified materials, and a new bridge coat.

Half Pint, Pick, and I took Wynken, Blynken, and Nod for a ride in a rented car. We drove the perimeter of the Yard, noting the gates and the fences. Then I took a drive on Interstate 395, which passed not fifteen yards from the CNO's second-floor office suite. When I pointed out the target and explained how they'd hit it, the men couldn't keep from laughing.

I took the guys to lunch at the Bolling Air Force Base officers' club, where I maintain a membership. For $7.95 it's an all-you-can-eat affair, with free wine and beer offered. They lost money on us, I guar-on-tee.

Afterward, as long as we were across the river, we stopped by the gym at the Anacostia Naval Station and stole three more ID cards. I lucked out—I became a two-star without Senate approval. In the parking lot behind the gym, two unlocked cars had their Military District of Washington gate passes mounted on placards instead of inside the windshields. We stole them, too.

We gathered at Shooter McGee's for dinner Sunday, and I made the assignments. I'd wanted to include Stevie Wonder in this little escapade, but he was out of town on business— masquerading as a U.N. weapons inspector while he planted No Such Agency listening devices in a Middle Eastern country whose identity must remain classified, but looks very much like Iraq on a map. His loss.

Nasty and I assigned ourselves NIS headquarters. I gave Duck Foot and Cherry the TSD building, with permission to take all the equipment they could. Half Pint and Pick would raid the CNO's office—I'd visit them there as soon as I finished at NIS. Wynken, Blynken, et al., got the Navy Yard police station and the power plant. They would also maintain surveillance while Nasty and I broke into NIS, sitting outside dressed like security personnel in a stolen Navy Yard police van.

Costumes were easy. We'd all be joggers. We'd wear Navy blue sweats emblazoned with Annapolis logos. We'd carry the base ID cards stolen from the gym.

The hit would begin at 2130 hours and end at 0100 hours. We'd stash our equipment and the goods from TSD in the van. Some of what we stole we'd transfer to a car parked on the GSA side of the fence—we'd simply walk through the gate that Pick and Half Pint had doctored, load up, and drive away. The rest of the loot would be driven off in the base police van.

Does that all sound too simple? Too logical? Too easy? Of course it does—which is why it worked so well.

On Monday, as directed, I filed my daily mash note to Pinky. It was chatty and innocuous. It said that we were proceeding as planned, and that I was going to visit the Navy Yard. I also wrote that I planned to talk to the security officers at the Yard. I did not say, however, that I would see them in person. After all, if I paid them a courtesy call, they'd realize that I'd shaved my beard—and my little surprise might be compromised.

Still, I was as good as my word. I dialed *un coup de téléphone* to the captain in charge of the Yard security detail. I introduced myself as the new CO of Red Cell and explained that we'd been tasked with a security exercise and survey.

Capt. Worthingham Washington Lewis told me he was absatively, posolutely ready for us: "We've got the scenario, and my men are raring to go, Captain."

I wondered aloud what the scenario was.

He actually read it to me. "You guys come through the Main Gate at ten thirty hours Friday and head for Building Two Hundred, the Navy Yard's HQ. You take the guard at Main Gate hostage. But he calls an alert before you grab him, and our rapid-response team is ready. We set up a roadblock, and you can't reach HQ building so you hole up in the garage with your hostage. We seal the place off, cut the power, and negotiate. In three hours, you surrender. It's a pretty cut-and-dry situation if you ask me."

I bit my tongue. "Sounds that way to me, too, Captain."

"We can do the survey afterwards. I've cleared the whole day for you, but I don't think it'll take more than half an hour. We're battened down pretty tight here, y'know."

"Really?"

"That's a roger. This base is as secure as any installation in the world. I've seen to it."

I believed him completely when he said that. "Okay, Captain. Seems to me you've got things under control over there. See you Friday."

Chapter

12

TUESDAY MORNING I DROVE TO ANNAPOLIS, WHERE I BOUGHT seven sets of Academy sweats and three varsity jackets. I bought myself a baseball cap that said NAVY in gold on a blue background and had lots of scrambled eggs on the visor. It hid my hair nicely. Then I went to a Laundromat and put the hooded sweatshirts and thick pants through two wash-and-dry cycles. While I waited, I dropped by the Academy bookstore and autographed their stock of *Rogue Warrior* hardcovers, delighted to see that they'd almost sold out. When the book came out, the Naval Academy's administration had refused to allow me to hold a book-signing on campus. The fact that middies were buying my book by the hundreds gave me a great sense of satisfaction. Maybe they'd even learn something from it.

At 1655 I stopped by the Pentagon long enough to deposit an envelope on the anal-retentive-clean desk occupied by Pinky Prescott's administrative assistant. He'd already left, as had Pinky. Only the OP-06 chief of staff, a bookish squirrel of a man named Myer, remained, shuffling papers. He looked up as I was heading toward the door.

"Anything I can do to help, Dick?"

"Nah—I left my daily report for Pinky on the AA's desk."

He waved absentmindedly and went back to his papers. "I'll let him know."

The message was, as I'd been ordered to do, addressed to His Royal Highness the deputy chief of naval operations for plans, policy, and operations. The gist of the message was: "Dear Pinky, unless otherwise directed, my unit and I are going to probe the Navy Yard's readiness tonight, in preparation for the upcoming security exercise. Love and kisses, Richard (NMN) Marcinko, Captain, USN."

I was grinning as I left the building to grab the metro. Probe, hell. I was about to perform a fucking proctosigmoidoscopy.

I met the guys at the Cave—the studio apartment I keep in Old Town Alexandria—and passed out their uniforms. We cabbed over to National Airport, where we rented a Lincoln Continental and a Ford Escort using false IDs and driver's licenses, just like real terrorists would do. Then we drove the cars to the Shooter McGee parking lot. There, we scraped the Hertz decals off the rear windows and placed the MDW placards on the dashboards. We stowed our equipment, which was contained in ballistic nylon bags, in the trunks, then drove over to Bullfeathers, a bar on King Street in Old Town, where we chowed down on Bullburgers and Coors Light and went over last-minute details.

By 2030 we were on our way. Wynken, Blynken, and Nod sque-e-e-zed into the back of the Escort and drove with Pick and Half Pint into the GSA compound. They were scheduled to park a hundred feet from the doctored fence. While the trio of newcomers stole a police van and set up shop outside NIS headquarters, Pick and Half Pint would break into Building 200 and use the keys I'd taken to open up the CNO's office. Their instructions were to neutralize any Marines outside the door. Nasty drove the Lincoln, with Cherry riding shotgun. I was tucked on the floor in the back, with Duck Foot's size nines on top of me. Sure, I'd shaved my beard. Sure, I was certain no one would recognize me. But why take chances?

Nasty slowed at the gatehouse, waved at the guard, and cruised through at fifteen miles an hour. We swung right at the light, then slowed as we took the curve around the Navy Museum. We parked just outside the First Lieutenant's Division, a Civil War–era warehouse directly behind TSD, two blocks from NIS headquarters. Nasty popped the trunk. We drew our gear and got to work.

Cherry took out the two streetlights in the area with two ball bearings from his Wham-O slingshot, which he then dropped back into the Lincoln. We waited to see if anyone had heard the smack of glass, but things remained all quiet. So Duck Foot used a pick on the TSD warehouse door—a single panel steel rig with a pressure bar on the inside. It popped open before we'd even cleared the scene. The kid was everything he was quacked up to be. I waved as they disappeared inside.

Nasty and I carried two black nylon rucksacks. We jogged slowly around the TSD building, toward Admirals' Row. As we came past the park, we overtook a short, squat middle-aged woman in running gear huffing and puffing behind a huge rottweiler. The sucker must have been 160 pounds of dog, and you wouldn't want to get on its bad side.

I waved at her. "Evening, ma'am."

She smiled back. "Evening. Out for a jog?"

"Yup." I nodded toward Nasty in his varsity jacket. "Gets the old heart pumping so I can keep up with the younger men like Junior here."

"I know what you mean. I run whenever I have the chance—especially on nights like this when my husband's working late. But I tell you, it gets tougher and tougher. I have a heck of a hard time keeping up with old Murphy here."

I slowed down. She made terrific camouflage. "Murphy? What a great name for a dog."

"My husband named him after Murphy's Law. He says that's the one rule by which the entire Navy operates."

How right she was. I laughed. "I hope Murphy doesn't live up to his name."

"Well, he's always along for the ride." She stopped and ruffled the dog behind the ears. "No—he's a good fellow. Getting old, like me." She peered over at Nasty in his Annapolis letter jacket. "What year?"

"'Eighty-nine," Nasty said with a straight face.

"Ah—then you wouldn't have known our son. He was class of 'eighty-three."

"What's his name?" Nasty asked.

She told us. I almost lost my cookies. We were jogging alongside CNO's wife. Talk about timing. *I* should have been named Murphy—Murphy the dog, meet Murphy the Frog.

We'd passed NIS Headquarters by now and were headed toward the waterfront, where the USS *Barry* was moored. I nudged Nasty's arm, and we veered off to the right. "Nice talking to you, ma'am."

She waved in our direction and kept going toward the dock. "You, too. Take care, now."

We picked up our pace and moved off. "Shit," I said after she was out of earshot, "talk about timing."

"Like the Polish comedian says, Skipper, 'timing is everything.'"

We ran around the block twice. It was all quiet. No security. No cops. No CNO's wife. No Murphy. We circled back to the Forge Building from the south side, looking inside the glass doors to where the security guards were sitting behind their console. There were cameras and monitors, of course—but the pair of watchdogs were more interested in the card game they had going than the bank of screens behind them.

Headlights from the east. We slowed to a walk to see who it was. Wynken, in a police windbreaker and visored cap, sat in the shotgun seat of a Dodge panel truck with a bubblegum light bar. He wriggled his eyebrows in our direction. Nod, serious face and all, was behind the wheel.

It was time to move. At the northeast corner of the building, an iron drainpipe about the thickness of a good-size sapling ran from the ground right up to the roof four stories above. I pointed at it. "Nasty, would you like to lead the way?"

Shinnying up a drainpipe is harder than it looks—but if you can press more than 300 pounds, it just takes practice, because your upper-body strength will get you through the ordeal. Nasty presses 475. He went up the damn pipe like a Tahitian going after a coconut. By the time I wheezed my way over the rooftop, he'd pulled on his surgical gloves and was already hard at work breaking and entering.

I slipped my gloves on and joined him in crime. First, we eased the TV cameras out of position very slowly. No need to alert the guards below. Once the lenses were turned six inches to the right, they'd miss us as we worked. Then we jimmied open one of the building's three roof vents, propped it with a collapsible tent stake, attached nylon climbing line to a stanchion, and dropped into the main electrical shaft.

From there it was only a couple of wiggles and a shimmy or two into a fourth-floor hallway. There, we'd split up. Nasty would take the top two floors, searching for souvenirs and leaving IEDs. He would then make his escape the way we'd come, link up with the bogus police van, and head for the hills. I'd take the bottom two floors and cut my way out through one of the first-floor offices that backed up on an alleyway. Incredibly, the street-level offices, which were used by junior officers, had single panes of glass in their windows. Breaking out would be as easy as using a glass cutter and a suction cup, both of which I happened to have in my backpack.

I ambled down the fire stairs to two, eased the door open, and walked into the linoleum-tile hallway. I knew a fair amount about the layout of NIS headquarters because I'd been interrogated there for weeks, during my own inquisition back in the late eighties. I knew, for example, that there are three SCIFs on the second floor and two on the third. SCIFs are Special Classified Intelligence Facilities, or in plain English, bug-proof rooms.

The SCIFs on three are used for taking depositions and doing interrogations of people like me whose operations are code-word-level secret. Two SCIFs on the second floor are where NIS keeps its sensitive files, current investigations, and other goodies.

The third bubble room on two is used by SLUDJ—the special investigation task force that concentrates on prosecuting flag-rank officers. SLUDJ, pronounced sludge, stands for Sensitive Legal (Upper Deck) Jurisdiction. It maintains a suite of eight offices on the second floor.

I guess the idea was okay. It was similar to the concept of

the special prosecutor—an office of professional, apolitical investigators whose job would be to go after those who ran the Navy. An internal affairs unit similar to those on most police forces. The only trouble was that it got corrupted early on and was used almost exclusively for political revenge.

It was SLUDJ that was turned loose on my sea daddy Admiral Ace Lyons back in the late eighties when he offended too many of his Annapolis classmates by his inna-you-face attitude. Using intimidation, harassment, and direct threats during a two-year investigation code-named Iron Eagle, SLUDJ forced Ace into premature retirement from his post as CINCPACFLT—Commander-IN-Chief, PACific FLeeT.

The week after Ace retired, his greatest rival—a three-star named Mike Dyne whom Ace had displaced as the starting quarterback of the 1946 Navy football team four decades earlier—was promoted to full admiral and given Ace's job. It was Dyne—acting with the blessing of the then-CNO—who had loosed NIS on Ace. Not because Ace had done anything wrong, but because Mike Dyne wanted to settle a grudge he'd held since Annapolis. He used SLUDJ to do it.

I know—you're saying that using an investigative service for political goals is immoral and wrong. So what's your point? That's the real world. NIS is commonly known as the Admirals' Gestapo—indeed, that is precisely what it's called on the Pentagon's fourth-floor E Ring, where all the three- and four-stars have their offices. They use NIS against each other all the time.

Anyway, if NIS is the Gestapo, then the legal terrorists at SLUDJ are the Gestapo's Death's Head SS unit. They're known as Terminators.

I began checking SLUDJ's doors. The cypher locks on the first three were tight as virgin pussy. I heard voices behind door number four. I was about to diddle with the punch keys anyway when I heard the voices getting closer. I looked around for someplace to hide.

Shit—I'd passed the point of no return. There was no way I could make it back to the stairwell without their seeing me.

Wild-eyed, I hauled ass down the hall until I saw a men's room sign, wheelied through the door, took refuge in a stall, and dropped my sweatpants.

I wasn't an instant too soon. Twenty seconds later the door pushed open and two pairs of black shoes headed toward the urinals. I heard zippers unzip, and two ahs in unison. They peed in silence. Then, one of the Terminators suggested they grab a quick pizza at the O Club across the street before they finished their work. That sounded good to Terminator Two. They shook off, then left without washing up. Typical.

I gave them three minutes, then slipped out of the head, went back to their door, and turned the cypher-lock handle to the left. It moved—the assholes had actually left the room open. I could have picked the lock—they take four or five minutes to bypass—but now I didn't have to.

I went inside.

This was too good to be true. Like so many offices at so many allegedly secure locations, from Capitol Hill to the Pentagon to the CIA, the series of cypher-locked doors were a sham. All the offices were interconnected—a row of eight, sans any interior doorways. Only the SCIF at the end of the hall was sealed.

The Terminators who'd gone for pizza had observed security procedures. They'd locked their files and their desks, although they'd left some notes on a worktable and the Xerox machine was still turned on. Others, however, had been less conscientious. Two offices down, someone had left the safe open. In the very last office I discovered a bunch of files spread out on a pair of long tables in the center of the room.

It was time to go to work. I checked the tables first, searching for anything that contained Grant Griffith's name. I found nothing, although there were quite a few that dealt with operations he'd mentioned to me. I took a dozen or so files, ran down to the Xerox machine, copied them, and slipped them in my rucksack.

Then I opened the safe and rifled through the file jackets inside. Each jacket contained one investigation. Two code names caught my eye. One was labeled FOXHUNTER—that was probably about pussy-chasing. My kind of investigation. I pulled the file. The other one to get my attention had HUCKLEBERRY HOUND in one-inch capital letters written across the front. What came to mind immediately was the jowly, basset-hound face of the retired four-star admiral named—well, I'll just call him Huck.

I opened the Huckleberry jacket first. Inside was a six-inch-thick sheaf of papers. There were photographs and there were transcripts. There were reports, memos, copies of letters, and telephone logs. There were interviews, depositions, and sworn statements.

The subject of the investigation was indeed Admiral Huck, a former chairman of the Joint Chiefs of Staff who had become actively dovish in his retirement. He'd endorsed sanctions against Iraq instead of action during his televised Senate testimony. He'd campaigned for the current president, whom many in the Navy detested.

Now, it seemed, the Terminators were out to get Huck for influence peddling during his term as chairman, and from the look of the file in my hands, they were going to do it. They'd put together a damning bunch of evidence. The problem was, none of it was true. It was a tapestry of lies, innuendo, and hearsay, all woven together with circumstantial evidence and unnamed sources into a convincing tapestry. Still, if the story was leaked to the press—which was one of the ways SLUDJ operated—it could ruin Huck's civilian career. Because currently, Admiral Huckleberry Hound, USN (Ret.), had just been nominated by the White House as our new ambassador to Russia.

I'd served as Huckleberry's SpecWar liaison officer during a six-month period just after I left command of SEAL Team Six. He wasn't my kind of chairman. A ship driver who'd left the fleet two decades before and become a systems analyst and a Ph.D. in education, he'd been inclined against using force.

But he'd always been a square shooter with me. He'd never lied or tried to screw me or, more to the point, screw SpecWar. And there was no way he was an influence peddler. This was a man who never took anything from the hundreds of lobbyists who tried to buy his favors with lavish dinners or offers of free trips. He always paid his own way. He picked up his own dinner checks. He turned down golfing weekends in Palm Springs and Boca Raton. He once threw—*threw*—a lobbyist out of his office after the man hinted about a six-figure consulting fee after retirement if Admiral Huck would simply lean in favor of a certain weapons target-acquisitioning system under consideration.

I took the cover sheets to the file, the list of hostile witnesses and sources, the phone logs, and several of the shorter deposition transcripts and ran them through the Xerox. Then I slid everything back in the file jacket and replaced it in the safe. Old Admiral Huck was about to receive a plain brown envelope in the mail.

Next came Foxhunter. Imagine my surprise when I discovered that the pussy-crazed flag officer under investigation was none other than my own dear new boss, Pinckney Prescott III. It seems that Pinky'd been turned in by a high-placed civilian source who, the report said, chanced upon him and his sweetie as they came out of an apartment house at Twenty-first and N streets, Northwest, at three in the P.M., or 1500 hours by the military clock.

Said source, the report continued, became suspicious because Pinky gave said sweetie a big wet one, then climbed into a Pentagon staff car driven by a naval enlisted man. Said source had obtained the license plate and motor pool number of the aforementioned vehicle and given it to NIS, which determined that the staff car in question was assigned to my old nemesis Pinky da Turd.

According to the file, said civilian source had gone directly to the head of NIS, who had deemed the threat serious enough to commence an investigation of the deputy CNO for plans, policy, and operations. Obviously, said CS had beaucoup clout. It's not everybody who can call up the head of NIS and get him scrambling on an investigation in—according to what the report said—a mere three days.

Indeed, a surveillance had been set up by NIS because the civilian source suspected that Miko Takahashi, the BIQ, or Bimbo In Question, was a foreign intelligence agent. Miko was a Japanese national who had in the past worked for her embassy's military liaison office. She lived in the Twenty-first and N Street apartment and currently worked as a freelance translator and business consultant to the Matsuko Corporation. Spell that B-I-M-B-O.

It was determined that Pinky had his assignations thrice a week at precisely 1400. He arrived, he came, and he left, all on a meticulous schedule. That sounded just like him—nothing spontaneous.

There were phone transcripts—obviously they had the place bugged—and pictures. Great pictures. She was a real brunette. She had small tits, but nice ones, especially when aroused. Pinky was not well-endowed. I ran copies of a dozen of the photos, then photocopied the file.

I made a mental note to Fax Miko's photo to Tosho and see what he could come up with. Then I dropped everything into my knapsack, put the file back where it belonged, and slipped out of the room. The elevator doors were just opening. I ran like hell for the stairwell and got there unobserved.

Shit—I'd hit the fucking jackpot. My instinct was to take off—Nasty was under orders to leave enough IEDs to show we'd been visiting—but I held back. I left the stairwell and worked my way around the atrium, keeping low so the guards couldn't see me. I went into the first office that had an open door, popped the lock on a file cabinet with my screwdriver, and placed an IED smoke bomb inside. I left the drawer open, with a Naval Security Coordination Team sticker—a Globe, with the letters RC (for Red Cell) super-imposed on it—prominently displayed.

I stuck another decal on the office door as I left. Then I went back to the stairwell and ambled down to the first floor, jimmied one of the street-level offices, eased the curtains back, and peered out the window. The alley was quiet. I licked the suction cup and placed it on the window, took my glass cutter, and worked it around the perimeter of the pane, then tapped. The glass came free. I put a Red Cell decal on the glass before laying it on the floor. Then I eased myself outside.

Shouldering my rucksack, I jogged around the front of the Forge Building, heading northeast. The panel truck was still parked near Admiral Willard Park. I gave the thumbs-up

sign to my two bogus cops as I chugga-huffed past them.
Nod nodded in my direction and switched on the ignition.
Their next assignment was the TSD building. There, they'd
pick up the goodies Cherry and Duck Foot were purloining,
stow them, and drive them out of the Yard, down M Street,
and into the GSA lot, where they'd be transferred into the
trunk of the Escort. Duck Foot and Cherry would make
their own way back through the gate. They'd change the
locks again, then head for the Escort, and haul ass for the
Cave.

I wandered over to Building 200, where Half Pint and
Pick were wiring the CNO's office with half a dozen IEDs. I
slipped into the dress blue jacket and white hat that the chief
of naval operations had obligingly left hanging on his
coatrack, sat behind his desk, and smiled into the camera
while Pick snapped a Kodachrome with his Stylus. Then we
booby-trapped the Marine guard and split. After all, there
were still fifty-five minutes before the bars in Old Town
closed, and I thought that the boys deserved a few cold ones
after a productive night's work.

Chapter

13

Pinky was glued to the ceiling when I paid my morning call. He descended long enough to jump up and down like one of those cartoon organ-grinder monkeys, screaming his head off about the fact that NIS was going crazy because their sanctuary had been violated, and that I was in deep shit and about to spend the rest of my natural life at Fort Leavenworth, Kansas, breaking big stones into little stones.

I'd disobeyed my direct, written orders by not taking a JAG officer with me to the Navy Yard. I'd broken the rules by not alerting the Public Affairs Division of my moves in advance. Worst of all, I'd violated the Navy's most sacrosanct rule: thou shalt not fuck with your fellow officers.

Do you realize, Pinky bawled, that CNO is currently reaming the Navy Yard commandant, a one-star admiral named Moosley, a new asshole? CNO was furious. It seemed he'd walked into his office at 0645 and found the door wide open, the files rifled, and the armed Marine guard tied to his chair and booby-trapped with a smoke grenade. For some reason Pinky couldn't comprehend, CNO wasn't mad at Red Cell, but blamed the Navy Yard CO for the fact that the Yard had such lax security.

"Teddy Moosley," Pinky said bitterly, "was my roommate at the Academy." Now, he continued, his former roomie was dead meat. "He was up for promotion this year—until you had to go and blow him out of the water with your asinine games."

CNO might think it was Teddy's fault. Pinky, however, knew who'd really fucked up—and the culprit's name was spelled M-A-R-C-I-N-K-O. He insisted he was going to see that I paid full price for my inappropriate, thoughtless, and ill-considered actions, too.

Doom on you, Pinky. I could prove my innocence. I pointed to the love note I'd dropped off the previous afternoon, which lay opened on Pinky's desk. "I spelled out everything I was going to do right there. It was delivered before close of business. We waited until twenty-one hundred hours to hear from you, Pinky. You didn't oppose the operation. I took your silence to mean that the preliminary probe was okay with you."

"But I wasn't even here," Pinky whined.

"Your chief of staff was. He was at his desk when I dropped it off. He didn't say anything either, and when you didn't call, we believed we'd been given a green light."

He sputtered some more. But, being the bureaucrat that he was, he knew I'd left a proper paper trail and there was nothing he could do.

It was time to make him jump through another hoop or two. I took an envelope from my briefcase and laid it on his desk. "Anyway, I thought you might like a look at this souvenir from last night's exercise." I said it with a smile.

Pinky slid the ten-by-thirteen envelope toward him as if it might be contaminated. He slit it open and pulled a single photograph from inside. His eyes went wide in horror.

"What the—" I thought he was going to choke. "You rotten son of a bitch! How did you ever—" He laid the photograph on his desk, still sputtering. It was my face that was smiling up at him—a color print of me in CNO's blouse and hat I'd had done at an hour-photo lab before coming to work.

"Keep it as a souvenir, Pinky. I've already sent one to CNO."

I know, I know—you're asking why I didn't give Pinky one of the better shots—the ones I'd found in the SLUDJ offices. Well, there's a time for everything, and this wasn't the time.

After all, I'd secured a treasure trove of information in SLUDJ's suite, and I didn't think they knew I'd been there. Pinky and his ilk see me as a knuckle dragger and nothing more. But I know how to use intelligence—and how to exploit it. I knew Pinky was after my ass. So were a dozen other flag officers—men I'd screwed when I had command of Six or the Red Cell back in the eighties. Base commanders whose careers were blotted by my escapades. Staff officers I'd bullied and terrorized. SEAL competitors whose toes I'd stomped.

Now that I was back, they all wanted a piece of me. So I had to protect myself. The SLUDJ papers were just the life preserver I needed. They were currently stored beneath the floorboards of the kitchen at Rogue Manor, where Stevie Wonder had built me a little hideaway. It's a neat job and so well carpentered that the CIA's top black-bag man, who's an old friend of Stevie's, came over and spent nine hours looking for it one day. He came up dry.

So this was no time to tell anyone what I had. Besides, with Pinky under NIS surveillance, things were taking a nasty turn. I wanted to learn who'd turned Pinky in—discover the identity of that highly placed civilian source. I wanted to see if Pinky was indeed involved with a foreign agent—because if he was, his ass was going to be *mine,* or if he'd been set up, in which case his ass was also going to be *mine*.

I wanted the time to think of a way to use the Foxhunter file and Pinky's provocative, passionate pecker-and-pussy pictures to my best advantage. It was better to let him spit nails about a photo of me trying to impersonate an officer and bide my time.

So, I made myself scarce. I bought the boys a celebratory dinner at the Chart House. I began working the phones, setting up the old network of chiefs and junior officers I'd used to get round the system in the past—I call it my Safety Net because it allows me to operate outside the system. I checked in with Tosho and slipped him Miko Takahashi's name. I even gave Joe Andrews a call to see how his minisub business was going. And all the while, I added a snippet here and a snippet there to my Grant Griffith file.

I'm a very instinctual person. In combat, instinct has saved my life—like the time in Vietnam when a voice in my head said "Duck!" and I threw myself onto the ground just as an AK-47 blasted at me from five yards away. There were hundreds of times during my career when life-and-death decisions had to be made. I made many of them "from the gut" and regretted very few. Now, my gut was telling me that no matter what Grant Griffith said, no matter who he knew, no matter how important he was to our national security, the guy was dirty. I just couldn't prove it—yet.

Meanwhile, my plate was full. I hung out at the Cave, checking over the TSD gadgets my nasty little devils had purloined. We probably had half a million dollars' worth of goodies—everything from a pair of fiber-optic TV cameras smaller than pipe cleaners, to a voice-stress analyzer, to a set of portable voice scramblers that were small enough to fit in your pocket. I had no intention of giving them back, figuring that somewhere, sometime, somehow, they'd come in handy. Toys like that always do.

I was summoned to OP-06 forty-eight hours later. Pinky was his usual abrupt and charming self. "Come," he said by way of greeting, grabbing his jacket and heading out the door.

I followed him like a dog, trailing behind as he strode admirally down the E Ring hallway, galumphed down two flights of stairs, and marched back up the D Ring to the hallway outside the Joint Chiefs of Staff situation room. He stopped in front of an unmarked door and punched a combination into the cypher-button lock. We entered a room directly across the hall from the JCS facility, a SCIF I'd used during the Tehran rescue mission.

Inside, an easel had been set up. Files were spread out on a long table. And a one-starred, four-eyed intelligence squirrel named Howard Rosenberg was pacing nervously. Two of Rosenberg's aides—weenies wearing captain's stripes and thick glasses—sat on folding chairs biting their nails. Pinky made perfunctory introductions, then we got down to the nitty-gritty. And there was a lot more grit than nit, believe me.

In essence, I was being given the unenviable task of volunteering to take my men into North Korean waters, where we would infiltrate the minisub pens at Chongjin, the site of the country's most secret naval installation, and place underwater "tracer" monitors on all the North Korean minisubs we could find, so their activity could be tracked by satellite. Chongjin was where DIA had pinpointed fresh nuclear weapons smuggling activity, by using, as one weenie put it, "several various clandestine monitoring devices that were built internally." Simultaneous translation: NIS monitors from the Navy Yard had been placed in the containers. Shades of Narita. This was déjà vu all over again. I wondered who was really pulling Rosenberg's strings. Was this another Grant Griffith goatfuck?

I asked whether the incident at Narita had any connection to the current mission. "Only in the most ephemeral way," Pinky said.

And what was that? I asked.

"It caused us to improve the manner in which the devices report location," Rosenberg sniffed. "All our internal monitors now have directional and signal-strength capability."

In English, that meant the bugs I'd stolen could tell you where they were, and how close you were to them. At least TSD had learned something from its mistake.

Rosenberg's nerds continued with the briefing. The mission was to be a sneak-and-peek, with visual evidence to be gathered by digital infrared cameras that would, after we returned to the sub, burst-satellite the information back to DIA. Yes, we knew that the North Koreans didn't have their nuclear program based at Chongjin. The reactor that made their weapons-grade plutonium and the labs working on detonators and other elements of the bombs were all located at Yongbyon, about a hundred miles up the Chongchon River from Chongjin harbor. But they were using Chongjin as a transfer point. Our intel came up with the following scenario: Stolen materials were smuggled aboard cargo ships or tankers, which sailed to the North Korean port. There, it was suspected—although not confirmed—that minisubs were used to ferry the goods from dockside to the military base, where hard-topped concrete sub pens had been built to conceal activity from satellite observation. Inside the pens, the nuclear materials would be unloaded, and from there the stuff would be trucked to Yongbyon concealed in other cargo.

It was, Admiral Rosenberg said, our mission impossible to determine what the North Koreans were actually smuggling, and to bring back substantive evidence about precisely how they were doing it.

Once the intel weenies had left, Pinky explained how the mission would work. We'd travel in mufti to Hawaii, then go on to Tokyo by civilian carrier, traveling separately. We'd form up at Yokosuka, the joint U.S./Japanese navy base closest to Tokyo, grab a plane, and head out to the Sea of Japan, where we'd HALO, drop into the water, get picked up by a nuclear sub that had been outfitted for special operations with a DDS, or Dry Dock Shelter clamshell housing to protect our SDVs, or Swimmer Delivery Vehicles. Then it would be on to North Korea, where we'd complete our mission, be picked up by the sub, then taken back to Japan, from where we'd come home on civilian transport.

Why us? Because, as Pinky explained, this was a real black-bag job. The Joint Chiefs didn't even know about it. This was a Navy operation. Its background lay in the fact that the CIA and the State Department had determined— and more ominously, the administration had accepted— that the North Koreans weren't in the nuclear weapons development business anymore and were striving for normalization. But *we* Navy types knew better. My mission would provide evidence that the Navy was right.

Pinky didn't say it, but I realized there was more of a political element to the mission than there was a tactical need. Proof that the kimchis were building a bomb would help the Navy keep its budget, which was being slashed by almost 25 percent in this new administration. More than thirty Boomer-class subs had already been dry-docked. Another twenty were scheduled to be scrapped. The fleet was being cut to less than three hundred ships—down 50 percent from a decade ago. If the North Koreans were nuclear capable, then the Navy would have a strategic mission once again, and we'd be able to keep our subs and our ships.

Pinky kept repeating that the Cell's mission was no more than a simple in-and-out. I didn't like the sound of that. In/out, in/out reminded me of fucking—except I was the fuckee.

Sure, it *sounded* simple—except we didn't have intelligence worth a fuck anymore (if we ever did), *and* today's naval commanders are extra cautious in all operational activity, let alone those that have serious political implications. And I knew something Pinky didn't: nothing is simple. Special operations succeed because of good intelligence, meticulous planning, and the ability to go balls-to-the-wall without being second-guessed by some asshole behind an E-Ring desk.

This intel was for shit. I pored over the stuff on the table. All the data in this squirrel locker had been picked up by satellites and analyzed by the new breed of young kids that didn't know fuck-all about war or what an enemy was. They may have been well schooled and have punched all the right tickets, but they didn't have the corporate knowledge to tell me anything I wanted to know.

All their data could tell me—if the weather was good—was how many of their SpecWar minisubs were in port. They couldn't say where they were going, what they were doing, or where they'd been. In fact, I'd be damn lucky to get sequential data so I could determine presence/absence, thus allowing me to estimate their mission range.

And as for planning, Pinky couldn't design a SpecWar op if his life depended on it. And his life didn't—it was my ass on the line and in the water. I told him as much, too.

He pouted and said that was too bad—nothing could be changed. I explained a few of the facts of life to him, and he actually gave in here and there.

But overall, I was being asked to do the impossible, by somebody who would have loved to see me and my men fail, or die. When I'd taken over the Cell less than a week before, Nasty had said that we were in a TARFU situation, because Things Are Really Fucked Up.

He'd underestimated things. As I mentally listed the clusterfuck factors, I realized we were almost all the way to FUBAR—Fucked Up Beyond All Repair. I explained things to Pinky in simple declarative sentences.

CF One: The Navy's intelligence—an oxymoron if ever there was one—was sketchy at best.

CF Two: Red Cell hadn't done a clandestine/covert lock-out/lock-in submarine operation since before the death of the Soviet Bear. Which put the Murphy probability at 100 percent.

CF Three: The relevant equipment had been used for administrative requalification dives only and hadn't been pushed to the limits in years. Why? Because, said the current crop of SEAL COs, we wouldn't want to authorize a potential safety violation—that might hurt our careers. Over more than thirty years of active duty, I could never convince my peers, seniors, or subordinates that the reason SEALs get hazardous-duty pay is because the assignment is inherently dangerous. Fact of life: people die on the job.

CF Four: With the Soviet Bear dead, SUBFORCE hadn't done any real snooping and pooping like in the good old days. (To be honest, their hands had often been tied for reasons of safety and/or political concern for potential risk or embarrassment, so I wasn't blaming them.)

But it was going to be a real mess. In effect, I was about to lead a kamikaze attack against some North Korean minisubs based on shitty-to-none intelligence, with old, tired diving equipment, and SEALs with more balls than brains, and do it all from a submarine that was smart but manned by an unchallenged, untested crew.

Then the negotiations began in earnest. For example, because of all the possibilities of turning the operation into a monumental clusterfuck, I wanted a dedicated sixty-day training period to get the guys up to speed; design some new beacons; work with the assigned submarine and her crew and turn loose some of my old contacts and find out what was really happening at Chongjin. Moreover, I wanted to scrounge up some trusty munitions that would get us out of a tight jam if we got compromised.

I didn't consider sixty days too long. In fact, it would be a squeeze if I planned to follow Everett E. Barrett's dictum of the Seven Ps: "Proper Previous Planning Prevents Piss Poor Performance, you geek dickhead," is what the old Frog would growl at me back when I was but a Tadpole.

But sixty days was not acceptable to Pinky, who wanted the mission done—now. Tomorrow.

He pressed me. How come I wanted to stall? Wasn't I the go-get-'em hard charger? He hinted that perhaps I was getting soft in my old age.

I had visions of murder.

Besides, Pinky's plan sucked. I had one top priority: bringing all my men home alive. I know I talk about cannon fodder and SEALs being expendable assets and all of that. But there is no reason to die needlessly. And if I did things Pinky's way, there'd be casualties. There were too many elements. All that flying and dropping and moving around made me nervous. I wanted to keep things KISS-simple. In my cantankerous old heart I felt we'd be better off heading for the North Korean coast in some shitty old indigenous fishing trawler, dropping off into the drink, swimming in and doing our dirty deed, then either heading to sea for a pickup by one of our subs, or—more to my liking—going balls-to-the-wall and heading inland, stealing an airplane, and heading for Japan or Hawaii, depending on what we stole.

Pinky, however, vetoed my loot, pillage, and burn scenario, reminding me that we had been assigned to accomplish our mission without alerting anybody we were in the neighborhood. On the other hand, we finally agreed that choppering out to the sub was less hazardous than jumping. Tally one for the good guys.

But if you're keeping a box score on this, Pinky was the big winner. I lost out on everything from the basic mission profile to the sixty days for training and rehearsing the men.

Pinky gave me a choice. I could go to Japan and commence the mission in forty-eight hours, or I could conduct six days of diving and equipment checkout in California.

I asked him what the catch was.

"No catch, Dick. Except, while you are in California, you'll be required to perform a three-day security exercise at the U.S. Naval Weapons Station, Seal Beach."

"Seal Beach?"

"Must I repeat myself? Seal Beach. And this exercise had better be done by the book. Letter by fucking letter. None of this UNODIR crap. No surprises, or your men all become yeomen. Do you comprehend, Captain?"

Am I repeating myself when I say I had visions of murder? Mentally, I crossed my fingers and gave Pinky an "Aye, aye, sir," spelling it with a *c* and a *u*.

I went back to the Cave and spent the next twenty-four hours in solitary, thinking about the problems I had to solve. And God, were there ever problems to solve. Why, for example, had Pinky assigned us to hit Seal Beach? The last time I'd been there, the Navy had been sued by one of the civilian security employees because of alleged roughness by Red Cell "terrorists." The trial had taken months and cost millions, and its outcome was unsatisfactory to everyone—the Navy settled, but for less than the civilian wanted. I was persona non grata in Seal Beach, and everyone, including Pinky, knew it.

Maybe it was a trap—catch Dickie with his hand in the nuclear cookie jar and send him to Leavenworth. After all, Seal Beach was a sensitive installation what with the strategic nuclear drawdown and the increased reliance on tactical nuclear missiles—Tomahawks—many of which were tested, maintained, and stored there.

Maybe Pinky really was concerned about the security at Seal Beach. Nah—that was too obvious. Maybe he was smarter than I gave him credit for being, and this was all part of some greater scheme that only he knew about. Fat fucking chance of that.

I pondered those questions for a while, but gave up trying to second-guess Pinky Prescott da Turd. There were more important real-life challenges to face.

The DDS I was going to use in North Korean waters was one. The DDS allows SEALs to launch and recover their

SDVs, Swimmer Delivery Vehicles, from a submarine that is submerged. But there are often snags. The rules mandate that a DDS be installed on a sub just prior to a mission and removed immediately after.

The problem is that by doing so you let the opposition know that you're up to something. It's inconceivable to the people who made the rules that bad guys ever look for a U.S. Navy submarine coming into port to have a DDS installed or watch for its return to have it removed.

This was one of the reasons I'd never been a big supporter of our SDV program. You had to be transported by people who never gave a shit about you, the DDS itself was as obvious as a fifteen-year-old's boner, and everyone knew when you'd finished your work and therefore could guess what you'd been up to.

Dry dock shelters are also complicated, Rube Goldberg affairs. The step-by-step outline of a DDS operation in the current NAVSEA—that's the NAVal SEA Systems Command—manual takes twenty pages of convoluted Navy speak prose.

Evidence? You want evidence, gentle reader? Okay. Let's get technical for a few minutes.

In general, and—very important to my well-being these days—*wholly unclassified* terms, the dry dock shelter, or DDS, consists of a hangar where up to four SDVs are stowed (think of it as the garage), the access sphere (the passageway we use to get to the garage from the sub), and a hyperbaric chamber for decompression and recompression of the divers.

The hangar is a cylinder nine feet in diameter, which is flooded during SDV launch and recovery operations, and drained when recovery operations are completed. Diver air-breathing manifolds, located on the hangar's port and starboard sides, supply breathing and scuba-charging air to the hangar.

While the SDVs are in the hangar, they are supported by a wheeled cradle on a fixed track. The cradle is rolled along the fixed track out of the hangar and onto an extended portable track during SDV launch and recovery operations. The hangar's outer door (the clamshell) is controlled by a hydraulic system in the hangar. The rate of movement of the outer door can be controlled by varying the stroke of a valve lever. The faster you hump and pump, the faster the door opens and closes.

The access sphere, which is seven feet in diameter, serves as a lock between the hangar, the hyperbaric chamber, and the submarine. The access sphere is also flooded to operational level during SDV launch and recovery. It has two watertight doors: one leading to the hyperbaric chamber, the other leading to the hangar. Each can be operated from either side by turning the hand wheel, which, through a system of gears, operates a locking ring. In emergencies, the access sphere can be used for decompression of divers if the number of personnel to be treated exceeds the space limitations in the hyperbaric chamber.

The hyperbaric chamber is a sphere seven feet in diameter that provides a sealed atmosphere for decompression of divers. The chamber remains dry at all times. Decompression operations are normally controlled by the divers using control valves located inside the chamber for pressurizing and venting. A Built-in Breathing System (BBS) provides pure oxygen for decompression treatment. A CO_2 scrubber/heater unit in the hyperbaric chamber prevents carbon dioxide buildup in the chamber and provides a warm environment for personnel during decompression.

Think of a DDS as a big, long cylinder that is fastened to the submarine's deck and is reached by going through a deck hatch that opens into the access sphere.

What happens is that with the sub hovering (nuclear subs cannot just lie still in the water, or bottom. They must, like sharks, keep moving because they must force water through their cooling systems), you move through the weapons shipping trunk (that's the place where they load weapons on a submarine), undog the access hatch, and enter the DDS access sphere. After you've done a check, you dog the weapons shipping hatch, enter the hangar, dog the inner door, get into the scuba gear or Draeger bubbleless lungs, flood the hangar, open the clamshell, assemble the track, unstrap the SDV, and roll it out. Then you attach a Zulu Victor Delta, or ZVD, homing-device buoy to the outside of the sub's hull, so your SDV chauffeur can find his way home in the dark. The whole process takes about half an hour, start to finish, complete with "May I?"'s and "By your leave, sir"'s and the requisite Murphy's Law screwups.

That's why I'm a believer in the indigenous trawler technique, or the airborne boat drop. There are fewer steps to worry about, hence less chance of your operation's becoming a major goatfuck.

But I had other, more immediate concerns than ruminating about the tactical problems of DDS operations. For example, I had to lay my hands on some HUMINT about our target area. (HUMINT is HUMan INTelligence in mil-speak. In civilian, it's the information you get from two-legged spies.) HUMINT would tell us something tangible about Chongjin harbor—news we could use when we went in.

It was time to activate the Safety Net. So I called my old classmate Irish Kernan. Irish and I went to the Air Force Command and Staff College in Montgomery, Alabama, together in 1976, and we've stayed fast friends ever since, collecting interest on the wages of sin, no doubt. He's a retarded Marine colonel who's double-dipping at DIA these days, and there's very little that goes on in this world of ours that he doesn't know about.

Irish, a feisty guy wid a tick Noo Yawk accent, was part of my early-warning system when I CO'd Six. He could assemble tactical intel that was fast and accurate. And, despite written instructions from half a dozen panjandrums at Langley, the Pentagon, and the Joint Intel HQ at 1776 G Street to the contrary, he never stopped acquiring human assets.

He didn't want to be seen with me at any of his regular haunts, so we met at Hanecks, a little bar about five miles from Fort Meade where they make great sandwiches and serve ice-cold beer. We sat in a vintage red Naugahyde booth with a fifties Formica table, and with Billy Ray Cyrus providing audio cover, I told Irish what I was doing and what I thought I'd need.

Irish, a chunky welterweight if ever there was one, drained

his Michelob Dry, shifted his knees under the table, and nodded. "Youse got it, pal."

He added that he'd be happy to set up secure comms with us anywhere in the world and wasn't surprised when I told him I had a secure satellite dish in my possession.

"I heard TSD lost one last week from the Navy Yard." He toasted me. "Nice work, Dick."

I tried to look innocent. Belay that. I tried to look not guilty. *"Moi?"*

We had to assemble equipment. That was going to be a problem. Pinky was still the same ball-busting pain in the ass he always was. He'd made it impossible to upgrade the OBE—standing for Overtaken By Events and spelled o-b-s-o-l-e-t-e—equipment that was left in the Red Cell inventory, and it hadn't been fully operational in so long that I doubted it would last through a full mission profile exercise let alone an actual mission that had human lives on the line—mine included. I brought that up to my two-starred boss.

His response was, "So what's your point?"

Then Pinky started playing dirty. He got the SPECWARGRU Two commodore to conduct an administrative inspection on Red Cell's gear to validate/certify its acceptability or operational ability. That process, which involves doing a complete inventory, wasted 72 hours of my men's precious time. The inspection was carried out by the COMSPECWARGRU Two's staff, who knew as much about what worked and what didn't as they knew about brain surgery. Besides, the inspectors—three lieutenants and a lieutenant commander—hadn't done any operating other than the "Nada Regatta" Parade in Coronado. They were too busy dedicating themselves to the winning of the Admiral's Cup for Small Command Participation in athletic events, or working themselves into a lather over EDREs —Emergency Directed Response Exercises—the no-notice exercises run by SOCOM, the Special Operations COMmand based in Tampa.

Well, I'd been stuck with this shit, and before I'd think of deploying it on a real-life black op, I had to wring it out. I wanted to know what was salvageable and/or what I really had to beg, borrow, and steal to get the job done.

Some things have never changed in my life. It seems I've been scrambling, lying, and cheating for better equipment since I was a seaman in UDT-21. I can still see the happy glint in Chief Petty Officer (Gunner's Mate Guns) Everett E. Barrett's eyes as I drove the first half-ton truckload of cumshaw gear—parachutes, parachute rigging tables, and a portable field kitchen, as I recall—into the UDT area at Little Creek. It had found its way onto my truck at Langley Air Force Base in Hampton, Virginia. (To be perfectly honest it wasn't my truck. It was an Air Force truck, but we fixed that with a little paint soon after it arrived.)

Soon after that, Ev promoted me to SFC—Scrounger First Class—and I earned my keep by liberating such necessities as vehicle parts from the Army Quartermaster Depot in Richmond, paint from LANTFLT headquarters in Norfolk, and pallet loads of ammunition from the St. Julian Navy Depot in Portsmouth.

Plus ça change, plus la même chose, as we used to say in Cambodia—the more things change the more they stay the same. Twenty years later, when I was forming SEAL Team Six, I had all the money I needed. But I still had to jump-start assembly lines, requisition items previously destined for other parties who had what I considered a far lesser need than mine, and in a few cases revert back to my SFC ways and just plain steal what I needed.

This exercise was closest to the early, impoverished days of UDT—when you had to make do with what you had or do without completely. I had absolutely no intention of doing without.

We had to get some "sanitary" weapons—lethal and untraceable. Pinky had wanted us to carry regulation arms and equipment. But you don't do that on covert operations. Because if something gets left behind, you don't want the opposition looking at it and saying, "Ah—American Navy SEALs."

So I called my old SEAL Team Six weapons maven, Doc Tremblay, for advice. Doc, a master chief corpsman by rating and a sniper by avocation, was currently in Cairo, serving a two-year sentence in Egypt courtesy of the U.S. government. Don't even think about asking what he was doing there. All I can tell you is that it combined both of his specialties.

As he pondered my request, I could almost see him scratching his big chin. He was a New Englander, and New Englanders like to scratch their chins. Anyway, he told me in his flat Rhode Island drawl about a couple of new Russian SpecWar weapons that sounded promising. He'd read about 'em. There was a 4.5mm pistol called the SPP-1, which fired long, dartlike projectiles underwater. The downside of the SPP-1, Al said, was that it carried only four rounds, and it was hell to reload at thirty meters down.

On the other hand, he continued, there was this new 5.66mm assault rifle—slightly bigger than the M16's 5.56mm bore—that had a twenty-six-round magazine and fired its projectiles up to eleven meters underwater at a depth of forty meters. Used as an out-of-the-water assault weapon, it allegedly had an accurate range of a hundred meters. "And shit, Skipper, I wouldn't use an AK-47 to shoot that far."

Doc, God bless him, said he'd try to lay his hands on two or three of the rifles, and a couple of hundred mags of dart ammo. He told me he was heading to the Defendory arms trade show in Athens in less than a week and said he'd see what he could find there.

Since he was going shopping, I asked him to buy three or four HK-93 assault rifles, and fifty thousand rounds of .223 ammo for them.

"How come, Skipper?"

"Because, as you know, the HK's probably the most ubiquitous combat rifle after the M16 and the AK, and since we can't carry U.S. weapons and I don't want to carry AKs, I'd like to have a few around just in case I need 'em on short notice."

"Aye, aye, Cap. That means you'll be wanting Euroammo, right?"

"Portuguese or Yugo surplus, Doc."

"That's a roger."

Doc said I'd find the goods on my doorstep in about ten days. I gave him a doorstep in California because that's where I'd be, told him to drop the invoices into the system in a month or so, then rang off.

It gratified me to have Doc on the case. But to be honest, another hurdle was even more important than operational intelligence or special weapons.

Red Cell had to learn to work together as a team. Remember all that preaching about unit integrity I did to Joe and the dweebs? Well, this was no war game, and these were no dweebs. But even seasoned professionals like Nasty, Duck Foot, Half Pint, and Pick would take time to gel into the kind of seamless unit I was used to commanding.

That was one reason that, despite all the bitching, I was actually glad to be doing the security exercise at Seal Beach. It would give us a chance to play touchie-feelie with each other under pressure. We'd be able to eat and drink and brawl together during a concentrated work period, a combination that had always worked in the past to build unit integrity quickly.

Indeed, we'd need all the unit integrity we could muster because none of us had done something like this "for real" in years. As I explained above, an underwater lock-out/lock-in is a complicated, dangerous operation that takes split-second timing and substantial concentration. To do it in hostile waters, where you are also concerned about protecting your butt because there are people out there who want to kill you, becomes even more hairy.

And I'd been ordered to do everything I've just talked about with a JAG legal officer and an NIS rep—neither of whom would be clued in to our real mission—hanging off our shoulders while we performed our scheduled security check at Seal Beach. Talk about potential for disaster—this was absolutely casebook stuff.

I knew I'd need some kind of diversion. So I called Mike Regan. Mike's the SEAL with whom I did that walk in the woods from Chompa Mountain to Tri Ton—when I first had the pleasure of meeting Manny Tanto. He's been retired for about twenty years now, but we stay in touch. He's a successful businessman these days, but in his heart he misses pushing the edge of the envelope. Sure, he's a sky diver and a spelunker and a bungee jumper, and he flies ultralights. But as he puts it, "Hell, Rick, it's not the same as when they're shooting at you." He's right, too.

In fact, Mike even went over to what used to be Yugoslavia back in the early nineties. He spent a month there, serving as a visiting and unofficial military adviser to the Croatian forces, so he could pop a few rounds at the Serbian Army through an Armalon BGR .300 Winchester magnum sniper's rifle he'd picked up in London. He claims he made a head shot at nine hundred yards.

Did I say he's making money as if he were printing it himself? Well, he is. Mike owns a boatyard, a hundred-slip marina, a three-hundred-unit waterfront apartment house, and two restaurants in Newport Beach, a chic waterfront community on the coast about a third of the way from L.A. to San Diego. He resides aboard the *Malevolent Frog,* an eighty-five-foot, twin-diesel Matthews, which dates to the mid-sixties, with his second wife, Nancy, a former Pan Am stew who's seven years younger than the Matthews and a hell of a lot sleeker.

Even so, the *MF* is a hell of a boat—it's all done in teak, with lots of leather and burled French walnut inside. There are four staterooms—two with private baths, as well as crew's quarters for six. The galley is state-of-the-art. So is the bar—which features Coors Light and Michelob Dry on tap. He's even got a sauna, a steam room, and a gym aboard. Of course he has a dive locker, too—as well as an escape hatch below the waterline for clandestine insertions. Once an operator, always an operator. The boat may have been built when Lyndon Johnson was president, but it's totally nineties electronically—right down to the same kind of radar used by U.S. Customs.

When I'd commanded the Cell back in 1985, Mike had been kind enough to let us use the *MF* as our seagoing base of operations when we tested the security at Seal Beach. He'd cruised offshore while we surveilled the installation through long lenses. He let Red Cell divers use his escape hatch for their penetrations. And we used the marina, where many Seal Beach personnel lived, ate, and drank, as our own on-site HQ.

He picked up on the first ring. "Regan."

"Doom on you, bro."

There was a slight pause, then a hearty laugh rumbled from 2,800 miles away. "Long time no hear, Dick-head."

"I've been busy. Cooped up."

"So rumor has it. I read your book—nice piece of work, for fiction."

"That's what the Navy spokesman said, too."

"It figures. Say, how come you didn't write about our little walk in the woods? I would have liked my fifteen minutes in the spotlight."

"I did—but the fucking editor cut it. He said it contained too much violence."

Mike laughed again. "Okay, Rick, so what's the story? You didn't call just to tell me to go fuck myself."

I gave him a nutshell dump—at least as much as I could tell him on an open line.

He was silent for a few seconds. Then he whistled long and low. "Tell you what. You bring the boys out here toot sweet and we'll get you straight. I still have some friends around—unlike one asshole I can think of who managed to burn all his bridges."

"What's life without conflict? Fuck you, Mike. We'll see you at the bar at Casa Italia—you know, the place in Huntington Beach we used as our HQ?"

I liked Casa Italia. It was run by an Old World mama-san named Mama Mascalzone. She cooked family-style meals for us that reminded me of the Sicilian food on Old Man Gussi's table back when I was a bare-balled kid in New Brunswick hustling for quarters after school. She gave us the run of the place and didn't mind a broken plate (or two or three) if the boys got a little frisky after an overload of tequila shooters.

Mike interrupted my reverie. "Sure. How will I know when you've arrived?"

"Same as always—just listen for the sound of breaking glass."

I made a couple of command decisions. Pinky would like neither of them, but then again, who cares. First, I fired off a UNODIR to the CO of the Seal Beach Naval Weapons Station, with info copies to the normal batch of admin pukes who wouldn't pay attention to the message for at least six or seven business days. That, of course, was allowing for their coffee breaks, stock market reports, lunches, and happy hours, all the patterns of bureaucratic, desk-bound Navy life that had not changed in the years I'd been gone. Anyway, the message let him know the Red Cell would be paying an unannounced visit shortly, and that instead of letting him decide who did what to whom, we'd play the same nasty-boy scenarios we did years ago, when we wiped the floor with the Seal Beach security force.

Since it was sunny California and near the weekend, I didn't expect a timely reply, although I could almost guarantee that Seal Beach's C²CO—that's a Can't Cunt CO—would list a litany of why-it-was-impossibles to do anything just now, starting with the fact that I was gonna screw up his days off and ending with a nasal whine about not playing fair. Well, too fucking bad.

Besides, our transportation was ready and waiting for us. Pick and Half Pint had staked out a Naval Reserve P-3 Orion that had been sitting on the apron at Andrews Air Farce Base for the past three days. That's the normal parking place for Naval Reserve air crews from across the U.S. who fly your tax dollars into Washington so they can lobby their sea daddies for their next job or slip up to their detailers and lick bootstraps, so the assignment officers will extend their tours in Hawaii or Bermuda.

The latest phenomenon, what with yuppie-scum, two-income families being fashionable and all that, is the long line of married-couple officers showing up at BUPERS—Navyspeak for the BUreau of PERSonnel—to explain that little Johnny and baby Mary were doing so well in school that a move at this time would be traumatic to the domestic tranquility of these two kiddies. Translation: if you move us around like Gypsies, you're going to turn the kids into antisocial psychopaths ten years down the line, and we'll sue.

Another ploy is to say that since it's Mommy's turn for first choice of assignment locations, and she's happy doing whatever the fuck she's doing shuffling papers at NAVSEA, there's no reason to uproot Lt. Comdr. Rufus Throckmorton Ballscratch and his wife, Lt. Comdr. Henrietta Bigsnatch Ballscratch from their Springfield, Virginia, Eden and transplant the happy family to NAVAIR Station Keflavík, where they'd enjoy a ten-month winter and all the Icelandic reindeer they could eat for three happy, isolated, alcohol-filled years.

Maybe I'm old-fashioned, but I always figured that if the Navy wanted you to have a wife and family, they would have issued you one. Anyway, the process is called *orders*. It's not a fucking invitation. End of sermon.

Okay, back to the P-3. We needed a plane because, courtesy of Pinky's bean-counting machinations, we were not going to be supported by Navy logistics. He insisted that detailing a C-9 transport plane for us was too expensive and memoed me to that effect, cc'ing the head of NAVAIR. So I took matters into my own hands. Besides, I decided that borrowing the empty P-3, which was gathering dust on the apron, was a true cost-cutting measure in these days of RIFs and downsizings.

To my way of thinking, by using the vacant plane, we could travel to Seal Beach without wasting another dime of the national deficit on nine full-fare, coach-class tickets, and half a ton of excess baggage. Then an air crew from L.A. could fly it back to D.C., thus getting their flight time for the month.

So, while the rest of the Navy was at happy hour, or busy bagging it for the weekend (it was, after all, Thursday), we talked our way onto the Andrews tarmac, fueled up using a bogus account, and headed for the West Coast, toward more fun and games. We were over Missouri when we discovered we'd somehow left our Legal Eagle and NIS officers back at their desks, and our radio wasn't working.

Quel dommage—what a pity!

Chapter

14

WE LANDED AT LOS ALAMITOS NAVAL AIR STATION AS THE SUN slipped beyond the horizon, putting everybody in the dark —both literally and figuratively. Nasty, Duck Foot, and Cherry slipped into a cab and headed for Long Beach Airport to rent three cars with their false IDs and driver's licenses. By 2000, we were unlocked, unloaded, and on our way to Huntington Beach to check into a motel and—more importantly—to hit the bar at Casa Italia.

I'd already decided to wait until morning before calling the NCC (that's the Navy Command Center to you civilians out there) back at the Pentagon to inform them where I was and what I was doing. Between the weekend, the UNODIR, and Murphy's Law, I figured I'd be able to string my little game out for somewhere between three to five days. That, incidentally, is about the same length of time it took a War Department telex to make its way from a yeoman's outbox to the telegraph operator back in December 1941. The telex in question was to alert the fleet at Pearl Harbor that a Japanese attack was imminent. That should make you all feel real confident about the Navy's ability to react to a crisis, right?

Mike Regan was sitting at the bar when we walked in at about 2100. He grinned and started to get up as I came through the door. But, happy as I was to see him, I waved him off. There was something more important to do first than say hello to an ex-SEAL—there was a woman to kiss. So, I strode behind the bar, swept Mama Mascalzone off her feet, and planted a big wet one on her lips.

Mama cuffed my ears. *Whaaap!* "So, Meesta Dick Marcinko—you back in town, huh?" *Whaaap!* She hit me again and laughed with joy. "Finally you come to pay your respects to Mama, huh?" *Whaaap-whaaap!* "Nice to see you after so long."

Tears in my eyes—she packs a real wallop for someone sixty-five years old who must weigh all of eighty-five pounds soaking wet—I set all four feet ten of her down and formally kissed the back of her hand. *"Mille grazie,* Mama. I always like to come back here." I rubbed my face. "It feels like home when you hit me like that."

Whaaap! "I know." She reached up and chinned herself on my cheeks. "You still a good-looking boy, Richard." She grinned slyly. "It was probably all that jail time. You meet any Sicilians in there?"

"You bet—a capo named Paulie. He looked like your son Anthony."

"Like Anthony? Then he must have had an *organo* a foot long." Mama laughed. I loved the way she laughed. None of your tee-hee's or polite ha-ha's for Mama. Inside her tiny frame were Ethel Merman's lungs. Mama guffawed—she'd throw her head back, open her mouth, and roar unselfconsciously. She wiped her eyes, adjusted her black dress, and looked over the kids from Red Cell.

"New batch of sailors, huh?"

"You know me—I wear 'em out. Like women."

"Well, if you still see Meesta Poosta Roost, you tell him I still got his nugget ring and he's gonna have to come and get it back personal." Her eyes flashed. "I tell you, Meesta Richard, if you was a couple of years younger . . . I give you the workout of your life, believe me."

The thought brought tears to my eyes again.

Then she nodded toward Mike. "Friend of yours?"

"Nah—asshole buddy."

"Good—because I've been insulting him like I insult you."

"And he's still here?" I swung around, hugged Mike, and introduced him to the troops. He looked great—tanned, fit, and expensively dressed, with thick black hair that was turning gray at the temples, giving him a distinguished appearance that I knew was just that—appearance.

It didn't take long to explain the situation to him. I outlined what we were doing in California, told him about my recommissioning, and explained about Pinky.

He listened, then he spoke. What he had to say made sense, too. Then, after an hour and a half of conversation, roughly ten pounds of Mama's lasagna, two loaves of garlic bread, and half a case of Coors, Cherry and Nasty took off in two of the cars for a preliminary sneak-and-peek, Duck Foot took the rest of the boys back to the motel, and Mike and I got off for a little quiet talk where we couldn't be overheard. I had favors to ask.

I returned to the motel just after midnight, unpacked, and waited for my two scouts to return and tell me about the walls of Jericho. It wasn't very complicated. The Seal Beach Naval Weapons Station is bordered by four major thorough-fares. Interstate 405—the San Diego Freeway—runs along the base's northern border. To its west, Seal Beach Boule-vard, six lanes of constantly moving traffic, runs in a north-south direction. Parallel to it is Bolsa Chica Street, the eastern edge of the station. Highway 1—the Pacific Coast Highway—is the base's south border. It doesn't take any effort to cruise around the perimeter and observe activity because there are no fences, vegetation, or other obstacles to get in the way. Moreover, most of the base is contained behind the most elementary eight-foot chain-link fences—easy to climb over. In other words, this was going to be the archetypal piece of cake.

By the time they got back, at 0245, their brief told me I was right. In fact, Nasty, who had been here before, con-cluded that access would be easier than ever, since the USMC security detachment had been disbanded. Why? Because Jarheads cost too much. Now, only sailors and rent-a-cops under the management of NIS were in charge of security.

* * *

I decided that we should start probing immediately, before someone back in Washington realized I was gone—and even more important, to make sure I wasn't being set up by Pinky. So at 0400—0700 Eastern time—I called Washington with my code word, a prearranged signal that told OP-06 I was now in play mode. I made the message brief and failed to give the sleepy four-striper duty captain a number where to reach me.

Then it was off to work. Cherry Enders donned his tights and climbed aboard a European cross-country bike he'd discovered unlocked somewhere nearby (I didn't want to know) and headed for the Pacific Coast Highway. At the Weapons Station's southernmost edge, there's an overpass where the Coastal Highway crosses an access road that is the only land-side access to the water ops section of Seal Beach. From the overpass, one can monitor barge and tugboat activity, as well as watch all the ammo trucks as they deliver ordnance to the barges.

On a previous visit we'd stopped all pursuit by the base security force by blowing up a stolen police car on the single-lane access road while we made our escape by water. I wanted Cherry to see whether history could repeat itself.

I preferred to hit the base from the south, east, or west. The northern border was the best-patrolled. Not by the Navy, of course, but by the old-timers who lived across Westminster Avenue at Leisure World. The retirees there were basically a little bored with life, and due to that and medication, they kept nonstandard hours of existence, making them unpredictable. They also wanted a little excitement in their lives. I discovered that they'd call the police or the base security at a moment's notice—I even got burnt once by them back in 1985. So I've learned to give them a wide berth.

It took Cherry half an hour to make his circuit. He reported that, due to the weekend, there was a lot of leisure-boat activity up the channel. Did I say that there is a civilian channel that skirts the barge anchorage? Well, there is—a channel that runs from the Pacific to the high-rent marina that sits to the southeast of the Station. That was where Mike would tie up the *MF* in about an hour.

I sent Half Pint and Pick to meet him and cruise the waterways. I sent Wynken and Nod to infiltrate the base itself and draw me a map of the nuclear weapons stowage facility to see if anything had been altered during my absence. Blynken and Duck Foot were dispatched to the marshland on the southern side of the base. And Nasty and I began to play with some of the monitoring devices that had been liberated from TSD. There was a pair of fiber-optic TV cameras I liked. I planned to drop them into the weapons locker so I could play the tape for CNO to show him how well NIS was doing at protecting his beloved nuclear Tomahawk missiles. We also had tracking devices— improved versions of what Grant Griffith and Pinky had used at Narita. And we'd also taken scramblers, which allowed us secure communications on our walkie-talkies, as well as a pair of secure cellular telephones.

We spent the rest of Friday and Saturday morning building our IEDs, gathering intelligence, and planning each step of the assault. After the first twenty-four hours on the ground, I was convinced that Pinky hadn't tried to set a trap. The base was operating at its normal—which is to say unprepared—pace. I shuttled between the *Malevolent Frog* and the motel, with an occasional side trip to Casa Italia so Mama could slap me silly between bites of lasagna. By early afternoon Saturday, we were ready. I let the guys grab rays, while Mike and I did some catching up.

I planned to start the strikes at dusk Saturday. I figured we'd do Saturday-night probes to check out the frequency of the roving patrols, monitor the fence line at the nuclear stowage facility, and place the first dozen IEDs on base. Then, bright and early Sunday morning we'd begin phoned threats to find out which one had priority—church services or the base's security.

I hoped to penetrate the stowage facility between dusk Sunday and sunrise Monday. That way, if they hadn't declared me missing in Washington by Monday noon, I'd still have time to fill out a report, sneak our P-3 back to the East Coast, and show my face in Pinky's office by 0800 Tuesday, complete with the videotapes.

At about 1800, Half Pint, Pick, Wynken, Blynken, and Nod and I repaired to Mike's boat, carried our gear aboard, and started a preflight checkout, while Mike maneuvered us out into the channel. There was no operational requirement to use diving gear on this exercise, but I wanted to find out what worked in a real-world environment. The boys' mission was an operational cakewalk: they would infiltrate the restricted cove where the ammo barges were moored and place limpet training devices on the hulls and screws of each craft they encountered.

Mike watched as I examined the Draegers.

"They look like hell, Rick."

He was right. I was leery about letting the men do even the most perfunctory admin dive, let alone allow them to precheck the equipment for a real-life combat situation, because the Draegers were in terrible shape. I fingered one of the rebreather bags. "It's probably been six months since this has been in the water."

"Then there's probably dry rot inside," Mike said. "Let me see." He fingered the harnesses and checked the gauges. "This is shit."

I had to agree. The gauges looked as if they hadn't been pressure-tested or recalibrated in years.

"What's the problem with this?" he asked.

I knew only too well what the problem was. I'd bought all the equipment we were currently using when I formed the Cell back in 1985. I kept it in top-notch shape back then, not to mention pushing it beyond its limits. The Draeger, for example, has an administrative limit of thirty-three feet— that means you're not supposed to go any deeper than that when the units are used. I took Draegers to sixty feet. But ever since the Cell had been authorized to do nothing but normal administrative requalification dives, the equipment hadn't been pushed. Hell—it had hardly been used. It also hadn't been maintained. Why should it be? It was only used every six months in the goddamn swimming pool.

Mike opened up his dive locker. Inside were six brand-new mixed-gas rigs. "My gift to you," he said. "Have fun."

We checked the gear out, then the divers slipped over the

side, took their sacks of IEDs, and disappeared into the channel. They had three hours to accomplish their mission. While they did their jobs, Mike and I cruised the channel, then moored the *Malevolent Frog* just off the wildlife preserve. We changed into wet suits, grabbed our haversack of IEDs, and slipped into the water. The perimeter of the base was about three hundred yards away. We slithered through mud and sea grass, pulling ourselves along foot by foot. Beyond the fence was the stowage area, complete with razor wire and a guard tower. There was a watch posted in the tower, but when we looked through the glasses we'd brought, we saw it was a rent-a-cop. The truck parked alongside told me he did double duty as a roving patrol. That meant *Screw* magazine up in the tower and snoozing and boozing in the vehicle.

Well, why pay attention in the first place? There are no more Soviets, the Japs are our friends, the Germans are busy with their own problems, and the Arab world is an East Coast problem. That's the Navy way of thinking.

I had digital timers attached to the IEDs. We set them for 2200 hours the following night, planted one close to the tower, one on the truck, and one in the grass close to where Mike and I had cut through the fence. The idea was to leave a noticeable trail—so we made lots of marks in the soft ground and tore up the sea grass as we made our escape. The only real problem we faced was the current. Swimming the last hundred yards back to the *MF* was a real chore because the tide was running against us, and we had to work like SOBs to make it.

At 0900 Sunday we called in a threat to the base Command Duty Officer (CDO) and told him we had already commenced activity.

I sent Half Pint and the Pick to check on our plane, just in case someone had noticed it. The rest of us packed for the homeward trip and prepared equipment for the night's assault. Cherry, Duck Foot, and I made a two-hour circuit to see how the base response was progressing.

The situation was normal—in other words, all fucked up.

There were no increased patrols, no intrusive gate checks, no disruption of the creature features such as the PX, commissary, or bowling alley. I called the base CDO to complain and was basically told to go fuck myself.

I hung up. Doom on them.

Pick reported back by phone that he was able to file a return flight plan. "And I sort of refueled, Skipper."

That meant he didn't have proper squadron billing data, so he took the P-3 on a checkout flight over to Long Beach Airport, where he refueled it using his personal credit card. Fuck—I didn't know who was going to be more pissed off, Pick's wife, or Pinky, when he got the bill.

I'd asked Pinky for an operational credit card like I used to have in the old days.

He sat there in his goddamn judge's chair and gave me his giggly faggot imitation. "Fuck you, Dick, tee-hee!" Of course he put it on paper, too.

I got a memo—Pinky cc'd CNO, the head of Naval Logistics, and the base commanders of the Washington Military District:

> If you cannot manage to operate within the system and in a timely manner, your operational needs will not be fulfilled. You have always been a second-rate planner and a slipshod leader, and the system will operate as it is supposed to, not the way you believe it should. Just to be sure you understand things, fiscal flexibility is no longer a term or capability within my glossary of acceptable terms.

By 1600 we were packed, the chariot was fueled and facing in the right direction, the base was wide-open, and I wanted to flay it, butterfly it, and char it. The master plan was to create mass havoc to cover the entry of Half Pint, Cherry, Nasty, and Duck Foot into the nuclear stowage facility. While they made their way through three sets of wire and two sets of doors into the warehouse within a warehouse where the nuclear Tomahawk missiles were stored, the rest of us would create diversions by racing around like Keystone Kops. We'd set off detonators, start fires, steal vehicles, crash fences, cut off communications to the outside world, and generally make nuisances of ourselves. It was the kind of thing you hate to get paid for.

I'd picked my two best pairs to go against the stowage facility. That way one team would get in if—by some unlikely event—the invaders got pinned down by the security response force. Half Pint and Cherry were ordnance experts, Duck Foot was a climbing specialist, and Nasty was a lock-and-cipher man. My instructions were simple: go for it.

At 1800 we checked out of the motel and headed toward the last rendezvous. We stashed our cars and started dispersing to do our separate missions. I started the clock with a phone call from a pay phone across from the main gate.

When the CDO answered, I growled, "This is the Movement for the Free Ejaculation of Palestine," in my best Yassir Arafat imitation. "We are going to kill you all. We are going to loot your women and rape your camels—or is that the other way around?"

He started to reply, but I hung up. It was show time. I gave the primary pairs time to get in position then started the hits, coordinating everything through the three-watt, scrambler-equipped walkie-talkies we all wore courtesy of TSD back at the Navy Yard. First, I activated a firing device down by the piers. That brought the base fire department and EOD unit on the run. Just as they arrived, I detonated the limpets Half Pint, Wynken, and Blynken had attached to the landing craft anchored just off the docks.

That commotion brought the base divers and the duty security patrol to the scene. As they arrived, I was busy cutting the phone lines, while Nod put a small charge on the base microwave tower—just enough to screw up the calibrated signals and scramble the load. Then, while everyone was focusing on the waterfront, Wynken and Blynken ran a stolen car through the main gate. They tossed smoke grenades right into the booth and—oops—set it on fire.

Chased by the rent-a-cops, they left the car—boobytrapped, of course—as a roadblock beneath the Highway 1 overpass, while they made their getaway by climbing up onto the highway and onto a cycle they'd borrowed from the BOQ and prepositioned. I listened to their progress and smiled. The kids were learning.

While Robin Hood and his band were creating havoc, Duck Foot was busy climbing the stowage-facility guard tower to immobilize the sailor on duty. Later, Duck Foot told me he could have had a cup of coffee and a cigarette before the kid knew he was there. Then, with an "All go" loud and clear on my earpiece, I knew we were right on schedule. I looked at my watch. Nasty would be sprinkling graphite powder on the cipher locks—that was the best way to see which numbers were used the most. Then he'd punch them into a pocket computer for the most likely combination variables. While he did that, Cherry and Half Pint were scheduled to break through the exterior vent screens and crawl down the air shafts.

I listened to their progress. They were making great time.

"Skipper—" It was Nasty's voice.

I pressed my transmit button. "Yo."

"You better get down here in a big hurry."

Nasty was not the sort to cry wolf, so I left my observation point just north of Highway 1, crossed the marsh, wriggled through the fence, evaded the IED minefield I'd put down, and went through the wire where the boys had cut it. I waved at Duck Foot, who was perched in the tower, dressed in a sailor suit, and went inside the stowage facility.

The place is smaller than you'd expect—perhaps one hundred feet by one hundred and fifty. The missiles are either crated or placed on racks for preflight inspection. The racks allow them to be forklifted onto dollies for transportation down to the barges that will carry them to the battleships, frigates, or submarines from which they're launched.

Nasty waved me over. There were three Tomahawks on the inspection bench for their preloading check, and half a dozen others in crates, with stamps showing that they were ready to go. Nasty—crazy asshole that he is—had one of the crates open.

"Look, Skipper."

I looked. Tomahawks are twenty feet long. They comprise four basic components. In the rear section, there's the engine—turbojet, with a seven-hundred-mile range—the aviation electronics systems, and the fuel tank. Just in front of the fuel tank is the payload, which can be either conventional high explosive or tactical nuclear. These were tactical-nuke Tomahawks. In front of the warhead is the navigation and guidance system, a computer-driven arrangement about the size of a PC that has target assessments programmed into it, and an infrared radar system to help contour-fly the Tomahawk a hundred feet above the ground, thus defeating defensive radar systems.

"Look, Skipper." Nasty had unscrewed the inspection compartment. I peered inside. There was empty space where the nuclear payload should have been. There is a technical term for my reaction: holy shit.

"I was gonna put a smoke bomb inside," he explained. "But damn, Captain—somebody got here before us and stole the fucking nuke."

Paranoia being what it is, the first thing I thought was that Pinky *had* set us up and NIS was about to bust through the door and arrest us for breaking into a top-secret facility. But there was no way he could have done it—not that he wasn't cunning enough, but the timing wasn't right. Besides, I'd perceived no signs of an ambush during our thirty-six hours of sneaking and peeking—and if I was good at anything, it was sensing danger.

So—this had to be for real. Somebody was stealing missile parts. My first reaction was anger. Goddammit, talk about your goddamn security being lax at the fucking Weapons Station—if this wasn't proof, I didn't know what was.

Then I flashed on Narita—was this another Grant Griffith sting, set up to catch Dickie and make him look bad? Or was Grant as dirty as I'd always thought, and he'd managed to pull an inside job.

An inside job? It wasn't impossible. The Russkies were selling their weapons—you could buy anything from an AK-47 to a SCUD missile if you had dollars, marks, or pounds. Some Polish asshole had recently been caught with an MRV—Multiple Reentry Vehicle—warhead from an old Soviet SS20 missile.

Was a similar enterprise going on here? If it was, I wanted to catch the dirty sons of bitches responsible and kill them.

Taking care not to disturb the seals, dimple the wood, or bend the nails, we opened all the crates. There were two warheads and three guidance systems missing. Given the fact that these missiles were slated to be shipped all over the world according to the destinations stenciled on the crates, it would have been weeks until they were uncrated and the missing parts discovered. It was a clusterfuck of the first order.

"Cherry—"

"Skipper?"

"You bring the TSD stuff?"

"Aye, aye, sir." He opened his rucksack. Inside were five passive monitors—the kind that transmit a locator signal once they've been turned on. They transmit for six weeks. And there were two fiber-optic TV cameras with lithium battery and microwave transmitters, giving them—I hoped—a thousand-yard range, and a two-week life span.

I had Half Pint place the cameras, concealing one above an exposed beam so that the crated missiles could be clearly seen on the mini-monitor, and the other behind an electrical outlet, so we'd have a floor-level shot that would hopefully capture the faces of the perpetrators. The extra-slow-moving tapes in the recording modules would last only 240 hours each—so I hoped the bad guys would visit again soon. Doom on you—you're on Candid Fucking Camera.

There were more crates than monitoring devices. My hunch was that if the place was going to be ripped off again, they'd come for the missiles that had been inspected. So we put monitors inside the navigation-system modules of the three Tomahawks on the inspection bench, replaced the dated seals, and then took the remaining pair of locators and concealed them inside the guidance systems of two in-spected, ready-to-go, but untampered-with missiles.

Then we resealed all the crates, careful to use the same nail holes as before. We policed the area, removing all evidence of our presence, and departed. To create confusion, I had Nasty and Cherry place some IEDs around the stowage facility, to create the impression that we'd been playing in the area but hadn't violated sacred ground.

Originally, I'd planned to use Seal Beach as training for our black-bag jaunt to Korea. Then, the exercise over, we'd been scheduled to fly back to D.C., where I'd make my report to Pinky, try to gather as much equipment as I could scrounge, then leave from Dulles International for Tokyo.

But that would be impossible now. Until we were wheels up on our way to Japan, I wanted to stay close to our TV surveillance cameras and see who the hell was stealing tactical nukes and top-secret guidance systems. One thing was certain: until I found out, everybody except the Red Cell and my old friend Mike Regan was a suspect. And that included the president, the vice president, the chairman of the Joint Chiefs of Staff, and CNO. Improbable? Sure. Impossible? Remember Rule One: never assume.

Two of the more likely suspects were closer to home: my favorite former SECDEF, Grant Griffith, and the deputy chief of naval operations for plans, policy, and operations, Pinky Prescott III. The one thing that made me feel good was the fact that, according to Navy regulations, the use of deadly force was justified for the protection of nuclear weapons. If Pinky and Grant were guilty, I'd be able to kill them legally. And there was no doubt I'd do it.

Part
Three

FUBAR

Dick Marcinko

Chapter

15

RED CELL WENT TO GROUND FOR THE NEXT FIVE DAYS. I CALLED the Pentagon once every twenty-four hours, just to let Pinky know I was alive—I didn't want him to know what we were up to, but at the same time I didn't want him calling out the Marines either. To keep him off-balance I filed an unclassified report on our security exercise and sent it back via FedEx, addressed to his administrative assistant. My evaluation was not going to do the base commander's fitreps any good, and just to make sure that Pinky couldn't bury my report, I sent CNO a copy, addressed to his residence at the Navy Yard.

We stayed away from our usual hangouts and lived aboard the *Malevolent Frog.* Mike and Nancy did the shopping. I did the cooking—a holdover from my days at Gussi's back in New Brunswick. Between meals, we all did the job, which in this case meant infiltrating Seal Beach's weapons stowage area on a random basis to see if anything had been disturbed. Nothing. It was doubly discouraging to come and go at will because we'd just performed a security exercise at the place, and one hoped that, at the very least, the C^{2}CO in charge of the weapons station would have learned *some*thing from all our efforts. Obviously, he hadn't. The place was still wide-open. I can't tell you how secure it makes me feel to have to report to you that virtually anybody with a little bit of imagination and energy can break into a Navy nuclear weapons stowage depot.

By now, my beeper was going off so often I thought the screen was going to burn out. And every time I looked at the digital readout, the number was the same—it belonged to the phone that sat on Pinky Prescott's desk.

After five days I returned his call. I let him jabber at me for three or four minutes about how my report was a load of crap, and I'd exceeded my orders again, and my ass was going to be keelhauled. Given the fact that I certainly wasn't about to let him know about the missing missile parts, I explained—after he'd quieted down a bit—that we'd run into some operational difficulties with the pus-nutted, no-load gear we'd been allotted, and before I was going to let my men commit hara-kiri in the open seas, I wanted to make sure that it worked to my satisfaction.

"Goddammit, Dick, this is a nonsecure line we're on." And he was off on another five-minute jabberfest about assets waiting and opportunities lost, and the fact that people above his pay grade were asking what the fuck was going on, and why wasn't Red Cell doing, you know, what we'd been assigned to do.

I growled right back and used the F-word a lot, and in the end it was decided we'd fly straight to our other destination (that was Tokyo) from Los Angeles, and that Pinky would airlift our equipment from D.C. He appeared to be mollified when I told him we'd move within forty-eight hours.

"Where can I reach you?"

"You can't."

He started to jabber again but I hung up on him. I needed time to think. Obviously, the mission to North Korea was going to be a complete goatfuck. We hadn't had time to obtain the right intelligence or get our hands on the best equipment. Our precious training time had been squandered because of what we'd discovered at Seal Beach.

So I made a command decision. We would go out and do what we'd been ordered to do. But we'd do it quick and dirty, then we'd haul our asses back to Seal Beach and finish what I considered our first priority—finding out who the fuck was stealing the Navy's nukes.

While the boys worked on their gear, I went up and sat on the bowsprit as Mike kept the *Malevolent Frog* on an even course paralleling the coast, three miles offshore, moving toward Huntington Beach at a steady five knots. The easy rhythm of the long, slow swells allowed me to think. Somehow, this entire series of events had to be connected— from the kimchis at Narita to the missing nukes at Seal Beach. The two constants were Pinky Prescott and Grant Griffith. One of them—or more likely, both—was involved every step of the way. They were both probably dirty. The thought of killing them gave me pleasure as I sat, Coors in hand, staring at the water.

There were other things to ponder as well. The Big Question, as they used to call it on the "Errors and No Facts" TV show, was, who could I trust when the whole Navy system was trying to screw me? Mike Regan, of course. And my Red Cell team. But who else? I mean, who could I really trust? The list was discouragingly short. Doc Tremblay? Bet your ass. Stevie Wonder? Absofuckinglutely. Irish Kernan? Maybe. Tony Mercaldi? I gave him a probably, too. With spooks like Irish and Merc you can never really tell. Still, I'd need some operational intel—which would mean calls to both of my spook pals before we left for Tokyo. I could make 'em on the secure cellular—it was untraceable.

Anybody else? It hit me like a ton of fucking sushi. Tosho. I could trust Tosho. He'd always been on the side of the angels in the past—a real straight shooter. And since events were about to carry me back to Jap-Land, I'd need Tosho's backup, not to mention his clout.

Those conclusions reached, I decided to call Tosh as soon as we docked. But I'd be careful about the way that I did it. People were probably listening.

Three hours later, I took down the number of a pay phone in a 7-Eleven three blocks from Mike's slip, went through my address book, and did some fast addition and subtraction.

The phone rang-rang in Tokyo. I asked for Lieutenant Inspector Toshiro Okinaga. The instant he said, *"Okinaga, hai!*" I said, "Fuck you." And before he could answer, I said, "Tosho—don't use names. You know who this is?"

There was a millisecond pause. Then: "Sure."

"Good. I have a couple of problems and need to talk. But we can't use these lines."

"Okay—what do you suggest?"

"You know our mutual friend who lives in the islands?" I was talking about Black Jack Morrison.

"The one who sent you here recently?"

"Yes."

"The big starred one and not the small striped one?"

In other words, Admiral Morrison of the four stars, not my old friend from Sweat Hog days, Captain Tom O'Bannion of the four stripes. God bless Tosho. "Yup. You have his private number at home?"

John Wayne's voice came across the international airwaves. "Bet your ass, pilgrim."

"Okay—when you subtract that number from the number I'm going to give you, you'll have an area code and phone number. Use a secure phone and call it in fifteen minutes." I read off the numbers. "Got it?"

"Roger." Tosho paused. "This is a great scheme. Where the hell did you pick it up—you're not smart enough to come up with it on your own."

"You're right." I laughed. "I got it out of a novel by a former assistant secretary of defense named Richard Perle. Talk to you soon." I rang off, then headed to the phone booth. The scheme Perle had devised in his book *Hard Line* was so KISS-simple that it worked like a charm. It would take anyone monitoring Mike's line—or Tosho's—longer than a quarter hour to come up with the right series of numbers. I didn't care that NSA's big ears would listen in—they monitor so many international calls that it takes them days to sort the information out. By then, I didn't care who knew what I was up to—either my mission would be completed or I'd be dead.

When Tosho called back, I outlined my situation. I told him I'd be coming through Tokyo in mufti with eight people and needed transportation from Narita to Yokosuka, plus weapons and ammo. I explained that we'd be bringing underwater gear, and one trunk of goodies I didn't want customs looking at. I added that he and I needed about half an hour in private.

"No prob, Dick—I'll meet you at the gate."

Tosho was as good as his word. He met us at the gate, smiling like the Littlest Samurai with a Brand-new Sword as he saw who I'd brought with me. He gave Nasty, Cherry, Duck Foot, Half Pint, and Pick *abrazos* that were *fuerte* enough to make me think there was some Jalapeño in this Jap. Then he herded us down a series of passages that led away from the customs and immigration areas. When we finally came to a halt, he eyeballed the new guys.

"The latest cannon fodder?"

"Yup," said Nod before I could introduce him. "I'm expendable."

He took Nod's hand and pumped it. "I'm Tosho—pleased to meetcha." Tosho extended his hand to Dale and Carl. "You expendable, too?"

"Nope—I'm Wynken," said Dale.

Tosho pointed his thumb toward Carl. "That means you're Blynken." He looked back at Ed DiCarlo. "And if you're Nod, nod."

He gave me the old inscrutable smile. "Which makes you Mother Goose. Or was that motherfucking goose shit?"

It was good to see him treat me with so much deference. It was so . . . Asian.

Tosho collected our passports and landing cards. "I'll take care of these. How was your flight?"

"It was pleasant, thank you for asking." I presented him with three bottles of Dimple Scotch. "They had duty-free, too."

Tosho's eyes brightened. "Ah—baksheesh." He accepted the shopping bag with a smile and bowed graciously. "You do know how to buy goodwill, Richard."

We made it from Narita to Yokosuka in about an hour and a half, in a convoy of three police cars with smoked-glass windows, traveling with blue lights flashing and Klaxon horns *ougah-ougahing*. I rode with Tosho in the first car. The normally ebullient policeman was uncharacteristically quiet as we traversed the superhighways, and I wondered what was bothering him. I put it down to lack of pussy, then concerned myself with more important things.

The vehicles' trunks were crammed to overflowing and we carried excess gear on our laps. I'd deep-sixed the Draegers back in L.A. Mike Regan, bless him, had donated his dive equipment to the cause. And the Russian underwater assault rifles, ammo, and HK-93s all arrived FedEx from Doc Tremblay, who'd disassembled them and sent them in a dozen different packages to defy the customs inspectors. The HK receivers—the part of the gun that actually fires the bullets—he'd labeled scrap metal. And they believed him. That should tell you something about the mind-set of most customs inspectors.

Allegedly, Pinky had limpet mines, a pair of infrared cameras, two dozen sensors, and nine MP5K suppressed submachine guns with twelve thousand rounds of ammo and fifty of the new lightweight plastic magazines waiting for us aboard the submarine. I wasn't about to hold my breath waiting to see if they'd all be there.

I used my ID to get us all through Yokosuka's main gate. Then we drove straight to the dock where a sub I'll call the USS *Humpback* waited for us.

The *Humpback* was a modified attack-class nuke. It held thirty-six Mod 7 Mark IV E-46 infrared-assisted, wire-guided torpedoes to destroy other subs. We would share space in the forward torpedo room with the weapons. Above our heads, through the weapons loading hatch, was where the DDS SpecWar platform was attached to the sub's decking. I went up the gangway and introduced myself while the guys unloaded our gear from the trunks of the police cars.

An ensign carrying a regulation Beretta sidearm greeted me at the top of the gangway. Well, he kind of greeted me. After all, I'd been letting my beard grow back—it was just past the Yassir Arafat stage right now—and my hair was as long as ever, and since I was in civvies, he had no idea who or what I was—except I was walking on his hallowed floating turf (or was that floating turd?) and he was gonna find out who the fuck this asshole coming up the gangway was.

He blocked my way. "Sir?"

"Captain Marcinko reporting aboard." I kept moving.

He stood his ground—no way I was going to get around him. "Sir, may I see your ID, sir?"

I liked that. I'd bluffed my way aboard so many submarines that it was actually refreshing to see an officer who cared enough to check the very best. I pulled my ID and my orders from my pocket. "There you go, Ensign. Good work."

He read every word and scrutinized the photograph on my ID card. Then he stepped back and saluted. "Welcome aboard, Captain."

I returned the salute, dropped through the forward hatch, and went to the conn. The skipper was working on charts and graphs. We introduced ourselves, shook hands, then retreated into neutral corners. His name was Kenny Ross and he had that bookish, computer-wonk look that all nuclear-sub drivers have. I had a slew of telexes as well as some useless intel reports waiting for me from Pinky. I watched Captain Ross while I leafed through them. He seemed to have a nice, easy rapport with his crew, and he didn't treat his enlisted men like serfs. Well, maybe he was one of those rare submariners who was more than half-human.

The intel briefs Pinky had sent were cursory at best and dangerous at worst. They provided no operational intelligence at all. Luckily, there were three messages from Irish Kernan that gave me some insight about the forces I was going to operate against. It wasn't much—but it was probably all I was going to get. Pinky's administrative rockets—two dozen of them—were all variations on a single theme, the theme being "What the hell have you been doing to me?" But his threats and invective didn't bother me. He was back there, and I was out here, and there was absolutely nothing he could do to me except use up paper.

Besides, I was reading his words differently now that I suspected he could be part of a weapons-smuggling scheme. Was he excoriating me because he suspected I knew more than I was letting on and he wanted to rattle me? Was he sending us into hostile waters to get ambushed? The puzzle was still too jumbled. Shit—I didn't even know what the fucking picture was yet.

I rolled the rockets up. Ken Ross closed his notebook. "Coffee?" he asked.

"Sure."

We repaired to the wardroom and drew two cups of strong submarine coffee. Sub coffee was the best in the Navy, but from the taste of this, Ken Ross had brought his own gourmet roast with him from the States. I had a second cup.

"You have some packages waiting for you," he said.

I asked what had come aboard and was somewhat surprised to learn that Pinky had actually shipped the weapons he'd promised us. That was good—because there wasn't an MP5 within a couple of hundred miles that wasn't attached to a Japanese policeman, and while Tosho had slipped me a box containing half a dozen Grock-19s in the car, MP5s would have been asking a lot from him.

Captain Ross and I felt each other out. He was polite, even deferential. But he also appeared jittery—uncommon for a sub captain. I guessed it was because he'd been read the riot act about me; told that I'd probably try something illegal—and if I did, he'd be the one to pay for it.

My suspicions were confirmed when he explained he wasn't about to take chances with a billion-dollar sub. I told him that I understood his point of view—all I was looking for was a quiet ferry ride in and a fast pickup when we'd done our job. But I emphasized that we'd need his crew's complete cooperation, and that so far as the mission was concerned, I was senior to him and my orders stated so explicitly.

It wasn't what you'd exactly call a meeting of the minds, but after fifteen minutes or so we reached what you might define as an operational understanding. So I went topside and got the Cell working.

It took them about three hours to load in. While the men toted and lifted, Tosho and I walked down to the end of the pier. We sat, legs dangling over the edge, and caught up.

Despite his outwardly warm welcome at the airport,

Tosho was pissed at me for not staying in touch better and let me know it.

I explained I'd been otherwise engaged. That was all very well, he said, but we'd made a deal. "You said we'd share information, Dick. It hasn't worked out that way—most of the flow has been moving in your direction, and I'm sitting in the dark. But I'm under incredible political pressure right now. Each time the Matsuko connection comes up—like when you called about Miko Takahashi and I started nosing around—somebody from the National Assembly calls my boss and bitches about me, and he feels constrained to haul my ass onto the hibachi and grill me about what the fuck I'm doing. It's giving me Excedrin Headache Number One."

He was right, of course. So, I brought him up to date. I didn't spare any details. I told him about my reentry into the Navy. I explained about my boss, Pinky Prescott, and my suspicions about Pinky wanting me dead. I talked at length about Grant Griffith and described how the former SECDEF had somehow managed to involve himself in the most sensitive national security matters. I told him about Pinky's liaison with Miko Takahashi, and how NIS had a file on him.

Tosho nodded, absorbing every detail.

Finally, I finished my monologue. "Now—you tell me, Tosh—what's the Matsuko angle all about? How come there's all the political pressure on you? I thought Matsuko was in a decline ever since it sold the Soviets prohibited submarine technology and paid a two-billion-dollar fine."

Tosho looked at me as if I were demented, then explained. Two billion bucks was chicken feed to Matsuko Machine. Anyway, that wasn't the point. The point was that Matsuko was run by a seventy-six-year-old named Hideo Ikigami. Ikigami, who had been a young lieutenant in an elite commando unit during the Second World War, was one of those old-fashioned Japanese who believed in the concept of a Greater Japan—a Japan that controlled the entire Pacific Rim.

His position as the head of Japan's fifth-largest corporation gave him influence and clout with whatever government was in power. Then, fifteen years ago or so he had founded—and still led—an extremist political party, the Society of Musashi, named after the greatest samurai swordsman ever, Miyamoto Musashi, a warrior, poet, and artist who lived in the seventeenth century. The Society was growing in popularity these days. It had started with only five hundred hard-core fanatics, but had obviously hit an emotional vein buried deep in the Japanese psyche, because today, more than a million Japanese paid ¥1,250 a year—about $12—to be members. "Remember when I told you how upset some Japanese are becoming about the loss of our classical culture?"

Not really. "Kind of."

"Well, Ikigami wants to banish Western society and reestablish the post of shogun, or military dictator. He wants to bring back all the old samurai ways, hence his Society. He's got the money to do it, too—he's founded a Miyamoto Musashi school for classical swordsmanship in Kyoto. And the Society has opened clubs all over Japan to teach samurai philosophy to youngsters. Except it's not pure samurai they teach—it's samurai mixed with racism, militarism, and autocracy."

That didn't sound so bad to me, and I said so. "We could stand a few more people who promote the warrior mentality, Tosho."

"Not this kind of mentality. Ikigami's a goddamn fascist and a racist. He's paid for a bunch of books written by kooks. Some of them put down Western culture because they argue it's racially inferior. Two more recent volumes endorsed anti-Semitism—and they were best-sellers here. The Society even holds rallies where they promote race unity—kind of like Klan meetings back in the States, or Hitler's Bund gatherings. The Kunika's been looking closely at Ikigami because we think he, or people working for him, are behind half a dozen bombings in the past three years."

Talk about information flowing both ways—Tosho hadn't passed this nugget on to me before. I'd been punching Griffith up in my databases. I should have been investigating Matsuko. I held up my hand. "Whoa. Say what? And *he's* in business with a former secretary of defense?"

Tosho nodded. "Old Japanese saying: 'There's more to this than meets eye.'"

"Roger that." My mind started to factor the possibilities. Like Griffith and Pinky working the scam to end all scams. I dwelled on that while Tosho rambled on.

"Ponder the possibilities. Griffith gets you recalled to duty. You tell me he's got some kind of hold over Pinky—what it is you don't know. Meanwhile, Griffith is also tied to Matsuko. And he was part of the sting you walked into at Narita—where two of the Koreans you shot worked for Matsuko as janitors." Tosho shook his head. "Once is happenstance. Twice becomes a pattern so far as I'm concerned."

I started to pay attention when I heard the word *pattern*.

"Yeah," Tosho was saying, "and your former SECDEF, Griffith, pops up half a dozen times—that makes it a fucking conspiracy."

Yeah, Griffith had been at the center of it all—from siccing NIS on Pinky and his Japanese piece of ass, to his relationship with Hideo Ikigami. "Right. The first time we heard about him was at Narita. He's been part of it since then—every step of the way." I scratched where my beard was starting to come in again. "So Narita's at the center of it—except we don't know why."

"No, but we better damn well find out."

I stood up. "Tell you what—you do the detective work. I've got to earn my Navy pay. I'll page you as we clear the outer marker on the way back. Maybe you can ride out on the pilot boat and we can talk then."

"Okay. Meanwhile, you watch your hairy Frogman's ass out there."

"I will." I handed Tosho what looked like a portable phone. "This is for you."

"Ah, so—verry interesting, American." He examined it carefully. "Is this what I think it is?"

"Yup. Scrambler phone. Cellular. Secure. Rechargeable. My number's programmed in as Zero One on recall. It'll find me anywhere in the world."

Tosho offered his hand, palm up. I slapped it and reversed

my hand. He slapped my palm, too. "Much grass, as we used to say in the fifties." He waved the phone in my direction. "Don't forget—let's be careful out there, Dickster."

"Yeah—I'll do it to them before they do it to me, Tosh."

After Tosho left I took a look at the DDS and the three SDVs inside. A cursory inspection didn't make me a happy camper. The coaming on the clamshell didn't look right, and some of the backup communications on the three modules looked as if they'd been patched together with chewing gum. But I didn't have any choice here. I was going to have to dance—or swim—with the one that brung me.

I left the DDS and went back to talk to the boys. We were bunking together in the forward crew's quarters. Captain Ross had offered me the XO's stateroom, but I refused it, saying I preferred to remain with the troops. It made me happier but it was a little unsettling to the rest of the caste-conscious boat. The Navy is like that. Officer country is for officers, the goat locker was for chiefs, and the mess is for the men, and never the opposites shall attract. I think the sub's master chief, a slim-jim named Bosiljevac, caught on to what I was doing and why, but then he asked me to inscribe his copy of *Rogue Warrior.*

I paid a lot of attention to Master Chief Bo because normally the chief of the boat is the key to how things will be. This one—we were on a first-name basis. I called him chief and he called me sir (and he spelled it c-u-r, which I liked)—was one of the new breed, a high-tech wizard who'd made chief because of his brains, not his fists. Still, he could quote Ev Barrett's law from *Rogue Warrior,* and his language told me he wanted to be a salty old chief, even if he was new breed. I liked his attitude.

We cleared the dock at 0-Dark Hundred and made our way down the channel with a pilot's help. He jumped into his tug at 0240, and we were on our own. I went into the forward torpedo room and spent some solo time, meditating on our situation and going over the probs and stats, which were considerable. Pinky was smarter than I gave him credit for being. If he wanted to get rid of me for good, this was the op that just might do it for him.

- Item: he'd made sure I'd have to use the DDS/SDV route, knowing how little I thought of the system in a tactical world.
- Item: I'd have to hope for the CO to be abnormal for a nuclear submariner, meaning that he'd actually want to take chances. The one thing in my favor was that with my four stripes on again I'd be senior to the CO because it was my primary mission, not his.
- Item: there would be no chance to test the equipment Pinky had sent from CONUS. Sure, we'd go over it with fine-tooth combs, but it would still be untested when we risked our lives using it. That made it clusterfuck material, so far as I was concerned.
  Why? Because:
- Item: Pinky had given me bad equipment in the past. The dry-rotted rebreathers we'd deep-sixed in California, for example, had come to us through my beloved boss. Was his other equipment equally FUBARed?

My reverie was interrupted by a page. "Captain Marcinko to the Conn." I went forward. Ken Ross and his enlisted naviguesser, a first-class named Hatfield, M.O., told me we were about twenty-six hours from a launch point. We wouldn't really know anything about the currents, tides, and other specifics until we arrived in the actual op area.

I thanked them for their info, then headed back to the men. We spent our remaining time prepping our weapons, working over the diving gear, and reviewing our pictures of the minisubs, harbor, and facilities in the immediate area. I gave Nasty the job of plotting an at-sea E&E route, while Cherry worked on inland evasion-and-escape plans. The inland route was a course of absolute last resort. If we had to go ashore, there was no way anybody from the Navy would be coming to get us. We'd be on our own—the expendables.

At 1845 the water temperature in the op area was forty-eight degrees, just cool enough to be invigorating. The currents flowed parallel to the coastline at approximately two and a half knots. That would present no problem for the

SDVs, but plenty for a swimmer. We planned to launch at 2030 to allow all transit in darkness so we could turtle the rigs—that is, surface them for a few minutes and breathe normally—if we had to save air. Nasty, Cherry, Duck Foot, Pick, and I loaded into the hangar at 1900. Half Pint, who was the dive master, had been there for two hours already, working over the equipment. Now, the rest of us began our preflight check. This would be a six-man op, with Wynken, Blynken, and Nod remaining behind to work the comms from the DDS. Why six instead of nine? Because that's all the rigs we had! Welcome to the New Navy—land of the politically correct clusterfuck.

I watched as the men began the ritual, praying that the unit's integrity had gelled sufficiently by now so that we could speak to each other in the "shorthand" that tight, efficient units use on the battlefield. The gritty determination on my men's faces told me it had.

We changed into wet suits. We packed our assault vests. We strapped knives and tactical holsters on. The homing beacons we planned to attach to the minisubs were charged and pinging. Our diving rigs all checked out. We loaded weapons: there were six Glock-19s with Trijicon tritium-powered sights. Each man would carry five seventeen-round magazines of Winchester Black Talon hollow-point ammunition. We assembled the four Russian underwater assault rifles I'd gotten from Doc Tremblay. I kept one and gave the others to Nasty, Cherry, and Half Pint. Duck Foot and Pick would carry the infrared cameras. We had three SDVs. The pairings would be Nasty and me, Duck Foot and Cherry, and Half Pint and Pick.

We performed our normal communications checks with the OOD—Officer Of the Deck—and received word from Captain Ken that we had permission from CNO to commence with the operation as planned. That was typical. Nothing without a "May I?" these days—even the most clandestine of missions. I hadn't bothered to check—but Captain Ken had.

We flooded the hangar on schedule. It's a strange dichotomy—on the one hand, you have to give submariners credit: they are professional. On the other hand, if it ain't on the checklist, they flounder like a dying flounder. We had a momentary pause because the shallow water was giving the planing officer trouble trying to maintain a steady depth. It wasn't a big deal—just one of those things I'd experienced before and he hadn't. As the *Humpback* fought to keep level, I remembered another op when the sub sucked in so much water while launching the SDVs that the boat stalled and started sinking at the stern. When we got back, the skipper's hair had gone completely white.

We left the main deck in our SDVs by 2042, only minutes off schedule. I'm sure the CO announced our departure with a coded signal on burst cycle from his trailing whip antenna. I wasn't keen on the trailing antenna. Pinky had demanded that he be kept advised of my progress. But I knew that in these coastal waters there are indigenous vessels that could get tangled in the antenna. It can also foul itself around buoys and nets—it was all just one more opportunity for Mr. Murphy to make his presence known.

Transit to the target area went smoothly—too smooth for me. We'd launched at one hundred and fifty feet, then come up to one atmosphere—about thirty feet—to conserve air during our twelve-mile run into Chongjin. We kept a loose formation during the run, but were still able to observe each other's position from the side-looking sonar display on the SDV dashboard. It took us a little less than two hours to penetrate the outer limits of the harbor area. There, we dove deep again. That's the normal operational profile: deep launch, shallow transit, and deep approach. Besides, we had enough problems with the mixed-gas rigs because we trailed bubbles, and I didn't want any kimchis catching on that we were in the area.

Even so, I had Half Pint surface his SDV for a peep just as we passed the outer-marker buoys so Pick could take infrared photos of the activity while we followed subsurface in trail. Half Pint was my waterborne point man—there wasn't a SEAL alive who could work an SDV better. After about ten minutes on the surface, he flashed back a digital signal that there were four targets in port.

That was promising. We slowed our approach to barely one knot and stayed at sixty feet depth for our final run, moving up the channel into the center of Chongjin harbor. We finally bottomed at forty-two feet of water, turned on the homing beacons so we could find our transportation home (it was, after all, a *big* parking lot), then said sayonara to our SDVs.

We broke surface about five hundred yards from the minisubs. Moored just past them was a small freighter— maybe five hundred feet or so. That was at first glance. As I paid more attention, I realized that the ship wasn't a container cargo vessel, but a mothership for the minisubs, made up to look like a freighter. I wanted to see more of it up close and personal. But our primary mission was to tag the subs and get our infrared pictures.

The minisubs looked a lot bigger and more sinister in the flesh than they did in eight-by-ten satellite glossies. These were German in manufacture—eighty-two feet long and about sixteen feet in the beam. It was evident they had a huge cargo bay—space for a lot of electronics equipment for intel work, rockets that could be surface-launched, or even missiles.

We split up in swim pairs and went to work. Cherry and Duck Foot, and Half Pint and Pick, each had two subs to tag. It was a piece of cake, so while they placed the monitors, Nasty and I dove and swam to the mothership, which was moored at the innermost dock. We approached cautiously. It was floodlit from above—there was enough ambient light to allow us to use hand signals—and the outlines of this big motherfucker were incredible.

From the number of kicks it took to pass her, she was indeed about five hundred feet long, and as broad in the beam as my ex-wife. We got under her and did a quick hull search.

Voilà! I knew it—she was equipped with a fucking hull recovery hatch door beneath the waterline. It was open and we snuck a look inside. There was a cargo bay big enough to carry weapons, electronics—our whole DDS would have fit inside with five yards to spare. There was certainly enough room to bring a twenty-meter minisub inside and allow it to offload its cargo.

Damn—so *that's* how the nuclear smuggling took place:

the minisubs would bring the goods in underwater. They'd off-load inside the mothership, which was camouflaged as a freighter. Once it was safely aboard, the mothership's crew would containerize the stuff and move it with the rest of the cargo. As usual, Naval Intelligence was an oxymoron—intel weenies relied on TECHINT, not HUMINT. TECHINT had developed the wrong scenario. But HUMINT—in this case, Red Cell—had discovered the truth of the matter. That's why I believe, no matter what the weenies say, you cannot discard human intelligence gathering. It's the only way to really find out what's happening on the ground.

I ran my hand along the mothership, caressing its steel plates. Shit, what a target—I'd suck a roomful of dick to break this baby's back.

Lightbulb. Let's sink this motherfucker and goatfuck the kimchi nuke program right into FUBAR. Why the hell not? We'd completed our mission—the one Pinky gave us to do—we'd tagged the subs and gotten lots of pictures.

But I've always felt that when God is good to you and offers a target of opportunity, you should take it. This was too good to miss.

Okay, I know you're saying that we were ordered to sneak and peek and do no more. And that in blowing up the mothership we'd alert the kimchis to our presence, and they'd take countermeasures—maybe find a new smuggling route. But frankly, hitting a target like this comes only once or twice in a lifetime, and if we hit them right, we could put them months, maybe years, behind their bomb-making schedule. In my estimation, the risk would certainly be worth it.

But later—not now. Now, we were getting low on air. It was time to get back to the SDVs and hightail it out of town. I circled my forefinger in the water. Nasty nodded in agreement. Together, we swam back the way we'd come, our digital locators homing on the SDV beacons.

"Absolutely not." Kenny Ross glared at me as he cleaned his glasses. "The mission profile is precise, and I'm not gonna deviate one iota from it, Dick. That's that."

I'd briefed Ross as soon as we'd cleared the locker and

gotten the pictures back to Washington via burst transmitter. While the boys recharged the systems, powered up the SDVs, refilled the compressed tanks, then took long, hot showers and ate a big supper, I went up to the conn and tried to convince the skipper that we needed another go-round in Chongjin harbor. But Captain Ross was having none of it.

I tried another tack. "Look, Ken, I brought some goodies with me just in case I ran into something like this. So we have the stuff on board." I paused and sipped my coffee—God, it tasted good. I'd been chilled clear through and was still cold from the water. "Besides, it'll give us a chance to plant some more sensors."

"You mean you didn't plant them all?"

I lied. "No. One of the subs was moving."

He thought about that. My mission was to tag all the subs. If I hadn't, then the mission wasn't complete, and he couldn't check all the boxes on his list. That made things different.

"Okay—you can go back. But only to plant the sensor on that last sub."

I smiled gratefully. "You got it, Ken." Then I told him I didn't think it was a good idea to ask Daddy if it was okay for me to go back. I explained that I'd draft a message to save his ass and he could send it UNODIR after I cleared the decks on the next launch.

Actually, I was doing Ken Ross a favor. For him to score—*really* score, like in this case sink a major vessel—in a support mission would demonstrate the need for both this class of boat and the DDS system. Furthermore, he'd be the only submariner in his pay grade with any tactical experience, which would naturally enhance his career.

I assembled the guys in the torpedo room, and while we were charging bottles, I explained about stage two. I told Pick to rig the device. He, Half Pint, Duck Foot, and I would horse the baby into place below the mothership's keel while Nasty and Cherry did a final hull search, took pictures, and suspended the hanging straps.

We'd use only two SDVs this time—less chance of getting spotted. I'd ride astride the bomb as we towed it to the target site—nothing like having a big bang between your legs.

Besides, if there was a fuckup I wouldn't have a thing to worry about. I never wanted to be without my nuts and pecker anyway. We loaded everything in the hangar area by 1200, grabbed a quick lunch, and crawled in our racks for a much needed snooze.

The chief of the boat held reveille at 1800. He was a little surprised that we hadn't completed our mission the first time. I think we disappointed him. Still, I was glad to know the CO hadn't told him what I was up to, which meant one of two things: either he was a typical submarine officer and didn't trust enlisted men, or he was covering his ass and wanted to be able to tell a board of inquiry, "I didn't know what that crazy Marcinko was doing out there." Either way, it was going to be my ass on the line.

We loaded the hangar area 1930 and commenced prep. I gave the XO my UNODIR message for Pinky.

Capt. Marcinko to RADM Prescott: We are returning on-site to complete attachment of beacons. UNODIR if we find a target of opportunity, we will take appropriate action.

Whatever the fuck that gibberish meant, the bottom line was, the system would be happy. If I died or there was a goatfuck, Kenny Ross's ass would be covered. I owed him that much.

We flooded the hangar at 2015 and opened the clamshell doors at 2100. We were approaching the target by 0012. At a range of about a thousand yards, Nasty went to the surface for a peek, just in case the mothership had shifted anchorage during the day. It had—now it was six hundred meters out in the harbor. I wondered about that until I realized that Chongjin's wide channel would allow the twenty-meter minisubs ample clearance for underwater docking. A ten- or twelve-meter minisub can sidle up to the dock and still sneak under the mothership. But these big twenty-meter boats needed space. And what looks more innocent than a freighter sitting at anchor in a harbor?

I ordered both SDVs to surface for a look. When we poked our noses above the water, we saw that the freighter had all its interior lights on, as if it was setting up for a load-unload sequence. The lights didn't bother me. I knew from all the Z-5-Oscar E&E exercises I'd ever done that illumination doesn't bother a swimmer unless he's on the surface, and even then he can function if there's a lot of flotsam and jetsam in the water. So we moved in cautiously at about three fathoms, then bottomed the SDVs in about eighty feet of water just outside the illumination limit of the hull.

Nasty and Cherry went up for the recon and observations while Half Pint, Pick, and I muscled the device onto the bottom and started filling the ballast tanks with air. We were hoping to get a negative buoyancy at about thirty-five feet, which was the approximate depth of the keel. I patted the device. It contained about two hundred pounds of C-4 explosive. When it went off, the shock wave would lift the ship right out of the water. The explosion would enter the cargo bay and rupture the ballast tanks, then drop the freighter back in the water with its asshole wide open, sucking water like an enema.

My reverie was interrupted by the seventh member of our assault team. Mr. Murphy had tagged along for the ride. I heard blade tonals and looked up to see a kimchi minisub approach from out of the darkness. I admit my first reaction was close to panic. Then I realized that the sub was operating blind—there were no TV camera lights on, and so we were safe. I watched, fascinated, as the sub slowly made its way alongside the mothership. Then it bottomed, settling on the harbor floor so the captain could begin the long process of ballasting, which would allow the sub to maneuver up under the cargo bay hatch opening.

Cargo bay hatch opening—shit—Nasty and Cherry were up there shooting pictures. I explained to Half Pint and Pick through our swimmer-to-swimmer comms what I was about to do and waited until they gave me thumbs-up. Then I left the bomb and swam up to see what was happening. I found Nasty at twenty-five feet, clinging to the mothership. Clinging is right. The mothership had started its own recovery sequence, and it was beginning to shift in the water. This was going to be much hairier than I'd thought. I explained what was happening with hand signals. Nasty nodded and pointed toward the stern, where Cherry had taken the camera.

We made our way back along the hull hand over hand, fighting the vibration of spinning screws and the sea suction that was coming from the induction ports. We discovered poor Cherry hanging on for dear life to a stabilizer, the cumbersome camera slung over his shoulder like a deadweight. I took him by one arm, Nasty grabbed the other, and the three of us kicked our way to freedom, heading down toward the SDVs and the explosive device.

We would have to wait until the minisub had actually entered the hatch and begun to unload before we could make a move. I have always hated this stage of an operation. There's nothing to do, you're getting cold sitting on the bottom on your SDV, and bodily functions still have to take place. Well, I'd shower later.

Finally, after two hours of what might be called sitting and shitting, the minisub made it up into the cargo hold and blew its ballast. Now it was time to move—quickly. I wanted to get the bomb rigged before the minisub changed position and snagged one of the girdle lines rigged to our device. Pick had rigged a triple-threat detonator: there was a remote firing device, an antiremoval device, and a tremble switch that would activate when water turbulence hit five knots. The six of us swam the device up under the mothership just aft of the underwater hatch, used our limpet-mine magnets to secure the girdle lines, then suspended the cigar-shaped, six-foot plastic tube about twelve feet below the keel, and about the same distance from the minisub's hull.

I sent Nasty and Cherry into the mouth of the cargo hold with their camera to try to get a snapshot or two of what was going on.

I pointed at my watch and held up five fingers. That's how much time they had. Cherry gave me a thumbs-up, his hand signal clear in the ambient light from the freighter. Then I pointed down toward the SDVs. That's where they'd go when they finished. Another affirmative.

Pick, Half Pint, and I swam around making a last check. Everything looked right. I gave Pick a thumbs-up, and he armed the device. We turned and dove. I checked my watch. It was 0300, and I was sweating profusely inside my wet suit.

Now all we had to do was get back to the *Humpback* before the motherfucker blew. Because if we were within half a mile of the explosion, we'd be killed by the concussion ourselves. I sat on the back of Half Pint's SDV and made the universal hand sign for a cavalry charge—let's get the hell out of here!

We'd been under way about thirty minutes when we were hit by the shock wave. You don't hear anything—it's like you're just picked up and slapped around by a big, angry bar bouncer. The SDVs bucked like broncos and rolled uncontrollably. The glass in the instrument panels shattered. That was incredible—no noise, but it was like they just blew up. Then my ears took one hell of a beating, and I almost lost my mask.

I signaled to surface, and we fought our way up from six fathoms. The chop was bad—about eight feet—and the wind was terrible. We bobbed like fucking apples on Halloween. I tried contacting the sub. Nothing. The fucking comms were out. Blown by the concussion. I pointed toward the compass. Half Pint gave me a thumbs-down. I saw the other SDV about a hundred yards away and pointed. Half Pint steered toward it. Riding the surface was like riding a roller coaster, and I felt like whoopsing my dinner. I would have if I hadn't shat it in my pants three hours before.

We lashed the SDVs together. If we were going to die, we'd do it as a team. Unit integrity to the end. I looked over at Nasty Nick. The motherfucker was actually smiling. I wondered why until he tilted something in my direction. It was a Silva compass that had survived in his waterproof container.

He verified our direction. God bless Grundle. Once a point man, always a point man. We turned due south, our backs to the harbor, submerged to twenty feet to get out of the chop, then hauled ass. I figured we'd go another twenty to thirty minutes, then surface again and sit. Maybe the sub would see us. Maybe, by some miracle, it would pick up our props. If not, we had our underwater assault rifles, and we could shoot each other. Or we could swim for land—a mere twenty miles. Neither prospect enthused me very much. We ducked under the surface and drove on south. After half an hour we surfaced again. Still no contact.

Maybe he'd see us if we stayed on top. So we bobbed like corks for another forty minutes. I was just about to take us down again when Cherry caught site of a periscope. My sphincter pucker factor increased until I discovered it was one of ours by looking at the cammo pattern. Damn— Captain Ken was doing one hell of a job. There was no way in hell we could have found him.

He slowed his boat to a hover; we cast a line around the periscope and waited for the recovery crew to surface to help us down and in. Frankly, we were too exhausted to do it ourselves. We left the SDVs and swam down to the hangar, went through the locks, peeled off our gear—God we smelled bad—then checked each other for lumps and bumps. I examined everybody's eyes for signs of concussion. Nothing. Nada. We were all okay.

That was when the pandemonium broke loose. Shit, we'd done what SEALs are supposed to do—we made a lot of noise with high explosives and probably killed a bunch of people in the bargain. That felt good.

We were still high-fiving each other when the recovery crew brought in two mangled pieces of shit masquerading as SDVs. Damn—Pinky was going to have a cow. Those vehicles weren't going anywhere—except as donations to the UDT/SEAL Museum at Fort Pierce, Florida, where my old point man from Vietnam, Jim "Patches" Watson, is the curator.

Showered but still hyper, I made my way to the bridge and thanked Kenny Ross for saving our butts. In my book he was a real hero, and I let him know it.

He took my gratitude modestly, explaining that he'd heard the explosion, changed course to place himself in a straight line with it, and cruised slowly, listening for the sound of our SDV screws, which he'd programmed into his computers. I told him I'd never make fun of computer wonks again, and the look on his face told me he believed me.

Then he held up a message that had my name on it. "This

came in about two hours after you left. I figured there was no rush to give it to you."

I took the envelope out of his hand, opened it up, and read. The words brought a smile to my face:

"RADM Prescott to Capt. Marcinko: Under no circumstances put any targets of opportunity under attack. This is an unequivocal direct order."

I showed Ross the message. "Captain Kenny, I swear that I had nothing to do with anything other than my original mission."

His expression was all business. "That better be the case."

"It was the case. Yeah—there was an incident. But I was there. I know what happened."

"Okay," he said with more than a little skepticism in his voice, "you tell me what happened."

"The Koreans had a foul-up during the off-loading process. A bad accident—a real clusterfuck. They actually lost a minisub and a mothership."

He looked at me intently. His career was on the line and he knew it. "Are you sure, Dick?"

I nodded. "Yes, Ken—that's the way it went down."

He shook his head, a perplexed, pained expression on his face. This wasn't the way things worked aboard nuclear subs. Improvs weren't allowed. The world ran according to the plan on your clipboard. But then, as slowly as a Pacific sunrise, a big, happy, shit-eating grin spread mile-wide across his face and he high-fived me. "It was a damn shame, too, Dick. A real damn shame."

Chapter

16

TOSHO GOT US OFF THE SUB. I GAVE HIM A GROWL EIGHT HOURS before landfall on my scrambler cellular, and he came chugging out on a pilot boat run by his Kunika boys. We transferred while we were still ten miles offshore. No need to alert prying eyes as the *Humpback* sailed hi-diddle-diddle straight up the middle of the channel into Yokosuka, the DDS sticking out below the sail like a sore deck.

I waved at Ken Ross as we headed northwest into the chop. Ross and his master chief, Bo, gave me a double thumbs-up from the sail. I made a mental note to send two SEAL wall plaques to the *Humpback,* one for the wardroom, the other for the chief's goat locker. He was the first nuclear dip-dunk—certainly the first Academy nuclear dip-dunk—that I'd ever actually liked. Pinky had sent six messages requesting my scalp, and Ross had actually deflected them. The shore patrol would probably be waiting for Red Cell when he docked—but thanks to Tosho, we wouldn't be available.

Once we were under way, Tosho and I talked in a corner of the wheelhouse, catching up. He said that despite word from above to lay off, he'd been taking a real close look at Matsuko, and he didn't like what he'd seen. He was running computer taps on the phones, he said—black-bag jobs—but wasn't picking up much because most of the calls were

247

scrambled and to unscramble them he would have had to go through channels.

"But there's been a lot of traffic between here and L.A., and here and D.C.," Tosho insisted. "They can't hide the numbers they call, just what they say."

"Who do they call?"

"Your old pal Grant Griffith gets a lot of the traffic."

That made sense. "Any other calls to D.C.?" I recited Pinky's number.

"Nope. Only to Griffith's law firm and the Matsuko offices."

"Too bad. Was there any time the traffic peaked?"

"Yeah, about eight hours after you cleared the harbor. By the way, whatever happened at Chongjin?"

"Where?" I played dumb. I trusted Tosho with my life—but not my operational secrets.

"Don't shit a shitter, Dick—I know where you've been, and that except for the North Korean reaction to what you probably did, you'd be in the brig by now."

"Oh?" I wondered what he meant.

"The evidence. Exhibit A." He extracted a piece of paper from his foul-weather gear. It was a top-secret DIA report that was based on findings from the Foreign Intelligence Service—the Russian successor to the KGB, which was now sharing information with its old American adversary. Its date stamp was three weeks old.

North Korea is performing applied military biological and nuclear research in a number of its universities, medical institutes, and specialized research facilities. It is receiving technological aid from German firms and has also hired a number of scientists from the former Soviet Union. The major port of entry for smuggled nuclear and biological material elements is Chongjin, where FIS sources report concentrated activity.

"And now, exhibit B for the prosecution." Tosho extracted a second sheet of paper and handed it to me. It was a CIA telex addressed to Japanese intelligence in response to a query about an explosion at Chongjin.

Satellite reconnaissance reports a massive explosion in the Chongjin harbor area. As already reported on open channels, official North Korean reaction is that a domestic NK container ship loaded with phosphates suffered a methane gas incident, hence problem was totally internal. Air sampling obtained through [NOFORN CODEWORD PROGRAM] detects no methane. Further, photo recon of area suggests freighter was broken in half by explosion, suggesting placed charge. Extensive damage also to 20-meter Seawolf-class diesel submarine. Source of damage is unknown to USINTEL.

"One plus one equals two. That's what the Jesuits at Notre Dame taught me."

"Look, Tosh—"

"Like I said, Dick, don't shit a shitter. This came straight from our intel liaison in Washington," Tosho snapped. He gave me the document. "Keep it. Kind of amazing, huh?"

"What?"

"First, that you Americans, with all your technogoodies, can't trace the source of the explosion. And second, which is more germane to you and me, old buddy, is that even the bureaucrats at CIA trust me—and you don't." He scowled at me. "Maybe your goddamn admiral should have thrown you in irons. He was on the phone to my boss, y'know, demanding that if we saw you, we turn you over to the CO at Yokosuka. Then, after the fucking Koreans refused to confirm anything, he had to call back and say it had all been a big mistake. Mistake, my Japanese ass."

I stuck my index finger in the center of his chest and pushed back slightly. "How the hell am I to know what you've been cleared on and what you haven't? Shit, Tosh, this thing's been a goatfuck from the beginning. A fucking former secretary of defense is selling secrets—or worse. He's probably the ringleader of a fucking nuclear-smuggling cabal. The admiral—my goddamn boss—*he's* probably in it with Griffith right up to his ears."

"Talk is cheap, Dick. I'm protecting your ass."

He was right, of course. "Okay, okay, okay—here's what

happened." I gave Tosho a thumbnail sketch of what we'd found—told him about the minisubs and the ruse used by the kimchis to mask the unloading process. He seemed mollified, but who could tell. I thought for a second, then added, "We got pictures, Tosho."

"Can I see 'em?"

Of course he could. I mean, this was a guy who'd protected my butt; a guy who trusted me enough to hand over a Glock—which was no small deal in this country, where pistol-toting *gaijins* were verboten. "Yeah, yeah—if you have the right computer equipment."

"Right computer equipment?" Tosho laughed. "This is Japan, Dick-head—land of the rising microchip."

The prints were a little fuzzy—Cherry's no Yousuf Karsh. But the images were clear enough for my needs.

I used a magnifying glass. "Tosho—"

"What?"

"Look at this."

He peered over my shoulder. "Holy Toledo."

The sequence was unmistakable. The minisub wasn't off-loading. It was taking on cargo.

Tosho scratched his chin. "I wonder where the hell it's headed."

"Me, too." The answer to that question, I knew all too well, was that we'd never know—because I'd blown the motherfucker, and its motherfucking mothership, to kingdom come.

Doom on me. There are times when I have been known to shoot myself in the foot. This was one of them. This time, Pinky's orders had been righteous. The original intelligence assessment I'd received at the briefing in Washington—which was, that the ships transferred nuclear materials to the subs, which then took them to their final destination—was probably correct. I'd screwed up royally.

Mike Regan met the plane at LAX. He'd taken care of hiring us three cars. I'd made Tosho a present of the Russian underwater assault rifles. In return, he'd made sure that our MP5Ks, Glocks, and the remaining C-4 explosive were all packed aboard the ANA 747 without a fuss from Japanese customs.

We claimed our luggage and three trunks, I used my ID card to get our stuff through customs, and we headed for Mike's place.

I'd spent my time in the air drawing lists of what I knew and what I didn't know. Now, with Mike heading for his house, I sat in the passenger seat of his Porsche and read what I'd scrawled.

I knew that from the minute I'd blundered into the Grant Griffith/Pinky Prescott sting at Narita, my life had become a seemingly never-ending series of clusterfucks, moving from SNAFU to TARFU to FUBAR. Narita was written in capital letters.

I knew that Grant Griffith had me recalled to active duty. Why? The answer was KISS-simple: because it was easier for him to keep tabs on me as Captain Richard (NMN) Marcinko, U.S. Navy officer, than it was to monitor Dick Marcinko, freewheeling civilian. And who was doing the tab-keeping? Pinky Prescott III. Pinky da Turd. Grant's probable partner in crime. Their names were also writ large.

And then all sorts of other things started to fall into place. I realized, for example, that Grant had tried to have me killed during the war game. Not for his vicarious pleasure, as I'd previously believed, but because he thought I was dangerous—someone who could upset the plans he'd so carefully crafted. Why did he think it? Because he knew what I'd discovered at Narita.

What had I learned there? That kimchis were engaged in a nuclear weapons smuggling program.

But I also knew that somebody was stealing pieces of Tomahawk missiles out of the Naval Weapons Station at Seal Beach.

I also knew that—wait a fucking second. How did I know the kimchis were trying to smuggle the crate *out* of Japan?

Answer: I assumed it.

What's the First Rule of SpecWar? Remember, I told you you'd see that material again? Okay—the First Rule of SpecWar is: never assume.

Why couldn't they have been trying to smuggle the

detonators *into* Japan? Or maybe, since they were switching crates, Grant was double-crossing Pinky and he was going to sell his own detonators to the North Koreans after they'd been "lost." Except I blundered into the switch. I started drawing circles around names, places, and events. The connections were real enough. Anything was possible. Anything at all.

Now I wanted to see the surveillance tapes from the weapons stowage area more than ever.

The pickup at Seal Beach went smoothly. No impediments to our entry or our extraction. I stayed aboard the *Malevolent Frog* while Nasty, Cherry, and Half Pint did the sneak-and-peek, with Wynken and Blynken providing backup. They were back within two hours, carrying the precious video cassettes.

I pulled the boys aboard. While they'd been out, I'd been working the galley, and I had big pots of sauerbraten, red cabbage, and boiled potatoes ready for them. While everybody chowed down, Mike and I went into the big main cabin and played the tapes on his VCR, using an adapter.

Mostly, I ran at fast forward, because nothing was going on.

But then—about one hundred thirty-four hours into the cassette—there was something.

"Look at this."

We watched as eight people made their way into the locker. They hadn't come the way we had, which meant they had a key to the place. Five were small—they looked oriental. It took me a minute, but I realized who they were—it was Team Matsuko from Grant Griffith's war game. The others were Americans. The point man was Biker Jordan—I recognized him right away from the bowlegged way he walked. The man keeping track of the Japs and holding a suppressed HK submachine gun was Buckshot Brannigan.

The last man in was a big, hatchet-faced son of a bitch who carried his HK in the crook of his arm and wore his hair in two flat braids. I knew him but didn't say anything. I wondered how good Mike's memory was.

"Geezus." Mike's jaw dropped about a foot. "I know that big guy—it's—it's—Manny Tanto, the fucking Jap Indian from Tri Ton who skinned the VC alive."

Give the man ten points. I guess some things you never forget.

Buckshot had a small knapsack slung over his shoulder. Manny Tanto carried a satchel. Biker Jordan had a canvas tool bag. Biker opened his tool bag, extracted a knife, and with Manny's help, began to open one of the crates, moving carefully so as not to damage the security seals. When he got it open, the Japs surrounded it like medical examiners at an autopsy. Carefully, they pointed at the Tomahawk innards, then engaged in an animated discussion with Buckshot.

From the body language, Buckshot seemed to be saying that they'd have to take bits and pieces. The Japs kept shaking their heads—they pointed at the crates. They wanted the whole enchilada.

When they finished talking, Manny sealed the crate, and the group made its way out, the head Jap still gesticulating in Buckshot's direction. I scanned the rest of the tape, but there was no activity.

"Nasty?" I shouted toward the galley.

He appeared, his plate piled high. "Yeah, Skipper?"

"They didn't take anything, huh?"

"Seems that way. All the monitors are where we left 'em."

"Okay. Thanks."

"No prob, boss."

That's what he thought.

By now Pinky had to be going crazy. He hadn't heard from me since I'd left the sub. Well, it was time to tantalize him a little bit. So about midnight I phoned the duty captain at the National Command Center and had a message relayed to him. I reported we were back in CONUS—that's the CONtinental United States to you cake-eaters—picking up supplies and devices in the Los Angeles region, and that we'd be disposing of excess ordnance we had cached on our way west to the Far East. I told the duty officer to pass the word that we'd be home soon, traveling commercial nonstop to Dulles, and we'd report to OP-06 as soon as we landed.

Depending on the duty captain's schedule, the implicit urgency of the message, or his whim, my report would either be called immediately to Pinky in quarters or would be hand-carried to his administrative assistant sometime the following morning. I'd phrased things so as not to ring any warning bells—that way, the message would meander through a bureaucratic maze of in/hold baskets. Starting with the AA, it would move to the admin secretary, thence on to the staff aide, from there to one of Pinky's executive assistants, then finally to the bottom of some pile in Pinky's office. This was one time the system was going to work in my favor.

Because I was hoping to be landing at Dulles about the time Pinky'd get around to it.

Meanwhile, I started playing Sherlock. Back at Mike's office I pulled out the L.A. phone books. I found Matsuko Machine listed in the West L.A. book, on the discreetly named Avenue of the Stars in Century City. Then I checked all the other usual suspects.

Centurions International, Buckshot Brannigan's security company, had an office in the same building as Matsuko. Gee, what a coincidence.

And guess what? Jones-Hamilton, the defense contractor that made the detonators I'd discovered at Narita, had an office in the very same building that housed Matsuko and Centurions International. Gosh and golly, Captain Midnight!

Grant Griffith had an office there, too. I called the number next to his name.

"Mr. Griffith's line."

Time to play solly, wrong number. "Oh—sorry, I thought I was calling Jones-Hamilton."

"You are—Mr. Griffith maintains an office here."

Gee whiz. "Is he in?"

"No, sir, but may I take a message?"

"I'll try him in Washington. Thanks."

Next, I called Centurions. "May I speak to Mr. Brannigan, please?"

"He's in conference. Who may I say is calling?"

"Snerd. Herman Snerd. From Petaluma. About Mr. Brannigan's insurance. I'll call him at home. No need to leave a message."

I rang off. Mike and I sat across his desk from each other and talked things over. It seemed to me that I had two choices. I could go back to Washington and deal with Pinky—confront him with the evidence I had and see what he'd do, or I could stay here and deal with the problem at hand—stolen tactical nuclear warheads, detonators, and guidance systems. Either way, I was going to be in trouble.

On the one hand, if I returned to D.C., I was going to be at a real disadvantage. If Pinky was dirty, if he was a part of this thing, he could sink me any number of ways because I was operating in his area of operations—the Pentagon— where he had a lot more clout and knew a lot more people than I did.

On the other hand, if I stayed in L.A. and staged a raid on the Jones-Hamilton offices to gather information that would sink Grant Griffith, I'd be breaking into a civilian facility—a court-martial offense under military law. Further, when I broke and entered, I'd be committing a felony under civilian law. And if I did get inside, there was no guarantee I'd find anything.

But on the third hand, if there was any real evidence about Griffith's involvement with Matsuko, or with the weapons smuggling operation, it would probably be found in his office—or Buckshot's. Besides, I rationalized, my ass was grass no matter what I did. Pinky would see to that. So I'd do what I do best when confronted with a tactical dilemma—I'd attack.

First priority was intelligence. You get intel through recon. I gave the job to Cherry, Duck Foot, and Pick. They drove to Century City, parked, and meandered through the lobby, making notes about the location of passenger and service elevators, emergency exits, fire stairways, and janitorial closets. They got onto the roof and discovered a cable rig for outside window-washing that could be used for emergency egress if necessary. I sent Nasty in a separate car with a portable scanner to detect ultrahigh-frequency transmissions that are common to all electrical cipher locks. That way we could break in without the telltale graphite dust. Once he discovered which frequency they used on the locks, we'd use a Motorola MX-360 radio, which would lock onto the cipher frequency and print out the sequence for us.

Half Pint was detailed to find a countersniper position in an adjacent building, just in case things really got out of hand. We didn't have the 50-BMG-caliber McMillan sniper's rifle I would have wanted, but Half Pint was deadly at five hundred yards with an HK-93 and a twelve-power scope—and Doc Tremblay had just happened to send us four HKs, one sniper's scope, and a bunch of hand-loaded .223 that was sniper-accurate out to 550 yards. I sent HP and his HK to the Beverly Hills Gun Club, an outdoor range on the site of the old Twentieth Century-Fox Studios, to zero the rifle in. Finally, Mike and I, dressed in suits, would reconnoiter the Jones-Hamilton offices.

I wasn't sanguine about this op. If Buckshot was as sharp as he used to be—and there was no reason to suppose he wasn't—he'd know I'd recon the area before I did anything, so he'd probably have watchers posted all over the high-rise where he and Grant Griffith had their offices. Sure, I could recognize Weasel Walker or Sally Stallion, but Buckshot wouldn't use them—he'd use retired L.A. cops or former FBI and Secret Service agents, the pool from which most security companies draw their talent.

Thinking logically, both Buckshot and the former SECDEF would probably figure that their L.A. offices were my third-choice target—after The Hustings and their Washington headquarters. It was true, too. I would have liked to have hit Grant's East Coast offices. But I hadn't had the opportunity—Pinky had kept me otherwise engaged.

But Buckshot would also know that target priorities change. Besides, Buckshot and his top lieutenants were here—not in D.C. They had to be because they were about to steal a bunch of missiles from Seal Beach.

So the odds were definitely not in Dickie's favor. That was an understatement. The odds sucked, the timing was terrible, and the chances of success ran from slim to none.

So what? I didn't have to like it—I just had to do it.

* * *

The Jones-Hamilton offices took up 15,750 square feet of the thirty-seventh floor of the Century Park Towers East, a forty-one-story high-rise that looked like it was the role model for the skyscraper in the movie *Die Hard.* Centurions International leased 5,000 square feet on the twenty-fourth floor, while Matsuko rented the entire twenty-second floor —26,500 square feet, bigger than a dozen million-dollar apartments in Tokyo.

Mike and I cruised the perimeter of the building in his Porsche, and the truth of the matter is that I was impressed. I look at things differently from the way you do. When I see a building, I try to think of the ways in which I could bring it tumbling down. This one would be hard. It was sturdy— built to withstand the earthquakes to which southern California is prone—and it was easily evacuated. There were two subterranean garages, each with eight lanes of ingress and egress. One emptied onto Avenue of the Stars, the other you got to by way of Santa Monica Boulevard.

It was imposing in a sci-fi sort of way. The facade was a mélange of shiny, black marble, polished ministerial-gray granite, and dull slate. The lobby, an atrium five stories high filled with forty-foot trees, two waterfalls, and escalator-hills alive with the Sound of Muzak, was about the size of a football field. The first three floors of the atrium were filled with dozens of fashionable boutiques, mini-cinemas, and the sorts of espresso bars and tofu takeout in vogue with the Armani-clad, designer-water-and-smoked-trout crowd that inhabited the building.

That was the front of the house. Backstage, it was different. All pipes and electrical conduits and gray paint over the concrete. High-rises are very much like hotels or ocean liners—an entire support network is hidden behind the gilded facade. And most of the residents never notice that it's there. They only know it if their trash isn't picked up or their lights go out or the air-conditioning screws up. And the people—the janitors, electricians, security guards, trash handlers, and maintenance techs—they're invisible. That's what made our job so much easier.

There were five service elevators. Duck Foot rode them all, dressed in a Federal Express uniform he borrowed from somewhere, and dragging a hand cart filled with FedEx boxes and envelopes. I like that boy. Imagination is what makes the difference between a good SEAL and a great SEAL. Cherry, carrying an L.A. Power & Light ID, worked his way into the electrical room and flagged the most important circuits—like the ones to the Jones-Hamilton, Matsuko, and Centurions International offices. Then he dropped by the phone room and placed half a dozen passive monitors where they'd do some good.

Pick, dressed in the ubiquitous blue overalls that render the wearer invisible to anyone in a suit and tie, worked his way through the building's air-conditioning and vent system. There were literally miles of conduit-lined passageways, accessible behind panels and locked shaftway doors, and Pick examined many of them. Like Theseus making his way through Minos' labyrinth, he left subtle signs behind so he—and the rest of my argonauts—could find his way.

After an hour and a half split between the car and a walk-through of two nearby shopping malls, curiosity got the better of me. Mike and I parked in the big garage off Santa Monica Boulevard, took the elevator to the lobby, and wandered around to see if anybody paid special notice to us. We seemed to attract no attention. So, after ten minutes, we rode up to the thirty-seventh floor and got off.

Jones-Hamilton shared the floor with a huge brokerage office. The defense contractor's offices lay to the left as you got off the elevators, behind massive French walnut doors. Alongside the door was a magnetic card lock. Instead of a cipher lock, you opened the door by running what looked like a credit card through the slot. The magnetic tape told the electronic lock to open. So much for Nasty and his radio monitor.

Mike punched the down button just as the door opened and two suits marched in lockstep unison out of the Jones-Hamilton offices. They were former straight-leg Army O-6s—colonels, from the broomstick-up-the-ass look of them. They wore matching West Point rings, cheap brown suits, and Hush Puppies. They carried black Samsonite attaché cases festooned with decals picked up at arms shows and expositions, and luggage tags that bore the Jones-Hamilton logo.

We all waited in silence. They looked me up and down. My beard was coming in nicely now, and my hair was shoulder length. I had it tied in a short pigtail. I wore black canvas slacks, loafers with no socks, a polo shirt, and my brown leather bomber jacket. The suits liked none of it—you could see it on their faces. They wrinkled their noses as if I hadn't bathed. Mike and I smiled and nodded at them. They nodded back somberly, and when the doors opened, they gestured that we should precede them into the elevator.

We rode down in silence—although I bit my tongue so hard I drew blood. But I saw no need to send up any flares. Too much was at stake. The elevator made five stops. By the time it hit Atrium Level Two it was jam-packed, everybody standing silently, staring at the digital floor-indicator and listening to the Muzak version of "'Round Midnight."

Suddenly, Mike pointed toward the door and started forward. We elbowed our way through the crowd, pushing and mumbling, "Excuse me, excuse me, pardon me, sorry," as we shimmied our way out.

The doors closed behind us. I turned to Mike. "How come you wanted to get off? We could have ridden straight to the garage on that elevator."

Mike didn't say anything. He led me through a series of stores and boutiques, window-shopping and chatting with salespeople as we went, then took the escalator down to the lobby. He waited as I noted the location of the security TV cameras, glanced behind the desk where the building's rent-a-cops did their monitoring, and peered at the elevator control panel. Then he beckoned me to follow. We descended to the third parking level where Mike found his Porsche and climbed in.

"What was all that about?"

Mike said nothing. He simply put his index finger in front of his lips and winked at me.

Then, as we drove out onto Santa Monica Boulevard, he flipped something into my lap.

I looked. It was a man's wallet.

Mike turned the stereo system on, and 120 watts of fifties bebop filled the interior of the car at about eighty decibels, all atonal piano, contrapuntal trumpet and sax exchanging riffs, and explosive drumming. He slammed the padded leather steering wheel in time with the music and grinned at me. "You might need what's inside," he said.

I extracted the embossed magnetic card that read JONES-HAMILTON.

A happy smile crossed my face. "God bless you, my nefarious son."

"The Muzak made me do it."

"Huh?" I was confused.

"In the elevator. I was influenced by Felonious Monk."

Chapter

17

BY THE EVENING AND THE MORNING OF THE THIRD DAY, WE'D gathered enough information to begin making a plan. I decided to hit both Centurions and Jones-Hamilton. It was risky. I'd be dividing my force, unable to provide either squad any significant backup other than Half Pint's sniping position. But I came to realize that we had to see Buckshot's files as well as Griffith's. After all, it was Buckshot, Manny Tanto, and Biker Jordan who'd gotten the Japs from Matsuko into Seal Beach, and I wanted to learn what their plans were for getting the nukes out of the country. So my new guys were going to get their wish—they'd be the cannon fodder going to Centurions, led by Cherry and Pick, while Nasty, Duck Foot, and I hit Jones-Hamilton.

That left things pretty thin for when Mr. Murphy made his customary guest appearance, but it was going to have to do. Mike volunteered to come along with us, but I turned him down. I didn't want to have to explain to Nancy why her dearly beloved was about to face twenty years in the slammer for breaking and entering. Instead, I assigned him as our mobile communications center and general backup.

He had a big, forest-green Range Rover that looked right at home in the Hills of Beverly, so he'd be able to cruise all night without attracting undue attention. We'd outfit him with one of our secure cellular phones, then turn him loose on the streets while we sneaked and peeked and shooted and looted.

Speaking of shooting, in one of those rare strokes of luck, it turned out that all the relevant offices faced west, which meant that Half Pint and his trusty HK would be able to set up shop on the roof of the tower next door and have a clear shot into both sets of offices. Thanks to Doc Tremblay, we had five hundred rounds of hand-loaded custom-made, armor-piercing ammunition, which flew straight, true, and deadly at distances up to five hundred yards.

Most factory loaded 5.56 ammo is effective only out to about 150 meters, after which it loses much of its punch—at 275 meters, for example, it has less than half the energy of a 7.62 NATO round. This stuff, however, was a real hot load. It was knockdown lethal, even in a crosswind—and Half Pint would be firing about 175 meters at most.

My original plan had been to strike on Saturday night, a move that gave us several tactical advantages. First, being a weekend, it was less likely we'd surprise people in their offices. Second, the weekend security people, who didn't see the occupants on a daily basis, would be less likely to realize that we were interlopers. And third, if we did our jobs well, it would be Monday before anybody discovered we'd come a-calling. And by that time, I planned to be back in my own king-size bed at Rogue Manor.

We had to alter our plans at the last minute. When Mike cruised the area at 1930 Thursday, he discovered a convoy of tractor trailers and mobile homes being parked on the far side of Century Park Towers East. He stopped, asked questions, and discovered that a movie company would be filming location scenes for some fucking action-adventure film on, around, and inside the building where Half Pint was to set up his countersniper position.

Mike called to let me know what was happening. "That's going to screw up your plans, Dick."

Not necessarily. "The revolutionary soldier," Mao Zedong once wrote in his Little Red Book, "should move through the masses like a fish through water." That is a doctrine I take to heart.

In Vietnam, my men wore the same sandals as the VC. We also wore black pajamas, carried AK-47s, and ate the same cold rice balls and *nuc mam* fermented fish sauce as Mr. Victor Charlie. That way he could not find us because, instead of sounding and smelling like Americans, we walked like he did, smelled like he did, and used the land like he did. We could find him, but he couldn't find us. Doom on him, because we killed him in great numbers.

Now, too, I saw immediately many advantages to using the movie set as a background for my own real-life production of Demo Dick goes to Hollywood.

For example, the place would be crawling with real cops assigned to security, as well as hundreds of extras in cop uniforms, SWAT battle fatigues, and tiger-stripe cammies. So, instead of sending HP and his HK into the area in mufti, at 1900 on Friday evening, I simply dressed him like a SEAL, gave him a lip-mike radio transceiver, and dropped him off carrying his HK in its Pelikan hard case—just like the other SWAT guy extras. It took him, he said when he checked in by radio, about sixteen minutes to get up to his position.

"How come so long, Pint?"

"I stopped by the catering wagon and picked up dinner, Skipper. I can recommend the tricolor pasta salad, the smoked turkey breast and garden peas, with cranberry-grapefruit coulis, and the tofu-pudding dessert."

I told him what he could do with his dinner. He said he'd prefer to ingest it from the top side.

He had to get off the air now—ten guys in SWAT uniforms were coming onto the roof. Extras—to be filmed from a chopper, he whispered five minutes later.

The pandemonium caused by the filming would give us wonderful camouflage. There were lots of bright lights, hundreds of strangers moving around the area, scores of vehicles, and enough confusion to allow us to do the job and get out without attracting any attention. So—we'd dress as if we worked on a movie set, mix and mingle to achieve our cover, then make our hit and disappear into the crowd again.

* * *

Mike dropped me a block from the Towers, then swung around to let Nasty and Duck Foot off closer to where the actors were congregating. We'd planned to rendezvous behind the building. I shouldered my way through the crowd of gawkers and watched as my Red Cell people climbed out of the Range Rover. It was like the Marines coming ashore at Mogadishu—lights, cameras, action. The sight-seers thought they were part of the cast because they started snapping away with their Instamatics and clamoring for autographs as soon as the pair of SEALs climbed out of the Range Rover.

I wasn't immune, either. On my way north on Avenue of the Stars half a dozen chattering teenage girls in $100 jeans with holes in the knees, po' boy sweaters, and imitation boondockers asked if I was Steven Seagal. No, I said, smiling, I really *do* kill people for a living. They thought that was hilarious and asked me for my autograph. I signed Pinckney Prescott III with a flourish and a lewd wink. "Come visit me at the CIA."

I linked up with my guys and stood watching as the director, an effete-looking bearded guy in sweatpants, a marijuana-leaf sweatshirt, and a Chicago Cubs baseball cap, rode up on a bright yellow, thirty-foot hydraulic crane to survey his empire strapped into what looked like an office chair. His domain was considerable. There were two choppers on the ground—a police Huey and a blue-and-white Hughes 500 camera chopper—a phalanx of police cars and fire trucks, hundreds of lights, and at least a dozen cameras. There were huge cranes and hydraulic platforms that allowed the camera to go ten stories in the air, and hundreds of yards of what looked like miniature railroad track, so the camera could move along with the police vehicles as they cruised up to the building.

Nasty and Duck Foot pushed ahead of me. I think they were a little uncomfortable with the crowd. I lagged behind, watching fascinated as special-effects technicians taped squibs and wires to a bunch of bulletproof vests.

"Who're they for?" I called over, pointing at the vests.

"Stuntmen," the tech yelled back. "For the gunfight close-ups."

So that was how it worked—the special-effects techs pushed buttons, the squibs exploded in sequence, and what the moviegoer saw was some guy being stitched by a submachine gun. Nice. Realistic.

I had a more effective technique, of course, but it would have meant working with disposable stuntmen.

Another tech was setting charges inside a car door. When he set them off, it would look like the car was being fired on. A third special-effects man was loading HK magazines with 9mm blanks. I guessed they'd be given to the guys playing SWAT teamers.

A good-looking blond-haired woman in a white Italian warm-up suit stood watching me watch the special-effects men at work. She was carrying a walkie-talkie and had legs about half a mile long. We made eye contact. I heard the trumpeting of mating elephants in my ears and headed in her direction. "Hi," I said by way of introduction, "what's all the ruckus?"

She was only too happy to explain the obvious. "We're shooting action sequences for *Terror Tower Two* tonight," she told me. "It's a movie about a bunch of terrorists who hijack a high-rise. Tonight, we're shooting the on-site stuff— the SWAT team assault, and the terrorists beating them back. We'll do the close-ups on a soundstage."

I nodded. "Sounds exciting." I looked her over. *Kreegah.* Tarzan want. Better looking than the herd of water buffalo he's been dating. I couldn't take my eyes off her chest, which was remarkable. Extraordinary. Noteworthy.

Her eyes wandered up and down, too. "Want to stay and watch? I could find you a place where you could see everything."

"I'd love to—maybe after work."

She scrutinized my face. "You look familiar. Work in the neighborhood?"

"I do tonight." I paused. "What's your name?"

"Melissa Gold."

"Like in Gold's Gym?"

"Yup. What's yours?"

"Dick."

She was staring at me quite intently now. "Is that a noun or a verb?"

"It's a proposition." I laughed. "And you're Gold, of the eighteen-karat variety, I presume."

"Twenty-four."

"My mistake." The name suited her—she had one of those perpetual tans you can find in southern California and other quasi-tropical places, which left her the color of precious metal. And she had great muscle tone, too. The thought of those legs wrapped around me was intriguing. I told it to her like it was. "I'd like to work out on your bench sometime."

Her eyes twinkled. "And I'd like to see your, ah, squat thrusts."

I winked back. "Maybe we'll get to wrestle later—if we're both lucky."

"Maybe—have a nice time at work."

"I will." I made my way through the crowd and continued north, to Santa Monica Boulevard. The line of semis and mobile homes stretched around the block, running alongside the back side of the Towers. I linked up with the boys and we made our way around the east side of the Towers, away from the lights and the crowds, and quietly talked things over one last time.

Then we slipped on our surgical gloves and set off in different directions. I led the Jones-Hamilton crew. Pick had found a nonmonitored service door during his recon. He'd flagged it with UV. I flashed my UV minilight until I found it, then we picked the lock and went inside.

We were traveling light on this one. We'd changed our appearance so we could blend in with the movie people. I wore a black turtleneck and chinos, no socks, soft shoes, and my hair tied in a short pigtail. Nasty and Duck Foot wore black SWAT BDUs and combat vests and carried suppressed MP5Ks inside ballistic nylon cases. Cherry, Pick, and the new guys wore black BDUs. Cherry and Pick had their SEAL Team Six undershirts—those are turtlenecks made of Kevlar similar to the fabric armor used to make everything from shark-proof diving suits to oyster-shucking gloves. I'd first seen the stuff in a *National Geographic* TV special back in the eighties and designed the high-collar shirts for my men. Nobody was going to garrote or slice them if I could help it.

We locked and loaded our HK submachine guns before starting out. I hadn't planned to carry automatic weapons, but since the Cell could pass as actors tonight, there was no reason not to. The only difference was that the bullets in our magazines were real.

We climbed six flights of service stairs, to another door that had been labeled by Pick. Duck Foot jimmied the lock and led the way into a huge shaft used for running electrical conduit, air-conditioning, and communications systems. This immense passageway was one of the benefits of modern construction: between fiber-optic lines, security camera and cable-TV cables, telecom wires, five long-distance and fifty private local telephone companies, burglar alarms, intrusion devices, telexes, fax lines, and computer network interconnects, you had to build these huge, wide, high passages inside every new office building, or your tenants couldn't run the wires to all their equipment.

In my earpiece, I could listen to Cherry and his people as they moved toward the Centurions offices. The reception was spotty. These were NIS radios, and they were second-rate. At SEAL Team Six we'd had Motorola build us transmitters that would work inside glass and concrete high-rises. These receivers were shit—they conked out when faced with too many electrical fields from too many computers, faxes, and other gadgets, each with its own transmissions. These radios had been designed for simple field ops, not urban warfare.

We moved down the passage, toward a second doorway that would take us to a set of fire stairs leading up. Duck Foot played with the lock and sprung it. We crossed the hall, opened the fire-stairwell door, and began the climb. No way would we use the elevators and let the rent-a-cops in the lobby know there was movement in the building.

We hit thirty-seven in less than five minutes, caught our breath, and then slid into the hall. The walnut doors were to my left. I held the magnetic card in my hand. I approached the Jones-Hamilton offices and checked the entrance out. I slid the card into the strip. The door clicked open. I hit the radio button and whispered, "Entering Target One."

We moved inside. It was dark, but not unnegotiable, as the glass walls were lit from the outside by the movie lights. We made our way past the luxurious reception area, down a long, thickly carpeted hallway, into the wing containing the executive suites. Like most offices, it had been laid out with no thought of security in mind. I saw no sentry lights or visible alarms, motion detectors, or intrusion devices. People prefer convenience to security—which benefits people like me, not to mention burglars, rip-off artists, and other assorted felons.

Nasty was on point, his HK at the ready. I followed him, and Duck Foot brought up the rear, protecting our butts. Griffith had the corner suite, facing north and west. The door to his outer office was locked, and Duck Foot went to work with his ubiquitous picklocks.

It took him less than thirty seconds to get the door open. I moved into Griffith's suite. "Inside," I told Half Pint across the street.

"Roger. All clear. No movement." There was static interference on Half Pint's line. Then I heard other voices in the background. One came through loud and clear. "Who're ya talking to, pal?"

Half Pint's voice came back in my direction. "Just getting into character, you asshole. Leave me alone."

I blinked. "Huh? Half Pint?"

"Actors," he stage-whispered. "There are a bunch of other actors here."

"Oh." He'd handle it. I had other things to think about.

I rifled Griffith's desk but found nothing. I started on the files. There were hundreds of account files—I snagged the one labeled MATSUKO—and lots of correspondence addressed to a lot of important people. But there had to be something—something. We pulled the pictures off the walls looking for a concealed safe. *Bubkes.* In frustration, I switched on the 486 Dell that sat on Griffith's credenza and ran a directory. I'll bet you're surprised that he hadn't locked the computer or set up a password access system. Well, in real life, secretaries usually follow the security procedures pretty well. But big-time executives are just too busy to keep passwords and other time-consuming stuff in their heads. So they don't. With the result that what's on their computers is usually there for the taking.

The Dell had one of those removable hard drives—and the drive bay was empty. Either he had it with him, or it was somewhere here in the office. I rolled the antique Oriental rug back—sometimes there's a floor safe. *Nada*. But the son of a bitch had to have something. You don't get to be Grant Griffith and not have a safe in your office.

I looked around the room. Desk. Credenza. Sofa. Two wingback chairs, between which sat a solid-block coffee table. I took a closer look. The "table" was actually a box made of inlaid wood. I lifted the box and discovered that it concealed a small document safe with a cipher lock.

Bingo. I pointed in its direction. "Nasty—"

He gave me a thumbs-up and went to work, powdering the cipher lock with graphite dust and playing with the keys.

While he played safecracker, I flipped through the files again. Duck Foot had the computer on, searching for files that might hold something. I pulled a Minox out of my pocket. The Minox is the original spy camera. It's about the size of a package of gum, it operates with 16mm film, and it has no bells and whistles at all.

There are newer cameras, like the ACMEL high-performance job with its electronic shutter and autofocus, but the Minox is a KISS camera, which is why I like it. You point it, focus according to a chain that stretches from the bottom of the camera to the edge of the document you're photographing, and snap away. It will give you razor-sharp pictures.

I laid the Matsuko files—both the Japanese and English papers—on Griffith's desk and started shooting them, working backward chronologically. Damn—the most recent date on an outgoing letter to Hideo Ikigami, Matsuko's CEO, was today. That meant Grant Griffith had to be in L.A. And that if we found the removable disk drive, we'd probably hit the mother lode.

We worked like fucking beavers for what I thought was about ten minutes—it turned out to be almost half an hour when I finally looked at my watch. I'd shot about one hundred pages, including a bunch of government documents stamped SECRET that even a former SECDEF had no business keeping around his office. That alone would sink Griffith—but I was in search of bigger things.

Nasty finally made it through the cipher lock and we opened the safe. I peered inside. There was the removable hard-drive cartridge. I picked it up. It was labeled TOMAHAWK.

I slipped it into the computer and ran a directory. Damn—we'd found the mother lode. He had the works here—everything from an inventory from Seal Beach to an Auto Cad program that gave us the entire schematic design of the Tomahawk-IA/n missile. This was CNWDI stuff—Critical Nuclear Weapon Design Information—classified in Category Sigma. That meant it was compartmented so far above top secret, even I couldn't imagine the code-word designations—and I've seen 'em all.

A second directory was labeled NAVY. I accessed it and discovered a mini-database of embarrassing details about the private peccadilloes and professional misbehavior of more than a hundred current and retired admirals—among them, Pinky Prescott III. Damn—I had hit the fucking jackpot. It was Griffith's blackmail file. I dropped the disk into my pocket and shut off the computer. It was time to move. "Let's close up shop."

I turned toward the window. "Half Pint, you hear that? We're moving."

HP's voice came through loud and clear. "Roger that."

"How's the other location?"

"Quiet. Haven't even sighted our guys yet."

How could they be that far behind schedule? Maybe the Centurions offices had better locks than Jones-Hamilton. Probably did. Probably had intrusion devices, motion sensors—the works. I chuckled to think of Pick and Cherry locked out of their target. I'd rag their asses when we caught up with them.

Half Pint's voice crackled in my left ear. "I've—" There was a break in the transmission.

"HP."

Another static crackle. "Can't—"

Damn—the fucking radios were fritzing. I moved to the window. The black Hughes 500 swooped low above Half Pint's location. They were probably filming. "You're gonna be in pictures," I told him. He answered, but his signal broke up. "Say again. Say again."

"—broken . . . window, Skipper."

Duck Foot and Nasty were stuffing papers in their combat vests. They stopped when they heard Half Pint's transmissions. Duck Foot saw the look on my face. "Skipper?"

I didn't know what the hell was happening. I couldn't see. I hoped he was shooting or doing something. "Get off the roof. Get off the roof. Get down. Link up outside the Towers. We're on our way."

Time to move. "Cherry."

There was no answer.

"Cherry—Pick—Wynken."

Silence. Static. "Blynken—Nod. Goddammit." Something was wrong. Very, very wrong. Feverishly, I started to put Grant Griffith's office back the way we'd found it. But there was no time for that. "Get the hell outta here—to the Centurions offices. This is turning into a clusterfuck."

They were in the service stairwell on the thirty-third floor, coming up as we were coming down. I almost took a round in the face. Somehow, I got out of the way. That's the way it's always been with me. In Vietnam, I remember stepping on a land mine. Nothing happened. The guy behind me put his foot in the same place—he lost his leg. Once I ran through a minefield barefoot. I could feel the detonators between my toes. Nothing exploded. The ARVNs behind me were cut to pieces.

North of Chau Doc, on the Cambodian border, the night before Tet, 1968, I was on patrol with my wonderful gang of shooters, Eighth Platoon. It was after midnight and I was on point. I'd stopped. Every molecule of my body was tensed and alert. My nose twitched like a bloodhound's, searching for the VCs' distinctive body odor, accentuated by the *nuc mam* they poured on everything they ate.

I knew there was something out there—I could fucking feel it. And then—I don't know what made me do it—I just dropped like a goddamn stone. At the instant I did, the muzzle blast of an AK-47 came straight at me from no more than ten feet away.

If I'd dropped half a second later, I would have been dead. What made me drop? I don't know.

Now, the same thing happened in the stairwell. I stopped. And I dropped. As I did, a bullet struck the cinder-block wall where my face had been a quarter second before. A shard of concrete cut my cheek.

There'd been no warning. The only sound was a *chuuuunk* as the goddamn thing thwocked. It was a fucking hush puppy—a suppressed pistol.

I flipped the fire selector switch on my silenced MP5 submachine gun to full auto and dropped over the steel-pipe stair rail, rolling toward the outside, the rough concrete wall to my back, firing three fast two-round bursts as I came, ducking as the rounds ricocheted off the concrete and the stair rails.

From below, somebody shot back, silenced rounds caroming off the walls and stairs.

We sucked concrete, rolled toward what cover we could find, and returned fire. For about fifteen seconds, the stairway became a goddamn shooting gallery, with hot brass flying everywhere and bullets coming from strange angles.

We poured it on—I used two of my three mags, then flipped the HK over my shoulder, drew the Glock, and fired an entire extended mag down the stairwell. The fucking explosions deafened me—and probably everybody else, too. Until now, all the fire had been from suppressed weapons—there'd been a lot of ambient noise from bullets hitting concrete and steel, but now I'd opened up with a fucking Austrian jackhammer and it was *loud*.

I dropped the mag, loaded a second, and fired six more rapid shots. When the echoes cleared, there was silence.

My antennae went up. I moved cautiously. Nothing. I stuck my nose over the edge of the stairwell. Silence. It was over as abruptly as it had started.

Nasty and I moved cautiously around the corner leading to the thirtieth floor, his MP5 and my Glock ready. We peered down. Empty. No sounds except for the spent casings that rolled everywhere, jingling as they fell into the stairwell.

"Everybody alive?" I looked them over quickly. Nasty had a ricochet cut on his face. Duck Foot's ear had been nicked. There was blood on the back of my hand, and I could feel wetness on my neck—but nobody'd been hit.

I pointed to the next floor. "Come on."

We ran to the twenty-ninth floor and changed stairwells. We were sweating when we got to the Centurions offices on twenty-four. The door was ajar. We went through in the approved manner I'd designed at SEAL Team Six. Nasty went first, HK ready. I went second, my Glock covering the opposite field of fire, and Duck Foot brought up the rear, his back to mine.

We swept office to office in total darkness, our flashlights probing the corners. The windows were blacked out— except for one office in the rear. When I knew we were clear, I turned the light switches. Nothing came on. I ripped the black plastic sheeting off the windows so we could see what the hell was happening. We found Wynken in what must have been Buckshot's office. He was lying in a puddle of blood staring at the ceiling, his throat slit deep across the carotid artery. From the position of his body and the depth of the wound, he'd been killed from behind.

Blynken was in the next room—the one with the broken window. He'd been shot in the head from close enough to leave a powder burn on his neck. Weasel Walker lay on the floor six feet away. Bullets had shattered the night-vision goggles he was wearing. The back of his head was blown off. At least my guys had got one of 'em.

Noise outside. We deployed, guns ready, and almost shot Pick, Nod, and Cherry.

"What the fuck—" Then I saw that Cherry was hurt—a lot of blood on his arm. Pick was dinged, too.

"Sorry, Skipper." Cherry collapsed on the rug, his back against the wall. "They were waiting inside—they'd blacked the windows. They must have had night vision. It was a clusterfuck."

"How many of them were there?"

Nod shook his head. "Don't know—four, maybe five. I'm

guessing. They made it real hard to get in—goddamn electronic locks and cyphers—then they rolled over us from two directions."

"We regrouped, then followed 'em as they headed for you—caught 'em from behind," said Pick, pulling a first-aid kit from his vest.

So the bad guys thought they'd been caught in a pincer. That was why the gunfight in the stairwell had stopped as quickly as it had started. "Then why the hell didn't we sandwich 'em and finish 'em off?"

"We ran out of ammo, boss," Nod said. "They didn't know it, but we were dry. Then Cherry got hit."

Cherry winced as Pick applied first aid to his arm and stabbed him with a morphine ampoule. "I took one round —just about the last fucking shot they fired before they bugged out. It went through clean, but goddamn it hurts."

I watched in silence. There was nothing to say. We'd been worked over by a bunch of pros. I'd probably been spotted during the sneak-and-peek I took with Mike Regan. Or maybe they noticed my men as they did the recon. However it had happened, we'd been sandbagged. The fuckers had shot up my secondary and had been on their way to get Nasty, Duck Foot, and me when we'd collided in the stairwell. Now, the bad guys were outside—waiting, armed and dangerous. We were in here—with casualties.

Instinct took over. My mission was the computer disk that was in my pocket and the pictures in the Minox. This was all secondary. Still, the place had to be cleaned out. Our KIAs had to be moved. No SEAL has ever been left on the field of battle, and I wasn't about to break the tradition now.

I snatched a trash liner from a wastebasket. Nasty did the same. We wrapped the corpses as best we could. No need to leave a trail of blood, and there was a lot of blood, believe me.

We worked without talking. Nasty draped Cherry over his shoulder in a fireman's carry. I took Wynken's body—damn he was heavy. Duck Foot grabbed Blynken and we headed for the hills—or more precisely, the stairwells.

I am not used to losing men in battle. In more than thirty years of active duty I lost only one. This made three. To make matters worse, they'd died on a mission the Navy wouldn't recognize—a black-bag job that had been my harebrained idea in the first place—which meant no benefits to their families. But I had more immediate concerns than survivor benefits right now. I had to get us out without taking any further casualties. I had to get the bodies into Mike Regan's Range Rover without anybody seeing them. We had to find Half Pint.

And then, once we'd regrouped and I'd put the disk and pictures in a safe place, we could start killing the people who'd been killing us. And kill them we would. The anger that burned inside me was brutal, white-hot, and violent. I'd felt similar rages before—and whenever I had, my enemies had died.

I punched Mike on the cellular and told him to cruise by for a pickup. He knew where to show up. I didn't mention the casualties—if Buckshot was waiting for us, then he damn well knew how to crack our communications. Maybe he even had the same NIS equipment as I did—courtesy of Grant Griffith and Pinky da Turd—so I wasn't about to say anything I didn't have to.

We made our way down the final three flights of stairs and waited inside, the door cracked. As soon as I saw Mike, we rushed the Range Rover and tossed the bodies and our knapsacks inside. I motioned to Cherry, Nod, and Pick to climb in, too. They hesitated, but I wasn't in the mood for backtalk, and when they saw the look on my face, they did as ordered. Mike's eyes went wide when he saw the corpses. "What happened?"

"No time to talk now. Cherry, Pick, and Nod'll give you a dump—just get to the boat fast and load up."

"Huh?"

What the fuck was he, dense? "Get moving. The boat. The rest of us'll see you at Zuma Beach in six hours. Light Cyalumes—we'll swim out. Keep these guys cool, Mike, and check your six regular because there are some real bad characters out and about."

I didn't give him a chance to say anything else. "Just go-go-go, goddammit. Get the fuck out of here."

Chapter

18

I DIDN'T SHOW IT BUT I WAS FRANTIC. I'D JUST LOST TWO OF MY men, I was missing another, and an unknown number of bad guys were out there. My tactical experience told me the only recourse was attack. SEALs don't retreat very well.

But my strategic sensibilities, not my tactical ones, took over. My mission wasn't shooting and looting. It was protecting the data I had in my pocket. Revenge would have to wait. Right now I had to find Half Pint and get the hell out of Dodge.

We locked and loaded, removed our surgical gloves, and moved out onto Constellation Avenue. As we rounded the corner on Century Park West, it was like we'd walked into Mardi Gras. The crowds had thinned in the cool California night, but there was lots of activity. The lights had all been turned on, and as the few hundred hardy spectators watched, the director marshaled his troops into action.

To our right, a path had been cleared so that two police cars could drive south from Santa Monica Boulevard, jump the curb, and come to a screeching stop in front of the main entrance of the hijacked skyscraper. Three stuntmen were pacing off the yardage. Beyond them, on the western side of the street, a knot of SWAT teamers stood next to an armored personnel carrier with the word POLICE stenciled on the side in foot-high letters. I scanned the SWATniks. I picked out

Half Pint and his sniper-rifle case hunkering in the middle trying not to attract attention. I pressed the transmit button on my lip mike.

"HP from silver bullet."

He looked around and came back immediately. "HP."

I told him where we were. He peered toward me and made me out. Even at that distance I could see something was wrong. "Three o'clock, Skipper."

I swiveled right and scanned the area. Beyond him, in the shadows where the light started to fall off, I saw Manny Tanto. He was dressed in the same kind of SWAT uniform Half Pint wore, and he carried a silenced MP5 submachine gun. Behind him I saw another familiar face. Sally Stallion. They were both wearing lip mikes and headsets similar to ours.

I used hand signals. I pointed at Nicky and Duck Foot and told them, "Enemy—three o'clock." They looked. They saw. They signaled back, "forming skirmish line," and moved out to my flank, using the sparse crowd as cover.

I gave Half Pint a high sign that moved him to his right—away from Manny and Stallion. He nodded and started to shift. If he could make it across eight lanes of Century Park West where the shot was being rehearsed, he'd be able to form up with us.

I shouldered my way through, up to the police line. Now, Half Pint was standing directly opposite me, one hundred and fifty yards away. I waved him on. "C'mon, dammit."

Carrying the Pelikan sniper's case, he vaulted over the barrier and got about ten feet, then he was stopped by a crew member carrying a walkie-talkie who stuck a hand in his chest.

I wasn't close enough to hear what was going on, but I could tell from the body English and gesticulating that the guy was saying something like, "You extras aren't supposed to be in this shot—go back and wait by the APC."

Half Pint just straight-armed the asshole, sending him butt-first onto the pavement.

That didn't deter Mr. Efficiency. He scrambled to his feet and set out in pursuit, shouting, "Hey—where do you think you're goin'?"

By now they were in the middle of the avenue, and I could see the face of the crewman trying to stop Half Pint. It was a face I knew—Biker Jordan's face.

I tried to catch Half Pint's attention, but he was intent on getting across the street. Now Jordan was right behind him, his hand dropping into the pocket of his windbreaker.

He must not have been paying attention because Half Pint caught him with an elbow in the solar plexus and dropped him like a hot brick. Then my little pocket rocket turned on the afterburners and sprinted the rest of the way across the street. He tossed me the Pelikan case and then vaulted the barrier.

Now Manny and the others were moving, too. I saw Buckshot. He was on the same side of the street as I was, perhaps a hundred yards away, dressed in a suit, pointing toward us and gesticulating to three men in LAPD uniforms. Were they real or were they Memorex? It didn't matter. Real or bogus, they were still trouble.

The cops began to walk in our direction. We had to move. My instinct was to steal a vehicle—there were certainly enough of them around—and head to Zuma. I signaled Nasty and Duck Foot to go west. They began to shoulder their way along the sidewalk. I backed away from the barrier, carrying the Pelikan case. "Rear-guard me," I told Half Pint.

"Aye, aye, Skipper." He dropped back, walking parallel to me about five yards behind. A familiar figure caught my peripheral vision as I made my way through the crowd. Melissa Gold saw me and walked over. "Hi again, Dick."

"Hi, Gold. How're you doing?"

"I'd be better if we could get this shot over with. Then we break for the night. How're you?"

"I've been better." I introduced Half Pint. She looked at his uniform. "You with us?"

"No, I'm with him."

She tapped the Pelikan. "What's in the case?"

"My dirty laundry."

She started to ask something, but thought better of it. There was an awkward pause while she looked at me intently. "Are you sure we haven't met before? I never forget a face."

"Well—maybe it was my book jacket you remember."

"Book?"

"Rogue Warrior."

Her face brightened. "That's it—I read it last month. You're Dick Marchenko."

"Mar*cinko.*" People are always doing that.

"You were a SEAL."

"Still am."

"No shit. I loved the book. Did you really do all that stuff?"

"Thanks—and yes." I looked down the street. The cops were watching us intently now. I had no idea where Manny and the rest of the Centurions goons were. It was time to go for it. "Melissa . . ."

"Yeah?"

"Look—this is awkward, but I need some help—real bad."

"What kind of help?"

"I've got Half Pint here, and two other guys, and we all have to get to Zuma Beach."

"Zuma Beach."

"Roger."

"When do you have to be there? I could take you as soon as we're done here—one last big shot tonight. I've got a Jimmy that'll hold us all."

I looked at the cops. They hadn't moved. That told me they were bogus because they weren't willing to come up to Melissa, explain what they wanted, cuff us, and take us away. That worked in our favor—but only if we acted right now. "That might not be soon enough."

She folded her arms and pondered what I'd said. Then she asked, "Is this official? I mean—are you guys working for the Navy?"

Well, we were, sort of. I nodded. "Yup."

"Can I ask what you're doing?"

"Well, I could tell you, but then I'd have to kill you." She looked at me very strangely right then. I realized she'd taken me seriously. "That was a joke, Gold. But it's better for you if you don't know."

She looked at me again and pursed her lips. "Come with me."

She ducked under the barrier and turned toward me. "Well? If you're gonna do it, let's do it—there's not much time."

I signaled Nasty and Duck Foot. They sprinted toward Half Pint and me. We vaulted the wood sawhorses and followed Gold as she headed back west, toward the long line of trailers that were parked around the corner.

Now the cops were moving again. So was Manny. So was Buckshot. But we were a hundred and fifty yards ahead of them. An air horn blew three times. I stopped to see what was going on. "Goddammit, Dick, move." Melissa's voice was urgent, and she began to run. I heard car engines growling off to my left. "Goddammit, get your asses in gear! They're starting the shot right now."

"Let's go." I sprinted after her. So did my guys.

We made the far side of the street just as six police cars and a big truck labeled SWAT TEAM came barreling down the wide street, their sirens and lights going full blast. They passed right where we'd crossed the street, then careened around the corner heading toward the front of the high-rise.

A hundred yards behind us, Manny Tanto tried to talk his way past a pair of LAPD motorcycle cops. He wasn't having much success. As we climbed into Gold's Jimmy, he stared at us through a small pair of binoculars.

We made the rendezvous just after 0300. Gold let us off on the Pacific Coast Highway after turning her lights off and slowing to a crawl on the shoulder. I wasn't sure whether we'd been followed or not, but I didn't want to take any chances. We rolled out of her Jimmy into a ditch, let her take off, and waited five minutes to see if anybody cruised past. *Nada.* I owed the lady a big favor—which I'd repay if I lived long enough to get back to Los Angeles.

When I decided the coast was clear, we made our way across the highway and into Zuma Beach Park, crept onto the beach, then down the rocks and into the water. It was cold and we were all exhausted, and we had to tow Cherry, whose right arm was cut and who'd lost a lot of blood. But I saw the *Malevolent Frog* riding out the swells about half a mile offshore. Mike had put out two pairs of Cyalume sticks—reds and whites—and we used them to guide us out.

He pulled us aboard, dried us down with big, thick towels, warmed us up with coffee and brandy, helped patch up Cherry's arm with surgical butterflies, then asked what the fuck was going on. He didn't like bodies on his boat, and he let me know it in terms Ev Barrett would have been proud of.

I wasn't keen on the idea either, but there hadn't been a hell of a lot of choice in the matter. We had two KIAs, and I was going to have to dispose of them so that it looked like they'd been killed on official Navy business.

The question was how to do it. The casualties would have to be caused within the realm of plausible denial. And the corpses would have to be discovered in a state that prevented them from being examined or autopsied.

The closest facility to where we lay at anchor was Point Mugu Naval Air Station, where the original Red Cell had one of its biggest triumphs. Back in 1985, we hit the base on Labor Day weekend and blew Air Force One off the map.

This time Red Cell's penetration would not be so successful. During the assault, we'd use some faulty IEDs—Improvised Explosive Devices—that would turn out to be a lot more powerful than we'd thought. There'd be a bad accident, and Wynken and Blynken would be killed.

My ass would probably end up in a court-martial, but I didn't care. It was all such a clusterfuck anyway—Pinky probably spent most of his time trying to figure out how to get me out of his hair and back into jail. Well, he didn't have to waste time on that, because between the North Korean mothership and this little op I'd done it to myself. Maybe he was right when he'd said that I'd fuck up, because I sure had fucked up right now.

But I had more important things to do than feel sorry for myself. I called the troops onto the fantail and ordered them to get as much rest as they could—things were about to get very busy. Mike got us under way at about 0445, and we steamed at twelve knots up the coast toward Pt. Mugu, some twenty-four miles from the pickup off Zuma.

The bodies had bled enough and swelled enough so that by daybreak they'd started to smell. We went dead in the water and took time to hose them off. It was an operational necessity—I didn't want seagulls flying over the boat, drawing attention to us and to our cargo.

We reached Pt. Mugu during morning rush hour and lay two miles off the coast, between the Vandenberg missile range and the Naval Air Station itself. We spent all day riding the swells. Mike dropped fishing lines into the water just in case a stray patrol craft or plane spotted us. Nobody said much. Nobody was in the mood.

At 1500, I assembled the troops in the galley and outlined our assignment. "This is probably the toughest thing you'll ever have to do," I told them. I said that we were going to stage a raid on Pt. Mugu. During the infiltration, Nasty and I would stack the bodies on top of a bunch of live IEDs and blow them up.

I explained why it had to be done.

It didn't go down very well with the men. But it had to be done.

I diagrammed the assault. Nod and Cherry would hit the police station, right outside the main gate. They'd cut the telephone lines and blow up the radio antennas so nobody could call for help. Pick and Half Pint would come across the beach and start a string of fires by the fuel farm as a diversion. Fires in California have a different meaning—especially when they're alongside a fuel farm that holds enough J-4 to ignite the area from Oxnard to Camarillo. Meanwhile, Duck Foot would cut the chain on the back access road and plant a series of artillery simulators along the fence line closest to the Pacific Coast Highway. While the authorities dealt with all that chaos, Nasty and I would plant the two bodies and a bunch of live IEDs behind the Air Station's explosive-ordnance-disposal facility.

We began the dirty work at 2130, going over the rail in pairs. Nasty and I towed the bodies in a raft. They'd begun to bloat by now and were pungent, stiff, and cumbersome as hell to carry. We grunted and groaned as we humped them through the marsh that bordered the Mugu Lagoon.

By the time we broke through the chain-link fence surrounding the EOD facility, the base authorities were already answering the call to the simulator explosions by the highway. As we found the perfect spot for Wynken and Blynken's funeral pyre, we could hear sirens wailing as all hands were signaled to turn to for fire brigade duty.

Nasty broke into the weapons locker with a crowbar and removed enough dynamite to bring down a medium-size building. Working in tandem, we set the charges, fuses, and det cords, and—as reverently as possible in a situation like this—we placed the bodies in position atop the explosives.

Nasty knelt to say a quick prayer. I joined him. We remained there for a few seconds, then resumed our work in silence.

I took care to partially cover the bodies with earth, making a mound that resembled a grave. You might think I did it to be decent. Actually, I did it so the corpses would act as tamping for the charges, which would maximize the dynamite's destructiveness. There'd be no way to salvage enough tissue from this explosion to conduct any autopsies or formal investigations of any real merit.

Nasty set the timer and we hauled ass, making our way back across the wildlife preserve, through the marsh, and down the lagoon. We grabbed the raft and towed it back out to the *Malevolent Frog.* The other teams were already aboard. Mike hit the throttle and we headed south. We were about three miles from the Air Station when a huge ball of orange flame rose into the sky.

It was done. Two more Frogmen to guard the gates of heaven.

As we passed Point Palos Verdes, I called Washington and told the duty captain who came on line who I was and what unit I commanded. I told him we had suffered two fatalities while expending live ordnance that we could not legally take on a commercial flight, while conducting a no-notice Red Cell penetration at Naval Air Station Point Mugu.

I told him a full report would be filed upon my return to Washington, and that, as Red Cell's CO, the fault for the fatalities lay entirely with me.

He started to blurt something back at me, but I pressed the off button and canceled the call. I wasn't in a very talkative mood.

Chapter

19

WE LEFT LOS ANGELES ON THE FIRST AVAILABLE FLIGHT—ONE of those short-body 737 locals that was scheduled to make seven stops between LAX and DCA. I'd stowed our HKs and most of the Glocks with Mike Regan—no reason to take them with us and create a lot of problems for airline security. He promised to send them on via Federal Express when we were back and safe. Safe. That was a laugh. As I sat on the first leg of our flight—Los Angeles International to Ontario, California—I actually developed the shakes. They were similar to the anticipatory tremors that had preyed on me before combat patrols in Vietnam—the knowledge that there was something out there that wanted to kill me transformed my whole body into a powerful, sensitive antenna. Back then, they made me a better warrior.

Now, sucking a half-cold Stroh's and staring vacantly out the window, I was getting the same vibes I'd had more than a quarter century ago when we left our base at My Tho after dark and went out into the Mekong Delta to hunt Mr. Charlie. But now the sensation was different. I didn't know what it was, or why it was. I only knew that something was wrong. Something was dreadfully wrong.

We took off for Scottsdale, Arizona, on schedule. I had a second beer. Then a third. I turned to look at my men. They were exhausted, wrung out, drained emotionally and physically. Cherry's arm was still virtually useless. From the way he acted, I feared Pick might have a concussion. The rest of them had developed thousand-yard stares.

I knew what was wrong. We'd lost two men and only taken down one bad guy. Those results were unacceptable. Their performance was unacceptable. They knew it—and I knew it.

We dropped into Denver just after 1155 Mountain Time. There was an hour-and-ten-minute layover at Stapleton International, and I suggested that we go and stretch our legs—find a bar and a few draft Coors Lights. That would be a fitting memorial service to the Frogs we'd left behind.

We found a generic bar about two-thirds of the way down the concourse but still inside the security zone. It offered computer-dispensed draft and was almost empty. The better bars were all in the main terminal, but I veered to the right and the men followed. No need to bother the Stapleton rent-a-cops with the few lethal goodies we'd managed to stow in our hand luggage.

I know, I know—you're wondering how we do that, what with all the concern these days about terrorism and fear of hijacking and the rest of it. Well, the answer's simple— when you combine minimum wage with lack of motivation, you get the kinds of people who are hired at airports to check your baggage. Remember Narita? Well—it was a hundred times worse here than it was there. Makes you feel secure, doesn't it?

We had about half a dozen rounds and I excused myself to drain the lizard, slipping out to the men's room about a hundred feet inside the metal detectors. As I came out, I fell in just behind two guys who, although dressed in pin-striped suits, were—to my practiced eye—carrying heat. I went to Threatcon Delta.

The mind stopped and the computer took over. Who were they? Obviously, they were either The Law or terrorists. I discounted the latter category immediately: they didn't fit the profile. In fact, from the way they dressed, they were feds. I drew closer without attracting attention. One of them was holding a photograph in his hand—a picture of me, the one on the jacket of *Rogue Warrior*.

Ah, fame. I slowed down and watched as they headed toward the gate where our flight was just getting ready to board again.

I jogged back to the bar.

"Let's go."

Nasty chugged the last of his beer, slung his knapsack over a huge shoulder, and swiveled off the bar stool. "Aye, aye, Skipper." The rest of the guys drank up and reached for their stuff, too.

Half Pint stopped short as I started down the concourse, away from the gate. "Hey—what's up?"

"Just follow—I'll tell you in a minute. We gotta move."

We went out past security, into the main arrival area. I herded the men through the doors and toward the cab line. "There's a Rent-A-Wreck franchise about two miles down Thirty-second Avenue. Grab a cab. Meet me there in an hour."

"What's up?" Cherry looked over his shoulder.

"Cops," I said as we walked. "Feds probably. Gone to the gate."

"For us?" Duck Foot wondered. "How—"

"Move, goddammit." This wasn't the time or place to talk. "I don't know whether they were feds looking for us or cops waiting to pick up an extraditee—but I'm not taking any goddamn chances. We gotta disappear until I can find out what the fuck is happening."

I called Irish Kernan from a pay phone about a mile from the terminal, but he wasn't in his office. His secretary said he had a meeting at the Pentagon and wouldn't be in until after eleven. "Any message, Captain Marcinko? Can he reach you?"

"No—I'll call him back later." Damn.

I tried to reach O'Bannion in Hawaii, but he was out, too. Totally frustrated, I dialed Stevie Wonder's private number at the Navy Yard. Two rings. Three. Four. I prayed in a way I hadn't since the nuns at St. Ladislaus Hungarian Catholic School used to rap my knuckles with their rulers.

On the sixth ring he growled, "Yo."

"It's me."

"Man, are you in a world of trouble, you sorry asshole."

"Moi?"

"Yeah—*twat.*" I heard him slurping coffee from the Big Gulp 7-Eleven plastic cup he kept on his desk to annoy the brass.

"Intel dump. Nutshell." I was in no mood for talkative.

"Mutiny. Felony murder. AWOL."

Nutshell indeed. "Shit."

"They sent the FBI after you."

"Do I have any friends left?"

"Aside from me? Maybe a couple. But not anybody across the river. E Ring went to DEFCON Five the minute you called from L.A. They'd been waiting. Sent people to every fucking airport west of the Mississippi."

"Anybody we know behind this?"

"The orders came from OP-06."

"That's not what I asked." I knew damn well who was behind it. Grant Griffith was behind it. Mutiny was a court-martial offense. And felony murder. That was a nice touch. Icing on the cake. Felony murder would put me away for, oh, fifty years minimum. That's a lot of time to steal Tomahawk missiles from the Navy.

And that's what this goatfuck was all about. Nuclear Tomahawk missiles. The stakes were fucking incredible—billions of dollars, not to mention the national security. And I was the fucking monkey wrench keeping the greased machinery from moving. So, I had to go.

And to make sure I was taken out of the picture, Grant Griffith and Pinky had loosed the entire fucking federal government on me and Red Cell. Well, screw Grant and Pinky. They were goddamn traitors who were selling our country's secrets and they didn't deserve to live. Moreover—and more immediate right now—was the fact that I'd lost two of Red Cell's best because of these arrogant, money-grubbing assholes, and I wanted to get even.

No—I wanted to get ahead. Grant's head. On a fucking pike. Pinky's ass—up the fucking river.

Yeah—what I wanted was to get my hands on those two goddamn cocksucking motherfucking dip-shit no-load pus-nutted pencil-dicked shit-for-brains sphincter-sucking asshole-kissing geek cockbreaths and kill them—not to put too fine a point on it—kill them very, very painfully. Very, very slowly.

"Any suggestions, Wonder?"

"Go to ground, bro. Don't call anybody. Lemme see which way the wind's blowing, and then we can make a plan."

That made sense to me. "I got a prob here, too."

"Only one?" I loved the boy's sense of irony.

"One of many. When you were in Iraq, we hit the Yard."

"I know. Bad juju. Lots of burned asses."

"Well, we borrowed some stuff from TSD. Monitors. I planted 'em, and I have a receiver in my war bag. But I got no way of picking up what they're putting out."

"Where are they?"

"L.A. area, I think."

"You think? You *think?* Shit, Holmes, ain't you got no brains?"

I told Wonder about Seal Beach. I listened as he slurped more coffee. "Lemme see what they can do out past the Beltway." He was talking about Vint Hill.

"Much grass, bro."

"Nada. Stay in touch."

I looked at my watch. "I'll check in at about eighteen hundred your time."

"I'll be here. Watch your butt, lard-for-brains."

"Eat shit and bark at the moon, asshole."

We got two cars for the seven of us. I'd wanted three, but we had only two credit cards that still worked. The others were Pentagon issue—which meant they'd probably been canceled by now. Anyway, there was no way I was going to use 'em and give the gumshoes a head start by letting them know where we'd begun our odyssey.

Nasty and I took Nod and Cherry with us. I chose a 1972 Monte Carlo—a real lead pig if you ever want to bust through a roadblock, chain-link fence, or other obstacle. Duck Foot, Mr. Bashful, selected a burgundy 1979 Fleetwood Brougham for himself, Pick, and Half Pint. We'd split up. Go south. I told the guys we'd meet up at a rest area

I remembered from my SEAL Team Six travels. It was about a hundred miles from Denver on I-25, south of Fountain and north of Pinon—just outside Pueblo, Colorado. Rendezvous h-hour was 2300.

If the feds were smart—which they weren't—they'd be holding the plane now, interviewing the crew to see if they remembered where we'd gotten off, and going through our baggage piece by piece to see what we'd been carrying.

I was glad we'd been subdued on the flight. No heavy drinking. No naughty banter with the stews. We'd also been fortunate because we'd boarded separately—not your usual, boisterous, surly pack of SEALs in search of fun and games. The war god was looking after us. I hoped he'd continue.

I let Nasty do the driving, while I put my head back and tried to sort everything out. It was like running the inside of a maze—I kept smacking up against dead ends and blind alleys.

Nasty pulled into a humongous mall just north of Colorado Springs so I could make the phone call. It was 1740 in Washington. I rang Stevie Wonder's number. No answer. We grabbed some chow from a pizza stand and wandered around, window-shopping and ogling the women. After half an hour I tried again.

"Yo." The familiar voice came through loud and clear.

"It's me."

"Remember this morning I tole you you was in a world of shit?"

"What's your point?"

"Fuck you—I underestimated the situation." Wonder snorted. "Here's the dump. You are persona non grata. The Navy wants your ass. The Pentagon wants you shot. The FBI has been alerted. Probably, so has ATF, Customs, Immigration, the Coast Guard—even the U.S. Mail."

"Anything else?"

"Yeah."

"What?"

"Don't try to call any of your alleged pals at DIA. They've

got digital tracers on all their phones and they'll find you in about thirty seconds."

"Like Irish?"

"Yeah—Irish and his shop have gone over to the enemy. A call to them is the same as a call to Pinky."

That was real bad news. The one thing I'd always been able to count on was the informal network of sources and contacts I'd built up over the years. That network was the reason I could run roughshod over the system. It was the reason I could say "fuck" to admirals and operate with impunity. Now, Wonder was telling me I didn't have my Safety Net anymore. "Is there anybody I can trust?"

His voice was even. "Besides me? I'm not sure, Dick. They want you pretty damn bad."

"Do you have any good news at all?"

He paused. "Well . . . I know where your monitors are and you don't."

Geezus—the asshole really knew how to keep a secret. "Wonder . . ."

He laughed. I could just see his head swiveling. "Okay, Dick-head. They're in southern California."

I knew that already and told him so.

"Yeah—but you don't know they've been moved."

That was news. "Where?"

"Not sure. I'm trying to get some friends to do me a real big favor. Call me back in two hours and I may have some news for you."

"Roger that."

We climbed back into the car and continued south. I had Nasty pull over at a Phillips 66 station just off the interstate and tried Wonder's number. There was no answer. We waited fifteen minutes, trying not to attract any attention, then I called again.

"Yo."

"It's me. Any news?"

"Yeah—you're in deep shit." He laughed. He loved to see me in pain. "Don't worry, I got a fix. The monitors are sitting in Long Beach Harbor."

"You sure?"

"Yup."

"Is it on a ship?"

"Don't know. There are a lot of ships in Long Beach Harbor. There are also a lot of docks."

He had a point. "So?"

"So, we wait, Dick-head. If the monitor starts to move west, then it's on a ship."

"If it is, we can track it, right?" I knew that all ships have navigation satellite transponders for position fixes, and that by matching the position of the monitor with the ship's transponder, we could identify the CIQ, or Craft In Question.

"Right—but there's been no movement yet." Wonder paused. I could hear him sip his omnipresent coffee.

"I'm on the move here. Lemme try you back in an hour."

"Roger."

He got me a fix at 2055. "The CIQ is a twin-hulled tanker named *Akita Maru*. Left at nineteen hundred today for Yokohama, says the harbormaster."

"Right on." A plan started to formulate. The first problem to solve was tracking the tanker. There was no way we could get to it if we couldn't find it. "Can you keep your eyes on the ship?" I asked Wonder.

"Maybe. If I can convince some people to look the other way while I play with switches and dials."

"Try."

"Wilco. Call me later and I'll have an update for you."

"Bless you, my son." I told the boy I'd buy him his own brewery when I got back to D.C. Wonder said he'd hold me to the promise.

He hung up. I wanted the ship and the missiles—bad. It wasn't that I lacked my own ammunition. I had videotape of Buckshot and the Japs from Matsuko Machine in my shoulder bag. I had Grant Griffith's computer disk in my pocket. Back in Washington, I had the NIS files on Pinky. Taken together, they became compelling evidence of a massive conspiracy reaching into the heart of the Navy establishment. But the evidence wasn't airtight. To make it so, I needed the stolen nuclear missiles on the *Akita Maru*. Then I'd have it all, and I could make my own fucking presentation to CNO.

We had a half-hour drive to rendezvous with the rest of the guys. While Nasty put pedal to metal, I sitrepped, trying to figure out why the fuck Grant Griffith would put the stolen missiles on a tanker when it would be just as easy to put them on a plane and fly them out.

The answer, I realized, had to do with technology. In this so-called New World Order, government agencies have become a lot more capable when it comes to sniffing out the smuggling of forbidden materials, such as explosives or nukes. Like Narita, where sophisticated sensors had been installed, all the major airports on the West Coast had installed the latest generation of explosive and nuclear-sensing baggage and cargo-handling protection devices.

Grant Griffith was not a man to take chances. He'd read my report on Narita, which had spotlighted the single bright side of the airport's security—its state-of-the-art detection devices. So there was no way he was going to risk a bunch of hijacked Tomahawk missiles by allowing them anywhere near an airport.

He'd move them by ship. It was slower, but it was also prudent.

We pulled into the rest area at about 2130. The boys were already sitting on the dew-covered picnic benches drinking cold Coors and working on deli sandwiches. I'd had plenty of time to think during the drive and gave the troops the benefit of my musings—a real no-shitter.

I told them it was my opinion we'd been set up from the very start. That every operation we'd been assigned—from the Navy Yard to Seal Beach to North Korea—had been a deception, a ruse, a psy op. We were the diversionary assholes—the force sent out to catch the enemy's attention, while the big flanking movement took place miles and miles away. Like Stormin' Norman Schwarzkopf did with Desert

Storm. And the real goal? KISS-simple. Grant Griffith and his friends were stealing nuclear weapons from the United States and selling them.

To the North Koreans? asked Duck Foot.

I'd thought about that. The kimchis, I told him, were a diversion, too. Griffith was using their nuclear program as cover. That way, while our entire military intelligence community was focusing on the Pyongyang putzes, he was shipping goods into Japan.

Japan?

Yeah—Japan. Probably to that fascist Jap asshole who ran Matsuko, what's-his-name. The guy Tosho told me about—Hideo Ikigami.

And guess what? Their plan had worked. I'd played right into their hands. Why? Because, I said, sometimes I am an egocentric asshole who cannot see the forest for the fucking trees. Because I often have this "stop me or I'll kill again" attitude when it comes to the system—which means I'll try to screw that system whenever I can—even if it is not in my best interests to do so.

Damn—Griffith and Pinky knew how I felt about the Navy. They knew how I'd react to taking over Red Cell. And I'd done exactly what they'd predicted I'd do: run a bunch of UNODIR operations that showed the world—the Navy world—that I was still a knuckle-dragging mustang, an uncontrollable rogue who habitually thumbed his nose at the chain of command.

I drained my beer and crushed the can in my hand. This was not a happy epiphany. "Shit," I said, "that's exactly what they fucking wanted me to do."

And what, I asked rhetorically, were the consequences of my playing into their hands? The most significant one was that I'd lost two good men, I said. Wynken and Blynken died because of me, and their wasted deaths were something I was going to have to live with for the rest of my life. Then there was our current situation. Here we were, renegades without friends. Fugitives on the run. Candidates for courts-martial. Meanwhile, Grant Griffith and his pals had loaded their nukes onto a ship and were sailing into the sunset—or in this case, toward the Land of the Rising Sun.

The Navy is unique when it comes to conferring command. When you assume command in the Navy, you assume it totally. You are responsible for your men. In every way. From their safety and well-being to making sure that their equipment works, to their morale, to protecting them from undue harassment from the system. I had let my men down. I'd been blind to the plot that now was obvious to me. That made me unworthy of them.

Now, I said, it was time for them to save themselves. I would take the fall because this situation was all my fault. My responsibility.

"I'm not ordering you to go back to Washington," I said, "but I'm suggesting it strongly."

"Shit, Skipper." Nod slapped his beer down on the table. "I'm only a fuckin' new guy, but it still seems to me that if we're gonna burn, we should burn together."

"Ditto," said Duck Foot.

"Look, Skipper," said Pick, "we're a unit. Units stay together."

"Okay," Half Pint chimed in, "so you got rolled by these assholes. But the point is, you were thinking of us. Fuck, Captain, nobody's been willing to cover our asses in years— not until you got back."

"That's the truth," said Cherry. "Goddamn officers— they all use us."

"Use you?"

"To get their fucking stars. When you were CO of SEAL Team Six, Skipper, that was all you wanted—to be CO of a kick-ass-take-names unit. Now, it seems like all officers want to be admirals. Command of a unit like Six is just another step toward flag rank. What're the consequences of that? Consequences are, we get screwed. They don't take chances. They don't protect us. They just cover their asses and do nothing. Well, Skipper, I didn't become a SEAL to do nothing. I'm tired of touch football and marathons and full-mission profiles. I want to go out and go fuckin' hunting."

"Me, too," said Nasty. "Shit, Skipper—it's time to avenge Wynken and Blynken. Let's take these fucking assholes down—no survivors."

There were tears in my eyes when Nasty finished. These were SEALs I loved to command—hunters in the tradition of crusty old Frogs like my sea daddy Roy Boehm, the first CO of SEAL Team Two—men who'd do anything to get the job done.

I examined their faces. The determination to triumph was palpable. The energy they radiated was incredible. Their resolve to win was absolute.

We had no weapons. We had no equipment. We had nothing but raw energy, guts, determination, and the will to succeed.

We would not fail.

I woke Mike Regan out of a sound sleep on the secure cellular phone just as the sun started to peek over the Dos Cabezas Mountains east of Willcox, Arizona. We'd been driving all night.

"I had the FBI here yesterday," was what he told me.

"No shit. What did they want?"

"Your scalp."

"What did you tell them?"

"That you'd left for Washington."

That was good. "And the stuff I left with you to post to me?"

"Still here."

That was as good a piece of news as I'd heard in a long time. It meant we had weapons and ammo. Now all we needed was an aircraft, a bunch of chutes, and an assault boat. All we needed—shit.

I explained to Mike what I needed. He grumbled, but said he'd take care of business for me.

"Great."

"One piece of coincidental news."

Coincidental? I didn't believe in coincidence anymore. "Yeah?"

"The movie set you used to infiltrate the offices?"

"Yeah?"

"One of the people working on the movie was killed yesterday. A woman. I don't recall her name offhand. She went off the road near Malibu in her Jeep and died. I only realized it when the obit said she'd been working in Century City the same night we were there."

I told you—there are no coincidences. I swallowed hard and added another score to settle with Manny Tanto. "Her name was Gold, Mike—Melissa Gold. She did me a favor. Save the obit."

"Roger that. When do I see you?"

"Hopefully within seventy-two hours. It's gonna be a tough trip. We need to move quick, but we also need to move quietly."

"Amen, bro."

"Stay close to the phone. I'll give you a call when I'm ready."

We'd been up for almost two days now. It was time to grab a combat nap and a hot shower. We checked into two motels so as not to attract attention. While the guys rested, I plotted. Obviously, we had to get to the tanker, hit it, bring the goodies back, and dump them—along with a couple of traitors named Pinky and Grant—right in the Navy's lap.

The top requirement was transportation. I needed a plane with three thousand miles or more of range. My first choice was a C-130 Hercules. They are stable platforms, and they are easy to fly. Pick could handle one by himself. Fortunately, there were a bunch of assets in the area. Near Tucson was Davis-Monthan Air Force Base, where the government graveyard for military aircraft is located. Thirty miles north of Davis-Monthan is a little town called Marana. That is where Christians in Action—the CIA—keeps some of its covert air force. I knew both bases because SEAL Team Six had trained there—we'd jumped near Davis-Monthan many times and had used the CIA's Marana planes during our deep-cover operations.

We recce'd Davis-Monthan first. There were a dozen C-130 birds in the graveyard. No good. Three other Hercules—they were EC-130 special-operations aircraft— were sitting on the tarmac waiting to be upgraded. But checking them out to find which were flyable and which weren't would have taken a week and I didn't have a week. Besides, EC-130s are crammed full of electronic goodies that weigh a ton, and we needed a bare plane that we could fill to the brim with gas—we'd carry only our combat gear and the IBS rubber ducky we'd need to make the jump.

Jump? Jump. My plan was KISS-simple. We'd fly out into the Pacific, locate the tanker using coordinates from Stevie Wonder, drop into the water, hit the ship from behind, and stage a classic takedown. Then we'd commandeer the tanker and bring it home. A piece of fucking cake, right?

So we moved up the path of least resistance, where they were more trusting, less bureaucratic—and the security sucked. We arrived at Marana just at sunset. There were a pair of commercial C-130s sitting on the tarmac outside a huge hangar. They were painted in U.N. colors—probably used somewhere in Africa, or one of the Balkan states that used to be Yugoslavia. Now they'd come home to be scraped and repainted. Maybe they'd become Red Cross mercy planes. Or camouflaged as military aircraft from France, Germany, Israel, or Egypt, depending on the mission. Frankly, I liked the way they looked right now.

Pick went through the fence. He was back in less than ten minutes. "I found one—it's perfect," he said. "It's been used for resupply—configured to make drops. Probably covert weapons to Bosnian Muslims, Kurds, or Azerbaijanis. Best of all, it looks like it's ready to go. All we'd need is fuel—and the fuel farm isn't even guarded. I saw it from the cockpit—it's right at the western edge of the field."

It all sounded good to me. I made a note of the number on the C-130's tail. We'd keep track of that particular bird. Okay—transportation was the easy part. It would be more difficult to assemble the goods we'd need to stage the takedown.

We couldn't grab the C-130 and fly to San Diego because it would be impossible to refuel there. Besides, we were the subjects of an intensive manhunt. So, everything had to come to us. What I wanted was to assemble everything I needed here in the Arizona desert, then in one big, sweeping operation we'd grab the bird, fuel her, and get under way before anybody knew what was happening.

Mike Regan would be arriving with our weapons within twenty-four hours. While I waited for him, Cherry and

Duck Foot—who had been instructors at the BUD/S school at Coronado—would visit some of their old haunts at SEAL Team Five and "borrow" (read *steal*) parachutes, an IBS (that's Inflatable Boat, Small, for you civilians), and a couple of rubber fuel bladders to increase the IBS's range.

Nasty, who'd survived his HALO accident not ten miles from where we were sitting, still had a key to the rigger loft at Marana on his key chain. I asked him to break in and see what was available for rigging the C-130 for the drop. Two hours later he came back with good news: there were pallets and cargo chutes. With luck—and some skill—no one would miss anything until it was too late.

We brainstormed all night. I figured that the maximum range we'd get out of the C-130 would be 3,200–3,300 miles. If it had been outfitted with additional tanks, it could go almost 5,000 miles. But the plane Pick had chosen didn't have 'em.

I checked in with Stevie Wonder. He told us the tanker was steaming at a steady 16.5 knots. That meant, after the thirty-six hours she'd been at sea, the tanker had gone about 680 miles. It was roughly 400 miles as the crow flies from Marana to the Pacific. If we could squeeze 3,200 miles out of the Hercules, we'd have 2,825 miles of range left before we went into the drink. A speed of sixteen and a half knots gave the tanker a daily run of 450 miles.

Allowing for Murphy's Law and all the other unknowns, I figured we had to do the rendezvous and takedown within six days after the ship had sailed, otherwise the *Akita Maru* would be out of range and we'd be fucked. That meant we had to be airborne within ninety hours.

Mike arrived on time. He was followed within hours by Cherry and Duck Foot, who'd not only brought the chutes, rubber ducky, and three fuel bladders, but also a trunkful of swim gear. Pick made five trips to the aircraft to check out its instrumentation and make sure there was enough fuel aboard to taxi us across the field to the tank farm. The only security he saw was jackalopes.

Nasty, Duck Foot, Nod, and Half Pint hit the Marana rigger's loft. They brought back one pallet, one packed cargo chute, and one set of rigging cables. Repack the chute? Yeah—if this weren't being done clandestinely. But there was no place to lay it out without being seen. So we decided to chance it. Backup? Who needs one? If this didn't work the first time, we'd all be dead anyway.

I examined the boat. It was one of the older ones, a rubber-ducky-configured IBS raiding craft with 125-horse-power outboard motor. It came sans radio. Well, that didn't matter—there'd be no one to call.

We had the boat. We had the plane. We had the guns and the bullets. What we lacked was some means to get from our IBS to the tanker. At SEAL Team Six, I'd designed titanium-hooked boarding ladders. But there were none of those around. We'd have to improvise.

Nasty and Duck Foot were the best climbers we had. I assigned the problem to them. Three hours later they came back to the motel carrying two expandable poles—the kind painters used to reach high ceilings. One was aluminum, the other was steel. We wrapped the components in electrical tape to make them sticky, designed hooks, and with the help of a local welder, fixed them to the top, then that night we assaulted a convenient water tower about eight miles down the road. The aluminum pole gave out, causing Duck Foot a nasty bruise. But the steel one worked fine—Nasty'd be able to set the hook, pull himself aboard the tanker, and then lower a knotted rope for the rest of us to climb.

There were air charts in the plane. Pick liberated the appropriate ones and began planning navigational routes. I decided—security be damned—that we were going to re-pack the chutes Cherry and Duck Foot brought back from Coronado. We'd all lost good friends on the Grenada operation doing this same kind of air-sea rendezvous, and I wanted no screwups. We laid the chutes out in the motel parking lot at 0300, had everything repacked in less than an hour, and no one was the wiser.

The way things looked, I guesstimated a 10-hour flight, plus three hours for a circle search (I hoped it wouldn't turn into a circle jerk!). If we launched at 0545, we'd be over the target in the late afternoon. We'd jump, assemble, track, chase, and take the tanker down at night. It sounded perfect. But I knew that Mr. Murphy would come along for the ride—and the best way to avoid him was preparation. Lots of preparation.

So, we put it all on paper and went over the details again and again.

- Aircraft launch at approximately 134 hours of ship steaming time.
- Overhead for a look-see at 144 hours (six days).
- Rubber ducky drop at 147 hours.
- Assault—at our first opportunity.

My preference would have been to track the tanker and make the assault at 0-Dark Hundred, when the opposition is always at its least dangerous. But with only a single boat I couldn't take a chance on the outboard engine's being flooded out by a following sea, the tanks giving way from dry rot, or any of the hundred other "normal" things Señor Murphy does during these types of events.

Indeed, I've had perfectly good engines die because they got flooded on impact. I've had my boats flip over when they hit the water. I've seen the wave action tear the engine mount right off. I've been there when the winds carry the boat a mile from the jumpers.

There are more ways for these ops to go wrong than right—which meant that along with our skill, our determination, and all our planning, we'd need a shitload of luck.

Still, I tried to leave as little to chance as possible. For example, I decided we'd hit the ship on the port side amidships, where the main deck is lowest to the waterline. The reason for going to port, versus starboard, is that more people are right-handed, and if smoking, will throw their butts away with their right hand—ergo they'll use the starboard side, and if you use it, too, they'll see you. Details, details, details.

At 2200 we assembled all our gear and set it up backward, so we could carry it onto the plane in reverse. The IBS—which was to be launched first off the ramp—was the last item loaded. I went over the stowage probs and stats carefully, then walked the men through—five dry runs on the ground.

Why? Because stowage can make or break an op. For example, if everything is not stowed just right, Mr. Murphy will find room to come along. If that happens, he might be able to loosen a strap or two so that when you go off the tail ramp (at between one hundred and two hundred knots), you lose your gear. You can wave good-bye as it disappears into the slipstream during the initial seconds of the drop or watch it sink on impact when you hit the water (which is damn hard). Or, he'll repack your combat vest so that when you reach for bullets, you come up with MREs.

Well, we didn't need those problems. We didn't have any spare gear, extra weapons, surplus bullets, or auxiliary boats—not to mention people. Talk about your bottom-line planning, bare-bones execution, and zero-based support. I had to laugh. So far as I was concerned, it was situation normal—all FUBAR.

Chapter

20

AT UNDER WAY PLUS 111 HOURS I TOSSED MIKE REGAN BACK into his car and pointed him west. We had no idea where Buckshot and his band of merry marauders were, and I wanted Mike to take Nancy and head to Hawaii or someplace else—anyplace else—for about a week. No need for him to wind up dead. He objected. He protested. He insisted he could take care of himself. I told him that wasn't the point—it was one against four, and the odds were in the bad guys' favor. Believe me, I said, there are ways of making you talk. Like causing Nancy a lot of pain—so why take chances with your wife's life? "Just get the hell out of Dodge for a while, pilgrim."

Besides, I needed my old Vietnam SEAL compadre alive. I entrusted him with the tapes, the computer disk, and my Minox and told him to take them with him when he disappeared. "Keep checking your answering machines," I said, adding that if he didn't hear from me within a week, he was to call "60 Minutes" and turn all the material over to Charlie Thompson, the producer who'd put together the Mike Wallace segment about *Rogue Warrior*.

I was certain that with the information I'd gathered, the Wallace-Thompson team would be able to ream Grant Griffith a new asshole from the inside out. They're both maverick Navy veterans, you know. And even in his mid-

seventies (he turned seventy-five in 1993), Mike Wallace—
who served in World War II—is as tough as they come. He
would have made a hell of a Frogman.

Charlie Thompson, who served in Vietnam, is that wonderful combination of ornery and adamant. Once he gets his
teeth into something he doesn't let go. He also hates crooks
and traitors. That's my kind of guy (even though he can't get
a decent table at the Palm).

Mike Regan finally saw the wisdom of my suggestions and
departed—grumbling. He'd be waiting for my call, he said.

Now we were in it for real. I called Stevie to see what the
Akita Maru was up to. He told me she was running a parallel
course to normal shipping channels, maintaining a consistent 16.5 knots twelve miles south of the normal lane. The
pattern had been consistent for twenty hours, which meant
the ship was on autopilot. If there was a major change,
Wonder said he'd be able to reach me on the satellite link
inside the C-130. All I had to do was contact him and give
the plane's call sign.

Then I asked him for a weather pic.

"Geez, is there anything ya don't want?"

"Not really."

He bitched, but told me he'd move quickly.

While I waited for his call, we ran another two dry-run
load-ins. We had it down to under twelve minutes from
cutting the fence to starting engines. Damn, these guys were
good.

Under way plus 132 hours. This was the worst time.
Nothing to do but sit in the motel room and wait, praying
that we hadn't attracted any undue attention. Hoping that
no one had called the feds or the sheriff or the state police. I
didn't want a Waco-style standoff on my hands, but my guys
were in no mood for surrendering and, more to the point,
neither was I.

No one said much. Each man concentrated on his job.
Nasty was working over the climbing pole he'd built. Cherry
loaded magazines. Nod sat on the floor, honing the blade of
his Field Fighter knife. It was big and mean and he wanted
to use it bad. I understood why. There are times when

killing is the only way to satisfy the revenge god. This was one of them.

At 133 hours we went through the fence. Duck Foot went straight to the fuel farm to pick the locks on the pumps so we wouldn't waste a lot of time fueling. We hadn't moved more than fifteen yards toward the flight line when I realized something had changed. There were security patrols out and about. We pulled back behind the fence line and hunkered in a gully, feeling exposed and vulnerable.

What the hell was going on? Had we blundered into one of the CIA's occasional security exercises, or were they piling on because they were looking for us?

Either way, we were screwed. I scrambled back through the fence and did a fast recon. The bad news was that I saw two separate patrols meandering up and down the tarmac, shining flashlights into dark places. The good news was they were rent-a-cops, not Marines, and they had no dogs or automatic weapons—just flashlights and nightsticks.

The situation was similar to the exercise I'd run at Narita. That thought brought a smile to my face. I wished I had a couple of the Fujoki Corporation stickers to leave behind. Remember them? They're the ones that read "Dead hostage —have a nice day" in Japanese and English. They would have been a real mind-fuck for any Agency asshole who tried to figure out what had happened.

Cherry tapped me on the shoulder, bringing me crashing back to reality. Silently, I explained the situation and the solution. There was one three-man patrol to our right, and another to our left, and they had to be silenced. I gave another sequence of hand signals and we split up to do the dirty deeds. Nasty and I took the port side. Pick and Nod had starboard. Six minutes later, we'd bound and gagged the rent-a-cops with tape and left them in a culvert like half a dozen mummies with sore heads.

But now we were also behind schedule. And we had to get the 130 to the gas pump without attracting attention. That meant we couldn't start the engines now. I sent Nasty to locate a mule—one of the small tractors used to tow aircraft—while we stowed the gear. It took him longer than it took us.

Finally, he drove up in the electric-powered tractor. "What the fuck took you so long?"

"This was the only one I could find that was charged."

We hooked up the C-130 and started toward the fuel farm, praying for no more security patrols. I walked alongside the nosewheel as we inched across the flight line, sweating although the temperature was in the forties.

Under way plus 133 hours 42 minutes. We crossed the field at a crawl. By the time we made it to the fuel farm, Duck Foot had the pumps running and was ready to start filling the wing tanks.

While Cherry and Duck Foot played gas jockeys, and Pick did a final walkabout, I had Nod locate an APU—that's one of those Auxiliary Power Units used to jump-start aircraft. That way we'd be able to wait until the last minute before we started making real noise—and revving engines make beaucoup noise.

It was a good thing we'd gotten an early start. Between the rent-a-cops, the crawl to the pump, and the pumping itself, we were almost forty-five minutes late before we closed the hatches. Damn. It looked as if the ever-popular Mr. Murphy had stowed away with us.

Well, there was nothing that we could do about that. Pick completed his preflight check and settled into the left-hand seat. I played copilot. Nod engaged the APU and we lit the big bird up. No problems. He disengaged, pushed it clear, then clambered aboard as Nasty raised the cargo ramp. Now we began the taxi. It suddenly hit me just how vulnerable we were as we made our way down three thousand feet of taxiway, seemingly crawling inch by painful inch. I stared down at the tarmac through the windshield. I thought about how I'd gotten here—and how I'd get out; what I'd do and to whom.

Pick's voice brought me out of my dawndream. "C'mon, Skipper—get with the program."

"Sorry, Pick."

"It's okay, boss, but I need you here, with me. Not a thousand miles away." He talked me through the throttle controls while he played with the flaps, and then we were rolling ka-bump ka-bump down the runway, sans lights, sans tower chatter, sans everything, and we growled into the purple sky at 134:18:22, loaded for bear, and wanted by lots of people who carried badges, guns, and federal warrants.

We cleared and climbed and the mission was going perfectly. At least the first six minutes of it went perfectly. Just as we climbed through seven thousand feet, the outboard port engine caught fire.

How did it happen? Don't ask. How does anything happen? It just happens. Faulty oil pressure? A mechanic's rag left behind? A ruptured line? Who knew—who cared. It was too late to do anything other than solve the problem and keep going.

The cockpit alarm sounded, and cool as a cuke, Pick steadied the aircraft and hit five of the hundred switches in front of him. A big plume of white smoke exploded from the outboard port nacelle as the dry fire extinguishers went to work, and the engine closed down.

"Can we fly on three?"

"Sure, Skipper. But we'll be moving much lower and slower."

"Which means . . ."

"We'll use more gas. You'll have to refigure the intercept point."

Great. I had no computer. In fact, I had no way of contacting Stevie Wonder—not without drawing attention to us.

Why? Because I'd assumed that, like most of the 130s I'd ever used, the one we stole would be outfitted with up-to-date communications gear. Where was my old UDT chief, Ev Barrett, when I really needed him to plant his size 10-D boondocker firmly up my butt. *"Never assume,* Marcinko, you worthless no-load shit-for-brains pus-nutted geek," is how Ev would have put it in his genteel, paternal manner.

After all, this was no military airplane. It was one of the CIA's covert-action craft, and it was outfitted with your basic 1970s communication gear—the sort of equipment you find in Third World aircraft. Bells and whistles? If they needed it, Christians in Action would bring portable SATCOM gear, burst transmitters, and all the other techno-goodies they love to travel with.

I climbed out of the copilot's seat and headed toward the naviguesser's rack. The phrase *dead reckoning* suddenly took on a whole new significance. I reckoned we could all be dead soon. I sat down, pulled out the charts, and tried to remember the basics of flight time/fuel consumption/range capabilities that I'd studied at the Air Force Command College in Montgomery, Alabama, almost two decades before. *Nada.* Zippo. My mind had turned to Jell-O.

Even with the possibility looming large that we'd all go down somewhere in the Pacific, I think we all felt relieved when Pick passed the word that we'd just passed the California coastline and we were now "feet wet," as the Airedales say, over the Pacific. Pick was going to fly manually for another hour then switch to autopilot so he could relax a little and double-check our newly revised and improvised flight plan. I sat in the radioman's seat and played with the dials and switches, scanning the airwaves for chatter. Radioman was my first Navy rating, and despite the fact that it had been three decades since I'd played with a radio seriously, the techniques came back to me easily. I spent fifteen minutes listening to traffic. Nothing mentioned us. At least we'd gotten away clean—thanks to Pick's flying us low and slow and threading the needle between flight controllers. At least that part of it hadn't been a total fuckup.

The troops in the cargo were in their normal long-flight mode—already asleep on top of anything that offered some comfort. I climbed down from the cockpit and looked at them sprawled out. It brought back memories of flying all the way to Vietnam from the East Coast in that same manner more than a quarter century ago.

God—had I been that young once? Idealistic? Believing that the Navy was a place of wooden ships and iron men, not the other way around?

Yeah—that was me all right. And it still was.

Why? Because I had iron men with me now—which was what kept me going.

I wish I could tell you I was a happy camper, but I wasn't. There were just too many loose ends to give me much confidence in anything but the ability of my men to respond to virtually any situation they'd have to face. So, giving myself over to the fates, I found a pile of canvas and lay down, forcing myself to rest. I'd need every bit of it.

139:52:15. I held a modified reveille. And after the requisite grunting and groaning, and after the guys lined up at the port and starboard piss tubes so they could drain their lizards at sixteen thousand feet, we began rehearsing our individual responsibilities for the ship takedown.

A tanker is both easier and harder to take down than your passenger liners, trawlers, or battleships. Easier because all the superstructure is aft, so it's like fighting inside a three-to-four-story apartment building instead of the maze of decks and passageways you find in passenger ships, Navy vessels, or freighters. On the downside, the decks and bulkheads are all made of steel, so ricochets can ruin your day just as easily as a well-aimed shot. Bullets tend to carom off steel bulkheads like balls on a pool table—except their paths are absolutely unpredictable.

Our goal would be to swarm the ship and take control as fast as possible. The hard part was that we'd be boarding right below the watchful eyes of the helmsman—who has an unrestricted view of the amidships area—plus whomever he had on the bridge with him. Still, we'd planned the assault for dusk, which was close to dinnertime, when things might be lax—meaning only one man on the bridge, maybe two.

I drew a rough diagram, pointing out the other complications we'd face, and the areas we'd have to secure.

The first problem was directly below the bridge, where the mess decks and crew quarters are located. That's where off-duty personnel relax. Because of the potential hazards of the cargo—combustible petroleum—they normally lounge around fully clothed, ready to respond to an emergency. On this particular voyage they'd probably be armed as well.

Below the mess deck lies the engineering space. In the old days, that meant a bunch of snipes working on boilers. Today, it normally means just one gauge-watcher, who sits monitoring the fully automated power plant. When the tanker enters confined waterways, there's usually also someone in the auxiliary steering compartment, which is aft, just to cover in case of a loss of steerage from the bridge.

There wouldn't normally be someone in the ASC when we did the takedown—but I wasn't about to trust "normally" because the steerage compartment is one of those hideaways sailors go to be alone or thump their lizards with a dog-eared fuck book. Other lockers that caused me concern were the forward boatswain's locker and chain locker. Both were pockets of privacy on long cruises.

What this all meant is that I had to run two shooters to the bridge to take control of the communications and the steerage, two shooters to the mess to secure the off-duty personnel, two belowdecks to control the power plant, two to sweep through the engineering spaces, one to clear the boatswain's locker and chain locker, and one to secure the bow. That made ten.

There were seven SEALs on the plane, including me.

Well, the superstructure was the key. Once the aft was secured, we'd be able to sweep the hold, the cofferdams, and the forward spaces. It would be a slow, meticulous, and most of all dangerous process—but we could do it.

141:22:25 I climbed back up into the cockpit and crawled in the rack behind the naviguesser position. I needed a combat nap. I don't sleep much—three, four hours a day will suffice. But once in a while I like to close my eyes for fifteen or twenty minutes and just let things go. This was one of them.

I woke up as I felt Pick change course and dip the wings. I went forward. He pointed to seven o'clock through the windscreen. There was a ship out there—a speck in the distance from our altitude of seventeen thousand feet. I threw glasses on it. It was a freighter. I went back to the rack.

Pick hit the jump Klaxon at 145:06. I rubbed my eyes and peered out the windscreen. Target in sight—tanker dead ahead, about six miles out. Damn—Steve's calculations and my revisions had been right on the money. I high-fived Pick. "Great work."

I clambered down and pulled the NIS monitor receiver from my war bag. I turned it on. No response. There were no bugged Tomahawks on that ship.

It was the wrong tanker.

I double-timed back to the flight deck. "Wrong target."

Pick didn't like what I was telling him. He tapped the gauges to emphasize the point. Even though we'd consumed less fuel than expected, he said, we were already brushing the edge of the envelope because with only three engines working we'd been flying lower, through thicker air, and we'd used up our gas faster.

"How long do we have?"

"Two hours. Maybe two and a half. Any ideas, Skipper?"

"Try a slow sweep to port." I'd plotted the tanker twelve miles south of normal shipping lanes, which were marked on my charts. Maybe it had veered farther south to escape detection.

"And if that doesn't work?"

"Then we're all in for a long, long swim."

The NIS monitor began squawking intermittently an hour and three-quarters later. I took it up to the flight deck. "We've got a signal."

"Let's follow it." Pick banked the plane to the right. The squawking stopped. "Nope." He altered course again, and we got a weak signal. Now he banked the other direction, and the squawk grew stronger. "They're way south of where we thought they were."

The monitor began to squeal loudly. I slammed Pick on the shoulder. Now we were heading toward the bull's-eye.

"There she is." I pointed through the windscreen. About eight miles ahead, a tanker was visible through the high clouds, her wake clearly marking her position. Pick held on the ship. The monitor left no doubt that the tanker I saw below was carrying the missiles I'd bugged.

We began a slow sweep, circling wide, putting fifteen to twenty miles between us and the *Akita Maru*. I would have preferred to go round one more time, but Pick showed me the fuel gauges. We were running on fumes—we didn't have enough to make another 360. In fact, we might go down before we came up on the tanker's wake.

"We've got to reach the wake." Indeed, to minimize the chances of failure, we had to go off the ramp just as we pulled directly behind the *Akita Maru*. I looked down at the water. The swells looked like they were running four to six feet. They were hypnotizing in the sun. Now I understood why P-3 pilots got bored—even hypnotized—during the long hours of sub hunting. The water is absolutely mesmerizing as it catches the light and the wave patterns move, undulating like a multicolored kaleidoscope. It's not just monochromatic blue or simple blue-green, but there are flashes of gold and orange from the sun, creamy wave froth, and even metallic glints from an occasional school of fish. It changes second by second in a pulsating, rhythmic syncopation. I could have watched it forever.

But there were other things to do first. Pick dropped to ten thousand feet, then descended another half mile. We'd go off the ramp at seventy-five hundred feet. High enough to make the jump interesting and low enough to make sure we'd all land in the same area. I wanted to drop astern of the *Maru* by twenty-five miles or so, which would put the C-130 out of sight during the maneuver. Jumping off the ship's port quarter would allow us to come up her wake—we'd be able to sense her presence in the darkness by the feel of the water. Then we'd slip up her port side and board at the gunwales just forward of the superstructure, where the decks are almost awash.

The men had their assault packages and chutes on. Cherry lowered the ramp. Half Pint, Duck Foot, and Nod set the cables on the IBS. Nasty opened the side door facing toward the *Akita Maru*. He'd spot the jump as soon as we crossed her wake.

I ran forward and slammed the ladder to the cockpit three times with a crowbar. That was the signal to Pick. Now he'd check the gauges, set the flaps, and slow us down to just over 110 knots, then slip the control onto autopilot and run like hell. He'd have to get into his equipment fast.

We all breathed easier now that fresh air was rushing through the aircraft. I looked down at the water below. It would be cold, and we weren't wearing wet suits—they were the single item that we hadn't been able to obtain during Cherry and Duck Foot's quick raid on Coronado.

I felt the aircraft slow down as it banked in a slow, easy counterclockwise turn. Then Pick slid down the ladder and ran aft. "We're going in," he shouted.

"Whaddya mean?"

"We're out of gas." Pick came even with the IBS. Half Pint and Duck Foot held his vest and chute harness for him. They swaddled, slammed, and smacked him into his equipment. Looking at them work was like watching a championship pit crew at the Indy 500.

Nasty was screaming that we hadn't crossed the wake yet, but ready or not, it was time to go. We launched the rubber ducky's extraction chute and ran out the greasy ramp right behind it, our static lines providing only the merest hint of resistance as we fell into the crepuscular sky.

The slipstream caught me and slapped me awake. I watched as the plane continued in its inexorable plunge to the sea. It hit, tumbled, cartwheeled, and disappeared beneath the waves before we'd descended through five thousand feet.

Now I paid attention to my risers. There were some twists, but I untangled them in short order and continued the descent. The IBS was falling nicely—no sign of trouble there. I looked at the water surface. There were crosswinds, but they weren't heavy. A heavy crosswind meant you could be dragged all the hell over the ocean. No fun.

I hit feet first and went under. The chilly water sent my balls into my mouth. Damn. I hit the quick-release, pulled myself out of the chute harness, and fought my way to the surface, dragging my combat pack with me. Quickly I uncoiled a length of nylon rope from my vest and swam toward Nasty, who'd landed about ten yards to my right. We linked up, both spitting water.

"Okay?"

"Yeah, Skipper—piece of fucking cake."

The IBS was about fifty yards from us, bobbing in the four-foot swells. Half Pint was already cutting the pallet away by the time we got there. He heaved himself over the gunwales and checked the equipment.

"All here," he shouted.

I gave him a thumbs-up. While the rest of us pulled ourselves aboard, he played snipe and began the engine-starting sequence. He pumped, primed, then pulled the starter cord. There were two sputters and a cough, and then the goddamn thing growled, roared, and settled into a steady, throaty purr.

Now it was time to go over the gear carefully. The assault pole had survived the ride in great shape. We had weapons and ammo. Cherry'd lost half a dozen flares, and Nod's survivor's kit had disappeared on impact. But that was all minor compared to what might have happened.

Even the extra fuel bladders had made the drop without rupturing—giving us an extra fifty miles worth of gas if we needed 'em. We shifted cargo until we'd achieved a working balance of men and equipment, then I rolled my forefinger above my head, pointed west, and we charged, Half Pint kicking the engine in the ass and almost standing the IBS's nose in the air.

It would not be an easy trip to the *Akita Maru*. All oceans are different. Each has its sphincter-puckering, nut-numbing, mind-fucking charm. The North Sea slam-dunks you in series after series of bone-jarring, keel-rattling shudders. Riding a small boat in the North Sea is like getting kicked in the balls again and again and again. The Atlantic has long swells that resemble roller coasters. You go up-up-up slowly, hit the crest, and look at the horizon, then down-down-down crashing into the frigid water. Riding a small boat in the Atlantic is like getting kicked in the balls punctuated by getting kicked in the ass.

In the Pacific, sixty-foot swells are not unknown. There are huge water-walls that can turn ships topsy-turvy. There are trenches so deep that nothing lives in them. Because of those trenches and the deep water, the ground swells are tremendous and powerful. One minute you're on the crest of a wave. Then all of a sudden your engine is sputtering and flooding and the water's looming ten feet above the gunwales and you're trying to fight your way out of a trough so fucking deep that it looks like one of those fucking Japanese prints with the stylized waves three stories high. Riding a small boat in the fucking Pacific is like getting kicked in the balls punctuated by getting kicked in the head. Am I making myself clear here through the use of repetition? I hope I am.

After twenty minutes or so my coccyx couldn't take any more. I had Half Pint cut the engine and we shifted ourselves around, moving onto the outside tubes, which distributed the weight better, allowing the boat to ride more evenly. That made all the difference in the world. Now, Half Pint was able to time the wave action without worrying about the IBS's balance, allowing him to push the boat forward as well as sideways and backward. I looked at it as one small step for mankind.

We kept pressing on. It was cold but nobody noticed. At times like this the adrenaline is flowing so fast and furious that even if it had been fucking freezing, we wouldn't have paid any attention. By the time we'd pulled within a mile and a half of the tanker, we were able to get a good view of the underway lights high on the ship's masthead about every third wave. I pointed and told HP to key on the lights until he closed in on the *Akita Maru*'s wake.

The wake is easy to follow and gives you the reassuring sense that you're really getting closer to your target, even though you may be more than half a mile off. The underway lights on the masthead do precisely the opposite. They're small and you can only see them when you're cresting the waves. Moreover, because of the relative speed between our rubber ducky and the *Akita Maru*—their sixteen-plus knots and our twenty-five—it seemed as if we were sitting still in the water and getting cold and miserable while they were steaming ahead full. I knew that once we hit the wake, however, there'd be a real feeling of progress. First, you're on a tangible track—like being on a dead heading. Second, as the wake reduces in size you can almost sense the heat from the ship's discharges in the water.

It was close to 2100 before we sensed we were riding in her wake—a subtle change of rhythm and motion that made our hearts beat just a little bit faster. Even though it was dark we could see her silhouette when we hit the crest. In my mind I heard the deep throb of those huge engines as we finally pushed through the wash.

Nod checked the extra fuel bladder and readied it for a

quick transfer. I didn't want to run out of gas as we made our attack run. Nor did I want to run the current tank down to empty. If I did, the line might vacuum up. That would take some minutes to clear, with us sitting within sight of the tanker like a fucking bull's-eye. *Merci, non, Monsieur Murphy.* But we had to change tanks. The first was too low to sustain us through our assault. So, when we got close enough to the *Akita Maru* so that her huge fantail towered above us like the ass end of four ten-story eighteen wheelers side by side, I told Nod to do his quick change.

Deftly, he switched the hoses and pumped the bulb, then watched horrified as the engine hiccuped, coughed, then died.

Unaware of his fuckup, the *Akita Maru* chugged on, pulling slowly away from us. Nod extracted the end of the hose, sucked on it, spat out fuel, reattached the hose, pumped the bulb, and yanked on the starter.

Nothing. We were up shit creek without a paddle, and the fucking tanker was getting away.

Duck Foot swatted Nod aside. He grabbed the starter cord, adjusted the choke, then gave the cord a vicious tug.

The engine sputtered, then died.

He tried again. Then again. It caught on the third try, and we all watched with a mixture of fascination and terror as he nursed the engine back to life by playing with the choke. Finally, it growled the way it was meant to growl. He threw it into gear, and we were back in the chase. It may have been cold, but I was sweating as much as if I'd been working the weight pile at Rogue Manor in August.

It was time to move. I wanted Nasty up the ladder first—he was the second-best climber in the group. The best, Duck Foot, would handle the boat and come up the ladder last, since he had the best chance of making it without help. And there would be problems in getting aboard. When you bring an IBS alongside a vessel the size of a tanker, you suffer additional ground swells. These come from the turbulence running down the sides of the ship, and they cause your small boat to be swept away from the ship's skin. It makes climbing difficult, to say the very least.

We came alongside. From the air it had seemed that the amidships deck was almost awash. Now, looking up at this fucking behemoth, I realized just how wrong I'd been. Pick extended the improvised caving ladder, set the hook on the rail, and tugged. It swayed like a fucking pendulum—but it held. Nod and Cherry swept the rail with their weapons. There'd be a crew aboard. We could handle them. We also sensed that Buckshot Brannigan, Manny Tanto, and the rest of the Centurions would be there, too, protecting the missiles. That was all right by me—we had a score to settle with them.

Nasty's HK was slung across his shoulders. He had a caving ladder coiled around his waist, and his vest was filled with deadly things. He looked at me in a way that told me he knew I was crazy and that he was even crazier. Then he started up the pole.

He got eight feet when one of the rungs we'd set into the pole collapsed under his weight and he fell ass over teakettle back into the IBS.

Luckily for him—and us—he landed on me.

"Shit, Skipper."

I rolled him off me and examined him quickly for breakage. He was okay—he'd only lost a tooth on the butt of my gun, so I kicked his ass and sent him back up the ladder. "Try to keep the fucking thing in one piece this time, will ya, Grundle?"

"Aye, aye, sir." Nasty gave me the finger. Then he actually scampered up the fucking pole, vaulted the rail, secured and dropped the caving ladder, and threw me the bird again.

I truly love the boy.

Now the rest of us could make the climb—anywhere from sixteen to twenty-six feet of it, depending on the swells. I let Nod and Cherry precede me, then I hooked an arm through the cable and started to pull myself up.

It's harder than it looks. There's the motion of the ocean; there's the bolt-covered skin of the tanker. The cable itself was wet and slippery, and you had to hook your arms and legs on each slippery metal rung.

There are exercises you do at BUD/S to make you

proficient at climbing cargo nets, but they do not prepare you for the unmitigated hell of an at-sea assault, hanging on to a ship under way with a bunch of bad guys aboard.

Still, consider the motivating factors. I could fall and break my back in the IBS. Or I could hit the water and be sliced by our outboard engine. If that didn't work, I could be sucked alongside the tanker, inexorably drawn toward the big grinding screw of the tanker, where I'd be turned into Dickburger.

Combine all those elements with the "normal" sphincter-pucker factor, and climbing on board becomes a piece of cake—you just go up the fucking ladder like a goddamn monkey with a tiger on your tail.

Over the rail. Nod, Cherry, and Nasty were spread out in a defensive perimeter, their weapons sweeping the deck. Not a soul out.

Finally, Duck Foot heaved himself aboard. I watched as the IBS slipped away, drawn aft by the current toward the tanker's screw. There were no lights forward, although I could see figures in the wheelhouse atop the superstructure.

I gave hand signals, and we moved out. Pick and Half Pint would scale the superstructure and take over the bridge. Nasty and I would seize the crew's quarters. Duck Foot, Cherry, and Nod would secure the engineering spaces, then work their way forward to the chain lockers.

We had no radios. We had no comms. All we had was us—and the knowledge that everyone else aboard the *Akita Maru* was a bad guy.

It was time to go to work. I watched as Pick and HP went up the outside of the superstructure, climbing hand over hand. HP rolled over the rail first, his suppressed submachine gun at the ready. Then Pick followed. I'd have liked to watch, but I was otherwise engaged.

Nasty Nick took point as we rolled through the first deckhouse hatchway. Inside, it was clean and white. Good lights. The Japs liked their ships neat. The passageway forked. I took the port side as Grundle moved starboard. There were six compartments, three to port, three to starboard. I tried the first. The knob turned. I eased the hatch open. No lights inside.

I went through the hatch, my back to the wall, closed it behind me, and flipped on the light.

The cabin was empty.

I turned the light out and slipped back outside, locking the door before closing it and moving to the second doorway. I repeated my actions. Clear.

Now for number three. There was a light behind this door. Slowly, slowly, I tested the handle. It worked. I turned the knob and pushed.

The hatch was locked from the inside.

HK ready, I applied a liberal helping of shoulder. The lock snapped and I moved inside.

A round oriental face looked at me quizzically from the bunk across the cabin. The expression turned to pure horror when he saw who it was and what I had in my paw.

"*I-ie*—" He raised his hands in surrender.

I knew enough Japanese to take yes for an answer. Before he could react, I was on top of him. I flipped him, slapped him with my sap, wrapped his hands, feet, and mouth with surgical tape, and left him trussed to the bunk, facedown and blindfolded, while I searched his cabin. His face was familiar. It took me a while to realize that I'd seen him twice before. Once at Grant Griffith's war game, the second time on videotape at Seal Beach.

That meant there were five of them. Okay—next.

Four and five were empty. Six had a light.

Another Jap—and he'd left his hatch unlocked, the sorry asshole.

Deep breath. Focus on the job. Don't take chances. Now, go—

Into the cabin. Sally Stallone's eyes met mine. He had a *Playboy* in his big hands. There was a Sig Sauer 9mm lying on his chest, and his arm moved toward it.

I stitched him up the side with the HK, knocking him into the back of his bunk. The loudest sound my weapon made was the soft *whoomp* of rounds impacting in Sally's rib cage.

He may have been down, but the son of a bitch wasn't out. He roared like a fucking wounded grizzly, rolled off the bunk, gun in hand, and came charging at me. With six feet between us I wasn't taking chances. I shot him with two more three-round bursts in the chest, and he went to his knees, falling toward me.

I sidestepped, kicked the gun away, and put another three-round burst in the back of his head for good measure. Now I knew the cockbreath was down for good.

I changed mags. I was covered with sweat. Had anybody heard the commotion? If they had, Nasty was out there working the opposite passageway.

I rolled Sally over and went through his pockets. I took the son of a bitch's straight razor and his wallet. There were no papers in the room.

Now back into the passageway. Nasty waited aft. I told him with hand signals that I'd killed one and taken one prisoner. He signaled that he'd taken three prisoners.

Americans?

No, he signaled, stretching the skin around his eyes. Japs.

We moved up one deck. There was no one in the laundry or the storeroom area. We secured each one and locked them up for the night. We slipped into the galley. The stove had been turned off—that was a good sign.

Carefully, we bolted the door behind us and moved along a short passageway toward the mess, where we heard voices speaking Japanese. I looked at Nasty. He looked back at me and gave me an "OK" with thumb and forefinger.

I was on my way to the bridge when I heard the first shots. Nasty'd stayed below to secure the six card-playing coffee-drinkers. I was halfway up the superstructure when I heard them. Slam-slam, slam-slam. Two double taps. Then a burst of automatic-weapons fire. Now they had to know they'd been attacked. I changed course. To play it safe I went up the outside of the deckhouse, mountain-climbing the white-painted superstructure, bolt by bolt and cleat by cleat. By the time I pulled myself over the top rail, I was huffing and puffing like an old fart.

I heaved myself into the wheelhouse. Pick stood there, his HK pointed at the body on the deck. A Walther PPK/S lay in the corner where he'd kicked it. "Pilot—a Jap. Sumbitch went for a gun, Skipper—got four rounds off."

"I heard. Where's Pint?"

"He's securing the radio shack."

"They didn't get a message off—" That would have made me very nervous.

"Nah—we prevented that. We got their codes—everything. They didn't stand a chance. They had fucking NSA ciphers, Skipper."

"No shit."

Pick nodded. "The real thing."

I free-associated. Four words came to mind. Pinky and Prescott, and Grant and Griffith.

"Shiiiit—" Pick jumped my bones. Just as he hit me, I heard an explosion from my six o'clock and felt the burn of his HK as he loosed a full mag over my shoulder.

"What the—" I rolled just in time to see Manny Tanto's big, ugly form disappear past the wheelhouse window. He was carrying a Benelli assault shotgun—nine rounds in the long tubular magazine.

"Pick." I rolled him off onto the deck. He'd saved my life, but he'd caught some of the blast. His ear was half-gone and he was bleeding all over me. Quickly, I sat him up, found his medical kit, jabbed him with morphine, wrapped his head, and tapped him on the shoulder. "You'll be okay, kid—gotta go." I slapped a fresh mag into Pick's HK, locked and loaded it for him, and put it in his hands. "Tell Nasty to hold the fort. Anybody comes through the door, kill 'em."

Outside. Where the hell had he gone? I checked the wing area, then circled the wheelhouse. Nothing. Then I saw it—blood by a hatchway. One drop. One of Pick's shots had nicked the son of a bitch.

I moved inside. There was more blood—the asshole had dropped down a scuttle from the looks of it. Now he was in the bowels of the ship and it would take me forever to find him.

It was time to link up with Cherry. I moved toward the engine room, sweeping each passageway with my HK as I went. I yelled down as I cleared the hatch and heard Cherry's voice come back at me: "All clear, Skipper." Good. That gave us control of the ship for all practical purposes—except there were still a bunch of bad guys prowling and growling.

I dropped down a metal ladder onto a long catwalk that ran above the main engine room. I whistled, and Cherry looked up. He and Nod were shackling three Japanese crewmen to a bulkhead. I pointed forward. Cherry gave me a thumbs-up. He and Nod clambered up the ladder to where I waited, and the three of us made our way forward, working our way through a maze of passageways, until we reached the tank hatches that sat just about amidships.

There were eight hatches in all. Six were bolted tight and hadn't been played with recently. Two others showed signs of use. In fact, one hatch was so loose we removed the cover without a wrench. Now, the three of us dropped into the darkness, climbing down the rungs welded to the side of the two-foot, cylindrical hatchway.

We went down five or six yards, ending up on a narrow catwalk that ran around the circumference of one of the ship's main tanks. I looked at the cargo tanks and prayed it was crude down there. Nod took point, leading the way around the cofferdams and into a series of short passageways punctuated by ninety-degree turns that ran athwartships between the tanks. It seemed to me that if the weapons were on board, they would be riding amidships in one of these passageways that ran port to starboard instead of bow to stern, where they'd take the least abuse from the seas and would be the most protected.

There were six of these mazelike athwartships passages, all of them dimly lit from above with sealed, low-voltage lamps that gave the passages a flickering, oil-lamp look. Above, the ship was spotless. Here, a perpetual veneer of grime had attached itself to every possible surface. The sickly sweet odor of raw petroleum permeated the atmosphere, making breathing hard. We moved slowly, deliberately. I studied closely for any sign of blood on the deck but discovered none. We pressed on. After fifteen minutes I exchanged positions with Nod and took the point to give him a break. Cherry patrolled ten yards behind us, providing cover.

I hadn't gone more than halfway down the third athwart-ships passageway when I turned a corner and saw what we'd come to find: a pile of wooden crates were secured against the tank bulkheads, and extra dunnage was used to brace them in place. The lettering on the crates read U.S. GOVERN-MENT PROPERTY.

Buckshot Brannigan and Biker Jordan were there, too. Biker was holding a grenade in his hand—the pin had been pulled and only the pressure of his fingers kept the spoon from popping. Buckshot had a suppressed HK cradled in his arms. His finger was on the trigger. I saw that the fire-selector switch was in three-shot-burst mode.

"Yo, Dick, long time no see—not since Century City."

I drew up. My HK hung from my right shoulder by its sling, the muzzle level with his chest. "Buckshot."

He moved alongside one of the missile crates, about five yards from me. I swiveled my HK as he moved. "Seems we have a problem here."

"Oh?" I didn't see it that way.

"Look, this'll have to be worked out between us. We can't have a Mexican standoff for the next six days."

"Sure, Buckshot—put the fucking gun down, have Biker put the pin back in the grenade, and we'll work it all out."

He shook his head. "No can do, old buddy. There's too much at stake. Far too much."

He was right. There *was* far too much at stake here—but the stakes weren't the ones Buckshot was thinking of. His mind was focused solely on money. What made me homicidal was the fact that Buckshot had killed two of my men. But while avenging Wynken's and Blynken's deaths was one major element of my rage, there were other factors, too.

Buckshot betrayed his country when he stole the Toma-hawks. Even worse, he betrayed all the other men who'd worn the same uniform he had, just as surely as if he'd knowingly led them into an ambush.

When you fight, you don't fight for abstract values like The Flag, or The Nation, or Democracy. You fight for your buddy. You fight to keep him alive and he fights to keep you alive, and you go on that way, day after day, battle after battle. And when one of your buddies dies, something inside you dies as well. But you go on. You fight, so that his death isn't meaningless, his sacrifice isn't for nothing.

That is the real essence, the nucleus, the core, of unit integrity.

But Buckshot had betrayed all that for money. There was no way I was going to let his perfidy stand unchallenged.

I saw Cherry coming up behind Biker Jordan, and I wasn't in much of a mood to waste Buckshot's time—or mine. So I shot him in the head. Once. Between the eyes. Not bad for instinct shooting. But then, Buckshot had killed two of my men—and the bitter memory of those assassinations made my shot go true. He dropped like a stone before he could say anything more.

Biker was still reacting when Cherry's hands closed around the grenade and twisted savagely. I heard Biker's wrist snap before the ex–Green Beret screamed like the proverbial stuck pig. In a millisecond, Nod was on the son of a bitch, his Field Fighter up Biker's solar plexus to the hilt. Nod was halfway to eviscerating the poor asshole before I pulled him off.

Cherry stepped out of the spreading blood puddle and held the grenade tightly. "Let's put a pin in this, Skipper— the fucking thing makes me nervous."

He wasn't the only one.

Now we had the goods. We had the ship secured. The only thing we didn't have was Manny Tanto. I knew he was wounded, but I didn't have any idea how bad Pick had dinged him. I had Nod, Duck Foot, and Cherry booby-trap the athwart ship passages so that if Manny tried to break into the area, we'd know about it. Then we cleared the bodies out and went back to the bridge.

I sent Nasty down to find Buckshot's cabin and bring back any paperwork he could lay his hands on. He returned in ten minutes carrying a locked leather attaché case. Half Pint checked it for booby traps, then we pried it open.

Inside there were ciphers and fax messages and a lot of cash. I went down to the mess deck and read the faxes. They were very interesting indeed.

Once everything had been secured, we went over the ship again, searching for Manny Tanto. Working in three pairs, we started in the forecastle and worked our way aft, locker by locker, tank by tank, passageway by passageway. I discovered compartments I'd never known existed. But there was no sign of Manny. It was like he'd vanished.

But of course he hadn't vanished. He was out there, somewhere, waiting. Well, we were prepared for him—armed and dangerous. In the meanwhile, we had a tanker to bring in. I assigned each of my SEALs a four-hour watch on the bridge. The ship was on autopilot, the logs gave us our course, and the cipher books allowed us to fax the right coded messages back to Japan. So the only thing to do was sit back and enjoy the ride. The hard part would come in six days, when we made landfall.

In the meanwhile, I made a few quick satellite phone calls. I called Stevie Wonder, who chortled that Pinky was having a cow because we'd dropped off the face of the earth. "Fuckin' feds are going crazy, Dick-head."

That made me feel great. I told him I'd be in touch soon, and to stand by for action.

"I thought you'd never ask."

Then I touched base with Tosho, just to make sure we'd have a proper welcoming committee when we docked at Yokohama. When he heard where I was and what I had with me, there was an audible gasp on the line. Then he asked me to call him back in fifteen minutes. When I did, Tosho said he'd briefed his boss and received permission to chopper a crew out to us thirty-six hours before landing. "We're gonna rock and roll, Dick—and have this all wrapped up before the fucking politicians know what's happened. No way they'll interfere now."

That sounded good to me. I also checked in with Mike Regan's answering machine to let him know we were all still alive. Then it was time to strip to Skivvies and lead PT on the *Akita Maru*'s huge flat deck. The air was clear, the sun was hot, we worked ourselves into a sweat, and life was absofuckinglutely perfect.

That is, it *was* perfect—until Manny Tanto paid me a social call the third night. It was just past 0200. We'd settled into our schedule comfortably. Too comfortably, it turned out—which is no doubt what he'd been waiting for. I had the conn, and Duck Foot was keeping me company. We didn't hear him so much as sense him—as if a ghost had passed through the bridge.

And then all of a sudden Duck Foot's hand was pinned to the map table by a stiletto. He screamed and yanked—which didn't do him any good. By the time I looked around and saw there was no way I was going to reach the HK that sat useless ten feet away on the other side of the bridge, Manny had opened him up like a chicken and was coming for me—a big, bloody knife in his hand.

The nasty thing about knife fighting is that no matter what you do, you're going to get cut. Make no mistake about it. All those movies in which guys go at each other with blades and slash and slash and manage to keep out of the way of the blade—they're so much bullshit.

The bottom line is that if you fight with knives, you will be cut. That's why I prefer guns. It's more effective to shoot someone at five yards than have him slamming into your face carrying a big, ugly sharp blade to do you bodily harm.

But I wasn't being given any choice here. The half-breed had chosen the time and the place—and all I could do was make sure he didn't completely control the venue.

He was out of control. He had his war face on—he'd striped his skin with camouflage cream and tied his hair back in samurai style, a black band knotted around his forehead. His eyes were like coals, reflecting the red, blue, and green instrumentation lights. His bare chest, painted in the same black and green tiger stripes as his face, rippled.

He nicked me good before I put a steel-frame chair between us—a long slash that cut me along the bone side of my left arm and drew a lot of blood. Then, smiling the same savage leer he'd had on his face all those years ago in Tri Ton, he stepped back to gauge his best attack.

He lunged. I dodged. He feinted. I parried. He slashed. I sidestepped.

All the while, wild-eyed, I searched for improvised weapons as Manny hacked away. I had a pocket knife on my belt. It's one of those Maritime lockback jobs—a big fat blade for cutting rope, and a marlinespike for making splices. I fumbled for it, holding Manny off with the chair.

One-handed, I opened the marlinespike and set the knife inside my right fist, the spike jutting out two inches. I used the chair like a lion tamer—jabbing to keep him away from me.

It was like some fucking scene from a deranged gladiator movie—a crazy half-breed and a bearded Visigoth going at it to the death.

"Come on, you son of a bitch," I taunted him.

The only sounds he made were his breathing and the scuff of his bare feet on the deck. He lunged at me, sinking the knife through the fiber seat bottom and soft cushion. I twisted away and popped him a quick one with my right hand.

He looked surprised as the marlinespike punctured his chest, just above the right nipple. "Uh—"

I gave him another. A trickle of blood began to run down his chest, dark liquid against the camouflage.

He roared and came at me; the knife cut through the chair seat again and clipped me in the side, drawing blood. But the son of a bitch had made a bad tactical error.

His right hand was stuck in the chair seat. He tried to wrestle the chair from me, but I pushed him back against the ship's wheel, put both of my hands on the steel frame, and went left—hard. I heard his right shoulder separate as he got tangled up in the wheel. Still, he wouldn't let go of the fucking knife. I pushed the chair as hard as I could and kneed him in the groin. He grunted. Now I hit him again with the marlinespike—once, twice, three times in the chest. I could feel the cartilage pop with each penetration.

He started to gargle blood—bright red blood. I'd hit his fucking lungs.

Now I got the goddamn knife out of his hands by the blade. He cut my fingers but I didn't give a shit. I was in a frenzy. I twisted the knife away, doubled it over, and sunk the point into his groin. He screamed.

I pulled away, reversed the blade, and swung it up between his legs like a sucker punch. It caught him squarely in the crotch. He doubled over.

Then I grabbed him by the long single braid and the seat of his pants and ran him through the glass door of the wheelhouse. There wasn't much of his face left when he hit the bridge wing rail. Not my problem. I picked Manny up and rolled him over the rail and watched as he fell sixty feet into the black water. I hoped the cockbreath liked to swim.

I staggered, my hand leaving bloody prints on the deck and bulkheads as I lurched back to the wheelhouse to get some help for Duck Foot and me. I made it as far as the intercom, then everything went black.

Chapter

21

TOSHO CHOPPERED ABOARD ABOUT EIGHTEEN HOURS FROM LAND-fall. He brought six of his best shooters with him, including Kunika's own punk-rock kid, Yoshioka, who dropped out of the SH-3 ASW helicopter complete with leather jeans, James Dean T-shirt, and motorcycle boots.

I gave Tosho a big *abrazo*. "Nice to see you, asshole."

He returned the hug and gave me a high five. "Welcome back to the Land of the Rising Sun, Dick-head."

While his troops unloaded their gear so the chopper could take off, I took Tosho and two of his men below so they could visit the Japanese we'd taken prisoner. Five of them were Matsukos; the rest were the tanker's skeleton crew.

Tosho wasn't bound by the same rules of evidence and interrogation American policemen are, and it didn't take him more than half an hour to sweat the story out of our prisoners. The crew had no idea what the ship was carrying. But the owners had been well paid by Hideo Ikigami to transport his precious cargo. According to the Matsukos, the tanker would dock at Yokohama, where it would be met by a Matsuko truck, which would take the Tomahawks to a Matsuko Machine warehouse in Yokota, an industrial city northwest of Tokyo. From there, the Japs told Tosho they had no idea what would happen.

From reading Buckshot's papers, I knew that his assignment was to remain with the shipment until it was safely inside Matsuko's gates.

"So what do you think?" Tosho asked.

"I think we have a golden opportunity here," I said. "I have Buckshot's codebooks. Let's send your pal Ikigami a fax. Tell him there's a bonus package in the shipment."

That brought a grin to Tosho's face. "Sounds righteous to me, dude. What're you gonna promise him?"

"I'll keep it vague but tantalizing."

He watched as I drafted a short message, encoded it, and rolled it through the fax. "Perfect. Now let's go upstairs and see my favorite *Amerikajins.*"

"That's topside, asshole, you're aboard a ship now."

"Topside, shmopside—whatever."

We climbed two decks and walked into the mess, where Red Cell was waiting. Tosho greeted them all effusively, especially Duck Foot, who really looked the worse for wear. He'd lost a lot of blood by the time Nasty and Nod got him down to the ship's infirmary, punched him full of morphine, and sewed him up. He was pale and frail, but full of fight. He'd insisted on being with the rest of the men when Tosho arrived. "I'm not gonna lose face on this one, Skipper."

And he hadn't. Tosho ruffled the hair on Duck Foot's head. "You do nice work as a bayonet dummy," he said, examining the wounds. "But the next time you want to try *seppuku,* you talk to me first, okay?"

The SEAL nodded. "Okay by me, Tosh."

"Good." Tosho looked my crew over critically. "You're all much grungier than I remember," he said.

"Lack of pussy," Cherry said.

"Lack of beer," growled Nasty Nick Grundle.

"Amen to that," said Half Pint. "We could use some good times."

"If you say so." Tosho barked an order in Japanese, and two Kunika shooters bowed, said, *"Hai!"* in unison, and bounded out the hatchway toward the deck. In a few minutes they returned carrying a huge chest. "For you, my honored guests," the policeman said, bowing toward Nasty.

Grundle opened the double clasps. Inside thick, thermal-plastic foam packing were three dozen two-liter jugs of iced draft Asahi Dry beer. The smile on Nasty's face spread from ear to ear. *"Domo arigato*—thank you, Tosho-san," he said gleefully, bowing respectfully and deeply in the Japanese policeman's direction.

Then Nasty turned around to address the rest of us: "So—what are you guys gonna drink?"

We made landfall more or less on schedule. I watched Tosho and his boys with admiration. The son of a bitch knew how to run an op. His men were lean and mean. They worked out—and it showed. They could start and finish each other's sentences, one sure sign that he'd built them into a real team, not a collection of disparate souls. And he'd given them all the latest and best gear. From weapons to clothes, they had everything they needed to get the job done. He'd packed all the right stuff, too—from scrambler telephones and secure portable radios to directional monitors, miniature eavesdropping devices, and tiny, fiber-optic cameras. The fact that he could get all his equipment so easily made me somewhat jealous. But I realized that in Japan, unlike the United States, they had to deal with terrorism on a daily basis. Thus, the government realized that a normal bureaucracy wasn't going to be able to handle situations of crisis proportion. So they allowed shooters like Tosho free rein. He planned and ran all his own ops.

In the United States, things are exactly the opposite. We have been largely immune from terrorism—although that will not be the case in the nineties, as we have already seen. Still, in the United States, it's the "suits"—the office-bound apparatchiki—who most often get to decide what, when, where, and how the operators will do their jobs. And when that occurs, you get situations like Waco, Texas, where four ATF agents lost their lives because the senior officials who planned and approved the raid against a heavily armed cult had no idea how such operations should be run.

In Waco, despite faulty intelligence, bad tactics, abysmal communications, poor leadership, no coordination, and advice from the raiding team that the op should be scrubbed, the "suits" in the choppers ordered their subordinates to go ahead.

If I were a cynic, I'd say the reason behind their decision was so that they'd get their faces on "Top Cops" or some other TV show, get still another Peter Principle promotion, another civil service bonus, and then retire to a cushy security job in a Fortune 500 corporation. You do not run special operations by thinking about yourself. You run them by thinking about your men. Like Tosho did. Endeth the sermon.

Three Matsuko tugboats met us as we came up on Uraga Point, about forty miles south of Yokohama. We let the crew wave at them and make chatter on the radio, with one of Tosho's Kunika boys listening in to ensure everything went according to plan. Docking was to be at 2200—the better to keep a low profile. Unlike a freighter, the tanker couldn't just tie up to a dock. It was too big and too ungainly. Besides, tankers don't usually tie up and unload their cargo the same way other ships do. Instead, we'd moor out in the bay, just below the main harbor, close to the crude-oil pipeline that sat atop a quarter-mile breakwater. Then one of the tugs would ferry the booty to shore and make the transfer.

We were ready to go. Duck Foot would stay out of sight, working communications from the tanker until we'd left. Then he'd link up with a Kunika squad and come with them. Tosho and four of his shooters, as well as Nasty, Half Pint, Pick, Cherry, Nod, and I, would go with the shipment. I mentioned to Tosho that one thing working in our favor was the fact that the people from Matsuko had never met Buckshot and his Centurions International crew—Buckshot had once told me he'd never deployed overseas.

"It wouldn't matter if they had," Tosho said. "Face it, Dick, you *gaijins* all look alike to us."

We weren't pretty, but we were ready to go by the time the Matsuko tug nudged up to our amidships port side, tied alongside, and the captain radioed that he was coming aboard. Tosho and I had had plenty of time to plan our moves, so when the tugster called, I answered his signal with the response I'd gotten from Buckshot's cipher book, and he in turn responded to me in the approved manner. Now we knew that we were both kosher.

Yoki, carrying an HK-93 with retracted stock slung over his shoulder, met the Matsuko officer and ushered him topside. I was standing just inside the wheelhouse, a Glock in the waistband of my black BDUs. My Notre Dame T-shirt was courtesy of Tosho. I waited until the tug captain had bowed at me. I didn't bow back. "We're ready," I said.

Tosho was standing at my side. He started to translate but the tugboat man held up his hand. "I understand English," he said.

"Good. Then understand this: I don't have any time to waste. Let's get this thing underway."

He bowed again. *"Hai!"* Then he turned away, plucked a cellular phone from his jacket, and made a call, jabbering away in Jap for a minute or two. "We are ready for you, Major Brannigan."

"You know who I am?"

"Your directness precedes you. I am told you are a very straightforward personage. Now we will begin the operation."

I gestured toward his tugboat. "Please."

We watched from the wheelhouse wing as they maneuvered the crates from the hatchway and lowered them carefully onto the tug's aft deck, piling them between the stern cleat and the starboard capstan and securing each crate with a separate line. There were five Tomahawks, and three larger boxes that Tosho and I had built—props for Mr. Ikigami's benefit. When everything had been loaded, Tosho and I made our way down from the bridge, and joined by four of his shooters and my quintet of Red Cell marauders, we lowered ourselves down onto the tug deck.

The trip to dockside took less than ten minutes. As we came alongside, I saw a flatbed truck, four Jeep Cherokees with smoked-glass windows, and the longest fucking Cadillac limousine I've ever seen, all parked in a row. I nudged Tosho with my elbow. He nudged back.

The Jeep doors opened, and two men carrying shotguns got out of each one. They stood guard as half a dozen gorillas in blue jumpsuits swarmed the tug. The cargo handlers moved the crates onto the flatbed, tied them down securely.

When it was all done, a tall, liveried Anglo chauffeur climbed out of the limo. He moved to the rear door and opened it reverently, then reached inside and presented his arm so that the car's occupant could lean on it as he emerged.

Hideo Ikigami was so short that he almost didn't have to duck his head as he climbed out of his car. He was a wizened little man wearing an impeccably tailored sharkskin suit in the sort of iridescent gray that oriental businessmen often favor, white shirt, dark tie, and buffed black shoes that reflected the moonlight. His hair—what there was of it— was slicked back along the sides of his head, trailing off in greasy wisps.

He stood quietly, taking the scene in, his eyes locked onto the three big shipping crates that Tosho and I had built. Then a big smile came over his face, and he began to walk in my direction, trailed by another suited man who'd appeared at his side like a shadow. He bowed when he reached me.

I bowed back. "Mr. Ikigami, I presume."

"Hai!" He bowed again and spoke in Japanese. The Shadow bowed as well, then said, "Mr. Ikigami says you must be Major Brannigan."

I bowed a second time. *"Hai!"* This was getting boring. I elbowed Tosho forward. "This is my associate, Mr. Tanto."

Tosho translated his own introduction and bowed.

Once the formalities were over, Ikigami bowed again and spoke in my direction. The Shadow translated. "Thank you, Major Brannigan, for your care and your concern in overseeing the transport of these precious materials to us. They will be well used. You may tell Mr. Griffith that I am very appreciative."

Would I ever. The son of a bitch had just hung himself— and there were witnesses, too. I glanced at Tosho, whose face was as inscrutable as ever.

As he spoke, Ikigami's eyes had never wandered from the crates. Now, the Shadow inclined his head in my direction.

"My employer wishes to know the nature of the extra cargo you communicated to him about."

"Ah," I said, bowing in Ikigami's direction, "I managed to locate a mobile missile launcher, and on my own I brought it as a special gift."

Shadow translated. Ikigami's eyes went wide. He bowed deeply in my direction, then he swiveled away and muttered a few words to his factotum before climbing back into the huge Caddie.

The Shadow closed the limousine door. "Mr. Ikigami says that you may accompany him."

"Thank you." I started for the flatbed truck. Four Matsuko nasty boys were covering the crates with a huge, blue tarp on which was the red, green, gold, and black Matsuko Machine logo—a stylized dragon bearing two swords.

Shadow blocked my way. "He means that you may ride with him. Your associates can ride with our security people."

Why didn't he just give us the keys to the fucking city while he was at it? I bowed. "He is very gracious." And he is a first-class shit-for-brains on top of it all, too, I thought.

We loaded up. Tosho came with me. We paired up the rest so each Jeep had one of Tosho's shooters and one American. Nasty elected to ride in the cab of the semi. I liked that—he knew how to drive one better than most professionals.

Tosho and I climbed into the limo. Ikigami had settled into the right rear side, nestled under a reading lamp, a folded Asian *Wall Street Journal* on his lap.

Sitting across from him was his Shadow—the translator —who, I now realized, carried a Walther PPK in a chamois shoulder holster. I started to sit next to Ikigami, but the Shadow gestured for me to take the other jump seat. Tosho settled in front next to the driver, beyond a thick black-glass partition. I couldn't see or hear him.

After about a minute we pulled out. I looked out the smoked windows and saw that we were leaving the dock area and easing onto an access road. From there, the convoy moved through a maze of industrial parks and warehouse complexes until it reached the on-ramp of a huge, elevated, six-lane highway.

We headed south for a few kilometers, then took an off-ramp onto a smaller but still-divided highway that swung west, then north. We rode in silence, Ikigami perusing his *Wall Street Journal* as we passed through Sagamihara, Hachioji, and Akishima. Just after dawn we reached Yokota and turned east, turning onto a two-lane road that led to a one-lane slab of asphalt that in turn followed alongside an eight-foot chain-link fence topped with razor wire. I scrunched my nose against the side window as the convoy slowed to a crawl. Up ahead was an unmanned gate. Beyond it, a huge warehouse loomed in the early-morning light.

I stuck my thumb in the direction of the warehouse. "So—this is where you're going to stow them," I said.

The slight businessman folded his paper back on its original seams, almost as if he were preparing it for an origami exercise.

"Yes, at last—we are here," Ikigami said in accented English. "The missiles are finally safe. I control everything inside this fence." He smiled at my reaction to his English. "And you, Major—you have done well."

The Shadow sitting across from Ikigami started to shift in his seat, as if he were about to stretch.

"Thank you," I said to Ikigami. "But please—never shit a shitter."

The Shadow paused and turned slightly toward me. I came around with my left elbow and slammed him up against the partition, smashing his neck and shattering his windpipe.

I leaned across his body and removed the Walther from its holster, dropped the magazine, and ratcheted the slide, extracting the shell in the chamber. I popped the rest of the rounds from the magazine so I could examine them, too. The PPK had been loaded with six Eley subsonic .22-caliber hollow-point bullets—the choice of professional assassins all over the world. They're quiet, and they're deadly. They're perfect for enclosed spaces like Ikigami's limo, where there's concern about secondary penetration.

Ikigami was looking at me with a mixture of fascination

and horror as I checked the weapon. "Don't worry, Hideo-san, I'm not gonna shoot you—yet."

I loaded the loose bullets back into the magazine, slapped the mag up into the pistol, chambered a round, then dropped the hammer safety to lower the hammer, flicked the safety off, then slid the weapon into my pocket. It fit very nicely there. Just as I finished, the convoy came to a complete stop just beyond the gate.

"I am not worried, *gaijin*," Ikigami said. "You are a dead man. You are all dead men. It is what Griffith-san wanted. You will simply disappear here."

"Don't count on it, asshole." I opened the limo door and rolled Shadow's corpse out. The driver's door opened and the big American chauffeur lurched out, too. Ikigami's eyes brightened until he saw that the man collapsed on the asphalt facedown.

I stepped into the cool morning air and stretched. "Everybody okay?"

Tosho came out of the limo's front door. "Fine here," he said. "Great day for the Fighting Irish."

I watched proudly as my shooters and Tosho's emerged from the Jeeps alone. We'd rehearsed various combinations of moves for ten hours. God, how I love teamwork.

"Oh, Mr. Ikigami," I said, "I think you better come on out and take a look at this. Seems some of your people just got terminally carsick."

Chapter

22

STEALING ANOTHER PLANE WAS OUT OF THE QUESTION. THE LOGI-cal place to go would have been Atsugi, the joint Japanese-American air base near Yokosuka. But we had too much loot to be able to slip onto the base unnoticed. There was the pallet-load of Tomahawk missiles. There was also a cross-section of missile parts, nuclear components, and other miscellaneous techno-goodies we'd taken from Ikigami's warehouse. Some of the materials had come from North Korea. I found that fact fascinating—and wondered, with some foreboding, what the kimchis had gotten in return for their help to Hideo Ikigami.

Well, Tosho would find out. He was a very thorough man. Especially when it came to traitors. He also solved our transportation problem: he made us a present of Hideo Ikigami's private jet. It was a Gulfstream-IIIA with auxiliary gas tanks. The plane's 5,800-mile range allowed us to fly Tokyo–Fairbanks, and then Fairbanks–Washington. Best of all, Matsuko would be stuck paying the gas bill.

Given the amount of evidence he'd collected at the warehouse, as well as the confessions from the five Matsukos he'd taken off the tanker, Tosho decided Ikigami-san could be kept on ice by the Kunika for about forty-eight hours without causing undue ripples either in the Japanese justice system or Ikigami's organization. The old man had been known to vanish from time to time, off on some private mission. This disappearance would fit his pattern.

Forty-eight hours was enough time for me, too. It would let me deal with Grant Griffith and Pinky Prescott. There would be no warning messages from the Jap kingpin to his pals back in the USA.

Red Cell slipped into Tokyo in a big closed van and showered and cleaned up at Kunika headquarters. Tosho opened the private bar in his bottom desk drawer, and fortified by a healthy prescription of Dr. Bombay, I called Mike Regan and asked him to put my goodies in a Federal Express box and post them to Stevie Wonder. Then I called Stevie and told him what he was about to acquire.

He was positively eloquent: "No shit. For what I am about to receive I am truly grateful."

I'll bet you are, I told him. Wonder had no use for people like Grant Griffith, or Pinky, either.

"What you want me to do with them?"

"Hold on to 'em." A plan was forming in my gin-numbed Slovak brain. "Remember where we had so much fun in the country last November?"

I could just see his head swiveling left/right/left, right/left/right. "Ah—near the old inn?"

"Bingo."

"Yeah. Nice place."

"I'm glad you approve. Rent two vans and leave them at Warrenton Airpark." The runway there was long enough to accommodate the Gulfstream, and I didn't want to land at Dulles, which was more convenient, but which also, according to Wonder, was crawling with feds. "Put the keys inside the bumpers. Chalk the vans so I'll know which ones are mine. Then go visit Uta and Don. Wait for me there with the FedEx package from Mike. Just remember to protect yourself at all times."

"No prob." Wonder, a combat-proven veteran of the USMC (which stands for Uncle Sam's Misguided Children), won two Silver Stars in Vietnam for doing unfriendly things up close and personal to Mr. Charlie and other assorted malefactors. He actually relishes that sort of stuff. Jarheads are all alike—they're crazy motherfuckers. That's why I like them so much.

Then we trucked out to Haneda airport, just south of Tokyo, where under Tosho's careful supervision, we packed the Matsuko corporate jet. It was a tight fit, but we managed to squeeze everything on board, including our weapons and ammo, as well as the evidence we'd gathered on the *Akita Maru*. Tosho sealed the most sensitive stuff with diplomatic seals—where he'd gotten them I had no idea. Pick would fly first seat with one of Matsuko's corporate pilots dragooned as his backup.

To make sure everything went smoothly, Tosho assigned his punkster, Yoki, to ride shotgun. Yoki, who came complete with diplomatic passport and fluent English, was the reason U.S. Customs wasn't going to give us any trouble about the weapons. So far as the Americans were being told, the Matsuko jet was on official GOJ—that's Government Of Japan to you civilians out there—business, and its cargo, suitably secured with diplomatic seals, was inviolable.

If there was going to be any problem, it was us American Navy people. There was, after all, an alert out for us. Moreover, we weren't carrying passports, and our credit cards and IDs were all bogus—and probably well-known to the feds by now. The plane and its cargo might be sacrosanct. We, on the other hand, were dog meat.

It took Tosho almost two minutes to solve that one. He came up with seven Costa Rican diplomatic passports. They'd been confiscated during a crackdown on citizenship-selling at the Costa Rican embassy. "They're real," he said. "The question is whether or not we can get them put together in time."

We sat at Haneda for six hours while a five-person crew from Kunika's equivalent of Technical Services Branch—they're the forgers and ID changers—took our pictures, pasted and sealed them into the passports, and then provided visas and entry stamps from Japan, as well as U.S. visas.

"How the hell did you get these?" I pointed to the red, white, and blue embossed seal on the fifth page where, according to a U.S. consul named Marilyn Povenmire, I had been given a diplomatic entry visa to the United States of America, and to the republic for which it stood.

"There are some things even you should not know," Tosho said. "This is one of them. But it's a real visa stamp."

Let it be known that I am willing to take yes for an answer. "Thanks, Tosh—fuck you very much."

He gave me a Japanese bow and an American hug. "You stay out of trouble, you no-load hairy *gaijin* asshole."

"Fat fucking chance, sashimi-breath."

"Well, in that case, at least have fun."

"Now you're talking."

There was an air phone in the Gulfstream, and once we were over Montana, I used it.

"Admiral Prescott's office."

"Tell him Dick Marcinko's calling."

There was an audible gasp. Then: "Yes, sir, Captain."

Pinky was on the line in no time, growling and threatening in language thick with wheretofores and what-the-hells. I let him rant. I wasn't paying for the call.

When he calmed down, sort of, I got a few words in edgewise. What I said brought him to attention. I told him what I wanted, and how I wanted it, and that if he didn't do it my way, he'd be breaking large stones into small stones out at Fort Leavenworth for the rest of his natural life.

Then I bid him a not-so-fond farewell. I checked my watch. Three hours until we landed at Warrenton. It was time for a combat nap.

We took out Grant Griffith's security force at The Hustings with no problems. They weren't expecting anybody, and in any case they weren't carrying meaningful weapons. So by the time Grant and Pinky arrived, the eight uniformed rent-a-cops from Centurions International, as well as Griffith's three houseboys, two butlers, his cook, his valet, and his stable manager, had all been trussed up and stored in a nearby barn.

I'd opened up the bar in The Hustings' huge atrium room and helped myself to a dollop or three of Bombay Sapphire. Stevie, who'd joined us for the festivities, sipped real

English bitter that was piped up from a keg in the basement. The rest of the boys stuck with Coors Light.

By the time we heard the cars outside, we'd set everything up.

Griffith was the first one through the door. He saw me, and reflexively his tongue played lizard with his lower lip. "Dick—"

"Fuck you, cockbreath."

As he moved into his foyer, Nasty came up from behind and frisked him thoroughly, then pushed him in my direction. "He's clean, Skipper."

Now it was Pinky's turn. Half Pint worked him over, removing a stainless steel folding knife from his uniform jacket and handing it to me.

Pinky glared in my direction.

Outside, there was scuffling. I checked through the glass in the front door and saw that Cherry, Nod, and Pick had apprehended the three drivers and six NIS security men Pinky'd brought along. The poor schmucks lay on the gravel driveway facedown, arms handcuffed behind their backs. It was raining, and they'd probably catch colds. Too bad. They weren't going anyplace, because Nod, his suppressed MP5 at the ready, stood under the portico and watched them. Shooting from the hip, Nod could hit a dime at ten yards with his MP5.

I led the two prisoners through the foyer, my heels tapping on the pegged pine boards, down the long hallway, through the arch, and into Griffith's atrium, where hidden spotlights shone down on the suits of armor. I pointed at two straight-back chairs I'd set in the middle of the space.

"Sit."

Griffith started to say something. I took him by the lapels of his chalk-striped Savile Row suit and raised him six inches off the ground. "I said sit, numb-nuts."

I put him down and he sat. That was gratifying. I like a man who can take direction.

Pinky didn't have to be asked twice.

Griffith adjusted the crease in his trouser leg. He played with his Roman ring. He shot the triple-button cuffs of his brightly striped Turnbull & Asser shirt. He ran a hand through thick white hair. I let him fidget.

I looked them over. "Y'know," I said, "this is like one of those fucking Charlie Chan movies, where Charlie—that's me—and his number one son—that's Nasty over there—and all his other sons—you met most of 'em outside—they assemble all the suspects in one room. Then Charlie goes over the case and tells us who's the guilty party."

I poured fresh Bombay into the cut-crystal glass. "Well, gents, in this case there are only two guilty parties—and you're both here." I helped myself to more ice. "And the unhappy fact is, not all my sons made it back."

I swirled the drink and sipped. "Gentlemen," I said, "I don't want to confuse you with technical language, but this has been one big solly clusterfuck."

Pinky's mouth opened. I raised an index finger in his direction and wiggled it. "Not yet. You get to talk later. As Charlie Chan used to say, 'Field telephone attached to admiral's nuts makes for interesting conversations.'"

"Good God—" His eyes went wide.

"Relax, Pinky, it was a joke."

"It wasn't funny."

"Neither is what happened." I sipped and set the tumbler down on one of Griffith's antique French tables. He gasped as the crystal touched the naked wood.

"Oh, Grant—I'm so sorry. Did Dickie make a nasty ring on your table?" I flicked open the knife Half Pint had taken from Pinky and buried half an inch of it in the table, punching right through the intricate wood inlay. "Now you don't have to worry."

Griffith started to rise. "That's a Louis Quatorze, you—"

I backhanded him across the face. A trickle of blood appeared in the corner of his mouth. I put my face about an inch from his. "I don't care if it was made by the fucking Sun King himself. I lost men because of you. I lost men because you are a greedy fucking traitor."

I waved at Pick, who removed the tarp from the crates of Tomahawks we'd piled in the atrium.

"He stole these from Seal Beach," I said to Pinky. "He

was selling them to his pal Hideo Ikigami, who owns Matsuko Machine. You remember them—that's the company that sold milling machines to the Soviets so they could make their missile subs as quiet as ours."

"I know he did," Pinky said.

"You did? Golly gee, Pinky, then why didn't you do anything about it?"

"It's a long story."

"I'll bet," I said.

Pinky sighed, then whined, "I didn't do anything—"

"You didn't do anything, Pinky," I interrupted, "because this asshole"—I stuck my thumb in Grant Griffith's direction—"was blackmailing you so you'd help him."

"What's your point?" Pinky said.

"My point is, you're a fucking traitor."

Pinky chose to disregard my accusation completely. "Frankly, Dick, I'm surprised that you haven't caught on to what's been happening yet. I thought you were smarter."

"I know enough." I picked up the Bombay and took a drink. "I know he was blackmailing you, and a bunch of others, too—I have his fucking files. But that's getting ahead of myself. You think I haven't caught on? Listen, numb-nuts, I catch on fast. I know that from the minute I blundered into those four fucking kimchis at Narita, my life has been a goatfuck. I know that you and Grant had me recalled to duty because it would be easier to eliminate me as a threat to your smuggling operation if I was back in uniform. I know you tried to set me up—tried to set Red Cell up. You sent us out to the Navy Yard to get caught."

Pinky didn't look convinced, so I continued. "When that didn't work, you assigned us Seal Beach. Why? Because when the next audit was done and missiles were discovered missing, we'd be blamed for what Griffith and his compadres from Centurions were doing."

I looked at Pinky again. He didn't seem worried. That was because he was an asshole. It made me happy to know I was going to kill him tonight.

"Then you assigned us North Korea. You hoped the kimchis could do what you hadn't been able to—which is, waste us all."

Pinky sighed. "You had it all figured out, then."

"Bet your ass."

His expression changed. "You'd lose."

"Don't shit a shitter, Pinky."

"I wouldn't." He stood up and walked over to a phone that sat atop a marble-and-walnut washstand. "Pick up the phone."

Okay, I was game. I picked up the phone. There was no dial tone. I said, "Hello?"

A voice answered me. "This is Colonel McCarthy."

Who the fuck was Colonel McCarthy?

He must have been prescient because he answered me right away. "U.S. Marine Corps Provost Marshal Command."

A Quantico gook. "What can I do for you, Colonel?"

"Put down your weapons. The compound is surrounded by an overwhelming force."

My face must have betrayed me. Pinky smirked. "I told you."

"You told me nothing, cockbreath."

"Pour me a Bombay, Dick."

That was the most intelligent thing he'd said all night. "Wonder . . ." I nodded in Wonder's direction. Wonder dumped an inch of gin in a glass, added ice, and handed it off to Pinky. "Enjoy, Admiral."

"Thank you." Pinky looked closely at Wonder's wraparound, mirror-lensed shooting glasses. "Do I know you?"

"I hope not."

Pinky took the glass and sat down on a comfortable chair. He sipped the gin. "Well—Wonder, is it?—you mix a hell of a drink." He turned toward me. "We knew about Griffith, but there was nothing anyone could do. He was wired. If anyone started an investigation that even hinted obliquely at Grant Griffith, it got shot down from above. He had too many friends in high places. It was worse than Tailhook, and potentially more damaging. After all, we're talking about our security, talking about nuclear weapons."

Pinky sipped. "So we needed a real rogue to stir things up."

"Me."

"That's a roger, Captain. I know how much you hate authority. I know how you operate. I could almost guarantee that when I gave you direct orders, you'd disobey them and go UNODIR."

Factoids and info-bits began to filter through my thick Slovak skull. "You wanted me to run amok."

"Affirmative. We knew something was going on. But frankly, Dick, the system has its limits, and as much as I'd like to be able to say otherwise, Griffith and his people knew how to manipulate the system. They were better than we."

He looked at me with a half smile, half grimace, kind of like if he had a bad case of gas, and sighed audibly. "You, however, are better than they." Pinky sipped his Bombay. "Dick—would you mind adding some more ice to this?"

I took his glass and walked toward the bar. His voice followed me. "I don't like the way you operate, Dick. Frankly, I believe that when the nation's not at war, you should be kept in a cage. But, sometimes, you need an animal to do the job. That was the case here. When Grant went to CNO about you, we saw a golden opportunity—and we took it."

I reached into the ice bucket, brought out a fistful, mashed the cubes in my fist, and dropped them into the glass.

"Oh," Pinky said, "no need to crush. Cubes are just fine."

I returned the drink to him. "Thanks, Dick."

I looked down at Pinky. He was a fucking geek, a bean-counter, a dip-dunk, a no-load. He was a prissy self-important pus-nutted shit-for-brains pencil-dicked asshole. "You mean to tell me you set this whole chain of events into play? You're not smart enough, Pinky."

He stretched his long legs out and crossed them at the ankles, sipped his gin, and waved me off. "Dick, Dick—don't do to me what you perpetually accuse the Navy of doing to you."

"What's that?"

"Underestimating you."

That brought me to a full stop. He had a point. "Okay, Pinky—let's give you the benefit of the doubt. How did you get me into this in the first place?"

Pinky explained. He'd heard about my involvement at

Narita when the cable from naval attaché/Tokyo landed on CNO's desk. Narita, Pinky explained, was a sting he and Griffith had set up with CNO's approval. But there was a twist to it: it had actually been designed to test the level of Griffith's involvement in weapons smuggling. If the detonators were lost in what was allegedly an airtight operation, then CNO and Pinky would add another guilty mark next to Griffith's name.

Then the cable arrived detailing my heavy-handed presence. A lightbulb went off when the CNO read my name. He'd called Pinky, who, after consuming a quart of Maalox, had called his friend Tony Mercaldi at DIA.

I said I found it surprising that he knew Merc, too. Pinky said that his circle of acquaintances probably ran a lot wider than I'd ever suspected.

Anyway, he continued, he knew that Merc and I had been friends for almost twenty years, since the Air Force Command College at Montgomery, Alabama, where the two of us spent most of 1976. So he asked Merc to act as a cutout and recommend me to a businessman who'd suddenly started getting death threats—a man Pinky knew wanted Grant Griffith to represent his company for Navy work.

So Pinky had been the one behind the Joe Andrews threats. It had been a "dangle" after all. "And then?"

"And then we let you run amok and let nature take its course."

"Just who is 'we,' Pinky?"

"Me. Me and CNO. We sent you where we hoped you'd find evidence to use against Grant. You came up dry at the Navy Yard, but you hit pay dirt at Seal Beach."

Well, I hadn't come up absolutely dry ay the Navy Yard. I had the NIS Foxhunter file with its pictures of Pinky in flagrante delicto buried below my kitchen floor. But this wasn't the time to mention them. "You and CNO came up with this? Just the two of you?"

"We're the only ones we could trust." He looked over at where Grant Griffith sat.

"You're the one who asked me to invite Joe Andrews to the war game," Griffith said, looking at Pinky incredulously. From the expression on his face, it was obvious that

Grant Griffith had underestimated Pinky even more than I had.

Griffith stood up. There was still a hint of blood in the corner of his mouth. "This is all idle talk," he said. "Nothing is going to happen."

Pinky looked at him. "Why is that, Grant?"

Griffith played with his Roman ring. "Because I'll never go to trial," he said confidently. "Face it, Pinky, I know too much. I'm privy to too many secrets. I've got information about too many skeletons in too many closets. Even if I am indicted, the fucking president will pardon me—*if* he wants to be reelected. I have tapes. Files. Documents. I have all sorts of evidence I can use as leverage."

Pinky indicated the crates. "So do we."

Griffith's expression grew contemptuous. "The missiles? They're nothing more than one link in a chain. And you can't display the entire chain without violating national security." Griffith smirked. "Face it—the Pentagon and the State Department aren't going to let you show what you have. Your 'evidence' would prove that the United States engages in covert operations. It would disclose sources and methods. It would demonstrate how you operate clandestinely in friendly countries without their permission. There's no way you can do that—not in a million years. It's not politically feasible."

He was right, of course. His leverage was blackmail—I had the computer disk to prove it. Our evidence was the nation's secrets. And because he knew we wouldn't be able to use them against him, the son of a bitch was going to buy a pass.

This sort of realpolitik has always bothered the shit out of me. I hate to see people like Grant Griffith get away with murder and other nefariousness when, instead of passing go and collecting their $200, they should go straight to jail. Still, it always pays to be a realist, especially when politics is concerned.

I looked at Pinky. "He's probably right, you know," I said.

Pinky nodded. "I'm aware of the delicate political ramifications," he said ruefully. He drained his gin. "So, what do you suggest?"

There was actually nothing left to say. So I didn't say anything. Instead, I withdrew the Walther PPK from my pocket, extended my arm, and put three quick shots into Grant Griffith's head, and three into his chest, from a distance of six feet. It was real quick—like, *pop-pop-pop, pop-pop-pop.* The former SECDEF blinked once. Then he collapsed in a bloody heap without a sound. "That's for my two men," I said to Griffith's corpse.

I turned his body with my foot and was pleased to see that none of the bullets had passed through him. The Eleys had performed just as advertised. I could write a fucking testimonial. Maybe I would.

"According to Navy regulations," I explained to Pinky, "use of deadly force is approved when the safety of nuclear weaponry is concerned." I pointed toward the Tomahawk crates. "And they ain't fucking chicken liver."

Pinky's face was white as chalk. But he managed to swallow, nod, then say, "You have a point, Dick. I accept it."

I wiped the Walther clean and tossed it on top of Griffith's corpse. The phone rang. That would be Colonel McCarthy wanting to know what was happening. Explaining was beyond my pay grade. I plucked the receiver, covered the mouthpiece, and handed it toward Pinky.

"Tell you what, Admiral. You clean this mess up—you're the fucking flag-rank officer with his own bunch of Jarheads outside." I thought about what I'd said, and what I'd done. Pinky had been awfully quick to endorse my deadly force justification. "You knew I'd kill the motherfucker, didn't you?"

"Moi?" He took the receiver from my hand. "Just a minute, Colonel, I have a final bit of business to conduct before you and your men can come in."

Now it was his turn to cover the mouthpiece. He gave me this innocent-as-the-day-he-was-born look. "When, Dick, have I ever been able to control you? You're a renegade, the ultimate rogue—and everybody in the Navy knows it."

He was a conniving, sneaky, deceitful asshole, and at that

instant, if I'd had another round, I would probably have shot him, too. But the gun was empty.

Besides, the true implications of what I'd done were just beginning to set in. "Well, fuck me again, Pinky, you're probably gonna get another star out of this."

He smiled his insipid smile at me. "I know. And I deserve it, too."

It was poetic justice. I wear nothing but scars, and assholes like Pinky get to wear stars. I felt like kicking him in the balls.

But frankly, I didn't have the energy. I was tired. Bone tired. I needed Rogue Manor, with the sauna and the Jacuzzi and the Bombay gin. "I'm going home," I said. "I'm taking my men and I'm going home."

I looked at Wonder, Cherry, Nasty, Duck Foot, Half Pint, Pick, and Nod. I looked at Pinky. He wasn't equal to their piss. "Let's go get shit-faced," I said, and started down the long hallway.

"Don't stray too far off the reservation," Pinky said. "We might need you again."

"Fat fucking chance of that."

Pinky waved a manicured finger in the air. "Never say never, Dick."

The son of a bitch was actually whistling "I Did It My Way" as we went out the door.

It didn't bother me in the least. I have his fucking NIS file.

Kelly Campbell

Glossary

ACMEL: intel camera for carrying on clandestine missions.

Admirals' Gestapo: what the secretary of defense's office calls the Naval Investigative Services Command (See: SHIT-FOR-BRAINS).

AK-47: 7.63 by 39 Kalashnikov automatic rifle. The most common assault weapon in the world.

Amerikajin: (Japanese) American.

APC: Armored Personnel Carrier.

APU: Auxiliary Power Unit.

ARG: Amphibious Ready Group.

ASW: Anti-Submarine Warfare.

A-Team: basic Special Forces unit of ten to fourteen men.

ATF: Anti-Terrorist Task Force, or Ambiguous (amphibious) Task Force.

Atsugi: the air base closest to Yokosuka.

BDUs: Battle Dress Uniforms. Now that's an oxymoron if I ever heard one.

BIQ: Bitch-In-Question.

BLACK TALON: State of the art lethal hollowpoint ammunition made by Winchester.

blivet: a collapsible fuel container, often used in SEAL missions.

Blowning: single-action 9mm pistol obtained in Japan.

Boomer: nuclear-powered missile submarine.

BTDT: Been There, Done That.

BUPERS: BUreau of PERSonnel.

C-130: Lockheed's ubiquitous Hercules.

C-141: Lockheed's ubiquitous StarLifter aircraft, soon to be mothballed.

C-4: plastic explosive. You can mold it like clay. You can even use it to light your fires. Just don't stamp on it.

C-9: Military designation for the McDonnell Douglas DC-9.

C²CO: Can't Cunt Commanding Officer. Too many of these in Navy SpecWar today. They won't support their men or take chances because they're afraid it'll ruin their chances for promotion.

CALOW: Coastal And Limited-Objective Warfare. Very fashionable acronym at the Pentagon in these days of increased low-intensity conflict.

cannon fodder: see FNG.

CAR-15: Colt's carbine-size .223 assault weapon.

Christians in Action: SpecWar slang for the Central Intelligence Agency.

CINCLANT: Commander-IN-Chief, AtLANTic.

CINCLANTFLT: Commander-IN-Chief, AtLANTic FLeeT.

CINCPAC: Commander-IN-Chief, PACific.

CINCPACFLT: Commander-IN-Chief, PACific FLeeT.

CNO: Chief of Naval Operations.

CNWDI: Critical Nuclear Weapons Design Information.

cockbreath: SEAL term of endearment used for those who only pay lip service.

COD: Carrier-On-board Delivery.

Combatmaster: palm-size .45-caliber pistol made by Detonics, often used during undercover assignments.

CONUS: CONtinental United States.

CQB: Close-Quarters Battle—e.g., killing that's up close and personal.

CT: CounterTerror.

DDS: Dry Dock Shelter. The clamshell unit put on subs to deliver SEALs and SDVs.

DEFCON: DEFense CONdition.

Dickhead: Stevie Wonder's nickname for Marcinko.

diplo-dink: no-load cookie-pushing diplomat.

dirtbag: the look Marcinko favors for his Team guys.

do-itashi-mashite: (Japanese) you're welcome.

doom on you: American version of Vietnamese for "go fuck yourself."

Dortmunder: great German beer.

Draeger: great German rebreathing apparatus.

DTSA (pronounced DITSA): Defense Technical Security Administration—the guys who try to keep complex, dual-use technology out of the bad guys' hands. They are often stymied by State Department diplo-dinks and Commerce Department apparatchiki.

du-ma-nhieu: (Vietnamese) go fuck yourself (see DOOM ON YOU).

dweeb: no-load shit-for-brains geeky asshole, usually shackled to a computer.

EC-130: electronic warfare–outfitted C-130.

ELINT: ELectronic INTelligence.

EOD: Explosive Ordnance Disposal.

FIS: Flight Information Service.

FMR: ForMeR, as seen on TV screens during interviews, e.g., Grant Griffith, FMR secretary of defense.

FNG: Fucking New Guy. See CANNON FODDER.

Foca: Italian minisub built with SpecWarriors in mind.

four-striper: captain. All too often, a C²CO.

FUBAR: Fucked Up Beyond All Repair.

gaijin: (Japanese) foreigner.

Glock: Reliable 9mm pistols made by Glock in Austria. Great for SEALS because they don't require as much care as Sig Sauers.

goatfuck: what the Navy likes to do to Marcinko (see FUBAR).

Grock: reliable 9mm pistol in Tokyo.

GSG-9: *Grenzchutzgruppe-9.* Top German CT unit.

HAHO: High-Altitude, High-Opening parachute jump.

HALO: High-Altitude, Low-Opening parachute jump.

HK: ultrareliable pistol, assault rifle, or submachine made by Heckler & Koch, a German firm. SEALs use HK MP5-K submachine guns in various configurations, as well as HK-93 assault rifles, and P7M8 9mm pistols.

Huey: Original slang for Bell's AH-1 two-bladed helicopter, but now refers to various UH configuration Bell choppers.

HUMINT: HUMan INTelligence.

Hydra-Shok: extremely lethal hollow-point ammunition manufactured by Federal Cartridge Company.

IBS: Inflatable Boat, Small—the basic unit of SEAL transportation.

ichiban: (Japanese) number one.

IED: Improvised Explosive Device.

Incursari: Italian Frogman unit based at La Spezia.

Japs: bad guys.

Jarheads: Marines. The Corps. Formally USMC, or Uncle Sam's Misguided Children.

JSOC: Joint Special Operations Command.

KATN: Kick Ass and Take Names. Marcinko avocation.

KH-11: NRO's spy-in-the-sky satellites, now superseded by KH-12s.

kimchi: fermented cabbage made with lots of garlic and hot peppers and the reason Koreans, who make and eat the stuff by the ton, have no sense of humor. In Marcinko-speak, any Korean.

KISS: Keep It Simple, Stupid. Marcinko's basic premise for special operations.

krytrons: precise timers used in making nuclear detonators.

Lacrosse: latest-version eye-in-the-sky NRO spy satellite with upgraded capabilities.

LANTFLT: AtLANTic FLeeT.

M16: basic U.S. .223-caliber weapon, used by the armed forces.

MagSafe: lethal frangible ammunition that does not penetrate the human body. Favored by some SWAT units for CQB.

MDW: Military District of Washington.

Mod-I Mark-O: basic unit.

MRE: Meals, Ready to Eat. Combat chow packed in waterproof containers.

MTBFR: (Dweeb-speak) Mean Time Between Failure Rate.

NAVAIR: NAVy AIR Command.

NAVSEA: NAVal SEA Systems Command.

NAVSPECWARGRU: NAVal SPECial WARfare GRoUp.

Navyspeak: redundant, bureaucratic naval nomenclature, either in written nonoral or nonwritten oral modes, indecipherable by nonmilitary (conventional) or military (unconventional) individuals during normal interfacing configuration conformations.

Nexis: private database.

NIS: Naval Investigative Service Command, also known as the Admirals' Gestapo (see: SHIT-FOR-BRAINS).

NRO: National Reconnaissance Office. Established August 25, 1960, to administer and coordinate satellite development and operations for the U.S. intelligence community. Very spooky place.

NSA: National Security Agency, known within the SpecWar community as No Such Agency.

NSCT: Naval Security Coordination Team (Navyspeak name for Red Cell).

NSD: National Security Directive.

OBE: Overtaken By Events—usually because of the bureaucracy.

OOD: Officer Of the Deck (he who drives the big gray monster).

OP-06: deputy CNO for plans, policy, and operations.

OP-0604: CNO's SpecWar briefing officer.

OP-06B: assistant deputy CNO for plans, policy, and operations.

OP-06D: cover organization for Red Cell/NSCT.

OPSEC: OPerational SECurity.

P-3: Orion sub-hunting and electronic-warfare prop-driven aircraft.

Phideaux: Cajun junkyard dog (or junkyard alligator).

poontang: capital idea anytime.

Pyongyang: capital of North Korea (see KIMCHI).

retarded: Marcinkospeak for "retired."

RHQ: Regional HeadQuarters.

RPG: Rocket-Propelled Grenade.

SAS: Special Air Service. Britain's top CT unit.

SATCOM: SATellite COMmunications.

SCIF: Special Classified Intelligence Facility. A bug-proof bubble room.

SDV: Swimmer Delivery Vehicle.

SEAL: SEa-Air-Land Navy SpecWarrior. A hop-and-popping shoot-and-looter hairy-assed Frogman who gives a shit. The acronym stands for Sleep, Eat, And Live it up.

Semtex: Czecho C-4 plastique explosive. Used for canceling Czechs.

SERE: Survival, Evasion, Resistance, and Escape school.

SH-3: versatile Sikorsky chopper. Used in ASW missions and also as a Spec Ops platform.

shit-for-brains: any no-load, pus-nutted, pencil-dicked asshole from NIS.

SIGINT: SIGnals INTelligence.

Simunition: Canadian-manufactured ammo using paint bullets instead of lead.

SLUDJ: top-secret NIS witch-hunters. Acronym stands for Sensitive Legal (Upper Deck) Jurisdiction.

SNAFU: Situation Normal—All Fucked Up.

SOCOM: Special Operations COMmand, located at MacDill AFB, Tampa, Florida.

SOF: Special Operations Force.

SOSUS: SOund SUrveillance System. Underwater detection system for finding submarines.

SPECWARGRU: SPECial WARfare GRoUp.

SpecWarrior: one who gives a fuck.

SSN: nuclear sub, commonly known as sewer pipe.

STABs: SEAL Tactical Assault Boats.

SWAT: Special Weapons And Tactics police teams. All too often they do not train enough and become SQUAT teams.

TAD: Temporary Additional Duty (SEALs refer to it as Traveling Around Drunk).

Tailhook: the convention of weenie-waggers, gropesters, and pressed-ham-on-glass devotees that put air brakes on NAVAIR.

TARFU: Things Are Really Fucked Up.

TECHINT: TECHnical INTelligence.

tiger stripes: the only stripes that SEALs will wear.

Trijicon: maker of the best radioactive night-sights for SEAL weaponry.

UGS: Unmanned Ground Sensors. Useful in setting off claymore mines and other booby traps.

UNODIR: UNless Otherwise DIRected. That's how Marcinko operates when he's surrounded by can't cunts.

wannabes: the sort of folks you meet at *Soldier of Fortune* conventions.

weenies: pussy-ass can't cunts and no-loads.

WIA: Wounded In Action.

Yokosuka: joint U.S./Japanese naval base, south of Tokyo.

Yongbyon: main site of North Korea's nuclear weapons program development, comprising eight major buildings and dozens of secondary structures according to current intelligence estimates.

Zulu: Greenwich Mean Time (GMT) designator used in formal military communications.

Zulu-5-Oscar: escape-and-evasion exercises in which Frogmen try to plant dummy limpet mines on Navy vessels, while the vessels' crews try to catch them in *bombus interruptus.*

Index

Abu Nidal, 8, 53
airport security, 3–34, 286
Akita Maru (tanker), 292,
    293, 299, 340
    Red Cell assault on,
    303–28
Allied National
    Technologies (ANT),
    41, 44
ambush, 120–21
Andrews, Joseph, 44–52,

64–69, 87, 90–91,
    96–97, 111, 114–15,
    116–17, 119, 347
    and Grant Griffith's
    party, 127–29,
    131–32, 168, 189
Aristide (deposed president
    of Haiti), 164
Aschenbrenner, Harold,
    63–64
Atlantic Ocean, 314

All entries preceded by an asterisk (*) are pseudonyms.

INDEX

Pocket Books
Proudly Announces

ROGUE WARRIOR III:
GREEN TEAM

Richard Marcinko

and

John Weisman

Coming in Hardcover
from Pocket Books
mid-March 1995

The following is a preview of
Rogue Warrior III: Green Team . . .

The first two floors were easy—no one in sight, no booby traps, and no cats, rats, bats, goats, sheep, or other miscellaneous animals to make our presence known. I crept up the dusty concrete stairs one by one, my black knee-length Pakistani 'Pasha' tunic covering the carbon-colored suppressed Glock 19 in its ballistic nylon thigh holster. The rest of my outfit was also basic black—from the thong sandals, to the Maharishi-style trousers, to the Titanium-framed Emerson CQC6 combat folder clipped to my waistband next to the Motorola beeper, to the lead-and-leather sap secured by a thick black Ace bandage to the inside of my right wrist.

My beard was full—reaching almost halfway down my chest. My mustache drooped Fu Manchu–like way below my upper lip. My shoulder-length hair, restrained by a thick black cotton band, was wild and crazee. If anybody ever looked the part of Islamic fundamentalist rogue warrior—the kind of maniacal Mujaheddin you used to see on the TV news shows when they sent camera crews into Afghanistan—it was me. Which is precisely why I'd volunteered as point man on this little jaunt, prowling and growling up the unlit stairwell of a Cairo slum at 0-dark hundred to catch my quarry napping on his bedroll.

I wasn't alone, of course. You do not meander into Islamic Cairo, home to some of the meanest Muslim fundamentalist sons of bitches in the world, without some fundamentally mean sons of bitches of your own to backstop your ass. That's why, half a yard behind me, Senior Chief Nasty Nicky Grundle, his suppressed Heckler & Koch MP5SD submachine gun at the ready, rested a huge paw on my shoulder. A yard behind him, Master Chief Boatswain's Mate Howie Kaluha's well-muscled Hawaiian back (not to mention his well-maintained Kraut submachine gun) brought up the rear.

A few streets away, cruising in the limo—it was actually a baby blue Peugeot 504 station wagon, but in Cairo, as the saying goes, almost anything that runs can be considered a limo—Doc Tremblay, handlebar mustachioed master chief corpsman and super sniper, waited, a Manurhin PPK/s loaded with seven rounds of .380 MagSafe frangible man stoppers tucked in his waistband and a disposable syringe filled with 200 milligrams of Dr. Nostradamus's best Ketamine Love Potion Number 9 in his hand. Behind the Peugeot's wheel sat Grandma Noel's favorite Peck's bad boy, MM1 Stevie Wonder, on indefinite leave from his classified job at the Washington Navy Yard. Wonder's carrot-colored hair was covered by a dark knit *fella-*

hin cap, and his tight frame was hidden by a shapeless *gallebiyah*. He was, however, wearing his trademark wraparound shooting glasses with lenses in the color named especially for him—bastard amber.

Wedged under Wonder's right thigh was a 9-mm hush-puppy—a suppressed Smith & Wesson semi-automatic—loaded with Doc Tremblay's best hand-loaded, subsonic hollowpoint. To his nightshirt-like garment was pinned a throwaway receiving device about the size of a pack of gum. When I pressed a chiclet-size button in my pocket, his gizmo would vibrate for thirty seconds. The tickle would tell him he had one minute to get his Mick ass in gear and pick me and the rest of the team up.

There's more: While Nasty, Howie, and I crept up the stairs, Chief Gunner's Mate (Guns) Duck Foot Dewey and Commander Tommy Tanaka were making their way up along a precarious path of irregular stonework, spindly balconies, laundry lines, and drainpipes that ran alongside the target's third-story dormer windows. I knew it would take every bit of their mountain-climbing expertise to clamber up thirty-five feet of brittle brick without snapping anything off and raising a ruckus.

I know, I know—you're asking what the fuck? What the hell's going on? What's Dickie doing back in the Third World when he should be home at Rogue Manor, just climbing out of the Jacuzzi clutching a tall, frosted glass of Bombay on the rocks in one hand, and something warm, wonderful, and remarkably full-breasted in the other.

Believe me, if there'd been time, I'd have been asking myself the same question. But there was no time for anything but the matter at hand. To whit: scratching and snatching then whopping and popping.

Translation: Our mission was to sit around and scratch our asses until the time was right, then snatch one Mahmoud Azziz abu Yasin, Islamic fundamentalist and terrorist asshole, from his beddy-bye. Then I'd whop him upside the haid with my handy little sap, knock him cold, and hustle his ass down to the Peugeot, where Doc would pop that 200 milligrams of Dr. N's Ketamine right into his upper deltoid, which would drug the shit out of ol'Mahmoud for a few precious hours.

Then we'd spirit the Tango Adam Henry (that's radio talk for terrorist asshole, for the uninitiated among you) out of Egypt on a thirty-two-foot fishing trawler Doc had rented in Alexandria, and after a pleasant ocean cruise, we'd rendezvous with a guided-missile frigate that had orders to be standing by, 75 miles off the Egyptian coast, during a six-hour window. From the frigate, we'd chopper to a carrier task force that sat another 125 miles out to sea. Then we'd use a Grumman C-2 Greyhound carrier on-board delivery plane to COD us all to Sigonella, Sicily.

Money being no object, we'd quietly slip Azziz aboard his own C-141 StarLifter aircraft and fly him back to CONUS (or the CONtinental United States, in civilian speak), where we'd drop him off in such plain sight that even the FBI would be able to find him. We would then disappear back into the shadows from which we'd come, leaving the feds to take all the capture credit when Azziz finally stood trial for his lethal part in a series of bombings across the United

States that had cost sixty-five lives in all, and disrupted the cities of New York, Chicago, Houston, and Washington, DC. for more than a month.

Piece of cake, right? Guess again. Snatch-and-grabs (or, as the Brits call 'em, cosh-and-carrys) like this one are precarious, risky operations. Probs and stats? Bad. Goatfuck likelihood? High.

GF factor 1: You're operating in a hostile environment with no backup.

GF factor 2: Your government will disavow your actions if you're caught.

GF factor 3: If the locals do get their hands on you, the odds are that you'll end up being dragged behind a car or truck for a few hours while they cut off significant pieces of your anatomy joint by joint.

So, you ask, how did I feel right now?

Brief answer: I felt as happy as a pig in shit, although you probably couldn't get something the width of a hairpin up my sphincter because the pucker factor was off the charts.

Above me, something moved. My hand went up. We stopped. I gave signals, and Nasty pressed himself against the stairwell wall, giving himself the greatest field of fire. His free hand grasped my shoulder. That way I'd know where he was all the time. Knowing where everybody is all the time is an important element of operations such as these. It's altogether possible to kill your own man if he's out of position by as much as a few inches. I know—because it has happened during training.

I kept moving in the same steady pace I'd set two floors below, progressing inch by inch, the fingers of my left hand sweeping carefully, caressing the stair treads and risers as carefully if they were virgin pussy. These assholes were SUCs—smart, unpredictable, and cunning. And they fucking *owned* this part of town—even government troops stayed away from this neighborhood.

We'd learned this fact—and others—during the past week as we surveilled our target. We'd infiltrated commercially ten days ago. Nasty Nick, Tommy, and I came through Rome, Messina, and Cyprus, catching a ferry from there to Port Said and busing the dusty road through Ismailia, south to Cairo. Howie, Duck Foot, and Wonder flew commercial—TWA to Frankfurt, changed planes for Athens, then straight on here.

Doc Tremblay had the toughest commute. He drove from his house in Maadi, six miles from Tahrir Square in central Cairo. He was on a two-year assignment here. And, glutton for punishment that he is, he'd volunteered to come along for the ride when I called him on the secure line and told him we'd be visiting.

That was a-okay with me. I always like to have a mole—a covert operator no one knows about—to wheel and deal for me. So, Doc took three weeks of leave and disappeared from the Mil Group. He told the embassy people he was taking vacation time in Alexandria, Suez, and Ismailia. Instead, he slipped into Cairo's back alleys to assemble our weapons and ordnance, buy a Peugeot and a pair of motorbikes, and arrange rooms at a local tourist hotel, all without alerting the Egyptian secret police, the local Christians in Action station—Navy talk for CIA agents—or the Foggy Bottom apparatchiki.

Once we'd arrived and set up shop it hadn't taken us

long to locate Azziz. Why? First, because we already knew where he lived. The Defense Intelligence Agency—DIA—had provided my boss, the Chief of Naval Operations, with a detailed map of the area. And second, because, as cops are fond of saying, a perp is a perp is a perp (actually, cops say that everywhere but New York, where they say a poip is a poip is a poip). Translated into English, that means perpetrators are creatures of habit. And Azziz the perp's habits were centered on politics and prayer.

Moreover, Azziz enjoyed a certain celebrity status on the local fundamentalist scene. No matter how low he may have wanted to keep his profile, the local mullahs singled him out, citing ol' Mahmoud as an example of righteous dedication to Islam's cause. He had defied the infidel. He had waged war against the Great Satan on the Great Satan's turf—and he'd won. So they showed him off. They displayed him at their rallies. They stood him at attention during their sermons.

So, finding our Muslim needle wasn't going to be hard—not in *this* here haystack. The challenge would be to snatch him up without creating a ruckus, in the same sort of low-key, quick-and-dirty kidnap operation I'd perfected more than a quarter-century ago in Vietnam.

We called them parakeet ops back then. We'd take four or five guys and hit a village, nabbing a VC paymaster or political cadre out of his hootch in the middle of the night with such quiet efficiency that the people in the adjacent hootch wouldn't hear a thing. They'd wake up the next morning, and Bin, or Phuong, or Tran, would just have disappeared into thin air. His bodyguards would still be there—dead, of course, and nicely, cunningly, lethally booby trapped. It was unnerving. It was intimidating. It was wonderful.

Parakeet ops took split-second timing. They also took good operational intelligence—you had to know how, and where, the bird lived before you could snare him.

So, when Doc showed me the latest *Cairo Weekly*—a newsletter published by the embassy's personnel office—and I read the listing titled Security Advisory, which said, quote, "AMEMB personnel should avoid the areas adjacent to the Rifai, Saiyida Sukayna, and al-Hambra mosques this Wednesday as DIPSEC has been advised that Islamic rallies have been planned," a 100-watt lightbulb went off in my thick-as-rocks Slovak skull.

All three mosques were in the general area where Azziz's family lived—the southern section of Islamic Cairo adjacent to the City of the Dead and below the Citadel. Odds were that Azziz would be featured at one or more of the rallies.

My plan was Keep-It-Simple-Stupid simple: Duck Foot and Howie would surveil one mosque, Wonder and Nasty would cover the other, and I'd handle the third with Tommy. We knew what Azziz looked like—his red hair and broken nose made him easily distinguishable. We'd shadow him at a discreet distance, check the opposition out, see what patterns he established, and once we could be reasonably certain of them, we'd go in and grab his ass. DIA's locals had no need to know we were in the city—which would protect their butts, bureaucratically, and our asses on the operational level.

We arrived Sunday. That gave us roughly forty-eight hours to become familiar with the territory. Not a lot—but it would have to do. Cairo, after all, is impenetrable to the first-time visitor. There are thousands of unpaved streets and muddy alleyways that run together in labyrinthine mazes. There are cul de sacs from which it's impossible to escape. There's the City of the Dead—six square miles of cemeteries turned slums, where more than half a million people live in mausoleums and mud hut shanties with open trench sewers.

I'd done time in Cairo back in the late '80s and was familiar with the city. Doc Tremblay, whose passion is shopping, knew it like the back of his hairy fucking hand.

But my youngsters had never been here before. I knew they'd have to get the feel of the place before they felt confident operating with the split-second timing the mission required.

There's a philosophical point about operations I should mention at this juncture. It is that you can't send a SEAL off to Cairo, Kabul, or Kinshasa and say, "Just do it." SEALs have to be able to blend in. Just like we learned how to use camouflage in Vietnam to render ourselves invisible to Mr. Charlie, you have to be able to hide in plain sight when you're in an urban jungle too.

One thing that often helps immeasurably is the ability to not sound like a Yankee. Me? I speak French and Italian, and get along in gutter Arabic, Spanish, and German. Tommy K is fluent in French, German, and Russian. Howie's Spanish is better than his English. Nasty Nick and Wonder *habla Espanol* too.

Duck Foot can pass as Polish if he has to. Doc Tremblay? His Farsi is passable, his Arabic's fluent, and his French? *Superbe.* Those linguistic abilities are what help make them dependable shooters overseas.

You send someone sounding like an American farm boy out in the Azerbaijani boondocks, and he's gonna stick out like a sore *szeb.* That will compromise your mission. Then there's the operational gestalt. You have to be able to blend in—whether it means passing as a tourist or a truck driver. If you 'read' like U.S. GOVT. ISSUE, you'll probably be dead-meat body-bag material before you get to shoot or loot.

So the boys and I took two days and played our own brand of tourist—familiarizing ourselves with the warp and weave of this huge, gawky city. I like Cairo, and I wanted my men to like it too. Sure, there are more than 15 million people living in a space barely adequate for half that number. Life is tough. The air pollution is horrible—equivalent to smoking more than a pack of cigarettes a day. The traffic is abysmal —which is why I'd ordered motorbikes for Tommy and Duck Foot. Sanitary facilities are often rudimentary—thousands do their bathing in the Nile —and millions do without such conveniences as indoor plumbing, sewers, and electricity. But Cairenes are special—they have a sense of humor that, at its best, resembles the droll, dry wit of New Yorkers. They treat life with a *maalesh* disposition—a sort of "whatever fate decrees, we're going to be forgiven" attitude.

We started at the mosques. All three sat in the shadow of the Citadel—the fortified complex built by

Salah al-Din in the twelfth century. The Citadel still dominates Cairo's skyline, accented by tin mosque domes that reflect the sunlight and a series of needle-like minarets that look skyward like ready-to-launch SAM-7 missiles.

Each two-man team, dressed like tourists and equipped with the requisite cameras, guidebooks, and maps, worked outward through concentric circles, charting alleyways and narrow passages, making mental notes about the decrepit three- and four-story apartment houses that sat cheek-to-jowl on narrow streets, laundry fluttering like flags from shuttered windows and shaky balcony railings.

Nasty and Duck Foot (and their sweet teeth) hit the neighborhood tea houses. They sat at window tables, Duck Foot tried his Polish on the waiters, and they maintained cover by sampling dozens of honey-covered cakes. Tommy and Howie wandered the souk, munching grilled meat wrapped in hot Arab bread, seasoned with fiery green pepper and chopped onion and sold by voluble street vendors dressed in the kind of sweat-suit pajamas common to backstreet Cairo. (Whether the kabobs were cat or rat they couldn't tell, but they're snake-eaters, so what difference would it make anyway?)

Wonder, Doc, and I poked our noses into small grocery stores, reveling in the pervasive smells of cardamom, cumin, allspice, and cinnamon. I tried my backstreet Arabic and was gratified to discover I could still make myself understood. Doc Tremblay—whom I first met back in Naples when he was a Second Class corpsman in search of a good time and I was working for the legendary Frogman Everett E. Barrett, Chief

Gunner's Mate/Guns, at UDT 22—was positively loquacious, much to the delight of the natives. Doc reminds me of Jim Finley, my utility man from Bravo Squad, Second Platoon, in Vietnam, 1967. We called Jim "the Mayor," because no matter where we went, he'd be out pressing the flesh and making friends within minutes of our arrival. Doc's much the same—he's the kind of guy who looks like he just belongs, whether he's in Chicago, Cairo, or Katmandu.

By the evening and the morning of the third day, we were ready. Each team knew its neighborhood; each pair of swim buddies felt they could move unhampered. And twenty-four hours later, having blanketed the neighborhood, Tommy T and Duck Foot finally sighted our quarry coming out the back of the Sidi Almas mosque just north of Saleh ed-Din Square.

Azziz, they said, was flanked by a pair of bodyguards who looked as if they were packing heat. He was in deep conversation with a huge black guy—could have been Sudanese, or Somali, but they'd dubbed him the Nubian—dressed in flowing robes and cowboy boots. The trio climbed into a huge Mercedes limo with blacked-out windows and drove to a coffeehouse, where the Nubian and Azziz sat for two hours in deep conversation, while the bodyguards waited just outside the doorway.

Tommy and Duck Foot gave them a loose tail when they left. Azziz was dropped right here at his apartment house. He was patting his pocket as he got out of the car, which told Duck Foot he'd been given something valuable—perhaps documentation, or money, or both. Tommy stayed with Azziz, watching as he and his shadows climbed the three flights of stairs to his flat.

Duck Foot followed the Mercedes, which wove its way downtown, finally pulling up on the long drive-way to the Cairo Meridien. The Nubian disembarked there. Duck Foot, ever patient, walked into the lobby and plunked himself down at the bar, watching as the Nubian took the elevator to the sixth floor. Six minutes later, the tall black man reappeared, now dressed in a fashionable Western suit and carrying an overnight bag. He paid his bill in cash, tipped the concierge handsomely, and climbed back into the Mercedes, which Duck Foot followed out to the air-port.

I duly noted Tommy and Duck Foot's reports. They indicated strongly that Azziz was about to do some-thing, which put pressure on me to act—right now—despite the fact that we hadn't prepped as much as I would have liked. My intuition was supported by the twenty-four–hour stakeout we maintained on Azziz's apartment. He started to receive a continuous stream of visitors. The first night, I had Duck Foot shinny up the power pole that also held the phone line and drop a passive device in place. We couldn't overhear Azziz's conversations, but we knew he was making lots of overseas calls from the number of blips we heard as he dialed.

While the squad worked overtime, I prepared a main escape route and two alternates. I went over my lists. I studied my maps. I ran my mental stop-watch. I tried to factor Mr. Murphy in at every stage.

I carefully made the sign the priests taught me when I was an altar boy: spectacles, testicles, wallet, and watch. Then I faced Rome, Jerusalem, and Mecca, and prayed to every deity I could think of. Because, ready or not, we had to act.

Look for
Rogue Warrior III: Green Team
Wherever Hardcover Books Are Sold
mid-March 1995